Ring On Deli

Ring On Deli

Eric Giroux

NEW SALEM BOOKS

Copyright © 2020 by Eric Giroux

All rights reserved. This book or any portion thereof may not be reproduced or used in any manner whatsoever without the express written permission of the publisher except for the use of brief quotations in a book review.

Ring On Deli is a work of fiction. Characters, businesses, places, and events are either the products of the author's imagination or used in a fictitious manner. Any resemblance to actual persons, living or dead, or actual events is purely coincidental. For example, there are no real-world counterparts to Chesley Brine Martini and Ernesta Martini, and the author is aware of no employee in any supermarket who shares the odious workplace habits of *The* Alfredo or Toothless Mary.

978-1-7342240-0-9 (paperback)

Book design by Dan Visel
First Printing: 2020

New Salem Books
P.O. Box 600672
Newtonville, MA 02460

newsalembooks@gmail.com
www.ringondeli.com

For Jasmine, Rose and Woody

"This is essentially a people's contest."

> Abraham Lincoln
> Quoted in Groof, C. Richard, H.S.D.,
> *Ideas of the Great Thinkers.*

BEFORE

Welcome to Pennacook

Hard to believe it had been five years since the crash. Ray hadn't needed the BAC test to guess who had caused it, or what. In the immediate aftermath, DCF plopped Patrick with a kindly foster family, the Rosenbaums of Waltham, who gave him a new clarinet and a Star of David necklace that he wore ever after. Ray had just turned 18, and he made a decision that felt both rash and fated: he withdrew his pending college applications so he could take care of Patrick, who was then only 11, through the rest of his childhood. He quietly wrapped up high school that spring and bade farewell to his friends, mostly honors kids who in the fall would disperse to the country's four corners. His grief made it awkward, and that summer they mostly avoided him. By mid-August the death benefit on Mom and Dad came through, but they sold the mortgaged house at a loss and that consumed the bulk of the death benefit. Finally, in October, he packed up the Buick and pulled out of the driveway in Dunstable for the very last time.

He stopped by Waltham to check in on Patrick and play catch on the Rosenbaums' lawn.

"This, little brother, is going to be the shortest, strangest episode of your life."

"Shortest" was a promise he'd made to himself, to get Patrick back as soon as possible. By "strangest" he meant being a foster kid. He whipped the baseball at Patrick. It landed in his glove with a snap.

"I'm fine," Patrick said. "It's nice."

Patrick threw a wild one and Ray chased it down the road. He knew from the Rosenbaums that there was more to this story. But since he didn't know what to say, he copied Patrick and acted stoic.

He crisscrossed the state looking for a cheap, new town with schools that Mom would've called "halfway decent," a job for himself, and not so many reminders of all they had lost—lost, and in the case of Dad, escaped. He was living in his car and in roadside motels, eating canned food for dinner and cheap pastries for breakfast. His days began early, when the sun was enshrouded in mist and diner lights were popping aglow for the morning crowd. He picked up coffee at gas-station convenience stores, and it sent icy jitters through his blood as he waited for the Buick to warm up. The Buick rolled through hills and valleys, and Ray found that he was enchanted, for the first time since he'd been a young kid, by the autumn colors and the smell of burning leaves. Gliding off an exit to another old mill town, he felt a very broad affection rise up inside of him, like a person who has returned to a native land after many months among foreigners. Things that had been only background—a chain restaurant, a postal jeep, a river running through a town center—suddenly became beautiful and hopeful to him. His burdens greater than ever, he somehow felt relieved, as if he'd decided to lower his ambitions.

But one Friday during Indian summer he made the regrettable decision to sleep in the car in a woodsy roadside spot in East Sturbridge just as the raucous parking lot of King Henry's Faire emptied out. Goths on Harleys, rowdies in pickups, scandalized families in sputtering sedans: each in turn paraded behind Ray as he attempted to sleep and gagged on the fumes. The next morning his lower-back muscles had some kind of bruising that would not be denied and he was all out of food and cash. He rose up from his blankets—only to lock eyes with ruddy King Henry himself. The King spanned an entire highway billboard, flaunting his smoked goose leg with the giant splintering tendons as if to hector Ray personally for his predicament. Unexpectedly, even disappointingly, the King's gruesome ad made no usage or punctuation errors for Ray to deflate. Mom, an English teacher who gave Ray his faith in words and books, had loved that snoot's game.

Back north, Pennacook didn't even make his good-schools list. But the state road was convenient enough, ran right up to the town center in fact, and a magazine said the place "could have potential." Somewhere between an orange-juice spill on his map and envying King Henry his dripping royal drumstick, he decided to give the small town a chance.

At first there didn't seem to be much work for the likes of Ray. What they'd soon call the Great Recession had just unmasked itself to the world, but it seemed to have gotten a head start here. He parked the Buick and walked the mall's length. The Pennacook Mall was dying, a caged-up, ribbed-concrete monstrosity with drained fountains, two feuding anchor stores—both part of larger chains plunging into bankruptcy (a fact their sales posters touted)—and nothing but one pizzeria between them to spice the shadowy air. Back in the car, he crossed over to Worcester Road and passed three Chinese restaurants and Jack's Four Lounge (additional Chinese restaurant? No, the little sign said: eighteen-and-over strip club that served only juice). Farther down he drove by a pine-doored cave called The Penalty Box, a bar. There were very few help-wanted ads in windows and plenty of helpless-looking able-bodied men walking around alone, some with their heads aimed skyward. Outside a gas station a kid in overalls stared into space like a figure in a Hopper painting. The women seemed to have gone into hiding. He cranked the window: the *air* was stale, a sneaker bouquet.

Town center held more promise. The Truble Cove Plaza and its optimistically immense parking lot interrupted a long line of dilapidated grand colonials, once inhabited, as Ray would later learn, by the pig-farm kings of Pennacook's heyday. Ray slammed the brakes for crossing boars and scoped out the plaza. He noted a large, well-lit supermarket, two restaurants (at least one of them Chinese), a ghostly storefront labeled only "T.A.P.S.," and a hardware store. A converted Pizza Hut at one end of the lot served as the Pennacook Walk-In, a medical clinic. In the hardware store a bearded, sleepy-eyed clerk pondering a German X-rated comic book said the store was going out of business, but he pointed Ray a couple of doors down to the supermarket, one of two Bounty Bags in town. Also in Pennacook, the chain's main warehouse was full up, but the large store in this plaza always needed an early-morning guy to set up the deli, a "real trouble spot," and they were willing to pay a premium for someone who actually showed up dry for the gig.

The clerk sized up Ray and elaborated, a little mysteriously, "It's a chain with a certain appeal for—how shall I put it? A person in need. Loyal in a crisis. Catch my drift?"

Ray didn't but nodded anyway.

"Owns half the town," the clerk added. He tilted his head. "More than half, actually."

Or, he continued, Ray could sub at Andrew Johnson High, just across the river. He sat up on his stool, visibly warming to his advisory role. "That is, if you're a thinking man." He looked Ray over again. "Or boy."

He tapped his temple with an index finger, licked it, then, as if for Ray's further enlightenment, used it to flick to the next page of his comic book where three nude blondes with red lips flared up grinning. In the real world their ballooned-out cartoon proportions would have tipped them over. Then, much like the men on the street and the Hopper figure at the gas station, the clerk leaned back and gazed out the window to space, as though some fantastical object (alien saucer? bamboo airship?) hovered overhead.

"What are you staring at?"

"The sky."

"Why?"

"In case it falls."

"What are you going to do then?"

The clerk shrugged. "Duck, I suppose. Hope it doesn't go down all the way."

For a flashing moment Ray saw the words emblazoned on a sign at the town's border, as if written just for him. "Welcome to Pennacook! *Duck and Hope.*"

But the clerk was right about the teeming supermarket. They took him right in.

"You look hungry," observed Stan Martini, the chipper store manager, eyeing him with a curiosity that seemed to extend beyond Ray's appetite. "Tell you what. I'll throw in a ham sandwich."

"Deal."

They shook on it, and with the solemnity of a childhood bonding ritual, Stan presented Ray with a maroon-and-white Bounty Bag clip-on tie. Stan was surprisingly young, had about a decade on Ray, who knew from the first they'd be friends of a sort. Ray folded the tie neatly, hatching a new vision of himself as a dedicated supermarket guy.

The next day he turned down a shabby tract-house rental, settling instead on a Rockport Lite Cruiser. "The Rock," as Patrick later dubbed it, was a travel trailer that Ray could buy outright for $18,900 of insurance money, nearly the last of it. It was powered by propane and replete with queen bed, double bunks, kitchenette, booth, and shower-bath. They moved it right into a lot at the Liberty Mobile Home Park in Pennacook's Oakhurst neighborhood. The Rock was the only trailer in Liberty. The other units were mobile homes, most of them double-wides, laid out neatly in a grid. Liberty proved a friendly neighborhood where people walked around and had events and kept tidy yards. The Rock was technically hitch-able to the Buick for regional excursions, and in a moment of very low self-knowledge he had purchased it in part for that very feature. But The Rock went nowhere, inspiring Patrick's nickname.

Little had changed since they moved to town, except for one thing that he'd noticed. Instead of staring up to the sky, Pennies were more likely to be found looking down at their devices.

Archie's Plan

DR. CHONG GAZED ABOVE ARCHIE TO *Napoleon Crossing the Alps* and her map of the solar system. True, she conceded, the adage the selectman had just cited half worked. But as a tweet typhoon would be happy to remind her, the town's real credo was simply "Don't fix it." Especially, it seemed, where her high school was concerned.

"But it *is* broke," she pressed him. "This is plywood!" She knocked the wall and a splinter glided in. "*Ow*. Look at these windows: you can't see out of them. They're all frosted, bottom to top."

"I know, but what's broken to you? Ask your average Penny, they'll say it's a matter of opinion."

"Sounds like we need to change some opinions."

"That's what I need your help with. What's that smell?"

Her office had a distinctive waxy cleaner smell that only sharpened after school when the day's buzz had died. The odor sometimes made her feel more lonely and confined than she would have thought possible outside an Idaho supermax. AJMHS had first opened its steel doors in 1945, and five other principals had occupied this office before Dr. Chong. She wondered how long the odor had been around and if it'd had the same wilting effect on her predecessors.

She swatted a mosquito on her neck and her palm came away wet and bloody. She wiped it on a napkin from her take-out lunch from Bounty Bag. It was mid-September, 2013. School was back in session, yet summer tarried like a pointless and tiresome houseguest.

"Wax."

"Love it. Smells like school."

Wrapped tightly and taped, the Bounty Bag chicken-salad sub sat on her desk. At 4 P.M., this was to be a late, late lunch, deferred by a fist-fight and three rounds of bracing interrogations.

She touched her sub. "Mind if I?"

"Bounty Bag? Best subs," Archie said with a grin.

So endearing at times, his almost canine enthusiasm could be rather taxing at others.

This was a special meeting, granted at Selectman Archie Simmons's request. Long ago, a line item in Pennacook's budget had been dedicated to the purchase of an ordinary digging shovel, a length of red ribbon, and a giant pair of cardboard scissors. These were to be brought out for the grand opening of the new high-school building. But while Pennacook's town-meeting reps favored the project, they disfavored paying for it. The reps were agreeable enough, just wholly inconsistent. Whole town meetings trotted round in circles. So here was Archie for a chin-wag on the upcoming tax-cap-override ("TCO") initiative. A majority of the board of selectmen opposed the TCO but had authorized a popular referendum as a buck-passing gambit. If the voters passed it, the TCO would unlock the funds they needed. Power to the people! Except... they'd tried this before.

She said a little prayer for Bounty Bag, unwrapped the sub, and started eating while Archie, always solicitous of her, quietly scanned local news on his phone.

The octagonal shield with "Bounty Bag" and the chain's motto was stamped on the sub's wrapper. *"Stretch your buck"* was right! Without Bounty Bag's revenue, Dr. Chong would need more than an override to fund a new school. Or current operations, for that matter.

It was an old story. When real estate was cheap in Pennacook, Massachusetts—it was always cheap but back in 1938 when it was *extremely* cheap—Antonio N. Martini, then-owner of the Bounty Bag stores, was seized by a vision of free-roaming veal (destined to be served fresh for a bargain) and ran all over buying up the town. When the farm didn't pan out, his son Ralph sold the livestock but kept the land, constructing a state-of-the-art warehouse on one enormous parcel along the Pennacook River. At first peripheral, it had become the main warehouse after the one at HQ burned down in the '70s. For some reason—speculations abounded of a wild-eyed supermarket theme park—Bounty Bag kept the remaining land too.

Two stores followed the land grab. A small one near the border served nearby Eaton's budget-minded few. The second, in Truble Cove Plaza, considered itself the flagship, staking its claim on location and size. Close to the warehouse, it was the largest in a chain of 74 stores, and its customer base fanned out from Pennacook, with its sparse and ever-shrinking population, to all of greater Leominster. The rest of the town's economy—the shoe and potato-chip factories, the small family storefronts, finally most of the mall—up and blew away, but this store's footprint *grew*. Viewed from Booth Hill against the dim backdrop of Pennacook-by-night, the store's lamps resembled a short string of pearls.

Today, Bounty Bag employed a remarkable one in three adult Pennies. It stood to follow that her high school, which property taxes in large part funded, heavily depended on the chain. But with Bounty Bag deeper in the black each year, it was a happy, happy equation for Pennacook.

She finished her sub and tossed the mess.

"You eat fast!"

From Archie, somehow, this wasn't an insult.

"Continue."

Archie heaved up a large black case, popped the two latches—*snap-bang*—and slipped in his fingers, removing a large tablet.

"Data-crunching whiz at *The Beat*, kid named Graham Bundt, tapped this out. M.I.T. grad who drove off a cliff into a linguistics degree. Then regretted it and started night school for stats."

"Hence Pennacook."

She scanned the graphs and multi-layered curves. They confirmed her worst fears.

Penny voter turnout was at the low end for county, state, and nation. So her strategy up to now had been simple: discreetly court their narrow base—teachers, parents, young new arrivals—and hope others stayed home. History buttressed this lay-low strategy. It showed that if you gave an override *too* much attention, Pennies might pass an *under*ride instead. This would reduce levy limits below the normal cap, not only emptying the till but drilling a hole in the till's bottom and placing Jesse James's hand under that hole.

But through an admixture of demographics and past TCO results, coupled with anecdotal evidence sourced to the juice bar at Jack's Four Lounge, the whiz kid had conjured a prophecy of doom. He set chances of TCO passage at a piddling 27%. Failure, in contrast, he pegged at 90%, the additional 17% factoring in that even if the petition passed, T.A.P.S. (Taxpayers Alliance of Pennacook Seniors) might corral the equity courts to enjoin it. Sound in theory, their whisper campaign would fail.

Lost matching funds made this all the more vexing. Bounty Bag, for one, had promised a major gift should the town break ground. Far more substantial, the state offered eye-popping grants that covered almost half the measly $14 million cost. Dr. Chong had done weeks of research to press the price tag down that far, ultimately settling on prefab architectural plans drafted by an Alabama firm for a Mississippi middle school. No frills, but all new systems and real windows (ornamental azalea trails excluded).

So different, this town, from where Dr. Chong lived. Each night after school she shuttled her Mini between Pennacook and Eaton through a dark tunneling road that only she seemed to travel. The very first thing she'd see as she emerged from Pennacook's gnarly brush onto the smooth moonlit pavement of the Eaton leg was the glittering spot-lit campus of the German-architect-designed Eaton High School. A monument to the town's school-lusting tax base, the $200-million palace was lavished with extras. An indoor-outdoor room, an eight-story climbing wall, a pro mechanics' garage. Rorsch School, at the town's other end, was a prestigious boarding school of global reach, managing an endowment even larger than Eaton High's final tally. When Dr. Chong first moved to Eaton the town also had: a ninety-year-old cheese shop; a bookstore; a one-screen artsy movie theater; a French-milled soap shop where Dr. Chong had purchased a new kind of rocky soap that was almost a sex act to apply (no kidding!); a small hardware store, Griggs Hardware, with a Japanese-garden-aproned hand-pumping proprietor; and a graveyard stocked with Transcendentalist corpses. Of these, only the cheese and the corpses remained. The others had flickered out one by one amid the double scourge of the Great Recession and Web 2.0, Griggs dragging his precious push-mowers off to a stand next to pumpkins on Rte. 2-W. In their place rose The Eaton of Tomorrow. Glass-walled banks; a hedge fund sharing downtown cottage frontage with a cupcake "creator"; two

S.E.C.-registered investment advisers; a fresh rash of realtors; bland fine art galleries touting Picasso's café-napkin detritus; a The Wall Fitness System; a cosmetic-surgery outpost from La Jolla; and in a condoized chunk of scandal-sapped St. Mary's, the Li'l Jack Harvard Admissions Salon at Hawthorne Corner, a made-up place. No one exactly *cheered* the Great Change but like some colossal Europan cryogeyser these places spewed rent and taxes. Meanwhile, the remaining pretentious older places, like the Eaton Bistro with its cold food and oddly angled tables that seemed to say, "Please, just... *go*," now unexpectedly drew Dr. Chong's sympathy.

"So they normally don't vote."

"Right."

"Except when they vote against money for school."

"Right again. Now I get why they call you doctor."

"So what am I supposed to do with this info?"

"I want you to campaign for the override."

"I am."

"I mean on Election Day—rather, the day before. Dec 17th."

She flipped her blotter forward to December. As it always did for special elections that threatened to boost revenue, the crafty town clerk's office had scheduled voting for a ridiculously inauspicious day for turnout: mid-week, mid-December. Looking up, she noticed that Archie was once more directing a hot stare at her legs. Admittedly as a power play Dr. Chong typically left these exposed—but that didn't make her a window-dangling rib rack! Of course... there was more to it. She'd had her eye on this handsome widower for years, and last Halloween she had agreed to a costume-party date. It had ended horribly with the selectman, clad in hard plastic as a Lego figurine, swinging wildly for a kiss on Dr. Chong's couch, before departing sad and empty-handed. She should have seen disaster coming because she had broken a cardinal rule in saying yes to Archie's invite: *Never date a man from Pennacook.* And during "Monster Mash" she had slipped her moorings and started grabbing Archie all over, potentially triggering the Lego-couch approach and breaking yet another cardinal rule of Dr. Chong's: *Control everything.* She'd given him the cold shoulder ever since but she wasn't surprised he was checking her out again today.

When he first floated this meeting, Archie's over-eager subconscious taking a not-so-sly peek over the hedges, he had e-mailed asking to "meat" her after school.

"I work. That's a school day."

"It is now."

"You want me to cancel school?"

"Not cancel. A walkout. Low turnout won't work. We need to shoot for high turnout now. *Very* high. The kind that only controversy can stir."

"And if I get fired you'll pay my salary to walk your Yorkie?"

This was disingenuous. In point of fact, she adored his Yorkie. Cornelius, a three-pound runt, traveled everywhere with Archie in his camper van.

"Think about it. Please. I'll be your biggest champion on the board. It'll be just like the '60s!"

"We were *nine* in the '60s. Do I look that old?"

She walked him to the door, noting once more his brisk, energetic step. Archie was in great shape due to his relentless pavement-pounding in support of various doomed Pennacook initiatives. She realized with a touch of admiration that true idealism (or else undiagnosed blood poisoning of the sort that undid poor Napoleon on St. Helena) motivated Archie's walk-out scheme. Recent redistricting by the board's then-tenuous pro-austerity majority had splattered the old Oakhurst, leaving Archie astride an ink-blot enclave that packed in the lefties. His seat safe, if politically quarantined, he had nothing personal to gain here. On the other hand, like most Pennies, he also had very little to lose.

Archie paused at the threshold and whispered some advice. "I know it doesn't come *natural* sometimes, mingling with Pennies. But I hope that you'll give it the old college try. We need you."

"I do try!"

Archie's words still stung at the end of the day as Dr. Chong exited Andrew Johnson onto Mediterranean Avenue, turning left on Baltic, then right on Oriental, pausing there to let a wild boar cross. At the end of Oriental (Pennacook had begun naming its streets after

Monopoly properties, but its signage budget expired on light blue) she hit the state road and steered her Mini into the Pennacook-Eaton wormhole. Tonight the wormhole was a brilliant green canopy, but she'd noticed that somehow even in winter alien fingers industriously patched over any light-seeping cracks, if not with swaying boughs and leaves then with snow, wind, and blotting fog screens.

Voters notwithstanding, Dr. Chong did not quite grasp why she had not yet won a new school because, above all else, Dr. Chong had faith in Dr. Chong. She considered herself administrative magic, with powers far greater than Archie's. The tricks in her hat, alien to the flesh-pressing selectman, leaned toward clever maneuvers — regulatory appeals to deep-pocketed state agencies, grant applications to string-attaching philanthropists, parliamentary legerdemain — that sidestepped altogether the Pennies and their elected representatives, or else made it more work for them to say "no" than to say "yes." In eight short years she had pulled rabbit after rabbit from that hat. State funds for Elmo projectors. Water-pipe-repair schematic and a preliminary budget for same. To everyone's surprise, she had also won an asbestos-and-radon pledge from the cagey school committee, even though this could spike their insurance. If her magic hat had produced all of this, surely somewhere in its red-velvet lining she'd find a new school. Perhaps Archie Simmons's walk-out proposal — kooky though it seemed on the surface — was just the spell to wake up these Pennies.

She switched her Mini to sport mode and revved the engine like a blender. Moonlight flickered in the wormhole's exit.

"I *do* try," she said again, with greater force, as if Archie were there to hear and believe her.

PART ONE

Loomings

PATRICK COULD LAUGH ALL HE WANTED. FIVE YEARS in, Ray appreciated the wholesome tasks, manageable and predictable, of supermarket life. If small by standards of the Lincoln administration, the work was far from useless. They *fed* people. Baking rolls, slicing meat. Neatly making sandwiches and forking them over to eager hands. Equally important, Bounty Bag's sparkling lights served as a reliable antiseptic to shadowy ruminations, on past, present, *or* future. You might even say that two of those dimensions barely existed in a supermarket; everything happened right here and now. There were problems, to be sure, but they were small ones, easily solved. Spilled grape juice, ma'am? No worries. We'll douse it with sawdust and mop the purple clots. Watch your step in the meantime. And have you seen today's specials? Best of all, supermarket life (if at times a bit of a grind) was stable, as if the store and all of the characters who worked there—even Deli's grotesques—were suspended in a gel. And since Bounty Bag took care of Ray, Ray could take care of Patrick and provide him a worthy home.

At least that's how he saw it in general and on average, for almost any given month behind the counter. But one Saturday in October these blessings started to flicker and dim like so many dying fluorescents. A civil war had brewed for years in the higher ranks, but on this day Bounty Bag began to really come apart and Patrick, as if conspiring, chose the same moment to betray him. Of course, Ray should have known something was coming—did know, in his bones—because bad omens abounded. As Ray duly noted at the time.

He got to the store before anyone else, clocking in at five-thirty on the button for Deli set-up. He flipped on the department lights, donned his Bounty Bag ball cap, and buttoned his forest-green Deli-assistant-management jacket over his dress shirt and clip-on. All suited up, he wheeled last night's extra rolls from Deli to the front entrance, where a small truck idled by the supermarket's curb.

"Twenty large and fourteen small," he counted off. "Slow day."

Dusty Grimes looked on glumly as Ray moved the rolls from his Bounty Bag trays to the pantry truck's cooler. A haunted-looking man, powder-faced and tumid in an orange jumpsuit, Dusty was the sole, part-time employee of the Pennacook Food Pantry. Ray recognized Dusty from when he first joined Deli, when Ray and Patrick were food-pantry shoppers themselves. The men weren't friends though because Dusty begrudged his shoppers and never forgot a face. Also, it had been Ray's idea, approved by benevolent store manager Stan Martini (who hadn't aged a day since Ray first met him), to donate the surplus Deli rolls to the local food pantry. This meant more work for pigeon-hearted Dusty.

"How's life at the PFP?" Ray asked.

Dusty shrugged. "Ten bucks is ten bucks."

"Someday you'll have to tell me what that means."

"Some *day* we'll both be dead."

Dusty hustled back into the truck and tore off for the exit. True to form he ignored the parking lanes and barely dodged around the last carriage corral before his engine went *bang* and he bent around the corner, swallowed by Pennacook.

Just then Ray heard a familiar rustle and his chin shot up. Five feral pigs trotted toward him through the mist. Bad omen—or worse, if Ray's courage failed him—the beasts had grown more aggressive of late, as if they could smell the trouble afoot at Bounty Bag. Ray reached for the broom and, twirling it, prepared defensive maneuvers. He looked down and spotted the immediate focus of the boars' interest: a large torpedo roll had slid from the trays and was splayed out neatly on a piece of wax paper, its white belly open and inviting. The boars became especially bold in groups... or when Ray's bread was on the menu.

In fact the boars were an ineradicable nuisance. They foraged through Pennacook in groups large and small. Sow-led families worked the outdoor-leisure circuit, terrorizing picnickers and teens getting drunk by the campfire. Other boars promenaded the streets at all hours and attracted a small tourist contingent of Eatonites slumming it. They brooked no accommodation for pedestrians and did not even make way for Bounty Bag associates, who could cut an intimidating figure as they stomped off to work in their many-colored jackets, scattering wild turkeys—but not boars. Howie O'Dell, the town's animal-control specialist (and an official, name-tagged Pennacook Ambassador) was a publicity hound, which hampered his technique, and he had recently executed a grisly downtown steel-wire strangling before children. That re-elected him and got him a new uniform, but Howie only downed one boar. Nobody in Pennacook seemed to know where the boars came from. Or if they did know at one point, they no longer remembered. Or if they remembered, they wouldn't discuss.

The supine roll was too much for the boars and they broke into a bouncing trot, then fell forward in an all-out charge. Ray switched tactics to the psychological. He scooped up the fallen roll and, gesticulating with it violently, declaimed in his loudest Deli-holler a muscular-sounding JFK line that he'd heard on a "Momentous Speeches of Recorded History" CD set that Patrick had spurned.

"Those who foolishly sought *pow*-ah…by riding the back of the *ti*-gah… ended up inside!"

It didn't really matter what you said to the boars so long as you spoke with force. This time he had, and mostly it worked. Camelot cast its twilight spell and the boars swiveled, scampered back across the parking lot, and swiftly scaled the hill. But they perched at the top and glowered through the lamplight, their bulky frames etched into the sky.

"Someday," they seemed to say. "Someday."

Safely back in Deli's glow, Ray shifted to torpedo-roll set-up. Ordinarily this was a pleasant task, purposeful and discrete. But last night Ray's lazy co-worker who answered only to *The* Alfredo had once more done a sloppy job laying out the frozen rolls, and when Ray pushed the rolls out front the cart's wobbly wheel caught on a wrapper that *The* Alfredo had failed to throw out—together with a half-empty beer bottle, a blunt, and, wrapped in a paper towel, what looked to be another used condom—and a whole tray spilled onto the floor.

"Fuck!" Ray shouted, the word bouncing off the refrigerated cases and echoing back in rebuke.

Bad omen number two.

For a time he had tried to befriend *The* Alfredo but he disliked how *The* Alfredo talked, strumming his chin and saying "indeed" a whole lot. It was hard to get a word in edgewise. *The* Alfredo would set a trap, and Ray would fall in. Next thing you knew he was off again, on some obscene topic like Doughnut Dayle.

"Who's Doughnut Dayle?"

"You don't know Doughnut Dayle!"

"I know who he *is*. Why's he called Doughnut Dayle?"

"He's *called* Doughnut Dayle because of what he does with doughnuts. First he applies two of his namesake confections, one honey dipped and one chocolate glazed, to his—"

Well he'd rather not relive it!

Another time, tripping, *The* Alfredo saw a monster climbing out of the boiled ham and had to go home. Last month, it was the saging of his new digs, a gratis hovel above Benvolio's, his elderly aunt's Italian restaurant.

"Turns out I got lingering residual lower energy," *The* Alfredo had said, regarding an audit performed in connection with the saging.

"No kidding," Ray said.

The doting aunt had a standing order. Benvolio's supplied *The* Alfredo with limitless spaghetti-and-meatballs in a pasta bowl, which they washed for him nightly. They also laundered his clothes. *The* Alfredo's Bounty Bag dress shirts tumbled together with Benvolio's wine-red napkins and tablecloths, and all of the shirts turned pink. *The* Alfredo was twenty-nine, which made him Ray's "elder" (by six years) as he put it, but he didn't outrank Ray, and over the pink shirts he wore the brown Deli jacket, showing that after all these years he was still a buck associate.

Rolls loaded, Ray turned to the slush machine, a fine and joy-bringing instrument that without proper care and maintenance turned quickly pestilential. He was busy cleaning it out, bearing down with a sort of wand with a yellow puff on the end of it that didn't scour well, when his flip phone buzzed, causing his leg to kick once like a horse's.

The text message read: "Did you read my e-mail? —Dr. RC."

Ray didn't recognize Dr. RC or the number and hadn't been on e-mail for a day. He slipped out back to the store laptop. It turned out the message was urgent.

Mr. Markham:

I am presently extremely concerned about your son Patrick. At the pre-season indoor track meet in Lowell this afternoon, Patrick was too intoxicated with alcohol to complete his leg of the one-mile relay.

Ray, I'd like you to come in to talk about your son. If you do not, then a representative from the Massachusetts Department of Children and Families will be in contact momentarily.

Thanks,
Principal Regina Chong, D.Ed.
Andrew Johnson Memorial High School

Although this news was alarming—perhaps *because* it was alarming—Ray, his mother's son, couldn't help but revise the e-mail as he read it. In the span of a single message Dr. Chong had managed to misuse both "presently" and "momentarily." Also, he was Patrick's brother, not his father (though he was his legal guardian), and why did she sign off with "thanks"? But any way you wrote it, Patrick was heading down Dad's path again. No doubt some other kid had sensed Patrick's easy nature and led him there. Lead suspect? Cashier Muscles Carbonara, Patrick's keen but shady comrade and a big question mark for Ray. Or maybe it was Ray's fault, for not paying close enough attention. Heaven knows he tried.

Patrick had always been the sweet one. There was that time at YMCA camp when Ray had forced him under the water for a ten count. Patrick wriggled free, not even biting, emerging not with the howls of outrage that Ray had expected but with stone-faced silence. Patrick's dark cloud lasted only until their picnic lunch, when it lifted in a vivid instant as his teeth worked their way down a corn cob gripped between his buttery hands. Patrick's muted reaction and forgetting spirit made Ray feel even worse.

But lately Ray worried that Patrick's charm was a glimmer of socio-pathology, an ailment he'd read about in the abnormal-psychology chapter of the doctor-written *Caring for Your Teen*. Ray kept this and other books of practical advice and allegory on a jam-packed shelf above The Rock's booth. These books were Ray's alloy-steel wrench set for Patrick's regular attitude adjustments. Core volumes were *Caring for Your Teen* and a paperback of mental calisthenics for the recalcitrant pessimist. Ray had given most of another shelf over to Mom's books. Literary classics (Dickinson and Keats, Ellison and Melville) shared pride of place with Ray's musty American history books and less-impressive syllabus standbys about prep school and stranded children.

"You're a worrywart and a fool," Patrick charged.

"This stuff is great."

"*Hamlet* isn't a moral guidebook. It ends really, really badly."

Ray removed *The Omnibus E. M. Forster* and chucked him at his brother. Patrick ducked, but the gentle Cantabrigian landed safely on The Rock's upholstered booth.

Also on the home bookshelf were the only books Patrick had actually embraced upon Ray's recommendation: *The Boxcar Children*. Ray had picked these up on a lark at a library fire-sale, not exactly grasping the intended audience until Patrick, pronouncing them "a riot," began reading one aloud over Ray's grilled cheese-'n-tomato soup lunch one Saturday. (*"Indeed, it is doubtful if collectors of rare and beautiful bits of porcelain ever enjoyed a search as much as did these adventurers in the dump heap."*) Actions perhaps spoke louder than words. Ray had twice caught Patrick smiling over the stories in his bunk. Characteristically, Ray's lighthouse of concern then spun in the opposite direction. Wasn't there something a tiny bit *wrong* with a sixteen-year-old who sincerely liked *The Boxcar Children*?

Ray now had to admit that his parenting approach wasn't working. He needed something firmer, with fangs and phases and crunched-bones bona fides. Less "To Autumn" or *The Boxcar Children* than the shape-clear-hold-build strategy that he had read about in a manual applying counter-insurgency theory to rebellious teens. Discouraged by his flagging literary campaigns, he'd already resorted to TV. He watched Patrick closely for habits and after noting his fixation on kids' shows in particular he had rushed off to the library for *The*

Brady Bunch box set. But *The Bradys* had been a total flop and had only led to another one of their confusing yet intense quasi-paternal arguments — all too common of late.

On purpose or not, Patrick had come home from the track meet only after Ray hit the sack last night. Then, this morning, he had slept through Ray's flip phone alarm. Soft tufts of Patrick's blue hair had over-spilled his pillow and his breathing was easy, warm, and deep, as if he had nothing whatsoever to hide.

Ray re-read Dr. Chong's e-mail alert about the track meet several times but he was at a loss as to the best, least revealing way to reply. He closed the store laptop and, returning to Deli, shot Patrick a wild string of unanswered texts. Patrick's continued silence all the way through morning set-up sapped him, and he leaned on the counter and put his head in his hands, daydreaming of Waikiki, which slowly but surely gathered substance behind his drooping eyelids. Bent palms and hula girls dancing. Diamond Head so close you could almost caress its volcanic folds. Ray had just gotten one uneasy knee up on his mahogany surfboard when he felt a sudden but familiar chill and turned to find Toothless Mary, Deli's manager, planted at his elbow. *Wipeout!*

"He*looo*, Mr. Ray," she said, flashing a ghoulish grin that did have some teeth but somehow appeared emptier for it.

"Hi, Mary."

In her blood-splattered apron and Elvis sunglasses, red hair blasting back from her head, Toothless Mary resembled some demonic rock-'n-roll garden gnome. Ever since Stan had reached through Toothless Mary to promote Ray to assistant deli manager, Toothless Mary had treated Ray as both her special confidante and her favorite target.

"Mind if I?" she asked, lighting up a cigarette.

"As long as I can breathe the second-hand smoke."

Mary ignored this, along with Ray's other "little cracks."

Every law and the Bounty Bag Code were against Toothless Mary's smoking in Deli, but before the store opened she did it anyway and left her hair unwrapped too. During business hours, she smoked on the Golden Mile, the long, wide lane out back used for trash and Deliveries. Sometimes she returned from the Golden Mile with little pieces of garbage attached to her. A paper plate, rendered partly translucent by pizza grease, pressed to her back. A noodle dangling from a sock like a tassel. The seemingly incongruous garbage made perfect sense when one accounted for her favorite pastime: dumpster diving. Lampshades, broken toys, other valuables: all went eventually into her bursting riverside shack, just a short walk from Bounty Bag. It got to the point that Ray was reluctant to deposit personal trash at Bounty Bag, so he sealed it up and carted it home. Proximity was essential to Toothless Mary's habit because she didn't drive or bike and even walked crooked due to her plantar warts (or *Planters* warts, as she called them, after the peanut company). These she sometimes froze in the break room using a special canned medicine from Aisle Nine that went *schwooooooop!* when she activated the nozzle.

Toothless Mary's cigarette dangled over the warm, square tins. She dropped in the macaroni and cheese with a wet cheesy smack, then mixed up some Buffalo-flavored chicken salad, a flailing trial item. Off to her side, Ray finished the rolls and refilled the lettuce, tomato, onions, and olives. He heard a gentle *plop* and slowly turned his head. Toothless Mary had dropped her cigarette in the Buffalo chicken salad and a plump, ungloved finger had chased it down into the salad's hidden depths. The finger, Ray guessed, had made the plop sound. Gradually, even delicately, Toothless Mary proceeded to press her entire hand into the salad, where it came to rest somewhere near the bottom of the tin.

Third bad omen. Although, now that he had the bad news about Patrick's track meet, shouldn't the omens have run their course? Ray wondered if something else, even worse, was headed his way. Or maybe, if he was lucky, Fate was just playing a little game of "I told you so," placing some of its omens *after* things went south.

"Oops," Toothless Mary said.

Schmoook! She suctioned free of the salad and stared at the surprisingly recovered butt, which she clutched between two mayonnaised fingertips.

"Have to dump it," she said uncertainly.

"I'll do it," Ray said, shouldering her aside and removing the tin from the station. He scooped the salad in the garbage and tossed the sullied tin in the sink. "This stuff isn't selling anyway," he observed, trying to make the best of an ugly situation. In fact, given the recipe for Buffalo chicken salad, which included an unappetizing combo of diced olives and pickles with a spicy-sweet mayonnaise overlay, you could almost count this a victimless crime. Though the salad had its fans.

"It is pretty gross," Toothless Mary said. Her Buffalo-chicken-salad-free hand reached for her Bounty Bag jacket pocket and removed another cigarette from her pack. Stuffed under her apron, Toothless Mary's jacket was the same forest green as Ray's but had a distinguishing bronze stripe to signify her higher rank.

Ray shot her a quick sidelong look.

"I think I'll take it out back," she said and hobbled off to the Golden Mile for her smoke. At this point she had to: at 9 o'clock, the store had opened.

In Ray's opinion Bounty Bag was the world's best supermarket and Store #28 the chain's crown jewel, its godforsaken Pennacook location notwithstanding. But on a sour day, as this was shaping up to be, Deli was like some Pennacook lesion on Bounty Bag's flank, welling and oozing with weak links and health-reg outlaws like *The* Alfredo and Toothless Mary. Deli had a chronic retention problem too, and they were currently hiring for at least a couple of slots. In just the past year they'd chewed up five associates, including fastidious full-timer Daphne Butterfield, whose milkmaidish charms had sparked a simmering crush in Ray—until *The* Alfredo wooed her away and wrecked her. Ray now wondered if he was no better than *The* Alfredo and Toothless Mary. Did he, too, have some defect that only others could see? Was he, like them, more Pennacook than Bounty Bag?

He noticed that the liverwurst was getting old and exercised some of his new executive muscle to write a note in red marker on the white board declaring liverwurst-and-Swiss the *Daily Super Special!* at the usual $4.75 per large sub. Bounty Bag encouraged local tinkering, and if something worked locally, they quickly scaled it up. Even Toothless Mary had imbibed these values and, re-emerging from the Golden Mile, she gave his special an approving nod: baby-manager

Ray's miraculous first twitch. For a breath he felt grateful for the gnome's company and her approval, but when he opened his flip phone, drawing from Mary a raised eyebrow that crossed even the ample threshold of her Elvis sunglasses, all his warmth toward her drained away.

"*Personal* call?" she asked.

"If I'm lucky."

One reason Ray didn't have a smartphone was that he was a technophobe. The other was that Bounty Bag quirkily didn't allow smartphones on the store floor. They had to be deposited in the breakroom's electrical-field-blocking Faraday cage, where most associates stored their keys as well. Ray approved of the rule, which thwarted distraction, but as Patrick's guardian he could use his flip phone (which Patrick called his "burner") to talk to Patrick and he could use the store laptop to check personal e-mail in emergencies. Toothless Mary strictly policed these exceptions, but she had no cause for envy this morning. Patrick didn't answer and still hadn't texted back.

Time stopped. The lights buzzed brightly, but few customers came this early and the quiet times were tough. Sometimes the place was packed from here to the Coke cooler. Then he could drop his head to the cutting board and work hard and the time would fly, Mary dimming to a fidgety orange smudge. He felt good about the work, feeding workers on break or, on summer days, families set on a long drive out to Gloucester for a beach day. Sometimes a whole afternoon, the best work time, would pass in this fashion, with one customer after another ordering a large Italian sub with everything plus hots, oil, and vinegar. It got so Ray felt like he was putting together a beautiful puzzle over and over again. Hypnotized by his own hands' motion, he'd feel the trance break and he'd look up and the customers would be gone and it would be day's end. All he'd have to do was sweep up and go home.

Mornings were different, slower. Today Ray's 10 A.M. coffee break came and went without happening. Toothless Mary seemed to have vanished through a time bubble in the pantry and was too busy reversing the assassination of JFK like that guy from the Stephen King novel or, more likely, diving into the nearest dumpster from 1963 to actually do a lick of work. Ray craved his missed coffee. He swallowed his resentment like a fly accidentally ingested and ate a pickle.

He was the first guy on duty and a fast worker and it once more occurred to him that he could have slept in and no one would have noticed. The punch clock would have automatically docked him some change for the lost time, but that was about it under Bounty Bag's benign regime. Ray shunned the thought. Better not to head down that road. Work was work, and he had his responsibilities. Cultivate your garden and such. Plus, sloppy work brought bad luck. On a day like this, who needed more of it?

He tried Patrick again on the flip phone. Again no answer. He snapped on fresh gloves and turned to take an order.

———

Abandoned once more by Toothless Mary — and still no word from Patrick — Ray fell knuckle-deep into an afternoon clean-up fury. He pushed the rag down hard against the counter and flossed and polished the slicers to a gleam.

In a small but welcome development, Gary Snow appeared over in Aisle Five, restocking canned veggies with aplomb. Gary had been a Bounty Bag associate since junior year at Andrew Johnson Memorial High School. All eyebrow and grin, he vaguely resembled Michael S. Dukakis, whom Ray had actually passed once on the Lowell Connector, driving his unassuming Dodge exactly 55 mph, tiny hands planted at 10 o'clock and 2. (Ray thought he'd never meet a more cautious driver than himself but by God there he was. The Duke!) But today Gary resembled less the petite former governor than an American robin harkening spring's arrival in northern Massachusetts. He wore his orange-and-silver senior-associate jacket, and as he stocked, his sleeves flapped up and down. Shelf to box, box to shelf.

Sure enough, the day soon brightened further. A surprise late run of polite customers — nary a leaner or finger-pointer among them — finished off the last of Ray's Canadian chili (steamed potatoes, beef chunks, carrots). Then the honorable Stan Martini arrived.

"How art thou?" he asked, his standard greeting, as he bellied up to Deli.

Stan wore the purple jacket, with golden stripes down the arms that signaled his store-manager rank. If Gary Snow was the American robin of a warm morning in late March, Stan was the regal purple martin of April return. An afternoon visit by his friend Stan was typically a highlight of Ray's day, leavening his mood at a time when the hard grind of morning prep and lunch service was mostly behind him. But today there was a weary squint to Stan's eyes that portended, Ray feared, some adverse corporate news. Suspiciously, Stan had stuffed something in his jacket's oversize chest pocket, causing it to bulge out like the purple martin's breast.

Ray sensed a fourth bad omen.

"'Don't make good the enemy of perfect.' —Voltaire," Stan said.

"No, sir, I won't." Stan always got it backward, but it kind of worked either way.

"'Better a diamond with a flaw than a pebble without,'" Stan added.

"I know that one: Confucius."

"Really? I thought that was mine."

"Not unless you're a twenty-five-hundred-year-old Chinese man."

"Or C. Richard Groof, H.S.D."

About two years earlier, Ray had left a copy of *Ideas of the Great Thinkers* on the toilet above the stairs out back. It was a nifty little volume by one C. Richard Groof, who, according to the bio, was a man unlettered beyond the high-school level with no philosophical axe of his own to grind, only a deep and abiding love for the truth and a knack for summary, compression, and pithy quote selection. (Groof's taxonomy was extremely loose, however. He strayed far afield of philosophy, to the arts, literature, history, and the law.) Ray had scored the Groof at the Penny Corporal. He had partly memorized it, recommending their home copy to Patrick, but hadn't tackled it in any systematic way. Stan partook of the book liberally and would dip into its well for tidbits of workplace wisdom. For too many questions about dress code or break time: "Trust thyself: Every heart vibrates to that iron string." —Emerson. For confronting a rash of empty toppings bins: "When you look into an abyss, the abyss also looks into you." —Nietzsche. This marked an improvement over Stan's pre-Groof quips, though these (the frayed tag lines of Popeye and Porky Pig) carried similar existential implications, if read a certain way. Stan was known to bend a quote to fit a work moment, and some made no sense from a managerial perspective, even sounding borderline tyrannical ("Do I contradict myself? Very well then, I contradict myself!" —Walt Whitman). But Stan was good-willed and Ray figured he didn't really mean or maybe even understand those ones.

Stan had quickly traced the gift book of wisdom teachings back to Ray. As a result, he came to associate Ray with intelligence and effective wordsmithing, when in fact Ray considered himself merely a competent reviser. By last winter, Stan was turning to him for all sorts of stuff. Editing his e-mails to HQ in Wilmington. Proofing, on occasion, the weekly deals flyer. He also asked Ray to revise his copy for in-store ads and intercom broadcasts. Stan would pencil a lead-in that was honest enough about what they were selling but that somehow made the customer's entire life sound shabby (*Kids in the mood for a box of cheap donuts?*), and Ray would replace it with a good-willed pun that insulted only the customer's intelligence (*Do-nut miss our super donuts special!*). Just last week, Stan had tapped Ray to review his draft poster for a new hot-menu item that Stan had devised in his home kitchen using Deli discards and an unlicensed Chocolatey Chip Eggo. Stan curled the Eggo into a cone and stuffed it with hamburger meat and blue-cheese crumbles. His poster featured a close-up of the wrap-sandwich's innards. Beneath that, Stan penned a slogan: "Lunch! (No, really.)" Ray persuaded Stan to scrap that particular ad campaign, along with the hideous culinary gallimaufry, but it was nevertheless a virtue of Bounty Bag that they gave local staff the freedom to try out their ideas.

"Let me bounce something off you, Ray," Stan now said, leaning in.
"Shoot."
"What do you think of this?" Stan asked.

He reached into his jacket's bulging pocket and removed a balled-up, brilliant-green T-shirt, which he proceeded to unfurl. It had the trademark Bounty Bag octagonal icon in the center of the chest. A new slogan in hot-pink lettering appeared beneath it and also on the back. "I ♥ My Job!" it said, italics wringing the heart symbol.

"This your work?" Ray asked.

"Take a wild guess."

"No."

"Yep. Order came down in the e-mail. The board says all associates, at all times. *Over* coats and ties. Four boxes of 'em were stuffed under my desk this morning. Chesley signed the letter himself, the big jerk. Here's yours—catch!"

Ray caught it. He had heard all about Chesley and, by extension, Bounty Bag's board of directors, from Stan and the Bounty Bag gossip mill. Stan, of course, had the inside scoop. His mom was the CEO.

Angelica Goode Martini ("Angie," to one and all) was, indeed, Bounty Bag's longtime and beloved CEO. But power shifted between branches of the Martini clan in a never-ending see saw, and Chesley Brine Martini, Angie's nemesis, currently controlled the board of directors, a state of affairs that did not bode well for Angie's long-term corporate fate.

Chesley headed up the family's playboy wing, which lived in upscale Eaton and shopped only at Great Foods. He was four times divorced, estranged from his two sons, and apparently friendless. Angie, in contrast, shopped only at Bounty Bag and beyond its doors lived the quiet life of a Billerica widow, admiring the portrait of her gentle Gerard, gone now these ten-odd years, idly playing her pedaled electric organ, and doting, whenever they'd allow it, on her ten grown children—including Stan, her last, whom she indulged as "*il bambino della famiglia.*" Every associate at Bounty Bag and every manager counted her a friend. Unlikely as it seemed, Chesley and Angie were fraternal twins, son and daughter of supermarket baron Ralph Martini and grandchildren of company founder and fresh-veal merchant Antonio Martini (b. 1894, Turi, Italy). The Martini line descended, it was said, from ancient Athenian migrants.

Chesley's domination of the board had its roots in Ralph Martini's will. When Ralph died in 1990, the will granted each of his children—Chesley, Angie, and baby-sister Ernesta—a one-third stake in Bounty Bag. For very different reasons that only later became clear, Angie and Chesley immediately began warring for control. Ernesta, however, confessed little interest in "pitching poor-man's prosciutto" and let Chesley command her board seats. Why him and not her big sister? It was generally believed that Chesley and Ernesta shared a searing envy of golden-child Angie. All of their lives, it seemed, they had been merely an audience in Ralph's theater of adoration for his first daughter. Well past the age when Angie fit, Ralph would stuff her into a grocery carriage and proudly parade her down Bounty Bag's aisles. Teenage Angie piously donned the sacker's smock at Store #2, but she also served in a more elevated role as Ralph's apprentice, sharpening pencils and charming grouchy vendors down at HQ in Wilmington. By her mid-thirties, Angie had climbed to the level of consigliere, and in Ralph's last days he verbally anointed Angie his successor—a stinging rejection for Chesley, who had his own secret plans for the family business.

Or Ernesta sided with Chesley because of an occasionally discussed incident that had nothing to do with Angie. In the late '60s, while Angie was sacking and learning the ropes at Bounty Bag, Chesley was a strapping Rocky Marciano fan-boy, merrily brawling in the streets of Everett. One day when Chesley was in this phase, he pleasantly pummeled Hank Speeney for prank-calling Ernesta after the St. Vincent's eighth-grade dance and making vague slurping sounds. For this (the pummeling, not the slurping) Ernesta was said to remain ever grateful.

Whatever her motives, Ernesta's decision meant that for many years in the 1990s Chesley called the shots at Bounty Bag. Chesley's actions at the helm during this period showed he had only one goal for Bounty Bag Grocers, Inc.: produce cash for Chesley and the other shareholders, typically by means of board-ordered "special payouts." These were to be spent on unimaginable luxuries seemingly tailored to elicit a gasp from commoners. Scuba-diving disco parties in underwater caves. Chiseled Thoroughbreds in the hundreds of thousands. Space-scraping hot-air balloon rides. To solidify his control, Chesley banished Angie from HQ, forcing her into a manager's slot in the smaller Billerica store.

But on Thanksgiving Day 1999—or so the story went—a Chesley misstep unwittingly yielded the upper hand, for years, to Angie. According to Stan, it happened something like this:

Chesley loved a fin-tailed Porsche. Freshly divorced from his third wife that year and feeling rather lonesome, he drove his latest model to Ernesta's Italianate mansion to glom onto her holiday dinner. He was already half in the bag when he arrived and parked half-on, half-off the lawn. By Chesley's lights this was half acceptable, hence totally fine, because Chesley always rounded up in his own favor. Chesley downed six more cold ones at dinner and after he passed out on the recliner the children climbed him to get a better look at the Nintendo 64. Late that evening, he rose in a daze and, opening a drawer, urinated into the veggie crisper of Ernesta's Meneghini La Cambusa, according to Stan one of the most expensive refrigerators the world over. He either mistook the veggie crisper for a toilet (with a drawer) or *just didn't care.*

"I'll clean it up after," Chesley growled.

Ernesta seized him by the arm and pulled him back from the Great Foods produce. Chesley swung around and sprayed Ernesta's L. L. Bean chukkas.

Many people don't work on the Friday after Thanksgiving, and Ernesta was not known to work at all. The morning after the soiling of her Meneghini La Cambusa, however, she was up bright and early, zipping off to the John Hancock Tower, where she ascended in an immaculate high-speed elevator to the crisp, hushed offices of Vines Hay LLP. She plucked two associates from the muffled hive and quickly removed Chesley's offspring from certain revocable trusts. After some prodding, the malnourished, pale-faced associates spelled out her broad discretion as a board member to vote uniformly against her now-despised elder brother. By COB, she had re-aligned with Angie's board minority, making it a new governing majority and opening the door to Angie's swift ascent, from adored store manager to the chain's CEO.

"We'll tie this up on Saturday," one of the young associates, blue under the eyes, croakily assured her. Though much older, Ernesta was smooth, cool, and fresh by comparison. An un-dimpled pudding of wealth.

By Monday Angie was pulling her manual Ford Fiesta into the CEO space at HQ, where she executed an oriental knot on her maroon-and-white man's tie before stepping inside to formally take the reins—to a sea of applause in the company cafeteria.

That was only the beginning. Angie proved a supermarket savant. In her first decade she added twenty stores, all of them highly profitable, including the one she had brilliantly planted just over Bourne Bridge on Cape Cod. Families stopped there as soon as they crossed the bridge, feeling they'd "reached the Cape" and could now relax and shop for the rental. Angie also increased employment by thousands and sales by over a billion. She was praised by customers for her maniacal commitment to lower prices ("Stretch Your Buck" was Bounty Bag's time-honored motto) and fresh food. She also kept the stores stocked with a deep bench of ethnic favorites, from Cuban to Thai, including Ray's go-to choice for sloppy winter days when he was too exhausted to cook for Patrick: Sicilian pizzas and Italian pastries shipped in from Matt & Amanda's in Boston's North End.

Plus the CEO spurned the tricks that other chains used to max-out short-term profits but that, like some of Stan's lesser draft slogans, made everyone feel a bit black-and-blue. Confusing aisles that led you to the expensive stuff positioned at the end. Sparse staff that didn't know where anything was. Automatic registers that never seemed to work, or club cards that prized certain customers over others.

The grocery business, Angie had said, was about "One human serving another." "Don't forget to be a person," she'd remind you if you met her—and if you worked at Bounty Bag, you probably had.

Ray's encounter happened one morning when nothing was doing and he had stepped out from Deli to fix something he had noticed in the freezers and didn't like. Bridge's Bacon had re-arranged their label so it went perpendicular to the length of their extra-long bacon. This made it hard to read the label given how the bacon had always been positioned in the freezer, which was horizontally. Ray turned them all 90 degrees so the label would be easy to read. Ray was still smarting from having just cleared another batch of *The* Alfredo's personal garbage from Deli's trash can and made this refinement quickly, even brutally. This created an extra step of tapping the bacon packages into line.

"Good eye on the bacon," a thick voice behind him said.

Ray turned to find the little Apulian billionaire at the end of the nearest aisle, her brown eyes impassive but staring.

She wore, as usual, an immaculate black pantsuit and the Bounty Bag man's tie, hers alone not a clip-on. Despite the formality, Angie looked to Ray like nothing so much as a humble deli woman herself—or deli man, for that matter. She had a high forehead and bushy black eyebrows and she badly slouched. Her hair, a jet-black Brillo Pad, was not only coarse but, once you made it past the forehead, aggressively bountiful and always in disarray. Her low voice rumbled, like one of her milk trucks crossing a covered bridge, and her thick Everett accent—immediately apparent to Ray when she addressed him—seeped into words that one passingly familiar with Boston accents might think inviolate because they had no *"r"* to leave out ("Fuji apples," for instance). It was the type of accent that taught you about accents, the kind studied closely by anthropologists or linguists. Or, in Angie's case, by a Sloan School student who had attempted to quantify the contribution that the accent had made to Bounty Bag's bottom line by cementing certain affinity ties to area shellfish vendors and honey-wine producers.

"Thank you, ma'am," Ray said.

"A word of advice, young man: a little less duty, a little more love." She spun on her heel and clicked off down the aisle. "Nice to meet you, Ray," she added over her shoulder. "My best to the kid. Patrick, ain't it?"

"Right, ma'am."

If some customers saw Bounty Bag as nothing more than a respectful, affordable grocer that knew how to align its bacon for easy reading, store employees—including even chronic underperformers like *The* Alfredo and Toothless Mary—tended to regard it as an extension of family. Associates got paid minimum wage for starters, but the company hired managers, even its top echelon, from within. And as Ray had been surprised to learn when he first signed on at Store #28, all full-time employees, even new hires, could draw on the company's expanding profit-sharing plan. Angie and her co-trustees conservatively managed the plan from the Wilmington HQ. Like some don of old, Angie cut regular checks from the plan for emergencies, such as unfunded funeral or medical expenses or a long sick leave. There were semi-annual bonuses too, and they weren't chump change. Ray had taken home $1,200 last Christmas!

The chain's swelling reputation drew not just M.B.A. aspirants, who'd churned out dozens of case studies of the company, but also art students. One Mexican visual artist from the Rhode Island School of Design had driven up from the East Side to gather a sampling of the sawdust that Bounty Bag had used since the '50s to soak up spills. Euclides Montoya brought the sawdust and assorted juice boxes back to Providence for a capstone-project installation that even the reserved chief judge had reluctantly agreed to allow in the federal courthouse lobby for a day.

In recent years, however, Ernesta began to waver. Though she continued formally to affirm Angie as CEO—given Angie's performance, it was financially risky to eject her—she also gradually softened her opposition to Chesley on other key issues. Chesley's first goal remained the cash payouts. His new and second goal was gradually to pulverize Angie with derivative shareholder lawsuits so he could better accomplish the first goal. Signaling her shifting allegiance, Ernesta stopped vetoing the cash payouts. But for the time being she still wouldn't let Chesley add her name to the lawsuits.

The nuisance lawsuits comprised various breach-of-fiduciary-duty and Chapter 93A claims. Chesley filed the lawsuits against Angie and her sympathetic directors every year on October 1st, the first day of the new fiscal year, recognized by Aisle Four's do-it-yerself promotion as National Homemade Cookies Day. (Which it was.) In response, Stan's mom would raise a dozen defenses and counterclaims. These included the company's own by-laws and the Massachusetts Constituency Statute, which said a company is not required to max out shareholder value; directors may instead favor employee, customer, or even community interests.

This whole legal situation—document requests that seemed endless, interminable depositions in windowless hotel rooms—was bad enough. But (Stan had explained about a month ago) it had recently gotten worse. The latest development was that Ernesta had wholly defected and could no longer be relied upon to prop up Angie's job. The reasons remained mysterious. Perhaps cheapskate Chesley had finally replaced her Meneghini La Cambusa (which had been sterilized but understandably brought back memories). Or maybe he had built her a whole new Italianate mansion. No matter the cause, Chesley's newly minted majority took up in earnest the firing of Angie so they could release cash wads for further space balloons. Given the woman's popularity they'd need a pretext or at least some delicate planning, of course, and that might take a little time.

In the weeks following Ernesta's fateful switch, agitated associates began stacking mellow-looking Angie posters in the back of Ray's store and, from what Ray heard, the 73 other stores too. A vague notion circulated in the ranks that they'd somehow use the posters to show their support for Angie if the board crossed the Rubicon and fired her. There were even whispers about a more aggressive resistance movement to challenge the wicked new board or even, somehow, replace it.

Ray didn't find the associates' threats credible. They were, after all, grocery workers, with very little power and even less money to throw around. Meanwhile, Chesley's governing majority had printed and mandated these horrible "I ♥ My Job!" T-shirts, a stomach-turning glimpse into the abyss of Bounty Bag's future (Nietzsche indeed!).

"'Men are disturbed not by things, but by the views that they form concerning things,'" Stan said. He pushed off from the counter, one wing-tipped toe and a knee aimed at the bread aisle, and pointed at Ray. "Wear it. Please. We can burn them later."

"When Angie comes back?"

"She isn't even gone yet! You know what? Do whatever you want. *I* won't wear it."

With a weary sigh, Stan drifted off to the bread aisle, where he began restoring the flat edge of the shelved product in an apparent attempt to cool himself. Ray said to himself, relative to Epictetus's sentiment, that it was beautiful but flawed. To be fair, Ray agreed with at least part of the aphorism. People are disturbed by their views of things, and maybe you can do something about that by slapping yourself in the face now and again. But you had to admit that sometimes we're disturbed by the things themselves. Like this T-shirt, which wasn't even team colors. He looked down at the cheaply stitched monstrosity resting in his hands and asked, with genuine uncertainty, "What am I going to do with this?"

Toothless Mary materialized at his elbow and yanked the "I ♥ My Job!" T-shirt away from him. "I'll tell you. Give me that shit. I'm gonna' throw it in the trash!"

And for the first time in Ray's experience, Mary brought garbage to the dumpsters instead of fetching treasures from them.

Toothless Mary went home and Ray dumped in the Goodwill bin the rest of the store's "I ♥ My Job!" T-shirts. He texted Patrick five more times and gave up.

In a quiet moment he slipped *Garner's Modern American Usage*, by Bryan A. Garner, out from under the counter. First he thumbed his way over to "picaresque" and "picturesque," a helpful distinction when accounting for Pennacook. Next he worked the tricky "lie/lay" verbs. Originally a prized birthday gift from his mother, *Garner's* was indispensable, right up there with Groof. Its mini-essays on everything from doughnut/donut to bologna/baloney came in super-handy for Ray's ad and flyer touch-up work.

Stan didn't disapprove of *Garner's* but, seeking to focus his young protégé on topics beyond usage, had given Ray some business books like *Captive-Ate: The Supermarket Handbook,* which he had just begun to tackle, along with *Supermarket Happenings*, the low-quality online trade paper. "Time to look up from Deli, pal," Stan had said, handing Ray the book-stuffed tote bag.

Four o'clock approached. The mid-autumn light declined in earnest, blackening the high-windowed storefront as Sheryl Crow sang "Soak up the Sun," interrupted mid-lyric by "CALL FOR SERVICE DEPARTMENT: LINE ONE."

Ray logged on to the store laptop and found a new e-mail from Stan, inviting Ray to a tour of the giant Pennacook warehouse, HQ, and ten sample stores from here to southern Maine.

"Standard practice for all new management."

An e-mail was a little odd. Stan walked the store constantly and was more likely to swing by in person with a message. Also, Ray had never heard of this management meet-and-greet program. Seemed a little premature for a mere assistant deli manager.

Ray sensed scrambling and unknown burdens related to Angie.

He hit "yes" on the invite and poked through the butcher's fridge. He wanted to buy something special for Patrick. If his records were correct, Patrick had once more broken from his *gotcha!* veganism, which — he recalled with a chastening chill of self-doubt — always seemed to take hold right after Ray had made a generous visit to the fridge, hauling home chuck eyes or discount burger trays. Tomorrow, Ray decided, he would risk it, on a big autumn barbecue with Bounty Bag beef ribs slopped with barbecue sauce the way Patrick liked them. After they feasted, if Patrick *would* partake, into the trash with the gristle and tendons! Then they would talk about his binge drinking.

His flip phone buzzed. He expected Patrick for certain after all these hours of ducking and answered without looking. "Ungh," he grunted, their standard fraternal greeting. His mouth steamed as he left the fridge for Deli.

"Um...hello. This is Dr. Chong, principal at Andrew Johnson Memorial High School. Is this Patrick's father..." Crinkling paper. "'Markham, Ray?'"

"Yes, ma'am. Markham Ray here, except it's Ray Markham, and I'm his brother."

"You sound like a kid."

Ray blushed and looked away to darkening sawdust tossed over raspberry jam. Dr. Chong's voice was husky but had a chime-like quality that was hard to reconcile.

"Did you get my e-mail?"

"Yeah, um, about that."

Tuck it in, Ray thought, *bring it back home*. Like they'd always done at Chateau Markham.

"I need you to come in. My office at 10."

Ray gulped audibly. It was the same gulp he'd made at several failed dinner dates these past years. Gulp of worry, gulp of lust. A confusion in the heart, but felt in his throat. It also plagued him in times of distress, like when *The* Alfredo left a bad mess or Patrick pulled loose a new thread of trouble. In short, times like these.

"I will," he said. "I'll talk to him too."

But when he got home, all bad omens of this day were fulfilled. Patrick had disappeared.

Patrick Disappears

THAT AUTUMN PATRICK DYED HIS HAIR, INCLUDING his eyebrows and armpits, electric blue and painted his nails the same color. His Andrew Johnson Memorial High School classmates accused him of "trying to look different like everyone else," since electric-blue hair wasn't all that uncommon anymore, and partly they were right. He had done it to feel different but not, as they supposed, to stand out. He had done it to escape. Escape what? Things as they were. Everything. *Escape Your Everyday*, like it said on the pop-up tropical-cruise ad, also in electric blue. Frankly the people in the cruise ad looked like they were doing pretty everydayish things even after embarking on their magical journey. Grazing buffets, sunning in crowds. Off camera they were probably stabbing one another over dubious beach-chair dibs or locked in their cabins, pinned to the toilet by some norovirus.

To the company's credit, at least their ad properly presented "everyday" as one word, albeit cornily mutating it into a noun. So often, ads and signs used one word where two would be right. As in, *Open Everyday*. Or *Everyday is Christmas at The Christmas Abyss!* Which always drove Mom nuts. That said, the incorrect two-word version of the cruise ad maybe better matched Patrick's animating mood for his hair-and-nails coloration: *Escape Your Every Day*. Ray didn't care for his blue hair and nails any more than Patrick's classmates did, but for a distinct reason that only Ray could come up with.

"You can't work at Bounty Bag like that. It's against the Code."

He didn't say more, but in the context of Ray's long crusade to rope Patrick into part-time employment as a sacker at Bounty Bag Store #28, Ray was charging bad faith. As if Patrick's only purpose for styling himself was to duck the glories of supermarket employment, the opportunity to mat down his hair with spittle, wear a clip-on tie and $10 shoes from Payless, shag carriages, and somehow keep a straight face for questions like "*May I hold those melons for you, ma'am?"* All for minimum wage. *No way*, he had concluded, not without guilt (because of that *other* thing he was doing to make money these days...).

Ray ultimately accepted Patrick's hair coloration with silent grace or else exhausted resignation. It was hard to tell the difference between those two qualities with Ray, if there even was one. Some nights Patrick would lose track of the time and stay up late reading or watching videos in The Rock's booth. If he stayed up late enough he'd catch his brother on the flip side of one of his occasional double-shift work days at the celebrated Bounty Bag. Ray would slump back into The Rock, fingers rendered gelatinous by a day's worth of rubber gloves and frequent washings, and head straight for the stove. Within minutes, he'd whip up something simple to munch on — fried bologna and canned beans — eyes off somewhere else and acknowledging Patrick only with a grunt. Ray's incessant homilies expressly concerned the morality of wage labor, but the message — question, rather — that his body conveyed was altogether different: Jesus Christ, does everyone have to *work* all the time?

Late Saturday night, he hopped off the yard-sale bike with the streamer-festooned handles and pitched it with zest into the shrubbery abutting the Pennacook Mall's entrance. Some spasmodic part of him hoped it would smash to smithereens.

His laptop bag swung low from his shoulder as he walked to the mall's pizza place. By all accounts it remained a flowering business, still only circling the mall's event horizon. Even so, it was hedging its bets and had recently unveiled a series of themed pizza deals and a chicken-wings side-menu. A canvas sign promoting the side-menu hung out front.

Jake's Joint: Wing's Headquarters

Well, asked Mom-in-his-head, *which is it?*

Mom was a befuddled submissive to Dad's drinking but she had been a pile-driver when it came to education. With Ray, an essay-writing medalist with solid verbal test scores, now off to Bounty Bag Store #28 instead of the Sorbonne, she left behind a captious ghost.

He whipped out Ray's twenty and got a souped-up version of the pizza joint's "Cinn-A-Deal." At the Cinn-A-Deal's core was a large jalapeno pizza slicked black like a terrorist-sabotaged oil field, a cinnamon-French-toast crust the only bulwark against the oil's further spread over the edge to his fingers. The war-torn pizza came with three cinnamon sticks (w/ frosting cup) and a cinnamon-dusted Coke. Patrick secreted his bundle off to the hollows of the mall where, following yesterday's aborted track meet, his reviving teenage stomach made quick work of the entire feast, oil pools and all. The aftertaste was more an after-material, a pervasive, dank adhesive. Something a dentist might spray to scope a surgical mold.

A thick iron ring, several inches across, with a single brass key on it, was clipped to Patrick's belt. The key clanged against the beefy ring while he chomped the Cinn-A-Deal. As he finished, it fell to rest against his leg.

He tossed the ravaged pizza box aside and took in the morbidly enticing dead mall. He popped open his laptop, withdrew his Local History notebook from his back pocket, and started scratching out figures and gathering notes for his essay on the mall's collapse. His first hurdle, a fresh thesis, was perhaps insurmountable (it was no secret that box stores and the Internet had body-slammed the mall years ago), but he pitied Mr. Grant, his Local History teacher, and not simply because of his terminal lung cancer, and wanted to do a good job for him.

Officially their text was *Haven's Pennacook* (1882), a book that Patrick defied anyone to read all the way through. He doubted Haven himself had; he seemed to have composed whole sections in his dreams. (*"Forged with slough-floundering brio by a lowly, soaring people, the Pennacook Mill's founding water wheel (c. 1842) daringly yoked the leaky waters of the majestic Pennacook for the first time since fishy Poseidon ascended his sparkly throne and divinely commanded them to ooze forth from noble Billerica."*) Haven mined boredom from even the late-seventeenth-century Pennacook Indian raid that slaughtered a quarter of Dover, New Hampshire, in the span of a single afternoon during King Philip's War. When he addressed other material of promise — a scholar's hypothesis that the Pennacooks' egalitarian ways had inspired early American democracy, from the New England town meeting to the federal project—Haven's attention lapsed altogether, his quill trailing off mid-sentence. *Ho hum, tyme 4 me porridge.* A page later, Haven's pulse miraculously reviving, he turned in his account of Pennacook's true claim to fame, *"The premier tarring and feathering of our revolutionary epoch."*

In May of 1774, Haven explained, a redcoat approached Pennacook farmer and gunsmith Jacob Pike with a musket for repair. Pike, grinning, set it on his sawhorse and, brandishing his hatchet, cracked it in two. Later that same morning the redcoat and his fellow soldiers, also grinning, returned carrying a tar bucket and rolling a barrel of feathers. They dragged Pike to a field at town center, later site of Truble Cove Plaza's parking lot, for application of their supplies to Pike's naked torso. Then they marched Pike all the way to Concord for display. At sunset they moved the party over to prospering Eaton for debriefing and pints at a popular royalist tavern where Pike, tied to a tree, expired. Patrick tried to understand why Haven found Pike's ordeal so historically important. All he could come up with was that, as Haven the snob emphasized, Pike was the first Penny recorded to cross the threshold of prestigious Eaton for a reason other than manure delivery. Though he died there too.

Pike was so celebrated that the town had elevated him to the Pennacook Rebels' mascot. During halftime at Rebels football games, the cheerleaders would select a Penny from the crowd, douse him in grape juice and plastic snow, and parade him around the track, an extraordinary display of self-flagellation that richly gratified the opposition. There had been mascot soul-searching on this account, talk of a "Pennacook Boars" swap-in, but it never went anywhere. Most Pennies found the ritual too damn hilarious to part with.

Patrick liked that Mr. Grant let them disregard Haven and make up a topic. He was a flexible guy. The assignment just had to be an essay, not some never-ending slide deck. Other classes Patrick found not so hot. Ms. Hamden's math class was worksheet heavy. Patrick would fold and peel her worksheets into snowflakes, not even realizing what he was doing until he was in the middle of one. American History, his second-period class, should have been a favorite, but his spirits flagged as he strapped on his snow shoes for the long march through Mr. Hitch's quiz blizzard. Mr. Hitch went hog-wild downloading the ones on the Progressive Era and the New Deal's Alphabet Soup. Stumped, Patrick improvised. He riffed off Pennacook's Polynesian-style restaurants, answering that W.C.T.U. stood for "We Cut Toothpick Umbrellas." In English, meanwhile, he read *The Boxcar Children* extracurricularly, wedging it into *A Separate Peace* and inflicting a satisfying *crack* on its preppy little binder. Mr. Papadopoulos's toad-and-potions take on science was okay, not requiring *Boxcar Children* self-medication, and Patrick was carrying a C in that one. If they graded winter track, though, he'd have an F. That was for sure.

He hadn't wanted to quit the one-mile relay yesterday, but at the opening gun his very first step veered off the track and his mouth was already dry from the nips that JV shot-putter Muscles Carbonara (a/k/a the Mad Crapper) had handed over in the back of the bus. The merciless blue heating machine beat down from the ceiling and baked his tongue into a parched flap that scraped his upper lip. He made nine of the twelve interminable laps around Lowell High School's indoor track but then scuffed the heel of the runner in front of him and tripped and stumbled over his own running flats. Rounding the corner for lap ten, he simply crapped out, his feet saying "no thanks" and running straight toward the bubbler. On the way he spotted his sophomore English teacher, Mrs. Modell, on the sidelines cheering on her son from the Chelmsford team, and deliriously tossed the baton into her surprised hands, blurting, "Great catch!"—just before he blew chunks into the bubbler. The vomit ran down the side and on an unlucky kid in pigtails sitting under the bubbler and it was a short dive from there to the gymnastics mats piled up in the corner, where Patrick collapsed, wishing they'd just leave him.

 Coach Gibson insisted on driving him home after the meet.

 "Your brother will want to know about this. Immediately."

 "He's at work." *Who cares anyway?* he thought. *It's not like I'm going to be a professional athlete or something.* The same thought hobbled every race.

"Principal Chong, too. An ounce of gratitude would do you good, you know."

"For what?"

Coach Gibson gave him his wide-eyed "Isn't it obvious?" look, and Patrick's stomach convulsed. He winced and banged his fist against the door. "Ouch."

Coach Gibson handed him a water bottle. "Sip this. Don't gulp: sip."

Coach Gibson had other looks, equally authoritarian. One was the skeptical raised-eyebrows look, which said both "Really?" and "I'm disappointed." Rather efficiently, Patrick felt. Another was the down-turned-mouth ("I'm very sorry to hear that"), which, when coupled with tented eyebrows and jangling digits below, said either "I don't know if I have enough change to purchase another Giant Alaska Cinnamon Roll from the vending machine" or "I'm airing out my nuts now." Coach Gibson used these various expressions so frequently that they had stamped his skin with an array of wrinkles that, in repose, said all these things at once less insistently.

"I used to be a drinker," wet-eyed Coach Gibson confided, not for the first time.

"Me too," Patrick said. Or was he just starting?

"Here's our stop."

Patrick approached The Rock's two steps and heard Coach Gibson bellow from the truck.

"You're a good runner, Patrick. Except when you're not. Like today. See you at practice."

The aching wind blasted through his green-mesh tank-top and fig-leaf racing shorts, and he felt stripped, alone. Inside he threw on a sweatshirt and jeans, then chopped an apple and crinkled it up in a paper lunch bag with some shredded lettuce for A. Lincoln, Eleanor Roosevelt, and Satchmo.

At the high school he hid his bike behind one of Ms. Chance's Thai rain drums and got in with the master key he had secretly copied for this purpose. Drills buzzed somewhere near, in the new building, as he slipped into Mr. Gherkin's office, flipped on the fluorescents, and approached the terrarium, humming loud and low a made-up, directionless tune. *Mmmm chicka. Boooom chicka.*

Mmmmm. It sufficed. The box turtles hearkened at the familiar vibrations and moved toward Food God Patrick. He unrolled the bag and hand-fed them the lettuce shreds and apple chunks, then fell into a beanbag to watch them.

They had a studied patience that Patrick admired. They ambled over the leaves, twigs, and rocks that Patrick had swapped in last week for the filth-smothered ones. The twigs cracked warmly like kindling as Satchmo made his way across a bundle and the terrarium hot lights dappled the box turtles' domed shells lavender and golden. A. Lincoln was a girl. They were Mr. Gherkin's, but Patrick had named them and cared for them ever since A. Lincoln turned the corner of Mr. Gherkin's doorway one day during the mad rush following lunch period, when bacon burgers richly perfumed the air, and Patrick stepped on her. Patrick sneaked in to feed them on Saturdays and Sundays. Some weekends he'd miss a feeding, clicking shoes or blazing hallway lights turning him back with his paper food bag still rolled up. He'd try to make amends the next time and offer something special like a jar of plump earthworms. Satchmo and A. Lincoln feasted on the treats, but persnickety Eleanor Roosevelt snubbed him. According to Ray's book of quotes, the real Eleanor Roosevelt said inspirational things like "the future belongs to those who believe in the beauty of their dreams." Perhaps.

Why had he tossed back nips before a race? Around his thirteenth birthday, when he began to think more broadly about things, he read a blog explaining that, given the laws of physics, everything he ever thought or did or *was* had a cause. So there was no such thing as free will. Now any time he felt like he wanted to feel good about something—French-kissing his first and last girlfriend, the sad-eyed Stacey Larusso, at Good Harbor Beach the morning after the sophomore dance last spring; assembling his clarinet for old time's sake and reveling in the G-blues scale, discovering that he still "had it"—he started to question why, and the answer ended up sounding like a chemistry formula. And when something bad like this happened, he felt powerless to stop it. With no one at the switch, could he ever really hope to? He drifted off to sleep, sinking in his dreams.

Hours later, deep undersea in a bean-bag nap, he woke to the drilling. It had grown louder as they worked their way down to the carcinogenic old building. Patrick kicked open the second door to Mr. Gherkin's office-nook and discovered on Mr. Gherkin's desk two new master key rings with new brass keys on them and a pile of discarded locks.

If you wanted to play around with physics and causation, maybe you could trace his drinking back to Dad. Some memories you could make a pretty good case for, but others stuck out for no clear reason.

Like in one of them, Patrick, seven, was up watching Conan's masturbating bear, and Dad was on the floor between the couch and the TV. Patrick had lifted his head just enough to slip a face cloth underneath it to give him a pillow. Later he drew a glass of water and poured it on Dad's ear. As he was returning the glass to the kitchen counter there came the *blitz! blitz! bliiiiiitz!* of the doorbell and Patrick, eager butler, hurried over.

"What?" he asked. He was very surprised because Ray had been talking this up, rubbing the sleepover privilege in his face for weeks.

Ray stood slump-shouldered, his knapsack over his back and his sleeping bag stuffed under one arm.

"Out of my way, shrimp," he said.

He shoved Patrick aside and stepped through the door.

"What's wrong?" Mom's reedy voice came from the hall.

"My stomach. It hurt."

"Too much pizza and soda," Patrick volunteered.

"It felt all twisted. So I came home."

"Is that what you said?" Mom asked.

"I left a note." He shook and twisted like a wet dog. He pulled back his hood with both hands and looked around. "Is everyone okay?"

Once the hubbub settled, Patrick returned to the television. The late-late-late slot was a '70s biopic of six-packed Bruce Lee. Fiercely alive to the slightest provocation, Bruce Lee vibrated and glowed saint-like around the fringes as he chopped, swept, and kicked through his foes, from West Coast suburbs to steamy Hong Kong. The final shot zoomed in on Bruce Lee's shiny grave. They cleaned it nearly every day; *it was really cool.* Beneath the televised grave, Dad's shadow heaved, and Patrick fleetingly marveled that Bruce Lee himself was returning from the dead.

He continued typing notes on his laptop and in his notebook sketched the nail parlor's sign, outlined in carnival-like light bulbs, and the frontier-themed log-cabin entrance to the Tobacco Shack. The sketch would be a valuable reference for his Local History paper, but maybe later he'd turn it into an oil painting for Art.

Two Pennacook boars crossed in front of him with their familiar rocking lope. There was no food here for them, but Patrick wasn't concerned. They were smart. They'd find their way out. Like Nancy's Shoes and nearly every other business that had occupied the mall.

The boars had been the subject of Patrick's first term paper for Local History. Tusked and ornery, the coarse-haired beasts had an average adult weight of 300 pounds and were a surly cross-breed. Some of their ancestors had escaped from the old pig farms of Pennacook's golden years. Others, more numerous, had like feral pigs elsewhere on the East Coast migrated from Tennessee, Andrew Johnson's state. They were Southerners, in a word. A third strain descended from the hefty Carpathian boar, infusing the cross-breed with a mean streak and a keen sense of bulk's advantage in a scrape. Gilmore Champs, the "Father of Finance," had imported this strain in the 1890s and fenced them into a park for hunting. But the park burned down in the late 1920s and only the fiercest boars survived, goring through the carnage to freedom. Today's largest boar colony numbered into the hundreds and occupied the woods between Ray's supermarket and the Pennacook River, rich with savory turtles. Patrick had pieced this all together easily enough from archived issues of the *Pennacook Beat* and Champs's turgid memoirs.

For this paper, Patrick could've followed a well-trod path and written yet another essay lionizing Bounty Bag, the local-hero employer of first and last resort. But something about this expiring mall drew him. He felt it had something to do with the boars, as if the mall's failure was an extension of their presence. Maybe it was a half-in-love-with-easeful-death type of situation. Who knew.

The dead-store signs in particular drew him. After their parents' wake, their detached Chicago uncle, their only known kin, had taken Patrick to a highway-side Dunkin' Donuts while Ray hung back at the funeral parlor. Patrick sat at the pink-stooled counter and peered through a curtain of rain at the store's towering sign. Its near permanence struck him. His parents' bodies could do nothing now, nada. But this sign might persist beyond even Patrick's lifespan, stolidly steering highway customers off Exit 27 to coffee and doughnuts and greasy wax wrappers. It was a remainder, in a sense, of his parents' world. As long as "Dunkin' Donuts—Next Exit!" called out, you could say that part of them was still around. They may have even looked at the sign, from this very stool.

As consolation this was not much better than the notion that they lived on in Patrick's memory banks, the standard shaky take on immortality that the more conscientious adults fed to atheist Patrick at the funeral, instead of thrusting the "they're-in-a-better-place" hardline on him. (Ray, as near as Patrick could determine, was a Catholic in ongoing negotiations with God over the latter's existence, a position that appeared to provide Ray with no consolation for anything.) Nor did Patrick find solace in the nutty stuff he read on science websites, much of it sounding more like death than death itself. Theories about how we never die because our quantum information is stored in the fabric of space-time, if not swallowed in a black hole. Or how even if your body shriveled, exploded, or was burnt to a crisp, your mind could be uploaded to a server and sheltered forever in a weatherless moon crater. *Where do I sign up!?!* Patrick did like space-oriented news though, the periodic viral post about alien signals, another kind of sign. It really made him wonder. Who was out there? When their message came through, what would it say? *"Hopefully something more profound than 'Jake's Joint: Wing's Headquarters,'"* said Mom-in-his-head, who abhorred commercial English even when it didn't misplace apostrophes. Patrick briefly considered working these odd ruminations into his dead-mall history but nixed the idea as personal minutiae, basically irrelevant.

Much like the track meet. Patrick couldn't even understand the event, let alone account for it to others. To explain why he had gotten drunk before the track meet, he supposed he would have to look back further than the moment on the bus ride when he downed the nips. Maybe the chain of events began Thursday after school, when they had the crazy argument about the Bradys.

Dinner Thursday had started out mellow. Ray was making tuna melts. His fare, generally, was simple and delicious junk. Burgers and dogs. Boxed pot pie. When Patrick was a vegan, Ray made clunky adjustments, but Patrick, always hungry, ate with the same gusto, tunneling into the food like he was trying to escape through it.

While Ray cooked, Patrick sat unhelpfully at the kitchen table, ravenous and wasted on Muscles Carbonara's Own. Muscles Carbonara's Own was Muscles Carbonara's brand-name for his pot brownies, which he sold at Andrew Johnson High. Andrew Johnson High was an alternative brand-name that Muscles Carbonara had considered.

Ray diced sweet pickles and plopped them in the tuna and mayo and mixed it all up, then put it all together and eased the sandwiches onto the pan.

"Check this out: garlic Texas toast. Provolone too, instead of cheddar. You want to flip 'em?"

"Sure, Ray."

Ray mussed up his hair. "*I* like you."

Patrick flipped the tuna melts and they sizzled in the hot buttered pan. He handed the spatula back, giving Ray the baby smile that he knew Ray craved. Also partly to flatter Ray, he pulled down from the shelf *The Boxcar Children (#10): Schoolhouse Mystery*, in which, it was promised, the irrepressible Benny used his curiosity to help them snag a swindler.

The thing about *The Boxcar Children* as they revealed themselves over the breadth of the series (my lord, there were over one-hundred volumes, each a distinct adventure) was their irreducible innocence and simplemindedness. Violet (favorite color: violet), who could charm any grouch. Adorable Benny, the littlest one, with his blueberry-stained cheeks, endearing remarks, and cherished chipped pink cup sourced to the dump. Unfortunately, the kids had other qualities that were less appealing and the author leaned heavily on sentimentality. For instance, they loved chores. Oh boy did they. But this genial submission — which must have been the big draw for Ray when he picked out the box set — felt forced and inauthentic to Patrick. Patrick also noticed that in the original version, from 1924, Father was a drunkard. But such gritty sorrows were swept away by the relentless good cheer of the 1940s series reboot.

As if to compensate for his earlier mockery, Patrick said, "These are pretty good," as he slid back into the booth.

But Ray had something else in mind.

"I was thinking we could watch *The Brady Bunch.*"

"Uh, do we have to?"

The DVDs were stacked high on the booth's table. Ray had pulled the Bradys from the library two weeks ago and had introduced them to Patrick over apple crisp. Ray confessed that he had never seen the program, but the box heralded a classic, with sound lessons and ample humor.

"Besides, I know you like kids shows," Ray had said, spooning an extra dollop of apple crisp onto Patrick's vanilla-ice-cream-smeared bowl. "Eh, Mr. McFeely?"

So what if Patrick streamed free videos of *Mister Rogers' Neighborhood*? No shame there. The show was indisputably great.

The Brady Bunch, in contrast, was a mite too slick. Patrick didn't trust these Brady characters, could almost feel the actor who played Father Mike chafing against his too-neat role. And Ray kept forcing him to watch the most chilling episode of all, "Father of the Year." They had already watched it twice last week, but now he restarted it, running it like a fight tape that Patrick needed to review scientifically for an upcoming championship bout.

Patrick's drowning eyes veered toward the screen. The episode interacted adversely with Muscles Carbonara's Own, and Patrick's heart thumped with mounting dread and paranoia, cold sweat bursting forth from his scalp and from the center of his chest. Once more, as in a recurring nightmare, step-dad Mike punished Marcia for invading his den afterhours, and after she failed to complete her punishment chores, Mike jacked up her sentence to a two-week grounding. Then when she sneaked out past curfew to a nearby mailbox—to mail in an essay nominating Mike for a local newspaper's "Father of the Year" award—he punished her *again*, excluding her from the family ski trip. At the end they all melted together when Mike won the award and learned that Marsha wrote the winning entry. But how believable was that after Marsha spilled glue all over Mike's architectural drawings? Mike didn't seem like the type to forgive.

"He should've just let her stay up late and work on her essay," Patrick said when it was over.

Ray retorted that the implausible set-up only proved the validity of the larger imperative. To obey family rules.

"Ray's rules, you mean. And we're watching this when I get home so, what? I have good morals or something?"

"A better attitude, maybe? Comfort and a laugh? A pleasing reminder that life's loose ends sometimes really do tie up?"

"You don't even believe that yourself! Besides, we're nothing like these people. It's a really big family made by two other families kind of smooshed together and plopped in an awesome house in California. And we're just one family, cut in half, stuffed into a travel trailer where it's freezing all the time. We're the anti-Bradys."

Come to think of it, maybe that was the key difference between Mister Rogers and the Bradys. With Mister Rogers there wasn't some fake-nice family-shaped box he wanted to nail you into for a quick and unceremonious burial. He was alive to the world, which meant, now as always, being alive to a world of suffering and change. Ray didn't know this.

"It's not freezing here."

"I mean outside. Outside it's freezing. Inside it's like a lava pit. Can we turn the heat down? Like, now?"

"Everyone's a critic. Hey, maybe you should be a critic."

"I don't do windows." Then, like a critic, Patrick picked up the DVD box and rendered a final verdict. "Beyond parody."

As if to sanction him for the squabble, Ray slapped onto the table a fresh optimism survey.

"*Do* this."

Patrick began reading the first question aloud. "*'You and several playmates belong to an after-school three-legged potato-sack racing club.'* What the hell, Ray!?!"

Mister Rogers supported Ray's inference that Patrick was more of a videos guy than a reader, but any number of book-based orphans held more appeal for Patrick than the wretched half-orphan Bradys. Tom and Huck, the Boxcar Children. Even precious Tony and Tia from *Escape to Witch Mountain.* Not to mention Patrick's all-time favorite storybook orphan, can-do heroine Dorothy Gale of Kansas.

The series high-water mark, hands down, was *The Emerald City of Oz*, a utopian vision of peace and abundance. L. Frank Baum mistakenly thought this his final Oz novel and he pulled out all the stops, from parallel plot lines to a brimming roster of exotics. Evil Nome King Roquat the Red excavated an underground tunnel to the Emerald City's inner sanctum, aiming to decapitate Oz as a prelude to its total annihilation. Meanwhile, Princess Dorothy, unaware, placidly toured Oz's back waters in a sagging "sawhorse"-drawn carriage. The politically inflected back story had Uncle Henry and Aunt Em fleeing to the fairy land from a farm-foreclosure nightmare in the States. In Oz, they discovered, Ozma provided for all, guaranteeing part-time employment to the able-bodied just for fun and retiring the Kansans to a ritzy urban pad. (*"Every one worked half the time and played half the time, and the people enjoyed the work as much as they did the play, because it is good to be occupied and to have something to do."*)

One bit didn't connect though. Professor H. M. Wogglebug, T. E. (H. M.: Highly Magnified; T. E.: Thoroughly Educated), Oz's answer to Ray's vaunted C. Richard Groof, H. S. D., had launched a new academy where he dosed students with algebra-and-Latin-bearing Education Pills, clearing the calendar for all-day athletics. Patrick would've taken a pill in place of Ms. Hamden's worksheets and Mr. Hitch's quizzes, but not if it meant more winter track. Besides, Professor Wogglebug's pill-popping pedagogy seemed pretty shallow. To Patrick's surprise, Baum thought he had a hit on his hands, basing an ill-starred stage show on the insect pedant.

Wogglebug receding to the background, Baum rallied for the closing chapters. The novel pre-dated Freud's influence but ended with an unselfconscious pacifying orgasm. Ozma could not subdue the Nome King and his minions by force of arms. After all, she had but one general, the affable Omby Amby, and zero soldiers at her disposal. Instead she used the Magic Belt to cloud their tunnel with thirst-inducing dust and then had them exit at her "Waters of Oblivion." One sip and her "horde of intruders" became "harmless as babes," "smiled innocently," and "seemed lighthearted and content." Their dark mission forgotten, they shriveled up and marched back home. " '*That was better than fighting*,' said Ozma."

All very stimulating. (Pun intended. Patrick didn't lust after Ozma, a mere girl, but sometimes cast imperious Principal Chong in her role, an unexpected turn-on.) Coincidentally, *The Emerald City of Oz* was the first book Mom had ever bought him, at Toad Hall Bookstore, on a let's-get-the-heck-out-of-here-before-he-blows daytrip to Rockport.

Night of the Bruce Lee biopic notwithstanding, drinking didn't always put Dad to sleep. One liquor-tinged memory was of a Cub Scout hike to Zealand Hut, in the White Mountains of New Hampshire. That time Dad was very much awake.

Patrick was excited by the bunkroom's wonders, the three layers of wood-cabined beds, the low dusky upper area where the bunks connected and the boys could play fort, and the opportunity, later, to witness stars, maybe even the Milky Way. He got carried away and hurled across the bunkroom an ill-considered disclosure.

"I don't want my bunk near you because I don't want to smell your stinky farts!"

Dad pounded across the planked floor. He swept in low and grabbed Patrick's hand, pressing hard on a pressure point at the base of his thumb. It was a devious trick that jolted Patrick and he folded over crying.

"What's wrong with you?" his father said hotly in his ear, whiskers scraping.

After roast chicken served family style, Patrick heard him guzzling in the next bathroom stall. He leaned over Patrick's bunk at lights out and, redolent of peppermint, kissed him on the lips.

"You're a good boy. There's nothing wrong with you. Do you forgive me?"

He did. Dad read *Red Rackham's Treasure*, one of his bedtime favorites, while the other boys rustled around them. He held a pen flashlight in one hand and touched the index finger of the other to each character's belly as he spoke their lines in the devastatingly funny voices he had made up for them: Tintin, with whom Patrick identified closely, chipper and high-toned; Captain Haddock, the hard-drinking man-child in whom Patrick saw his father sympathetically portrayed, gravel-voiced, apoplectic at Professor Calculus, whose obliviousness to his own deafness fueled much of the humor. Thomson and Thompson, the twin-doofus police investigators, bumbled their way through the pages, and Dad cursed them with a kazoo-like whine.

"They remind me of Ray," Patrick interrupted as Thomson and Thompson took turns getting bitten by crabs, Thomson on a toe, Thompson by the nose.

"I *know*," Dad whispered, heavy hand resting on Patrick's chest.

In the morning Patrick and some others climbed the steep rocky riverbed to survey the beaver pond. Patrick had sopped his boots in a trail-crossing brook, so he wore spare socks and school sneakers.

Dad stood below, shouting.

"Get down. You can't go up there with sneakers! We don't have another pair if you get those wet and it's not safe with sneakers!"

Patrick ignored the command, but his heart soared at the protective note of terror as he followed the other boys over the mossy rocks, sidestepping the icy flow. Back in the cabin, Dad wrapped him in a blanket and sniffed his warm head.

On the drive home, though, Dad shouted at him in front of the rest-area bathroom men.

"Just take the towel and stop waving your hands at the goddam machine!"

The machine wouldn't let out another paper towel until he tore off the first. Patrick saw this, but his fingers were slow on the uptake.

"Can't you hold it in, pal, when there are people all around?" someone muttered.

Dad ignored the man, but after Patrick tripped over his unlaced sneakers and fell face-first in the parking lot, he asked, "What's wrong with you?"

Patrick closed his notebook and laptop. He considered that it wouldn't take much to evade Murph Dooley, the night guard, and crash the whole night here—avoiding Ray once more, as he had last night with the turtles. A couple of quick moves ought to do it. Into the long hallway that had led to a bathroom, under the broken metal grate covering Slipt Disc, the expired CD store. Or he could sleep in the curved hall that once served as an entrance to Great Times, the closed arcade where, his online research showed, Gauntlet's four-colored wizards and pink-bowed Ms. Pac Man once romped for the youth of the '80s. A giant peeling silver arrow still pointed around the curve to the vacant arcade.

The Great Times arrow would probably flummox Murph Dooley, sending him in the opposite direction. The hapless night guard's job had survived three rounds of graffiti and one assault-and-battery "situation." Murph explained to the *Pennacook Beat* that while the first graffiti hit ("IT COULD BE WORSE?" the pink spray-paint asked), he was outside, and while the second graffiti attack was happening outside the mall (in a more scornful vein, the artist wrote "MURPH'S A EUNUCH" in flaming red, followed a tad redundantly by "4-EVA!"), Murph was inside picking through garbage pails for "potential devices."

The third graffiti attack occurred in the mall's main drag. ("I KNOW: RIGHT?" was all it said.) That one happened simultaneously with the A&B, a couple fist-fighting in the parking lot over which Chinese takeout place to choose. The lovebirds explained to the P.P.D. that they had just suffered a shock, having arrived for dinner only to find a bright-yellow Pennacook Board of Health sign posted on the Jingo Chef, their favorite Chinese spot. It was all downhill from there.

The Jingo Chef had once occupied a large mall storefront. But in the '80s it had retreated to the mall parking lot, to a primordial former Kodak booth where it magically produced hot enumerated meals from, it seemed, an underlying manhole. Jingo Chef the restaurant was no more, but his likeness abided. A thirty-foot statue, an Old

Hollywood yellowface in full chef's regalia, still loomed beside the water tower overlooking the mall. Booth renovations were underway to convert his former demesne to Pennacook's lobotomized version of a Starbucks, two chairs and a drive-thru.

"When asked for his location at the time of the simultaneous attacks," *The Beat* reported on the incident, "one inside the mall, the other outside, mall security guard Murph answered that he was inspecting the part of the mall's roof that was behind the mall's false front. 'You can't see anything back there,' Murph was reported to have said."

Ray had read *The Beat* article aloud to Patrick with growing dismay.

"Why don't they use his last name?" Ray complained, folding the paper down and looking at him. "What if I don't know the guy?"

"It's a small town."

"It's improper," Ray pressed, Mom's ghost emerging. "And why 'reported to have said'? They *are* reporting."

"Probably they had a tight deadline or something."

"And what kind of people fight over Chinese take-out in this town? We've got six more places just like Jingo Chef within a four-mile radius."

Here he had a point. Pennacook hosted an unusually large number of Chinese restaurants for a vanilla-white burg of just 15,000 souls. On Worcester Road alone the A-framed Tiki Shed and the murky, low-slung Wu Doon Mang, lit in blue and pink neon, offered the standard fare: pork-fried rice, lo mein, and pu pu platters of chicken fingers, bland white pork disks for duck-sauce dousing, boneless spare ribs, and egg rolls. The aptly named Sichuan Surprise, a newer place on Governor Hutchinson Road, was more authentic than the other restaurants and chemically charred the unsuspecting mouths of Pennacook's sugar-tamed palettes with spicy unfamiliar regional cuisine that was impossible to order without the menu photos. Sichuan Surprise was rapidly gaining a loyal following but without a liquor license it couldn't compete directly with Chopsticks, the umbrella-drink hole-in-the-wall next to The Penalty Box. The Penalty Box was less a bar than a rock-walled den for drunks to start fights in, or end them, but on weekends

Chopsticks and The Penalty Box catalyzed a modest plaza nightlife, a two-stop pub crawl of exotic drinks and beer. *The Beat* had written it up in a staycation feature: four stars. Ray and Patrick had never been to Chopsticks, but, driving by, Ray had more than once panned the uncreative name, saying that was like calling an American joint "Forks."

Jade Sunshine, a fifth Chinese restaurant, had cornered benighted Oakhurst's market. Its sole competitor was a shapeshifting minimall insert that cycled through names and niche-sniffing strategies at breakneck speed—buffet begetting hot-pot yielding to dumplings—yet earned points for pep. Last check its specialty was dim sum and they called it *Golden Dragon III*, but its implied predecessors' existence was considered a dubious proposition.

A *seventh* Chinese restaurant, Pat's Café, had snagged a sweet spot in the well-trafficked Truble Cove Plaza, which a late-'70s growth spurt had mercilessly carved from the town center's bleeding colonial heart to make room for, among other establishments, Ray's store. Menu-wise, Pat's Café was practically identical to Tiki Shed and Wo Doon Mang but it had other distinguishing virtues. Pat Feng, the chummy proprietor, knew everyone's name and he offered a popular lunch buffet marred only by his wife's surveillance. Coco Feng perched during lunch hours high up on a bar stool overlooking the buffet dispensary and clamped down hard on those she called "big boys" with the mid-meal imposition of "four entrées only" and "no more spare ribs" restrictions. Patrick and Ray had once witnessed a buffet-side legal debate between Coco Feng and defense-side divorce attorney Joe Delahunt over Coco's no-nos and the Rule of Law.

"Ad hoc," Attorney Delahunt said.

"*Bú shì* ad hoc. Hoc," Coco replied, an index finger sprouting.

Ray shook his head. "I don't think either of them know what that term means, but I think she's winning."

Sure enough, Attorney Delahunt retreated from the entrees and meaty sides, heaping a veggie medley on his platter.

"Better for you," Coco said, not without kindness. She may have been frugal but she wasn't cheap, really. Strategic eaters were endemic to Pennacook, and if you weren't careful they'd eat your shirt.

Attorney Delahunt scratched his side with his loose hand as he passed their booth with his greens-mounded platter, little onion cubes of uncertain origin affixed to his sleeve. More beatdown RMV road tester than Atticus Finch, Attorney Delahunt appeared to have been balled up in a dank fetid corner somewhere. He was a defense-side divorce attorney, it was commonly understood, because Pennacook had two divorce attorneys and everyone preferred the other.

Pat's was their favorite. Like other Pennies, Ray and Patrick worked their "Best Chinese Restaurant" pick into discussions of any length about their adopted hometown. In fact, now that Patrick thought of it, a historical account of Pennacook Chinese restaurants was another good topic, if the dead-mall essay didn't work.

All these restaurants, plus Jack's Four Lounge. Jack's Four was not a Chinese restaurant, but it had been one for several decades after the Second World War, and the residual Polynesian atmosphere confused and attracted forgetful Pennacook seniors, who, once they had stumbled inside, were not entirely disappointed to happen upon the Cambodian- and Irish-American strippers and the still-wider juice selection. More rarely, Jack's was mistaken for a French restaurant on account of the sign on its mansard roof reading "Mon Amateur Night." Several Pennacook Chinese restaurants echoed the Polynesian décor of Jack's Four. Tiki Shed, with its flaming torches and Easter Islandish totem poles; Jade Sunshine, its rear wall a clumsily painted fantasy mural of bending palms, lounging nude bathers whose hips appeared dislocated, flying cranes, and, in one corner, a miniature dinosaur, hopping.

When Ray and Patrick crossed the bamboo threshold of one of these places, cozily aglow with Christmas lights, food trays sailing toward vigilant Penny-packed tables, he was occasionally reminded of the Disney trip.

They had called it the Disney trip, but Patrick's eye was on the Animal Kingdom, and he made a constant drumbeat about it.

"Isn't this terrific?" Mom asked, regarding the fancy airport limo, which had soft drinks and a TV — Mom had won the trip in a hockey raffle — and it was clear she needed a "yes."

They easily filled most of the first day in one section of the Magic Kingdom standing in hour-plus lines and dodging scooters. By noon on the second day Dad had settled onto the park bench outside Walt Disney's Enchanted Tiki Room.

"Best ride in this place," he said, looking up at Patrick.

Patrick could see him hurting. It was a dry park, something Dad hadn't cared to research, so no pineapple nips were on hand to compliment the Tiki Room's terrific park bench, but he made up for it the next day at EPCOT, where he informed the bartender at the little faux British pub that it had "no feeling" but did sell his "favorite beer."

"Which one is that?" the bartender asked, sliding a napkin and coaster in front of him.

"One next to your hand."

While Dad had the one next to the bartender's hand and Mom stood behind him, arms folded, frowning, Ray and Patrick escaped. They wandered the sad dead-ended miniature version of where Mary Poppins "happened," where Ray, succumbing to Patrick's play for souvenirs, bought him a red double-decker bus in the gift shop, followed by a beret in France, a Moroccan basket, tea in Japan, American fries, Italian chocolate, schnitzel in Germany, Chinese chopsticks, a Norwegian troll, a sombrero in Mexico, and Canadian maple candy. It wasn't enough. It was *never* enough. Then the world was done ("Where's South America?" Ray asked) and Dad was done with the one next to the bartender's hand and the day was done. Rose & Crown: fine pub.

Dad hopped the campground bus and the three of them explored the rest of EPCOT as the sun went down and the parts came together on the lake for the closing show. Patrick had a special fascination, similar to his later affinity for Pennacook's dead mall and its commercial ghosts, for the failures on or near the perimeter between the World Showcase and Future World: the vague, desolate Odyssey Center, its cavernous dark-windowed building that resembled a restaurant but appeared abandoned; the Journey Into Imagination with its lusterless mascot Figment and his flibbertigibbet side-kick Jules Verne (whoever that was); and a little farther out the aquatic attraction that, despite fusing itself to the Nemo brand, had failed to crack the fish-boredom problem. At Patrick's insistence they hit repeat on the non-line Figment ride until its manic song and hazy script scrambled their brains into oatmeal.

The next day was the last day of the trip, with a mid-day flight home and the Animal Kingdom already open at nine. But Dad didn't come out of the tent-cabin for the Spam-'n-eggs breakfast Ray fried on the gas griddle while Mom pretended to put the site in order, looking back and forth between Patrick and the tent-cabin while Patrick looked back and forth between the tent-cabin's flaps and her.

"Don't give me that," she said. "Don't you see this is your father's way to *relax*? Can't you even *grasp* that?"

"Makes perfect sense," Ray said, looking at Patrick. Understanding what the question would ignite, he added, "So, no baby elephants?"

He heard a ruffling and looked across the mall to where white flakes whirled like nuclear ash down a purple cone of light toward a park bench. A raised Bounty Bag deals flyer, paper-thin disguise, obscured only the face of the one-and-only…

"Muscles Carbonara," Patrick said.

Muscles Carbonara balled up the flyer and threw it on the floor. Perpetually overheated by 'roids, he wore his standard tank top, cargo shorts, and unlaced construction boots, a black fisherman's cap his only nod to October. An orange neckerchief trumpeted Muscles Carbonara's membership in Boy Scouts of America's Troop 555, Pennacook, MA, Greater Worcester Council. Patrick also was a Troop 555 member, in the Tiger Patrol led by none other than Muscles Carbonara. He sporadically attended the weekly meetings under St. Mary's, his khaki uniform displaying, under his left breast, the lowly First Class badge. The red badge with the trefoil, eagle, scroll, and two stars signified unmistakably that Patrick, at the ripe age of sixteen, was most definitely not on Eagle track. That was no matter. Muscles Carbonara was a Tenderfoot, a rank they practically gave you for turning eleven.

"Are you aware that butter quarters are running two for five dollars at my place of employment?" Muscles Carbonara asked.

"Jiminy Christmas! You could jack off a whole day on that."

Muscles Carbonara flexed his ample right bicep in response. Despite the plural nickname, it was his only real muscle of note, a globular tumescence, itself resembling a shot put, that gave Muscles Carbonara the tipsy, asymmetric profile of a male fiddler crab. Muscles Carbonara had purpose-built the bicep for use in the JV shot put circle. This being high school, however, alternative masturbatory explanations for its bulk were compulsory, and Muscles Carbonara embraced these with the robust glee of a shameless roué. Adjusting to his audience, Patrick turned extra vulgar in Muscles Carbonara's presence.

"You brought it?" Muscles Carbonara asked.

Patrick held up the giant metal ring with the single key, the ring shining golden. "Pried it off my cock five minutes ago."

"I want it sterilized before you return it, bro. I need that to keep me snug when I'm flaccid."

How long would this go on? "Too bad it's all stretched out from when mine, totally limp, burped ever so gently during his afternoon nap."

Dick jokes exhausted, they got down to business.

Muscles Carbonara worked the register part-time at Ray's store, where he ran two scams. He carried out the smaller one right there at the register. When Muscles Carbonara's chums happened through his line, they didn't pay. Muscles Carbonara simply sailed their items over the scanner's range and bagged them. Muscles Carbonara didn't get any groceries or money out of this and risked ready detection—black-glass half-spheres scattered over the ceiling, concealing a battery of cameras and an elevated hallway overlooked the whole store—so this scam was little more than a status-boosting stunt. The cashier's equivalent of a drag race.

The back-store scam was for profit. Muscles Carbonara had arranged with one of the more corruptible elements on Ray's deli line, the cosseted *The* Alfredo, to smuggle frozen chickens after hours. When Muscles Carbonara picked them up, he compensated *The* Alfredo in the in-kind manner he preferred, twelve-packs of beer and boxloads of condoms.

"Magnum only, please," *The* Alfredo specified, *sotto voce*. "Smaller ones would harm my unit."

Muscles Carbonara then loaded the chickens onto his uncle's pickup for delivery to The Kluck Klucker in Oakhurst, a Buffalo-chicken dive bar willing to take a chance for cheap birds. The Kluck Klucker was one of those places that seemed normal enough except when Patrick was in a vegan phase. Then Kool Bird, the establishment's sunglasses-and-flip-flops-wearing chicken mascot, struck Patrick as grotesque, even cruel. Kool Bird even seemed to be mocking the avian lives, starting with his own, snuffed out by Pennies in their never-ending quest for wings and drumsticks. Muscles Carbonara pocketed the difference between what The Kluck Klucker paid him and what he paid for *The* Alfredo's suds and comfortably expansive rubbers, diverting a small final sum to Patrick for Ray's schedule. Which he now turned over.

Muscles Carbonara reviewed it.

"That boy works *hard*."

"I know."

Muscles Carbonara unrolled him a twenty. Feeling rather shitty, Patrick took it. Patrick would later add the twenty back into Ray's emergency meal-money box, but that didn't exactly undo the bad deed. After all, they were still robbing the store, and who did Patrick think would slip the same bill back out of the money box the next time Patrick was cash strapped and wanted to hide from Ray?

Muscles Carbonara needed the schedule from Patrick because, aside from Toothless Mary, Ray's supervisor, only Patrick had it. Ray closely guarded the information, afraid that *The* Alfredo would exploit Ray's schedule to slack off. Ray had confided this to Patrick one Sunday while handing it over and asking him to post it to their ghastly "Simpler Days" wall calendar (fluffy sleigh-ride and ole-fishin'-hole paintings by "Nebraska's Harken Cornblower").

"You see, he's like a builder who wins a zoning-code tweak that allows him to add another 2,000 square feet vertically. So he starts throwing up McMansions every-which-where. Like that new development in Maynard where they tore down the driving range and put up 'Maynard Estates'? Except it's not space *The* Alfredo maxes out. It's *laziness*. If his schedule overlaps with mine, he'll show up an hour late saying, I dunno, karate practice went over. And then I can't go home, and you can't eat right."

We don't eat right anyway, Patrick almost inserted, but he didn't want to slit his own throat, imperiling through nutritional sarcasm the steady supply of discount Bounty Bag private-label Oreo equivalents ("Genoreos," Patrick called them) and such that anti-junk food hypocrite Ray packed into their shelves.

As for the matter at hand, a normal supermarket would have stored Ray's schedule online, where at best anyone with Ray's password could hack it and at worst Ray would be forced to share it with all his co-workers on the deli line, together with his home contact info and maybe even an "employee fun fact" about himself. (*"My interests include being tired and hopeless and not planning for my own future while lecturing my brother Patrick that he's headed nowhere and force-feeding him* The Brady Bunch.") But then Bounty Bag wasn't normal by any means. The company pulled down $4b a year but, as Ray kept raving, it still didn't own a website.

"Got it," Patrick had said, when Ray told him to keep his schedule private.

And yet here he was, turning Ray's schedule over to Muscles Carbonara—for *The* Alfredo's benefit.

"Now let's test that key," said Muscles Carbonara. He slipped his money clip back in his cargo shorts.

In reply, Patrick said what was beginning to rate as his least-favorite word in the English language. "Okay."

At the Pennacook Mall's entrance, he hailed Muscles Carbonara to halt bikes (Patrick had a license but no car; Muscles Carbonara owned a trashed $450 BMW from 1994, but didn't even have a permit). He reached into his bag's zippered pocket, lifted open the blue-box maw, and dropped in Ray's Hampton College application.

That last spring, the spring of the accident, Dad put on another show, at the Dodgers v. Tigers Little League game.

Coach Mowder had tried to un-teach him, but Patrick, the Dodgers' worst hitter, always positioned his hands far apart on the handle and chopped downward like a caveman with his club. He developed a compensating strategy, swinging at nothing and hoping the faulty pitching that afflicted the Little League would tilt the odds in his favor enough times that he'd enjoy a respectable number of walks to first base and not strike out at every at bat.

"Swing, goddammit!" Dad shouted from the bleachers. "Swing! Swing! Swing!"

"Leave the kid alone," someone said.

"He's my son, goddammit, and I'll say whatever I want to him."

The fourth ball zoomed wildly overhead, and Patrick took first on a walk.

"Your dad's a real ass," the first baseman said.

"He's not my dad."

Patrick leaped toward second. His one card was that he ran fast, was a good stealer. As if to punish him for the lie, the first baseman not only ran after him with the ball in his glove but when it was clear that he would not be able to catch Patrick and tag him out, lifted the ball out of the glove and threw it at Patrick's back. It landed with a hard thump against his spine. Patrick hit the dirt between first and second.

"Ow!" he shouted. He curled and uncurled like some terrified worm stripped from its hole. Something took hold of him and rather than pull himself together he indulged the humiliation, spinning around and spawning a dust cloud over the sunburnt field. The other boys, on both teams, gaped at this history-making display with a mixture of horror and savage amusement.

"Ow!!"

"Get up!" his father roared, rising in the stands.

Coach Mowder had admitted to the Dodgers in a season-opening speech that he did not deal well with conflict. "It shall be one of my limitations as your coach," he had rather formally told the boys. Now, after he'd scrambled back over the ridge from the portable toilet, he took in the scene with one glance and bolted for the woods, shirttails flapping. Patrick decided to follow his coach's lead. He got up from the dirt and ran for the outfield fence, hopped it, and disappeared into the path that led into another part of the woods.

The path led to a brook where Patrick hurled his baseball cap into the water and sat down on a rock. His tears gradually subsided and his senses came alive to the wet earth and the murmuring brook and the chill. Famished, he crossed the brook and continued along the trail until he broke out near a convenience store. At the front counter—thinking, *"I'll do something bad now"*—he brazenly lifted some Twinkies from under the teenage clerk's homicidal-looking eyes and asked if he could borrow his cell phone to call home. The Twinkies went down smooth in the restroom. Then Mom arrived.

"My son's been delirious," she lied to the clerk. She put the back of her hand to her head.

"Going around. Hope the fever breaks soon."

Mom rushed out of the store, but Patrick was surprised by something in the clerk's tone. Short of sympathy but in that same general direction. He looked back over his shoulder and saw the clerk's open mouth, golden sponge cake and creamy filling churning.

"Brotherhood of thieves," the clerk said and gave him a wink.

The long night drew to a close. They had finished up at the high school—the new master key worked—and Patrick was ensconced in a hammock in Muscles Carbonara's basement ("Can I live here awhile?" "Suit yourself."), laptop open and wedged in his lap. He was just about to give up and turn off his computer when he stumbled across a choice *Pennacook Beat* clipping that he realized immediately would be the lynchpin for his Local History research paper.

It was dated November 12, 1965. The lead story, it recounted the Pennacook Mall's grand opening, which closed out that year's Veterans' Day parade. The veterans from the Second World War were in their robust prime, and it was clear from the double titles, military and civilian, of the local dignitaries that the cohort dominated Pennacook's government. The article bullet-listed the many zoning exemptions, revealing that the town had practically melted its book of ordinances to make way for the mall. It was as if the exemptions themselves were an honor roll of veterans or of those KIA'd.

A large photo of the ribbon-cutting ceremony stretched across the page, just under the masthead. A dense crowd of uniformed World War II veterans and jacketed Bounty Bag associates and managers of every rank and stripe—some WWII veterans also wore Bounty Bag jackets, over their uniforms—crammed onto a many-flagged platform, overflowing onto the steps and out into the parking lot.

Sharp-cornered U.S. Navy hats rose up in small, irregular groupings like flotillas on choppy waters. They brushed up to and blended with Bounty Bag ball caps and Bakery hairnets.

Farther down, the reporter recounted lesser details, including the erection of the Jingo Chef statue, which concluded the festivities. A smaller photo showed many hands together, raising the Jingo Chef like the flag at Iwo Jima. The author used the Jingo Chef as the hook to round out the piece, exhibiting a historical interest absent from the fear-and-failure-haunted pages of today's *Pennacook Beat*. In the process, he neatly resolved a longstanding point of curiosity for both Patrick and Ray.

> With the Jingo Chef's successful installation, the village of Pennacook now touts two Bounty Bag supermarkets and a remarkable seven Oriental restaurants, each offering a colorful menu of exotic cocktails. Five of the establishments opened their doors between 1949 and 1957.
>
> The prevalence of Oriental restaurants is a mystery to many residents. Its cause, however, is a point of general agreement among Pennacook historians and barroom wags. Though their food is based on Chinese cuisine, the restaurants are styled primarily according to the popular Polynesian fantasy aesthetic called "tiki." This heavy ornamentation caters to the nostalgia of Pennacook's large population of naval veterans returning from success in the Pacific.
>
> In fact, state records show, Pennacook is home to the third-highest per capita concentration of Second World War veterans in the Commonwealth. Casualties were also profound.

The essay for Mr. Grant would not be about the mall's collapse after all. It would focus on its birth and on the great tiki-restaurant boom of the '40s and '50s. Today's Pennacook restaurant scene, it turned out, was the commercial residue of the largest party the world had ever known, the one among the Allies after Hitler and Tojo's defeat. It didn't take Patrick long to type out a draft. He'd bike the Pennacook restaurant trail tomorrow morning, after the kitchens opened for the Sunday buffets. He'd ask to interview some current owners and staff as primary sources. Through them, he could maybe reach back to former owners too.

He felt philosophical again after he completed the rough draft and looked over his hammock's edge to where Muscles Carbonara, hunched over his Xbox controller, bathed in green light.

"Let me ask you something. Do you feel free?"

Nonplussed, Muscles Carbonara swiped at his fisherman's cap in a simian gesture but soon gathered himself for what was the obvious answer, given that Muscles Carbonara was Muscles Carbonara.

"As a bird, of course. Don't you?"

Patrick didn't answer, but by the time he closed his eyes and flew off to dreamland at 2:30 A.M., he had almost forgotten that he was the Mad Crapper's accomplice, a Bounty Bag chicken thief, and a drunk like Dad.

Faculty Meeting

DR. CHONG HAD PROMISED ARCHIE THAT SHE WOULD try—even harder—to muster support for the TCO to fund her new school, and at the October faculty meeting she did.

She arrived a few minutes late, mounting her strap-on cushioned seat and planting in front of her a miniature American flag, a little patriotic boost for Archie's idea. While she settled into place, the grinding faculty babble fell flatly into the tamped-down carpet.

"I wish potato skins would be entrees."

"You just order them to come with the meal, and then you don't order a meal."

"If they put it on the appetizer menu, then I feel embarrassed to order it as a meal."

Potato skins. *Lordy*. Last month it had been fried mozzarella sticks. Though the Red Sox appeared headed to another World Series this month, they were not the leading topic in this forum. Most faculty were locals, and Pennacook's passion for the franchise had withered after the Sox won the championship in 2004 and broke their relentless and, to Pennacook, alluring curse.

"Anyhow, I don't like potato skins. I think peanut-butter toast should be an entree."

"It is, at The Penalty Box."

"What about allergies?"

"There's peanut butter, and *then* there's Jif."

"Agreed!" Dr. Chong interjected, slapping both palms on the table. "Jif offers a fine product! Now, if we can please get moving."

She set out Archie's proposal.

"Isn't that illegal?" Ted Canyon immediately asked.

"You're the union rep. Grow a spine, man!" said Tito Tiggs, a muscle-bound gym teacher who tracked five miles through the halls of Andrew Johnson High—bounding over the occasional stray boar—between 6:15 and 7 each morning.

"We could all get *shit*canned for this," said Carol Modell, sophomore English.

"Dr. Chong is right. We need to fight for this school, personal risk be damned," said self-styled "Americanist" Bobby Hitch, pink lips moving in his oily black handlebar moustache.

"Are you serious?"

"Fudge no! I love my job."

"Ha! Ha!"

Tito Tiggs stood up and pressed his knuckles to the table.

"Listen, I know we'd all rather be talking about Jify's Extra Smooth and limitless 'tater skins right now but nobody knows this school better than I do and we need a new one. We got water leaking through the ceiling. Loose tiles. Cancer clusters in the old wing — I think we all know there's still asbestos down there — and when I run through this place it's like touring a goddam *paper* mill, such foul stenches."

"And that's coming from a gym teacher!" Bobby Hitch exclaimed.

Bobby Hitch's tight green cords had torn cuffs and circular buttcheek erosion, making them a clear breach of dress code. Dr. Chong wasn't above publicly carding him for the infraction if it proved necessary to bring him in line.

"What do you think, Brand?" Bobby Hitch added, turning to an ally, the school's librarian and IT teacher.

"I don't get paid to think. Just teach."

Both of these fellows were skating on thin ice. There were questions about Bobby Hitch, but you could call them harmless ones. Like: What did he *do* all day? As far as Dr. Chong could tell, he downloaded quizzes and hosted history-themed Jeopardy. But the kids idolized him, proclaiming him "the smartest person ever!" in teary-eyed graduation speeches, because he let them chatter through the semester and eat Italian-style meals in class.

The suspicions circling buddy Brand Welch — who after valiantly opposing uncompensated thinking had returned to twiddling his thumbs — were of a more sinister stripe. Dr. Chong had nailed the librarian at the recent Parent-Teacher night for hanging up and spotlighting a vintage movie poster of buxom motorcycling girls, nearly sparking a salacious "On Your Penny" feature in the *Pennacook Beat*.

Dr. Chong gave Brand a scalding lecture and tore the girls down leaving no fleshy traces, but under the librarian's name in Dr. Chong's mental roster the poster left a decided gray mark not so easily removed.

So far, motorcycling vixens aside, Brand Welch had been the subject only of un-actionably vague, though identically worded, complaints that during their library visits he had made several female faculty members "feel uncomfortable just because of the way he is." It seemed to Dr. Chong rather a standard feature of men to make women feel uncomfortable just because of the way that men were, but her eyes remained peeled.

Too bad she couldn't just fire these two and hire nephew Tommy instead.

She was always looking for ways to save Tommy. A skilled archer with untreated dyslexia, Tommy had dropped out of Springfield College under a mountain of debt, only to land in the workshop of Dr. Chong's dad, a floundering Flushing tailor.

A blunt and fractious man at least since his tender wife's death when Dr. Chong was three years old, Ba had called Dr. Chong "doctor" for as far back as she could remember—until the day she earned the one doctorate that in his view did not merit the title. In a burlesque of a graduation-day celebration, he hauled her to a taco truck parked on Commonwealth Ave. and, turning on a dime, started using her first name.

"Which taco, Regina?" His erect finger stabbed the laminate menu in time with his words. "*I. Haven't. Got. All. Day.*"

Within the hour he'd mounted Peter Pan and headed back to Queens and the urgent business of loosening crotches.

Now Ba and Tommy were predictably at loggerheads. Ba made Tommy walk an extra block for sandwiches on account of bad blood with the Chins' neighboring noodle-soup shop. Then Ba charged Tommy with time theft because this put him over the twenty-minute limit.

One day he screamed at his apprentice, "You bloodstained this man's shirt!"

And maybe Tommy had. He had kept up with the archery, competing in tournaments through the tri-state area and madly shooting five hours every Saturday at Bayside Archery. Perhaps this was a healthy outlet, but tailoring scabs atop archery calluses made a gruesome and unruly pile that, when torn, bled relentlessly.

More worrisome, a Chinatown gang called the Flying Turtles, deeming Tommy a modern-day Ho Yi for greater NYC, sponsored him in tournaments. Steeped in Chinese mythology, the gang's leader explained that in the earliest times Ho Yi had shot down surplus suns with his bow and arrow, cooling the Earth and making it livable.

Tommy denied he was a member of the Flying Turtles. "They won't let me in. I said I'd never use it on a person," he claimed. But then why practice on person-shaped targets?

Now Tommy said he wanted out of that world, but as a high-school principal she had nothing good to offer. He still hadn't graduated college and much like his auntie on faculty-meeting days, Tommy was too restless for a school.

Why did she care? Because he admired her unfairly, with a love built on the collective mound of Dr. Chong's top-shelf Christmas gifts (his widowed mom, Dr. Chong's sister, fried carp and had nothing). Tommy mistakenly and touchingly regarded Dr. Chong, who gave him his first bow, as a font of lovingkindness.

"Could relate to the second agenda item," someone observed.

"It's not just the smells," Tito Tiggs pressed. "This is a sick building. We got low Vitamin D up the kazoo and water that tastes like cement or earth clay. We have whole hallways with not a single classroom properly lit anymore the wiring's so old. I run by 'em every day. Mr. C, you know what I'm talking about. Speak up."

"Sure do," said Mr. C, the gregarious health teacher who was known for pushing things too far and flinging condoms around his classroom to desensitize the kids. "We also got water bubblers that are known herpes vectors. Why don't we stand up for that?"

"Yay herpes," muttered one of the sarcastic young English teachers, twirling a finger.

"I can't speak to cancer clusters," Dr. Chong said. "That's a big fat maybe, but I second all the rest."

"They'll slam *dunk* us," Ted Canyon said. "If we walk out, we'll lose our jobs."

"Coward," Tito Tiggs said.

Tito Tiggs's verdict on the union rep was sound. Pennacook's teacher's union and its reps were weaklings, easily cabined or lured into management's camp by a chintzy management-union tube-steaks picnic. Case in point: on the school committee's austere marching orders, Dr. Chong had once more prevailed in last year's salary-scale negotiations, hogtying the critters and padlocking them in the hold, below-decks of inflation for yet another two-year contract. Yay! *Why* were teachers such marshmallows? She had a theory. Unlike, say, your insured dentist or your test-hardened actuarial accountant, teachers and their families had little purchase in the world and nothing to fall back on. Or maybe it boiled down to character. They taught school to hide from life, and now they had to negotiate? Good grief! Perhaps one day something terrible would happen (a teacher famine?) and things would change. Here in 2013, that didn't seem likely.

The room fell silent at Ted Canyon's grim prognosis, and Tito Tiggs sat back down and returned to the solitary corporeal pleasure of massaging his own pecs and biceps with his flat, clamp-like hands. A *chuck chuck—kaff!* crossed the table. Mr. Grant, Stage IV lung cancer, had worked in the old Sick Building for four decades. His hacking cough drew morbid, accusatory stares, most of them directed at Dr. Chong, but others aimed at Mr. Grant himself, as if he had uncorked a dark village secret.

"What about Hallenbuck?" said Coach Gibson, finding yet another thorn. "We've got the best Turtle in the state. I'd hate to lose all that."

Point taken. Hallenbuck ice time held near-sacred status with voters. The Turtle, their deluxe ice resurfacer, could reach 18 mph, about twice a Zamboni's top speed, and was the finest friction-reduction machine on the market. It smoothed ice for Friday-night free-skate, when Pennies from all quarters skated with the joy and release of a holiday. It was like on the ice they became a different town, a town in graceful motion. Andrew Johnson could crumble into dust for all anyone cared, but Hallenbuck and the Turtle, which were adjacent to the high school, must be preserved.

"Well, we have time to think," Dr. Chong said, delay her best hope for faculty buy-in. "Vote's not until December 18th. Next item, the Mad Crapper..."

"I love these meetings," someone chirped. "Always make me feel like I'm part of something smaller."

"Mad Crapper remains on the loose," Head Janitor Kyle Gherkin said. "Latest and greatest: center of the gym floor, before *and after* b-ball practice."

"Suggesting an accomplice," Tito Tiggs re-emerged from his musculature to muse reasonably. "I mean, twice in one day? I, uh—forget it."

Handsome and sad, Tito Tiggs fell back into the shadows. At root a gentleman, even a prude, he poorly fit this rough-and-tumble world of faculty blab and Mad Crappers. Andrew Johnson High or any cold and impersonal institutional workplace was not Tito Tiggs's true métier. No, the place for a tender Tito Tiggs was garbed in a loincloth at Dr. Chong's feet, attesting regularly to his everlasting fealty as her leading and most loyal concubine. There, or among the pedestaled classical Greek statues at the MFA, with Dr. Chong at *his* feet. Why was it always Archie Simmons? Why didn't Tito *Tiggs* ask to "meat" her after school? Answer: he was happily married, unlike his lecherous captain.

Also, she was 4'11", weighed precisely 110 lbs., and her chest was a nipple-studded plank. Not exactly hot stuff in these parts! Exposed—might she add well-toned?—legs notwithstanding, Dr. Chong held for most Pennies the erotic fascination of the twig-boned parakeet, and she gave Archie reluctant kudos for concluding otherwise.

In contrast to Dr. Chong, the small cohort of Asian female students in her school, all Korean adoptees, were a real hit. Perpetual front-runners in the prom-queen stakes, the Korean-American girls had swept the crown from 2006 through 2009. Dr. Chong chalked this up to their perceived exoticness and to the boys' unconscious association of them with good times at Pennacook's numerous Chinese restaurants. Also, the Korean girls were larger than Dr. Chong. One of them, passing Dr. Chong in the hall, had mistaken her for her adoptive little sister, a petite freshman, and gave Dr. Chong's head a sympathetic pat that left her with a rosy glow for the rest of the day.

"Other recent victims were the science labs," Kyle Gherkin continued. "Band room: tuba. Art department: papier-mâché squirrel, thematically integrated."

That earned a laugh from this crew, and just then Dr. Chong noticed the quivering bear-like back of French teacher Benny Delacroix (*pr.* Della-CROX) emerging from under the table at the other end of the conference room. Under cover of the faculty's laughter, he gunned for the exit. Delacroix was pushing thirty years at AJMHS. He taught French but couldn't read it and barely spoke it in the outrageous accent of Pepé Le Pew. Come June, his energies completely spent by months posing as fluent, he was known to pad the last weeks with back-to-back screenings of charming family epics *Jean de Florette* and *Manon des Sources*, with English subtitles so everyone could understand the films (instead of no one). *Let him go*, Dr. Chong thought as his tired body bent around the door frame. *I'd have ADHD too after three decades in this place.* If anything, Benny's sly exit earned her begrudging admiration for its boldness. Though if one of his colleagues blew the whistle on him and forced Dr. Chong's hand, she'd collar him in the parking lot and herd him back to his stool.

She looked out at the sea of mostly hangdog faces. There were stars among them. Moral Tito Tiggs. Scholarly Keith Grant, her temperamental Local History workhorse, now cancer riddled. Janice Chance, her sole African American faculty member, who honchoed the hands-on environmental-science electives and her popular new journalism course. Teachers of this caliber were unfortunately the exception at AJMHS, and the good ones rarely lasted. Pennacook's stingy salary scale had something to do with it. Her gaze drifted to the slack, cattle-eyed underperformers—a finger in a nose, a paranoid palm swatting an imagined fly—and she wondered once more, Whose fannies would be in those chairs if we upped pay and shrank classes by half?

Or—a quiet angelic (dissenting) voice in Dr. Chong's conscience whispered—*if you stopped pressing that super-duper IN ONLY intercom button to spy on them and then sprinkling their evals with harvested tidbits? Not to mention the careless spill of rumor. Or that sprawling new surveillance system, which even Archie doesn't know about.*

I can't help myself, the majority replied, its decision binding.

In any event, she had more pressing concerns than faculty ennui right now. This Mad Crapper character, for instance.

"So what are we going to do about it?" Dr. Chong asked her head janitor.

"Mad Crapper may escape," Kyle Gherkin conceded. "But we've thwarted future mayhem. Took darn near all week, but we've changed all the locks and molded a new pair of masters."

"Where are the masters?"

"Oh, I got 'em. Here—here's one for you, and the other—the other"—hands swimming over his many janitorial pockets as in an exotic dance—"It's in my office. Yeah, that's where it is. Oh no, it's right here!"

He bent forward, daintily reached behind him, and tugged from the middle of his rear end a large ring with a single brass key.

The Mad Crapper's unchecked infiltration of Dr. Chong's high school seemed all the more bitter when she reflected on her first encounter with Pennacook, in her nauseating past life as a sewage-treatment-plant inspector for the state of Massachusetts.

It was long ago, sunny and prosperous 1998. Inspector Chong, then a bushy-tailed thirty-eight-year-old, five years into her DEM career, was on site for a surprise review.

"Howdy," said Harry Grimes, Pennacook's plant manager, his left thumb hooked in a pocket as he leaned back with "look what the cat drug in" amusement. He wore reflective aviator sunglasses and his right hand was a dry, fingerless stump, potential cue to a past plant accident—and underlying safety gaps.

Grimes escorted her to his tin hut for some pre-inspection chit-chat.

"Not often we get visitors from your department."

"All the more reason."

"Coffee?"

"Had some."

"Lemonade?"

"No thank you."

"Fudge?"

"No!"

"Up we go then!" Grimes slapped his left thigh and rose.

Grimes's stance shifted to lordly languor as he led Inspector Chong grandly to the wheel that greeted the city's inflow. "First, we sort," he said. The wobbly wheel bucked and lurched, crudely separating from the rest of the flow reams of shredded toilet paper and a motherlode of rubbers. Grimes touched her elbow and changed gears once more, jazzily promenading her alongside a five-fingered canal network to a watery grid that expanded over most of the plant's backside. "Next step: settling. Let Mr. Poop take a dip in the hotel pool. Shake *off* those traveler's blues." Grimes stepped to the edge of the last pool and pointed to where the liquid stream drained off to a capped bin that resembled a grain silo. "Secondary treatment: protozoa are our friends!" he exclaimed, his inner caged nerd busting loose. Gradually clearing to effluent, the wastewater would be poured into the Pennacook River, where it would add a certain creamy buoyancy to kayaks rounding the pipe-side river-bend. "Now for the *grande dame* of wastewater treatment: biosolids." He swung his arm around and pointed to some troughs where the mucky, hole-black sludge crept like a burglar toward the whirring centrifuge, which scooped it up and prankishly flung it around, caking the walls. "Would you eat carrots plucked from that? I would."

It was the end of the inspection and Grimes halted Inspector Chong on a platform above the secondary-treatment pools. Feral pigs watched with longing from a nearby hill.

"Pause," he said. He punched his stump out to the side, a hunter's call for silence in the midst of elusive prey. "Smell anything?"

Inspector Chong pinched her nose.

"See: nothing. Poof."

"Poof," she repeated nasally.

Either Grimes was faking it or due to some sort of sensory death he had no inkling of the plant's true sorry state. The over-eager flywheel that Grimes had regarded with such pride at the beginning of the tour had catapulted toilet-paper globs and slimy used condoms over the metal gates to civilian terrain, and the canal work channeling the effluent and sludge was more like a harum-scarum theme-park flume ride than a proper conveyance for potentially lethal waste product. She could hardly match Grimes's unbridled enthusiasm for munching Pennacook-sludge-dipped carrots!

Back in his hut, the gentleman's C- drew a frown but, interestingly, no formal protest from Grimes.

"Where's everyone else?"

"Lenny fell in. Joke!"

In fact, Grimes explained, Pennacook had slashed the plant's budget, forcing Grimes to send Lenny off in style with two-dozen glazed chocolate cake sticks from Dunkies.

"You're looking at this," he said, brandishing his stump.

"No."

"You want to know how I got it."

"That's okay."

"I'll tell you: voting."

Grimes elaborated as he walked her to the gate. It turned out that his injury was but one of many suffered in the teeth of Pennacook's voracious undercapitalized machines.

"Distracted," Denise Hamden, Math, reported, regarding the third and final item on the agenda: troubled junior Patrick Markham.

"My best student," Keith Grant, Local History, said between coughs. "Really cares."

Local History was a state requirement and a bit of a dog. No one wanted to teach it, except, for unknowable reasons, Mr. Grant. Mr. Grant had even *requested* Local History this fall, which he had taken to calling his "terminal semester."

"Curious," said George Papadopoulos, who taught an all-inclusive course called Science for kids who had long ago slipped the college track. "Enamored of bonobos. Elephants too."

"Animal lover, definitely," said Kyle Gherkin. He nodded at Mr. Papadopoulos. "Always checking on my turtles."

Against her better judgment, Dr. Chong allowed her head janitor to keep an office terrarium. Kids weren't supposed to be in there, but the spacious office was Gherkin's realm of ultimate autonomy, affording much-needed respite from cleaning others' messes. She could sympathize. Let him rule his turtles!

"Kid's a slacker," Mr. Hitch said. "Never turned in the 'Andrew Jackson: American Hero' quiz. He at least could've guessed."

Dr. Chong recounted Friday's track meet where Patrick had collapsed drunk mid-race and this morning's follow-up meeting with Patrick's dad—brother, as it turned out.

"That's bad," Mr. Hitch said.

"The right word is 'sad,'" said Mr. Grant. He coughed once, drily, into his fist.

There was an underlying animus between these two that transcended Patrick Markham. She couldn't quite put her finger on it, but it had something to do with Mr. Hitch's disdain for Mr. Grant's course subject and his snooty aversion to teaching it himself. Mr. Hitch had thrown a fit last year when the spring Tetris game called Scheduling nearly landed him with two sections of Local History in his loose third period. Dr. Chong would've forced him, but happily for Mr. Hitch the colored blocks fell his way after the school committee once more exacted punishing cuts from her music program.

This had become an annual tradition. The all-male school committee waited until April break, when the opposition was dispersed on family excursions, and then gathered at the Kluck Klucker to scarf piles of Buffalo chicken wings, trimming the figurative fat of Dr. Chong's music budget while they unbuttoned their pants for incoming poultry. An appalled Rife Dobson had a term for it: AJMHS's music program was "testing new lows." Rife was her one-man Business Department and an avid supply sider. But he had soft spots for the recorder, which he tirelessly tooted straight through the AJMHS faculty holiday bash *every last December*, and the Eastern Marching Band Association. The school committee's Music Department belt-tightening, which Rife uniformly opposed, had assorted downstream effects, like last spring's *Brigadoon*, which was super-light on atmospherics. The kids had no costumes, wearing black T-shirts and blue jeans instead, and for a backdrop they recycled the blood-curdling Dracula's Castle, scarcely evoking the vanished romantic Highlands.

In a way, though, the musical had been perfect. Pennacook was a kind of Brigadoon with malaise. Pennies kept up with modern gadgets, like smartphones and tablets—in fact, the town was a well-known technology test market—but didn't seem to do much with them. They seemed always to be peering into the past on their devices or wishing for something (or wishing for something to wish for).

"I think we should expel him," Mr. Hitch said.

"That's harsh," Tito Tiggs said.

"I'm not seeking advice. I'm only informing. Patrick Markham will be out for three days."

That morning's meeting with Ray Markham had been brief. He had shown up fifteen minutes early, yet when she swept into the office he was still standing in front of the guest chair like he needed permission to sit down. Cynthia, three feet away at her secretary's desk cruising Facebook, could have stopped smacking her gum for half a second to grant him that permission, but then she'd be deprived of the pleasure of watching him wait for it. He wore scuffed black dress shoes, battered-soft khakis, and, over his shirt and tie, a grease-stained buttoned green jacket with a familiar octagonal patch on the pocket. Ah, the boy worked at Bounty Bag, her favorite taxpayer. Wacky costume explained!

"Hello," he mumbled.

"Please step into my office," she said, shaking his damp, scrubbed-red hand.

He moved stiffly and his shoulders slumped forward, as if to say, "Hit me please."

The meeting had its thrills. Dr. Chong's legs elicited a brief but appreciative glance from the lad—whom she now recognized from the deli section; he made the best chicken-salad subs—and she felt the familiar power surge as she successfully imposed Patrick's well-earned suspension. "In light of his prior history of misconduct, and the health and safety concerns we presently feel, both for him and for..." She would've liked a TV show. Ray zoned out while she spoke, his eyes half closed, reeking of provolone, vinegary Italian roast beef, and the half-dried sweat of his interrupted work day.

"Understood," he said, his sopping-wet hand now cradling hers.

The boy was a bit of a paradox. The predominant vibe, certainly, was let's-hurry-up-and-climb-in-the-grave-while-supplies-last. Standard-issue Penny. But there were certain incongruous pieces too. Some of it—the studied patience, the eye-to-eye contact, when he managed to pry them open—she chalked up at least partly to Bounty

Bag's positive influence. He acted like a clerk behind a deli. Tired, but eager to communicate and, as needed, serve. It was an effect she had noticed in some of her more hardscrabble students after they took employment there, some of them going overboard into a fusillade of "yes, ma'ams," which at first came off sarcastic to her ears, Bayside, Queens, via B.U. and Eaton. Other of Ray's appealing qualities were, she supposed, genetic. An abundant soft mat of flat black hair. Paper-white skin, smooth and unblemished. Wide, sensuously sad blue eyes. Viewed from a certain angle, when he wasn't paying attention to himself, the boy radiated the freshness and vulnerability of a puppy.

"I like puppies," Dr. Chong said.

"What?"

"Now, if there's nothing else, meeting adjourned."

Palpably relieved, the faculty herd sighed and rose. They pushed to the door, clogging it at first, but then, clumping together like Harry Grimes's adored biosolids on their way to the humming centrifuge, they released themselves to the hall in a series of blobs.

On her way back to her office Dr. Chong mulled once more Archie's walkout idea and potential alternative approaches to the TCO campaign. But a peculiar development interrupted her thoughts. She tried Kyle Gherkin's new master key—the one that was supposed to end the Mad Crapper's reign of terror—on several passing locks and discovered that it didn't work on any of them. Nevertheless, she felt perversely sanguine, presuming that mere locksmithing incompetence, not foul play, was responsible. In Pennacook, after all, nothing except Bounty Bag ever seemed to work.

PART TWO

New Kid

PATRICK DIDN'T TURN UP DURING HIS SUSPENSION, not even to pick up the Luau Stuffers that Ray had pan-fried and left in the fridge as a lure, texting Patrick news of their completion. Ray had invented the Luau Stuffer on a snow day a couple of years back. At the time, Patrick had admitted that the specialty sandwiches (pineapple, cheddar, mayo, and ham on overpriced Queen's Hawaiian rolls) had brought "tropical relief" to his "winter-weary soul" and declared them a favorite. So their continued presence in the fridge, beside an apple and a bottle of Patrick's oft-requested, rarely supplied strawberry milk, set off early alarm bells.

After work on Friday he brought a box of groceries to the Carbonaras' dilapidated ranch house. He shooed the yard's boars—hissing *phhsstt phssstt*—and rang the bell and waited. Nobody answered, so he opened the outer door and set the box inside. He crossed the road and climbed a small dirt mound. From there he saw Patrick's knobby frame doing pull-ups in the basement, but then the light went out and all fell silent.

The next week he picked up whiffs of Patrick in certain telltale items removed from The Rock. Running clothes. Snow pants (which had become a fashion at the high school, boys walking around in big swishing snow pants like overheated babies). The marked envelope with a small cash allotment. Patrick had also taken a box of Oz paperbacks that for some reason he kept under his bed, leaving a cartoon behind as mock compensation. The cartoon depicted a mushroom cloud in the background and two figures in the foreground. One of the figures was on fire and screeching. The other, wearing a green Bounty Bag coat labeled "Ray," stressed in the caption, "It's *pronounced* /**n**[**y**] oo-klee-ər/." Another night Ray found his work schedule on the floor, bearing Patrick's track-sneaker print. Because Patrick had swiped the family laptop, Ray used the library's computers to write him, but he didn't write back.

At the stores during this period the board imposed a series of controversial new orders. New badges timed, and thus "reasonably restricted," bathroom visits by associates, who were re-designated as "cast members," and opaque inserts concealed cast members, "affording a comfortable separation" for customers, who were now "guests." Right next to Ray's ear in Deli they put in a talking idea box and nonsensically called it "Enervation Station." Whenever a guest passed its scanning red waffle, Enervation Station spouted, "Share your enervations with the new Bounty Bag!"

But Angie was ready. Each time the board gave an order, Angie called its bluff and undid it. The badges were collected. The opaque glass was dismantled, and, over in Bakery, a bewhiskered Leo re-emerged squinting to order another of his non-personalized birthday cakes. Enervation Station came down, sparing Ray's sanity.

Chesley backed down on these small-potatoes matters and didn't fare much better on the big stuff. The board's first attempt at firing Angie ended in disaster after four-hundred off-duty associates turned up in protest. "Still bedecked in jackets, aprons, and funny paper hats," *Supermarket Happenings* reported, they deployed Bounty Bag courtesy to skirt the capped bellhops at the Chesley-owned General Cornwallis Inn in Danvers and gathered outside the Arnold Room, where the board met to consider a motion to fire Angie. The associates chanted pro-Angie slogans and also demanded that the board re-commit to the profit-sharing plan and promise not to sell the company.

The board budged, a little. It tabled (4-3) the motion to fire Angie. But it ignored the protestors' other demands and instead ordered a $200 million payout to shareholders, whose "pent-up demand for liquidity," it was said, "required swift and merciful relief." Time to put the boat in the water!

According to *Supermarket Happenings*,

> As Angie exited the meeting, the crowd of associates seized her, raising her in a human chair.
>
> "I love you all and never want to go away," the typically non-demonstrative CEO Martini said. Associate Arnie Tebbetts, stocker,

Store #36, Grafton, utilized his regulation-maroon clip-on tie to dab away Angie's tears and his own.

Similarly moved, this reporter kept his honor!

The pretentious verb "utilize" was typical for the corny trade paper. Both *Garner's* and *Strunk & White* disapproved.

Ray could have panicked at these developments and started seeing more bad omens everywhere again. Instead, taking a cue from his advice books, he resolved to take a different approach. Why not look on the bright side? When push came to shove, nothing *that* big would change at the store. Sure, there might be some dreaded musical chairs at the top, and if Chesley prevailed there'd be more promotional gimmicks and tightfisted bennies cuts to contend with. But all in all, for someone at Ray's level, supermarket life surely would abide.

At Store #28, Stan rode the surf, bucking up associates with unflappable good cheer. The general message, which only bolstered Ray's refurbished optimism, was that life would go on, and that Bounty Bag's spirit would not perish from the earth.

As if to prove this, Deli recruitment continued apace.

Doreen Robinson appeared for her interview garbed in a frilly ensemble ripped from the wardrobe of Little Bo Peep. Her father, wearing a tattered cobalt-blue three-piece suit, closely trailed her into the tiny interview room. While they interviewed Doreen, Mr. Robinson roosted on the edge of a folding chair, leaning forward on a decorative cane crowned with a silver hawk.

Doreen competently answered all questions, including Stan's disorienting latest, hijacked from Groof.

"Why is there something rather than nothing?"

"Because there can be," Doreen answered, in a heavy Southern drawl.

Stan wrapped up the interview and swiveled in his chair to face their spectator.

"What line are you in, Mr. Robinson?"

The suit and the cane seemed to invite the question.

"Ribs. We *country* folk. We from *Grand* Bend."

He broke into a broad smile that, on account of the smoldering eyes above it, excited Ray's suspicion. Mr. Robinson's drawl was stronger than his daughter's, and "folk" crossed Ray's unschooled ears as the f-word, briefly conjuring a naked barnyard rumpus involving everyone in the room plus *The* Alfredo, Toothless Mary, and ravishing but quarrelsome cashier Natasha Romanov.

"He mean Alabama," Darleen interjected. "Daddy, don't nobody know about that stinky place."

She frowned at her father, who glared right back. Ray and Stan exchanged worried looks.

They walked the Robinsons out to the parking lot, where Mr. Robinson's eyes shifted to a small herd of Pennacook boars tearing into a trash pile, some illegal Penny dumping.

"What a waste," Mr. Robinson said quietly.

Very peculiar.

Stan reassigned Ray temporarily to his office-box overlooking the store for some post-interview sleuthing. When Ray was done he hailed Stan on the walkie-talkie and debriefed him amid the jungle-like mists of Produce.

"Dad's no harmless bumpkin, that's for sure. Barbecue man down to the pig's foot. Grand Bend, Alabama, yes—by way of Peebles Bar-B-Que in Auburndale, Florida, Mamma Brown's outside of Charleston, Austin's The Salt Lick, and City Market in Luling, Texas. Seem to be a lot of prizes in this BBQ area, blue ribbons and such, but every place he touched pulled down dozens. Must mean something. Family lives in South Oakhurst."

"And?"

"Moved north to exploit a perceived barbecue vacuum. Set up shop across Worcester Road. After 'the ball' drops, doors open wide. Then it's anyone's game."

Stan frowned. "Name?"

"'Shorty's Rib Cage.'"

Stan bent like he'd taken a hit. "I like it."

"Me too."

"Why come to us? Why doesn't she pull pork for Poppa?"

"Polish, to begin with," Ray said, relaying a plausible account from a friend of a friend of a friend.

This was no shocker. Many Bounty Bag associates found it a novel and sobering experience to put on a tie or modest skirt and a buttoned coat for work. Force wasn't popular at Bounty Bag, but you had to dress and groom like you gave a hoot, Henry David *beware-of-all-enterprises-that-require-new-clothes* Thoreau be damned. For most local associates, it was a first look up from the Pennacook muck.

Patrick's blue hair meant he couldn't work at Bounty Bag in any of the capacities that Ray had repeatedly suggested might be worth his while. Indeed, the dye job violated a clarion prohibition on spooky hair contained in *The Bounty Bag Look*, the hygiene pamphlet that set out Bounty Bag's dress code and style restrictions. (Feeble Stan illustrations accompanied the pamphlet's injunctions but were non-binding to the extent of a textual conflict.) Patrick may have even dyed his hair precisely to avoid Ray's open offer of employment. Ray's judgment having lapsed, he had left *The Bounty Bag Look* on The Rock's bookshelf, right next to Groof. Patrick probably found it there, read it, and after his big laugh hit CVS for the hair gunk.

"What else? C'mahn!" Stan pressed, apparently noticing Ray's blush.

"My sandwich-making may have played a small but decisive role."

"No surprise there." Stan touched his shoulder. "You're a trade secret, chum."

No farther than Pennacook itself, Ray was well regarded for neat, fresh sandwiches made very quickly, and your average sandwich-lover at Store #28 wasn't too shy to clamor come lunchtime for Ray's magic hands. "Nah nah nah, gimme the *other* guy," they'd say, looking at Toothless Mary as *The* Alfredo stood at the ready, holding a knife and feigning chagrin. Mr. Robinson, it so happened, wanted daughter Doreen to learn some tricks of the trade from sandwich-ninja Ray. Then, both Ray and Stan were certain, he'd sweep her off to Shorty's Rib Cage — Ray's Carolina Smoker the first target in her sights. Only fair. Karma for what Ray had been doing to Hungry Tiger Pasta for weeks.

H. T. Pasta was the Italian restaurant next to Bounty Bag. Vic Ardell, the proprietor, got to work super-early. By the time Ray pulled in, Vic was already inside stirring his gargantuan marinara vat with his ogre's spoon and pumping the saucy scent through his kitchen vents to the sidewalk. H. T. Pasta's aroma stoked not only Ray's appetite but his newfound competitive flame, which his recent promotion had unexpectedly lit. He decided to escalate. With Stan's permission, he ordered a used Carolina Smoker that he'd found cheap online and wheeled it out front for lunch service, 11:00 A.M.– 3:00 P.M. But the Robinsons now held a trump card: a full-blown barbecue restaurant plan.

Stan mulled Ray's info briefly, then snatched the pink application form from his hands and scrawled a red "H" in the top corner.

" 'Long as she makes sandwiches here, that's where we'll sell 'em."

"Understood," Ray said. He took the good news upstairs to the red phone they used for new hires.

Ray supposed the red phone had other uses but he wasn't aware of any. The phone represented a red mark, or line, down the center of a Bounty Bag associate's life. Once a Bounty Bag associate, always a Bounty Bag associate, it was said. Some requested a certificate suitable for framing; Stan obliged with a loopy cartoon that was quietly put away in the closet. Now Doreen would have that line through her life, even if it harmed them. Ray understood why Stan made the hire. Did we really need an enemy in the neighborhood? Or did we want a friendly rival worthy of the name? Fear simply wasn't Stan's thing. Nor was it Bounty Bag's—yet.

Angie explained more at a board meeting a couple of years back. By court order the board's meeting transcripts were a matter of public record, and Ray had read them all as part of his self-imposed managerial-training regimen, but also out of curiosity. In this one, Angie refused to sign on to end-of-year cash-filled bathtubs for all major shareholders, despite bumper third and fourth quarters.

"Impossible," Angie explained, given Bounty Bag's "other commitments this fiscal year."

What were those?

Three percent across-the-board discount, appropriate for "these hard times." Profit-sharing payouts for associate doctors' bills and other sundries. Expanded food-bank donations because lines had grown "like snake firecrackers" of late.

The reporter included narrative details not strictly required by court rules. In this case, Angie's interlocutor was Jowls O'Grady, The Trash King of Mississippi and one of Chesley's staunchest board allies.

```
Q (O'Grady): Angie, exactly what are your priorities as CEO of
this company? [Exasperated hand chops in the air.] Cuz I'd like to
know. I mean, who comes first around here? [Much table pounding,
felt in the thighs.]

A (Angie): The customers. Next, the Bounty Bag associates. After
that, the communities. They're our moral responsibility. Then, I
suppose, the shareholders.

Q (O'Grady): [Rage, indistinct.]
```

Hiring Doreen was good business. It also fell into the "communities" part of Angie's equation. After all, the Robinsons were likely to encounter all sorts of social isolation as transplanted African American Zion Methodists (unasked, she'd written her religion on her application) in chalk-white Pennacook, suffused with wary Catholics and creedless skeptics, with Ray falling somewhere between these two categories. Plus, Doreen was more than kitchen-qualified, with raving references from Grand Bend to Luling.

So here was Ray the following week, training the competition. As always, he wore the Bounty Bag maroon baseball cap for his hair covering. It had the logo, the "Stretch Your Buck" slogan, and the word "fresh" stitched into brim and face. Doreen had wrapped her hair tightly in a hairnet, bunching it up in a big ciabatta-like ring. Ray noticed something new and unpleasant on her: Doreen's nametag included not only her name and years as an associate ("0") but a personal factoid ("Ask me about my pogo stick trophy!"). Chesley, surely, had cooked up this one. But Angie would reverse it once word circled back.

"Apply cheese, then your wet veggies. On top of the veggies? Pile your meats."

Slop slop. Making sandwiches was probably Ray's #1 transferable skill if the Bounty Bag apocalypse *did* happen. He was only a fledgling manager but down in a deli he could always make a mean meatball. Of course, he hoped that if it came to that his new employer didn't use one of those cutesy alternative verbs for the task. "Handcraft." "Build."

"Sounds simple, but you wouldn't believe the mistakes people make. Repeatedly." Ray flicked his chin at *The* Alfredo.

Ray had a big fear regarding Doreen Robinson, that in a quiet moment, when Ray was distracted, *The* Alfredo would successfully seduce her and radicalize her to a Deli work life of sloth and indifference, just as he'd done to Daphne Butterfield last summer. After it was too late, little traces would emerge, seemingly harmless gossip-threads becoming far more consequential in retrospect. Fruit smoothie double-date sightings at Jack's Four with *The* Alfredo, Doughnut Dayle, and Doughnut Dayle's latest prey. A Benvolio's napkin poking from Little Bo Peep's lunch basket as, red-cheeked, she skipped into Deli thirty minutes late of a sunny morn'. All culminating—inevitably—in mutinous laughter behind the deli counter and a frantic "shh, shh, here *he* comes" or a "Look busy!" landing on Ray's ears as his heavy tread approached. Leaving Ray to ask, "Why didn't I notice and do more to save her?"

He'd rather not be in that position again, even if she was marked for better things at Shorty's Rib Cage. Hence the effort to marginalize *The* Alfredo up front.

"Never put the veggies against the bread directly," he continued, "unless you enjoy soggy bread and wet fingers. I see that you are laughing: this isn't obvious. Cheese and meat provide your insulation, and cheese insulates better than meat."

"Why you don't cheese up both side the roll?"

"Because that's not a sandwich."

He paused to let the preposterous image of a sandwich with cheese on both the top and the bottom of the filler sink in.

Doreen nodded but then wrinkled her nose.

"How about grilled cheese? That's got cheese up both side the roll."

"Exception proves the rule," Ray muttered quickly, looking down. "Grilled cheese has no filler. Then once you've wrapped it you print out the price and slap on one of these."

He showed her the wheel with the "Ring on, Deli" stickers. He mentally noted once more the erroneous comma and the resulting hortatory miscue but balked at a punctuation tutorial. Fact was, Doreen's African American vernacular had slammed Ray headlong into a thorny internal usage debate that threw into question his whole unofficial curriculum for associates on such matters.

His hesitation had to do with something in *Garner's*. The usage dictionary's intro tuned him into the basics of a long-running argument between Prescriptivists and Descriptivists in the field of linguistics. The Prescriptivists, who dominated the high-school English-teacher faction and included Mom, said there was a right way and a wrong way to use English — and one should enforce the right way. Some Descriptivists, however, said there was no wrong way; there were just many different ways, each following its own rules. No native speaker, it was said, could err.

Garner was something of a modified Prescriptivist seeking a truce in the language wars and he addressed this tension with at least three important moves. First he explained in a note on class that, on many entries where usage diverged, his guidance typically reflected the preferences of the upper-middle class, the class where most of his readers fell or wanted to end up. He similarly wrote in his entry on dialect that his book was restricted mainly to Standard English. If you *want* to get to Rome, to strain a metaphor, use English as the Romans do; if you don't, read another book. On dialects, he referred several.

Garner went further, evolving a sliding scale that promoted new words, even erstwhile slang, through the ranks as they gained acceptance. This implied a certain agnosticism about ultimate judgments. A new form or usage might begin at the first stage but as it met with broader success it could work its way up to the fifth stage, where it was totally acceptable. An asterisk condemned forms that should never be used, as when Stan described *The* Alfredo as "lacksadaisical" instead of "lackadaisical." Or when Stan had typed the double bobble "reak havoc" into an e-mail, coupling a misspelling of "reek" with a misuse of "reak" for "wreak." "Reeks of havoc," Toothless Mary's precise variant — as in, "Chesley's self-checkout plan *reeks of havoc*" — hadn't even made Garner's tome. (Angie had fought self-checkout registers for years, calling them a job killer that stripped yet one more human moment from the day.)

But Ray still didn't know how to care about this stuff and *not* be a squirming snob in his chosen life, a provincial deli-slinging snoot with only the airiest goals of extra-grocery ascent. What difference did Toothless Mary's errors make if she could take and tag a ham-salad-with-hots order? And if Toothless Mary's fractured English ("exspecially," "breakfases") had ultimately left Ray's troops along the Descriptivist side of the de-militarized zone, too battle-weary to fight, didn't the same go double for Doreen's English, which wasn't flawed, just built on a different chassis?

Embarrassed by his ignorance, Ray had read up further on the topic. Doreen spoke a version of African American Vernacular English, or AAVE. AAVE wasn't slang or "broken" English. It was a dialect with its own rules, just not Mom's or Garner's—a whole other language system afoot in Deli! He *guessed* you could still argue that, as Doreen's Deli supervisor, he should step into Mom's empty shoes and wave the schoolmarm's ruler over her vernacular to smooth her dealings with the store's AAVE-deaf customers. But since nitpicking associate usage—in particular with a transplant like Doreen—didn't just make him out to be a snob but, far worse, risked the fellowship so central to the Bounty Bag way, wasn't it better to refrain? Let Pennies figure *her* out if it came to that. They could swing it! Besides, Ray liked the way that Doreen and Mr. Robinson spoke (*we country, both side the roll*), a fresh departure from the Pennacook familiar, and he wanted to hear and understand it more. Not muffle and thwart it for some foggy business interest.

Garner's rules had their place, he concluded, but to "correct" Doreen seemed a larger betrayal. Not only of her and of Bounty Bag values but, in some way he couldn't pin down, of language itself. His gut told him that Angie would agree.

Doreen returned from her restroom break. Creepy Peter Rollins appeared like clockwork at 11:15 for his daily sriracha corned-beef, a/k/a the Corned Beef Rooster (Ray's own coinage), from the hot menu. He took a seat at one of their two small folding tables and battled the sandwich quickly into submission, his knee wham-*bang*ing against the table as he rose to wipe his mouth with his puff jacket's sleeve and slither back to the Hallmark Gold Crown Store.

A pocket of silence opened. Ray shifted into low gear — the girl was practically training herself — and Doreen revealed that she was in the same grade as Patrick. She also had Mr. Grant for Local History. Did she know him?

"Blue hair, kinda pale."

"Oh he sweet."

"Can be."

Training wound down, and Doreen asked to try her hand at a large Italian sub. It was their most loaded and colorful sandwich but not their most difficult. That prize might go to the Turkey Gobbler (Thanksgiving in a torpedo roll), deceptively simple but easily overdone in several directions. Either that or the Yee-haw! Cheeseburger, a burger topped with cheddar, fried egg, and a hash brown, all within a Portuguese muffin. The Italian was a better choice for trainee confidence-building. He liked her instincts.

"Mine as well," Ray said. "If you're ready."

"What did you say?" asked Doreen, eyes widening.

"I said you mine as well make one."

"Oh, Mr. Ray. Don't nobody say 'mine as well.' "

"No?"

"Oh, Mr. Ray," she chuckled, "I guess it don't matter none, but it *ain't* 'mine as well.' It's '*might* as well.' "

Ray stared at her dumbfounded, torpedo roll in one hand, three slices of boiled ham draped over the other.

After work, Ray sidled up to the long, glowing wall of computer terminals at the Pennacook Free Town Library. He was still smarting from his linguistic misfire when he snapped open *Supermarket Happenings*, only to read a post that highlighted a whole other arena where Ray's ineptitude at communication was profound: the Internet.

> Bounty Bag associates have started a web site, SaveBountyBag.com, to gather signatures in support of Angie Martini amid rumors that the company's board is again considering a motion to terminate the embattled CEO. They've also started a Facebook page.

Leroy Soots, 56, a meat buyer for Store #12 in Lawrence, Massachusetts, reported difficulties purchasing the URL and populating the Save Bounty Bag website.

"I'm more of an old-fashioned newspaper man myself. Though sometimes I read the whole thing and the only section that makes sense these days is the funny pages. So I asked my nine-year-old to set me up. Took her five minutes."

The online petition garnered only forty-two signatures during its first week. But after Janine, Mr. Soots's daughter and a fourth grader at John Kenneth Galbraith Elementary in Methuen, Massachusetts, finished troubleshooting the site, it went live again yesterday. Within hours, it attracted over 10,000 "siggies." A board vote is expected within weeks.

Hey, Leroy! How's about a Bounty Bag slushie for Janine?

Local History: Oneida

PATRICK TOOK A SHORTCUT TO LOCAL HISTORY. HE passed through the cafetorium, where cheeseburger and stringbean steam clung to his skin. C Lunch was slated for a far-off 12:30 P.M., so Patrick sneaked into the lunch line and cadged two fatty cheese sticks. These came unlimited and free with school lunch, which he planned to buy later, so he didn't consider it stealing. Nor, vegan that he was, did he consider the clumps cheese. Mostly sawdust, probably.

Screaming red paint on the cafetorium's wall had turned the former president's initials into a didactic acronym.

A=Achievement
J=Joy

A couple of the Tennessee Tailor's quotes were up there too.

I am sworn to uphold the Constitution as
Andy Johnson understands it and interprets it.

And:

The goal to strive for is
a poor government but a rich people.

Patrick walked down the stairs and his eyes fell on the familiar heart-shaped crack, third step up from the landing. The crack was an emblem of humility to Patrick, a refreshing confession of vulnerability by the imposing public-school system with its attendance mandate and the cops to back it up. Even Patrick, who had run away from home, had to go to school or hazard the orphanage.

A boar turned a corner, trailing some kid's backpack from its hoof. At Room 164, Patrick slipped into his half desk and looked up at the spectral Mr. Grant. The worst thing about being a teacher had to be dying in front of cackling teenagers. Jelly pouches cascaded down his wrecked face, his body a Muppet's. Patrick wished he had grabbed a couple of extra cheese sticks for him. There was no medicine in sight, except for a cough-drop package, but make no mistake, here was a guest from the land of the sick.

Mr. Grant leaned forward and began his lecture in earnest, but lung cancer had reduced his voice to a rattle.

"Much of American history fits into one word: Oneida."

Kaff.

Mr. Grant was supposed to teach *local* history but he regularly veered off the bread-and-butter topics — the boar infestation, the abiding urban myth of a Bounty Bag theme park in the works, persistent unicorn sightings "potentially indicative of something in the Oakhurst water" — to American history writ large. The advantage of teaching Local History, he had explained, was that state standards for the subject were pretty low and shaggy, unlike those for American History (though these failed to deter Mr. Hitch's ziti dinners). So Mr. Grant played Br'er Rabbit and got tossed into the Local History briar patch, freeing him up to teach American History in his own way, which was unusual. Among other peculiarities, he typically went backward, digging for the roots. "Sneaky," Muscles Carbonara had said approvingly. Today's lecture, however, was thematic. It went in chronological order, putting a tracer on the word "Oneida."

"Part of the Iroquois Confederacy," he continued, "'Oneida' started as an Indian tribe whose basic features included matriarchy. Each clan had a different animal symbol."

Kaff.

"Turtle meant patience."

Kaff.

"Also solidarity, perseverance, and Mother Earth, or motherhood."

Kaff kaff kaff kaff kaff.

New tissue, old one red.

"The Oneida people lived communally, as extended families under the wife's family line, in longhouses with smoke holes. Cooped up for the winter months, they developed a real knack for storytelling."

Muscles Carbonara tapped Patrick's shoulder.

"Stuff this in your bottom lip."

He held out a Red Man tin.

"Brought special for today's lesson."

Patrick reluctantly stuffed in the dip and felt his glands squirt with delight at a new drug system. The potency and quick delivery jolted him. His stomach turned and he spat the junk out into his hand and looked at the thing, wet, brown, and ugly. He had no place to put the turd and slipped it in his pocket where it soaked his upper thigh. Muscles Carbonara spat in a wax cup.

"The tribe is a federally recognized Indian nation. In a recent controversy"

—*kaff*—

"a Wounded Knee victim's descendant and other Indians challenged an Oz-themed Oneida casino in Chittenango, New York, because of controversial remarks made by L. Frank Baum, the man who wrote *The Wizard of Oz*. As a young newspaper editorialist, Baum had called for 'total annihilation of the few remaining Indians' as the 'best safety of the frontier settlements.'"

Mr. Grant put up a slide with an excerpt from Baum's editorial.

"In the 1890 piece for the *Aberdeen Saturday Pioneer* he further characterized the remaining Indians as 'a pack of whining curs who lick the hand that smites them'; '[t]he Whites,' having conquered, were now the rightful 'masters of the American continent.'"

Increasingly alarmed, Patrick folded moral pretzels for Baum. The times were different, there were Indian wars, a massacre. He probably outgrew this, certainly by the time he wrote *The Emerald City of Oz*. Mr. Grant added that elsewhere around the same time Baum had condemned "bigotry" and preached "tolerance" as key to America's greatness. Patrick dug deep into the negative-capability larder, determined to both condemn and absolve Baum, or at least suspend judgment on the man's whole life.

"Oneida took on a different meaning in the mid-nineteenth century with John Humphrey Noyes's Oneida Community, a Christian utopian experiment. Memorable characteristics included free love, equality for women, and a well-stocked library."

Plus, plus, plus, thought Patrick.

"Others included mutual criticism, eugenics, extreme male continence, and an unwieldy and time sucking bureaucracy."

Minus minus *minus* minus.

Mr. Grant drew loose analogies to bonobos and to the Mosuo people of China with their walking marriages. Muscles Carbonara fired up his phone and flashed an obscene primate video.

Footnote on bonobos.

Mr. Grant's allusion to our closest genetic relatives, tied with chimpanzees, brought to mind their recent primates unit in Science.

Unlike chimps and humans, bonobos don't kill one another. Horndogs that they are, they prefer to use sex—"missionary position, please," the dominant females often insist—and sharing, rather than violence, to resolve disputes over things like food and territory. A bonobo would even unlock a stranger-bonobo's cage to share some newly discovered food, even though the bonobo could've hogged it all! Chimps, the bastards, you couldn't even get to share a bucket of food with a relative if doing so would require the dominant chimp to let even a little itty bitty of the prize go to its subordinate.

Bonobos show compassion for other species too. True story: a bonobo had captured a starling in her hands. When a zookeeper asked her to release it, the bonobo climbed a tree, wrapped her legs around the top, opened the bird's wings, and launched the starling up to freedom.

How did bonobos end up magnanimous? Nobody knows for sure, but maybe it happened because during their evolution the Congo River had shielded them from threats and they'd enjoyed eons of abundance.

Unfortunately there are only about 50,000 max of bonobos left in the world. All the wild ones still cluster in one little area, in forests south of the Congo. Scientists project only further declines given poaching and other pressures. There is so much bloodshed and hatred and menace in the human world. Gas attacks, oceanic garbage patches, nuclear fire sticks abounding. So many high principles not lived up to. Are people more bonobo or more chimp?

TBD. Some days we release starlings; others, we vivisect one another. Maybe it would have been better if bonobos had evolved larger brains instead of us, traversing vast spans on solar-sailboats, bringing to the void their message of peace. With the rare exception — your Mister Rogers, your Eleanor Roosevelt — maybe we should all just *die.*

It sometimes got him down.

"Predictably unstable," Mr. Grant continued, "Oneida Community"

—*kaff*—

"degraded to a carnival-type attraction for urban tourists of the Gilded Age."

Mr. Grant drew up on the Elmo an 1870s promotional poster, its thrust being: *Come see our weirdo kids hop, skip, and jump fer yer amusement. Bolt a hot meal, then flee on the train!*

"The Oneida Community converted from a Perfectionist utopia to a for-profit. Soon enough, animal trapping and silk and silverware production replaced the social experiments of the Noyesian Mansion House. The company paid members seven percent dividends in 1899, a princely sum for the time."

As he transitioned to Oneida's early twentieth century, Mr. Grant passed out a scattershot index of a few seemingly unrelated terms from that era. Erik Weisz. *Lochner v. New York* (Holmes, J., dissenting). Colorado Coalfield War. The Great Molasses Flood.

"During the world wars," Mr. Grant continued, "war-horse Oneida armed the Allies with ammo clips, gas shells, combat knives, army trucks, and jet engines. Oneida's corporate heyday stretched from WWII through the 1980s, when it was known the world over for its stainless-steel flatware.

"Oneida more recently stepped into the pages of yet another well-known American story when it transitioned from manufacturing flatware in America to marketing and selling from America flatware produced not in America or by someone else on contract. It declared bankruptcy, was swallowed by some hedge funds, merged, and became one of several brands of the extant Oneida Group. Which today has a website.

"Wall Street is still something of an old boys' club. Culturally speaking, it is close to the opposite of the original Oneida Nation. At 8-to-2, the male-to-female ratio of major-firm executives is comparable to that of our violent-crime inmate population, roughly 9 men for every woman. Racially, though, Wall Street's quite distinct from our prisons."

Up went the charts.

"PC malarkey," Muscles Carbonara said as the Oneida lecture wrapped up. Declaring himself "hot in more ways than one," he marched over to the tiny fold-in window and jammed his head and his pimply red arms through the narrow slit.

Patrick wasn't so sure about Muscles Carbonara's accusation. Patrick had easily ruled out certain political identities for Mr. Grant. He was not, for example, an anarchist like Muscles Carbonara, a large-banks enthusiast like AJMHS business teacher Mr. Dobson, or a card-carrying member of the revanchist League of the South. But for all Patrick knew he could be a socialist, a libertarian, the PC Chief of Police, the *anti*-PC Chief of Police, or a burrowing mole for the progressive left. One minute he'd rip the white man for treating Indian treaties like such much gossamer when it suited them, but the next his coal-black eyes would flare up red at them for being complacent about free speech, for slandering the Gettysburg Address as archaic, or for crudely assuming historical bloodbaths.

"Do any of you recall what happened at the real first Thanksgiving?"

"Didn't we like slay them?"

"Wrong," Mr. Grant thundered. " 'They' joined 'us' for a three-day harvest festival. Earlier in 1621 the Pilgrims and the Wampanoag reached a peace agreement that lasted fifty years. Don't make it up!"

On weekends Patrick kept to his old schedule, sneaking into the school to feed A. Lincoln, Eleanor Roosevelt, and Satchmo. Muscles Carbonara had copied an extra set of the new master key for his own doings, which, as best Patrick could piece together, no longer involved just the Mad Crapper. (Indeed, though with Patrick's purloined copy of the new master the Mad Crapper had free rein at AJMHS, he teetered on the edge of retirement, on account of the joke getting old.) Patrick watched the turtles from Head Janitor Gherkin's beanbag and often thought about Mr. Grant and his class. He decided that if he had to pick one word for Mr. Grant, it would be "patriot." Granted two to play around with, he'd add "tormented." It sometimes seemed that what Mr. Grant was really teaching, with a last-gasp desperation, was how to be that way too.

In Local History Patrick held an A–, his highest grade and some kind of fluke.

Escape to Castle Eaton

D R. CHONG PLANNED TO CHANNEL ALL OF HER energy into the tax-cap-override campaign, but with the TCO vote still two months off she started an affair instead.

It all began on a Sunday afternoon at the Eaton Bistro. Dr. Chong was having another sad meal alone, listlessly poking through cold barbecue chicken and bitter greens while the antique-bottle glass windows distorted her face, reflecting it back purple and weeping. While she ate, she flipped through *Lung Cancer Monthly*, a magazine that she had swiped from Thoreau Hospital and tucked in *Eaton Living* to conceal it. The magazine offered some shiny palliative-care equipment that Dr. Chong was thinking of buying for Mr. Grant's classroom. It wasn't much of a gesture, but what more could she do? Time travel back to the 1990s and win him a non-carcinogenic classroom before it was too late? She also found *Lung Cancer Monthly* useful for some admittedly shameful downward comparison. At least she wasn't in physical pain or dying!

A prematurely white-haired man sat across the dining room. She guessed from his light, almost carefree movements that he was just cresting 40, a mere babe, and found him attractive in a sweeping, tall-sailboat way. At this point Dr. Chong stared like a man at any man who might interest her. This man noticed and, clanging his fork down loudly against his china, marched to her table, sat down, and flagged the waitress for wine.

"Skip LaBoeuf. I'd like to meet you."

"Then do." She held out a palm. Under the table, her other hand dropped her magazines.

Skip LaBoeuf was cleanly shaven and dressed mostly right in a tight-fitting sport coat and polo, pressed dress jeans, and purple suede sneakers that looked brand new. A shade too sprightly and neat for her taste, the outfit made Skip resemble a disabled adult wrapped by a loving caretaker. On the other hand, it was thankfully devoid of the abyss-evoking bloodstains and hard-liquor stenches that she had encountered with other bold men moving in for their close-ups.

She liked that he didn't probe her incessantly for common interests but told her things instead.

"I teach Spanish at Rorsch School," he said. He chuckled and raised a fist. "*Vincere Semper!*"

In Dr. Chong's mind the Rorsch School affiliation instantly vaulted Skip high above her own faculty at Andrew Johnson Memorial High School. *Vincere semper*, Rorsch School's exacting Latin motto, translated as "Always win." Once a Yale pipeline, the elite boarding school still looked like Yale and continued to produce enough all-star alumni to lend its motto credence. Recent graduates included a hawkish U.S. Senator busy halving immigration and doubling nukes (Dr. Chong opposed these policies) and a pair of start-up founders attempting a cure for aging (good, but hurry please!).

"Always lose" was more like it at Andrew Johnson. You couldn't exactly blame Pennies. There wasn't much work in town anymore, aside from Bounty Bag, Pennacook's guardian angel, and the well-paid jobs outside of town that they landed—toll-booth collector, for instance—seemed damned by obsolescence to dissolve in Penny hands. The problem solved itself for her top kids. They left. Drafted off to Holy Cross or Brown, never to return. Pennacook had also offered up a pro hockey player, his Hallenbuck ice time paying off in a one-way ticket to the Canucks. But what was Dr. Chong, high-school principal and designated local booster, supposed to tell the other kids about their vanishing economic futures? Eat less and dress in layers? Cheer harder for the flag? It was a conundrum. Certainly part of the answer was a new school building that didn't ooze amber substances and (it was hypothesized) kill.

Skip executed an increasingly intimate series of touches as he spoke, tapping Dr. Chong's elbow and seizing her upper arm for a mid-joke squeeze. She watched his tendons ripple in his shirt. On the way out the door he took a big risk and lightly touched her lower back. She let him.

"This was a nice surprise," she said after, and sort of it was. But her back ached and as so often happened these days the man had petered out early. Her focus, now, had shifted from romance to humiliation control. At the moment, her most urgent hope was that the ceiling leak would hold off until Skip LaBoeuf departed.

Skip stared at her ceiling as if sensing her anxiety's target and expanded upon life at Rorsch School. They lived, he said, in a recently renovated four-floor unit. Part of an all-girls dorm, it had a wood-burning fireplace, spacious bedrooms, and hardwood floors. It overlooked a nature preserve and boasted a balcony. The millionaire's pad was free and the job came with meals, utilities, and access to a world-class gym and pool. For the special occasion of the annual on-campus class reunion the head welcomed the faculty into his striped tent for a clam bake, allotting two lobster tickets, bibs, and limitless corn cobs to each faculty family. It was a real highlight of the school year, and Skip's little family—Skip, Kat, and their boy Blake—never once missed it. Blake went undescribed, but he featured in Dr. Chong's imagination as a sailor-suited towhead of impeccable manners (*"I'm having a splendid time, thank you very much, and I'm very glad to have made your acquaintance!"*).

The campus was a verdant park, designed by Olmsted's relations. It abutted a double-yellow-lined road, but a trick entrance that veered off to the side produced the desired medieval-forest effect. Old oaks swayed over sanded Gothic dorms in the famous Rorsch Oval. They had a camera obscura, a koi pond, and a zoo. Field-hockey and lacrosse fields skirted the dorms, providing a thick green margin for sunlight. The head of school lived—Dr. Chong's heart fluttered—in a breathtaking hilltop mansion.

With all of the commitments boarding school was busy, Skip confessed, "but in an invigorating way."

"*I* like it, but I guess it might seem a little *funny* to an outsider. Dorm living, at age forty-six."

Dr. Chong didn't see anything wrong with that and wondered why he did. "My condo's underground and hosts rats," she said, sounding more bitter than she intended. "Not *now*," she added. "We're under contract."

Dr. Chong had moved to this seeping basement condo in less-to-ny West Eaton eight years back but she had never intended to stay here. Her plan had been to trade up to an Eaton Center bungalow once her salary hit the grid's upper ranges. As fate would have it, the soaring local market priced her out. She could still buy a house in Pennacook of course, but she didn't want to. She wanted to own in, even under, a special town like Eaton. A town where Pennies could be trusted not to visit.

"Of course we don't live in the dorm *all* year," Skip continued. To the contrary, he had four weeks of vacation during the academic year plus a three-month summer. Skip's family retreated during this ample time off to their California-style Cohasset deck-house, where they "did nothing, basically," except "grill out."

The easy life, the good life.

At the door she kissed him. "Well, come again."

Local History: Reconstruction

THEY HAD BEEN PREPARING FOR *Reconstruction Role Play: Artificial Congress* for days and it was discouraging to find Mr. Grant slumped in his chair, too weak to interrupt as he usually did, their god-like referee.

Fortunately, he had set them up well with detailed instructions. In round one, Mr. Grant had jiggered the numbers so Congress consisted of four groups: Freedmen, white Radical Republicans, Conservative Republicans, and white northern Democrats, each apportioned according to its respective adult male population in 1865, the year that the Civil War ended. He excluded southern whites, who had offered near-universal support to the rebellion. He also left out women, because the idea of them voting was at the level of a mainstream joke in those years.

The Freedmen and the Radicals joined forces and naturally dominated. Their Congress gave 40 acres and a mule to every former slave family, guaranteed all civil rights irrespective of race, and seized and carved up plantations, classifying them as contraband with the moral stink of Nazi concentration camps. They stripped all Confederate leaders, military and civilian, of the right to vote and branded them traitors. To enforce it all, they established a standing army, lopped off the former Army of the Potomac.

They accomplished all of this despite Mr. Grant's inclusion in their primary-source packets of some fetid ammunition for the opposition. On September 3, 1866, for instance, Andrew Johnson had bitched in Cleveland that the Freedmen's Bureau cost too much.

> You had already expended three million dollars to set them free and give them a fair opportunity to take care of themselves—then these gentlemen, who are such great friends of the people, tell us they must be taxed twelve million dollars to sustain the Freedmen's Bureau.

Translation: *Sorry, Negroes: I know it's only been, oh, eighteen months since emancipation but the cupboard's bare. Maybe if you pinch your potato-sack trousers together with binder clips it'll make 'em last longer!*

Years ago the kids from Woodshop had hammered together a stained-pine judge's bench at the front of Mr. Grant's classroom. Patrick, presiding from the bench as Senate president, was pleased as punch with the outcome of their Congress. He swung the gavel hard on the last of their two-part session and returned to his seat while the class buzzed smugly all around him.

Mr. Grant bolstered himself with one hand on the arm rest, pulled himself up, and worked his way to the center of the room, where he leaned on his foam-gripped quad cane.

"This"

—*kaff*—

"is not what really happened, in the end."

To a sea of rolling eyes he slapped down the revised profiles and assignment sheets. He removed the Freedmen and swapped in the Redeemers, the white anti-civil rights coalition that replaced them in real life once they'd voided the Freedmen's voting rights and gotten their own restored.

"C'mon, folks. Once more time around the mulberry bush."

In this round, as in American history, all the property redistribution fell by the wayside, as did the civil-rights protections for blacks, which the Supreme Court gutted. The standing army retreated. Disenfranchisement, Jim Crow, lynchings.

"That's more like it," Mr. Grant said bitterly.

Patrick returned the gavel to its sound block and descended from the judge's bench with a sigh. As he passed her desk he glanced at Doreen Robinson, the only black kid in the class and she even came from Alabama, one of the states they'd offered up to the Redeemers. Patrick was crestfallen, but Doreen only shrugged at him, like it wasn't any kind of news.

Kaff.

Then in the twentieth century, Mr. Grant continued, the American government made sure that if you were black you probably couldn't buy a cheap house in the suburbs during the post-war boom. To get

LOCAL HISTORY: RECONSTRUCTION

Federal Housing Administration support for a massive suburban project like Levittown, New York, or Lakewood, California, developers had to exclude blacks. The FHA also redlined black neighborhoods, which meant the families who lived there couldn't get mortgages insured when they tried to buy homes. Meanwhile, America's cities and towns zoned toxic waste and industry into the black ghettoes the government had created. Flash forward to today and African American families, largely because of these and other such policies, have, on average, only about 14% of the wealth of their white counterparts.

So it didn't just end with Rutherford B. Hayes.

As Patrick walked home from school that day, his brain teemed with angles on Reconstruction and how it and everything after could have been so different. Backpack-laden, he filled with dread as he made the turn onto Governor Gerry Road and caught sight of the Carbonara manse. Unlike the Oneida, bonobos, Oz, or the Mosuo people of China, the Carbonara family was not a matriarchy, but it wasn't patriarchy either. It was chaos.

Gnarly vines had laid siege to the side of the house, encircling windows and striving up mightily to the hanging rusted gutter. Animal nests dangled over the roof and raccoons prowled and dislodged shingles. Like an earthquake-stressed bridge, the rotting split-rail fence oscillated in and out in a wave all the way down to the lawn's end, where, with a final flourish, it crashed spectacularly onto the sidewalk. "We surrender," the fence said, on behalf of the whole grand estate. Pennacook boars had made a plaything of the fence and, indeed, of the entire yard, despite sporadic bursts of firepower from Mr. Carbonara's window. As Patrick had recently witnessed, this was the kind of property that attracted a special fascination come Halloween, that frightened children crossed the road to avoid, only to gawk at it from the other side.

This was something of an achievement in Pennacook, a town with a hardy brand of trick-or-treaters and more than its share of murder houses. A murder house was any house that, from the exterior, looked like a murder had been committed in it. There were no specific requirements for a house to become a murder house, but newspapered windows, two of which the Carbonaras had, were a big boost for any candidate. Patrick had created the murder-house concept while running what amounted to hundreds of miles through Pennacook's streets for track. The term had sufficed up until now, but the Carbonaras' place demanded refinement. It looked not only as if a murder had been committed in it but like another was in the offing and a third probably happening right now. "Triple-murder house," perhaps.

Patrick had been spared such a home before. Mom had kept their house a safe distance from murder-house status, and Ray's spit-shined The Rock never came close.

The Carbonaras' interior, for which Patrick had yet to coin a master term, was little better. The Carbonaras had done no maintenance, unless you counted the installation of tin buckets. It seemed that the Carbonaras had selected the buckets for their booming resonance when they caught the seeping rain. The washer was broken and the hallway carpet had beer-stain constellations. Cabinets missed knobs and loose screws made for trick doors that either couldn't be locked or didn't need to be. Sundry garbage including empty mini junk-cereal boxes and soda bottles bespoke a family that had abandoned both healthy eating and budget-minded bulk-buying strategies. The living room was like some constantly erupting male ego of slasher films and porn screened from a projector. A samurai sword hung on a wall splattered red. In one corner, a barrel of cookies and cylinders of meat snacks. Over the floor, a newspaper carpet, smeared with something brown.

Back in Oakhurst, Ray and Patrick's neighbors maintained their homes with some basic level of care. Most had added personal touches. A patch of plastic turf and some tables. A flower box on a kitchen window. Religious statuary. A POW/MIA flag. Showing somebody in there cared about someone or something. Mother-hen Ray not only provided basic maintenance but went the extra mile, hosing and polishing the shell and whitewashing the inside walls every other year. He chopped the ice, shoveled the snow, and in the summer swept the yard like a Southerner. Come holidays, he heavily decorated. It defied description, except to say: walk blindfolded into your local party store's holiday aisle, remove the blindfold, and look around. That's what Ray did to their place. It was embarrassing, but not like this.

The house's condition became less mysterious once you met the "staff," Muscles Carbonara's term for his family.

The first time Patrick saw Chigger and Skeet, the two middle brothers, they were stationed at the kitchen table raping a bag of Bounty Bag chocolate-chip cookies—first of many Bounty Bag products that, extracted from Ray's care packages, the Carbonaras appropriated for the commonweal. Cookie crumbs swirled around them in a cloud as they joylessly dragged on a pair of cigarettes, their ash tray brimming over. Patrick and Muscles Carbonara hung up their jackets and the rumpled brothers, resembling a pair of dehydrated bus-station denizens, watched with jaundiced eyes.

"Hey, numbnuts," Chigger said.

"Hey, fat tub o' lard," said Skeet.

The smell of dogs was overpowering.

"I didn't know you had a dog," Patrick said.

"They're dead," Chigger said, giving Patrick a long, hard stare.

"Four years gone," Skeet said.

"One killed the other."

"So *we* killed *him*."

"It still smells like dogs," Patrick said, uncowed.

A couple of weeks had passed since then. Today, Chigger and Skeet were again munching Bounty Bag chocolate-chip cookies and smoking in the kitchen when Patrick entered. It was like they hadn't moved or—since Patrick had been through the kitchen dozens of times since that first conversation—like they and their cookie-clouds and cigarettes had been teleported from that afternoon to this one. Chigger's eyes bore into Patrick. It was like his one thing. Finding nothing there, Chigger shifted his attention to Muscles Carbonara, who had popped out of the basement and now snatched from Patrick's outstretched hand the printout Patrick had made of his report card.

Chigger pounced. "A little bird told me it's report-card day. Is this *true*?"

"You're not my mom or my dad," Muscles Carbonara said. It was a lame retort, wholly out of character, but Patrick had said it dozens of times to Ray.

"I think Dad's home," Skeet said. "You don't challenge his claim of parentage, do you?"

"Dad never leaves," Muscles Carbonara said.

Skeet ignored this and asked, "Why don't you show it to him?"

"We could use some live entertainment," Chigger added, locking eyes with Skeet. They hacked up some mirthless titters.

Just then a scream—"*Haaaah!*"—followed by a loud *CLANK!* came from down the hall. It was Curtis, the eldest brother.

Curtis lifted weights and hardly came out except to go to work, yet he commanded a kind of silent respect from the family, which he basically single-handedly taped together with his solid mechanics' salary at Newman's Repair Shop. Unlike the rest of the Carbonaras, Curtis was not indifferent to proper maintenance and nutrition, but clearly he was a man in retreat. When Patrick first moved in, Curtis had briefly lit up, bounding down the hall to grip his hand. His apparent assumption was that the new recruit offered better raw material for physical training, a skill Curtis was working on, than his own blood kin. But he was wrong. Almost as soon as Patrick entered his well-ordered chamber to learn a few tricks, like the knee-high bands and the boxes for jumping, Curtis shoved him right back out, citing too much irony. "*Don't* be a little asshole," he had said, pointing through the wall toward his brothers' rooms. "I would never intentionally do that," Patrick replied. Aside from Curtis's income, the family also garnished Muscles Carbonara's Bounty Bag paychecks, but it wasn't much dough. This left Muscles Carbonara only his drug money to spend, plus what he made stealing chickens.

"Go to Jack's Four and whack off all night for all I care," Muscles Carbonara said to Chigger and Skeet, but he looked worried, an emotion Patrick had never seen in his friend. As if on cue, Muscles Carbonara's dad shuffled in, moving unsteadily into the room, the dark-beer smell of Michelob steaming from his pores. Oh how this brought back memories for Patrick. One never forgot Dad's favorite beer.

Muscles Carbonara was mostly mum on the subject of family history. He had that in common with Ray. He did explain once, though, that after his father's tailspin his mom had left with a fireman neighbor ("Fireman Dick," Muscles Carbonara called him, in what was surely another of his phallic puns) who still worked for the PFD. Mr. Carbonara had long had bad luck work-wise. He drifted from electrical-equipment assembler ("People will always need help putting the pieces together," he said optimistically when accepting the position) to bank teller ("People will always need help with their money") to holiday mail carrier ("People will always need help with their Christmas mail"). He got up earlier and earlier in the morning and drove ever farther from Pennacook for these jobs, while taking a pay-and-bennies cut with each switch, ultimately landing part-time with no benefits in food services, where he remained — at Kluck Klucker, as it happened, frying Ray's stolen chickens ("People are always going to need help with their food"). Somewhere along the line he snapped a rib playing ice hockey and found oxycodone. When the dogs died he stopped walking around the block and put on 40 pounds. His wife left, and the house fell apart.

"Pathetic," Muscles Carbonara had said in summing up. But faced now with the real thing, he assumed a very different stance.

"It's grades day, Dad," Muscles Carbonara said.

"Grades are your future."

"Yeah, Dad. I know."

He lowered his report card to his dad's open hand.

"What is this crap? English, a C? What do you have between your ears, a pile of horse manure?"

"C means 'average,' Dad. I did okay."

"I know what C means these days: terrible. You should be getting A's in that dump."

"Sorry, Pop. Next time, okay? You want a glass of water, Pop?"

"Why? *Why* would I want a glass of water, MC? You think I'm high or something? Well, so what if I am? I'd be a hell of a lot more impressed with your C if I knew you were high when you got it!"

Chigger and Skeet traded amused looks. Mr. Carbonara seemed to notice Patrick for the first time.

"What about him? What'd he get?"

"The same," Patrick said, though he'd done a little better. "Only I was high for most of it, so I guess I must be a genius."

Which was not true. Despite his earlier self-diagnosis as a drunk he was finding himself weirdly untempted ever since he ran away. Sure, he'd knock back a few in the basement with Muscles Carbonara, but he didn't take him up on dumb ideas like getting loaded in school or before another race. He didn't know why, but now that he had broken from Ray's clutches, beer and liquor just didn't tempt him anymore. Nor did Muscles Carbonara's Own, at least not as much as before. Sometimes they still provided needed relief, driving a numbing pike through the overheated Ray side of his brain. But most days now he gobbled the pot brownies reluctantly, like doing so paid his basement rent.

For business reasons, Muscles Carbonara had moved beyond brownies to other edibles, including an in-development banner product, pot bacon made from Pennacook boars, which he'd first need to learn how to catch. In Muscles Carbonara's opinion innovation was now paramount for "the little man" in this industry, the principle of "everybody needs someone to grow their pot" being also under siege, by the specter of legal Big Pot. Muscles Carbonara also hedged his bets and had a small but growing cache of heroin. This traveled a circuitous route from New York City to Rutland, Vermont, to Pennacook. Muscles Carbonara had just begun to trickle it out to Pennacook's bloodstream and early reviews were enthusiastic. Patrick *did not* and *never would* touch horse. Too many famous junky deaths, bullets to the brain or falling out the window. Muscles Carbonara had dabbled, then retreated—or so he said—from the cusp of addiction to pot, beer, and shrooms. This was happy news for Patrick, who didn't want to have to lock up his stuff and hide it every time he left the basement for fear that Muscles Carbonara, having exhausted his cash with moneys still owed to Rutland, would steal it. He hoped Muscles Carbonara's restraint held.

"Another wiseacre," Mr. Carbonara said. He gave Patrick a twisted smile, which Patrick interpreted as provisional approval.

This being the way of things, Muscles Carbonara and Patrick passed most of their time, and slept, in the basement den—where they now fled to. While Muscles Carbonara clipped his toenails, *The Origin of Species* open on his lap, Patrick told him how the Reconstruction

Role Play went down. He was more than ready to contrast some of Andrew Johnson's repulsive speeches with those of fire-breathing radical Thaddeus Stevens. He went a little overboard for a few hours after Mr. Grant's class and felt like this stuff was happening right now and was of the utmost urgency. But as usual Muscles Carbonara was entirely uninterested.

"Did you hear anything funny at school today?" he asked.

"Like what? A joke? Did you hear about the man who overdid it at the Chinese restaurant?"

"What about him?"

"He had 'All You Can Eat' and dim sum."

"That's dumb. No, I mean sounds. Creaking doors. Howling wolves. Things like that. Did you hear it?"

"No."

Muscles Carbonara frowned. "Bum connection."

He scooped up his toenails and put them in a jar thick with them.

"The notion of parting with any residue of my biology, even my toenails, is too distressing to someone of my caliber," he said, closing the jar.

This was also why he cut his own hair at home. Down in the basement, where he was ever so bold.

Escape to Castle Eaton

WHILE THE SKIP LABOEUF ADVENTURE LIFTED off the tarmac, Andrew Johnson's troubles accumulated like a week-old dish pile. Dr. Chong realized that further delay would only harden the grime and plunged in with gloveless hands.

The news was bad and in the special Pennacook sense that *nothing was happening*. The *Pennacook Beat*'s online $14 million thermometer with the explosion at the top dramatized donated funds already allocated to the proposed new-school building. If the TCO passed, *The Beat* would color in the entire thermometer and the explosion. The thermometer's low red mark symbolized a $250,000 contingent gift by Bounty Bag Grocers, Inc., plus a pathetic $20,000 of Pennacook's budget and a 5¢ pledge by some Penny joker. *The Beat*'s iconic cartoon of Jacob Pike, tar coated but armed, rubbed up to the thermometer and scowled at it, his Brown Bess raised to one side as if he would shatter the thermometer with a whiff of musket-ball at the slightest hint of further taxes.

Many comments shared Pike's radiant hostility.

'Only the best' for their little darlings. And they want me to pay for it!

Trojan horse for socialism

I hate school. Always halve.

If convertible to Pennacook revenue, Dr. Chong's rising ire at the comments would have topped up *The Beat*'s thermometer in seconds, sparking a serious skirmish with Jacob Pike.

She logged back into her Andrew Johnson account only to find that eight-hundred members of T.A.P.S. wished individually to let her know that "no new taxis" were to be levied against Pennacook.

She hit "reply" on one of these messages and typed: "What's wrong with new taxis?" Possessing a drop of political sense, she deleted the draft e-mail.

Other comments supported the TCO, but they drew scalding rebukes from the more active never-TCOers. Far from complacent, the TCO opponents had finally forced a competing tax-cap-*under-ride* petition — the dreaded Question Two — onto December's ballot.

It's not like she'd done nothing for the TCO campaign while all this unfolded. She did press faculty flesh for a few days after the meeting where she'd raised Archie's walk-out idea. But the faculty sensed, correctly, that she didn't really like them very much and probably wouldn't like them appreciably more if they did stick their necks out for the TCO. Most of the teachers hemmed and hawed. If she lingered too long in their classrooms, they steered her back to their own concerns, which were legion.

Can we get more paper towels for the breakroom?

How about instant coffee?

Unpaid leave to finish my novel? It's a doozy.

As if she were God! Didn't they understand that if there was no budget for walls, ceilings, and floors, in all likelihood there was a bit of a pinch when it came to supporting fiction-writing forays, complimentary crystallized coffee, or extra napkins for these tenured slobs?

"You're a tough cookie," said Archie, dipping his Buffalo wing in a blue-cheese cup.

He was sitting across from her at the Kluck Klucker. It was their Tuesday business lunch on the TCO campaign and she'd just filled him in on the latest.

"I know."

"But you spill."

He handed her a napkin and slid across his water.

She looked forward to these weekly lunches, though she'd never tell Archie that.

Back in her office that night, Dr. Chong launched another line of attack, hatching an imaginary activist and giving him an angry webpage with some slap-dash graphics. By this means she gathered three e-signatures in support: her real self, Archie, and a Pennacook boar.

On the Friday before Halloween she went to Free Skate and spotted Archie up in the Hallenbuck stands as she entered. He was pitching a small group of Pennies who appeared variously amused or frightened. But they did lend an ear, and one man gave a weary Archie a friendly pat on the shoulder, saying, if she read his lips correctly, "Hang in there, bud."

Dr. Chong rented skates and wobbled out onto the ice. Soon enough she found herself sprawled out like a starfish as a toddler wearing a pumpkin cap eased by on an overturned crate. No voters down here! A burly old man and two of her Korean-American sophomores gracefully skated toward her from opposite directions, picked her up, and re-set her, but she collapsed like she was boneless and waved off further help.

A few days later, knees and spirits bruised, she cornered Graham Bundt, *The Beat*'s data whiz, at Jack's Four Lounge during Monday's amateur night. A wet T- shirt contest was in progress as Dr. Chong entered the lounge wearing a curly wig and sunglasses. The ludicrous disguise was essential. After all, half the senior class was eligible to frequent this eighteen-and-over establishment.

She snagged a hula-girl juice cup from the bar and found the whiz kid at a small circular table up front.

"I can't believe that's the shirt," Graham said, watching the women. "Though maybe it's true?"

"It's Amateur Night. It's *not* their job."

"Why's there a Bounty Bag logo on it?"

"This doesn't concern me."

"For what you want? Thirty of your American dollars," Graham said, handing one of his own to an amateur dancer.

Outside, she hooked the whiz kid's bike on her Mini and drove him to *The Beat*, where he turned a crank and spat out a map.

"I'm glad you hit the Hallenbuck," he said, sounding disappointed. "That was first on my list."

She scratched off Hallenbuck as "done." On Saturday, she took Graham's other recommendations, marked by color-coded icons on his map, and hit the social clubs. She started with the older men's clubs, the Elks and the Knights of Columbus. But their memberships had dwindled. The forlorn Elks fed her a couple of boiled hot dogs and a bag of Bounty Bag caramel popcorn and invited her to try again next week (no thanks, guys). The KOC gave her a blank plaque drawn from a vat. She rang the head of the bowling league too, but it turned out the Pennacook Ballers was a shell of its former self. It had no meetings and its president said even their lane times were staggered. The Pennies preferred to bowl in pairs now, or alone. Was she supposed to chase them from lane to lane all day and night?

She might have tried the churches and the Pennacook Checkers Club next, even though Graham hadn't flagged them. Not to mention hundreds of doors concealing lonely voters. She might've knocked on those doors, opening her life, as punishment-loving Archie did, to hours of inane, empty-headed Penny conversations about preferred snacks, recent sports games, and clever YouTube videos. Some would be crackpots. All her fault, their problems. Since they paid her salary with their taxes.

But after these initial attempts she re-claimed her evenings and Saturdays for herself. Rather than kiss the sunken rings of Pennacook's 15,000 lords and ladies, she loafed around Eaton, sipping coffee and window-shopping high-return CDs she couldn't afford. She skipped the Eaton Bistro and in November became something of a regular at the faux hipster restaurant called Vodka Pete's. A thirty-two-year-old hedge-fund retiree had started this place. It attracted a younger crowd, mostly male. Dr. Chong turned a vampire's eye to the budding financiers and programmers and got buzzed on Vodka Pete's gimmicky platters of fritters, fried chicken, and vodka shots. She settled on a park bench and crunched through antacids, hangover creeping.

Come Sunday afternoon, she was Skip's. For privacy on one early date, Skip took her through an alternative wormhole to the Chelmsford Burger King. Their neglected burgers with their peculiar physics unwrapped themselves on the table as the lovers touched fingers and plotted.

They bypassed the burgers and instead had creamed spinach and chopped chicken breast, "a picnic," Skip called it, that Skip had smuggled out of the Rorsch School dining hall and characterized as "higher quality" than Burger King's vittles. The dining-hall food wasn't bad, but it wasn't very good. The Tupperware containers full of lukewarm, smuggled food reminded Dr. Chong of similarly packaged vomit secreted on the closet floor of the heroine of the AJMHS Health-class film warning against bulimia.

He told her about his brother-in-law, an investment adviser and board member of several area companies. The brother-in-law managed their money. "He got this great deal with this Cambridge biotech company that the family owns a big chunk of. It's a can't-lose proposition."

Due to this thing called buybacks, Skip explained, management — the brother-in-law was the company's treasurer — had been able to discreetly plow profits *right back into the company's own stock* instead of wasting it on another polluting research lab or on excess worker compensation that labor-market forces didn't advise. This constricted the public's share supply and zoomed the family's holdings into space. Recommendation: strong sell.

They tossed their untouched Burger King in the garbage pail. Dr. Chong noticed, at the Eaton end of the Chelmsford-Eaton wormhole, another of the new construction signs on which a little man, hip tilted to the side like he was dancing, lowered a shovel. A bulb blinked beside him on a stick. The town had approved the invasive-species aquatic barrier overwhelmingly and without any "no new taxis" fuss in its own tax-cap override (82%: yes). The project was proceeding swiftly to completion with six miles already dug out and filled. It would be tube-able in the spring and summer, and they'd be laying down bike paths along its extent, spokes extending downtown for Eaton's cycling value creators.

"Effing moat," Dr. Chong said. "What next, murder holes?"

"Priceless."

Of course both of them had voted for it and they heartily approved.

Skip's Prius wheezed and rattled across the wood-plank bridge to Eaton.

Home for the Holidays

LATE OCTOBER PAINTED THE TREES AND THE ROCK'S recycling bin swelled with college brochures addressed to Ray. It had been an especially rich harvest this fall. They must have scooped up every H.S.D. above ground.

Although after five years at Deli the prospect of student life was daunting to Ray, each year right around this time college dreams clouded his mind like squid ink. Ray would be covering Seafood, ice-bedding trash fish or carving up a cod filet, and find himself lost in a college bookstore. Or as he lifted lobsters from the briny tank he'd suddenly inhabit still another Ray, even less familiar, sprawling in a well-lit diner, newspapers spread and hot tea steaming. Once he had strolled through an oak-lined college campus delivering finger-sandwich platters to an orchestra soiree. It made a pretty picture in more ways than one. My, these girls are *clean*, he thought, his Pennacook hanging out. That night he looked up the corresponding lines from Mom's Chaucer, about the prioress who didn't stick her fingers too deep into the sauce or dump food on her lap. *Exactly.*

If Ray's college plans for himself were the stuff of Seafood Department fantasy, on a par with Honolulu, those he had whipped up for Patrick simmered on his mind's back burner like New England Portuguese Fish Stew, a piquant trial item that Store #52, New Bedford, had recently devised. Ray would spring the plan next summer, just as Patrick was adjusting his tie for the twelfth grade, but the basic ingredients, the personal statement and financial-aid application, had already floated into view like alabaster cod chunks. Even stripped of hypothetical Bounty Bag heroics of the type that Patrick might've acquired as a sacker (*"That Wednesday started like any other. I brushed my teeth, slurped my Honey Nut Cheerios, and caught up on my math. I never would have guessed that this was the day that I would successfully perform the Heimlich on a man over-sampling cocktail wieners."*), the sad tune of Patrick's tragic childhood, parent deaths followed by galley-slave life under Emperor Ray, practically sang itself to Admissions. Toss on top a couple of art certificates and Ray's shabby financials and Patrick would be golden. He might even draw a scholarship from some non-exclusive "art institute," like the ones Mom had slammed as "not really college." That is, if the kid could pull it together and, for the next nineteen months, *execute bare minimum*.

On Halloween, Ray joined Mr. Orlando, an amiable neighbor and Vietnam vet, for a haunted-house puzzle and to help him hand out candy to Pennacook's trick-or-treaters. Mr. Orlando loved the holiday but this year, his replaced knee failing, he couldn't personally service all comers with his assorted miniature chocolate bars.

Knock knock.

"I'll grab these guys," Mr. Orlando said and reached for his cane.

"Trick or treat."

"What are you?"

"Trash."

"And what are you?"

"Trash."

"You're both trash?"

"I'm white trash. He's just trash."

"Trailer trash, actually. I used to live here."

Mr. Orlando closed the door with a sigh. "Same thing every year."

Ray hustled over.

"Patrick!" he called into the shadows.

Someone bounced a mini candy bar off Ray's forehead, and they shuffled away in their garbage-adorned trash bags. Boars chased them.

Five more Pennacook trash heaps came that night, none of them Patrick.

Thanksgiving approached and Ray had hopes, brittle ones to be sure, of another Patrick cameo and baked a vegan turkey roll in anticipation.

Thanksgiving had always been a sort of Upside-Down Day for the Markhams, a time to suppress family conflict in favor of a well-worn script that placed Mom on top. Indeed, she had cordoned off the holiday and dictated its terms so thoroughly that it had become fixed in Ray's memory, all those Thanksgivings blending into one.

She rose in the dark to pop the turkey in the oven. Dad got up and she handed him a beer, a small one and the first of several distributed evenly over the day. Dad sipped the first glass, chuckled, and leaned on the counter.

"Anything I can do?" he asked buoyantly, admiring his wife.

"You can chop those onions and mash those potatoes."

"Lickety-split!"

Dad slipped behind her on the way to the cutting board and pinched her fanny and she hopped.

"Oh you bad man. Shoo!"

Patrick looked up from his train set, beaming and bobbing his eyebrows twice. *Hubba hubba.*

Dad helped Mom at the cutting board, then dropped to the floor and played trains with Patrick. At dinner he was spick and span in a sweater. He scraped his pie plate dry with his fork and set the fork neatly to the side.

"Anyone up for a walk?" he asked.

"Walk? I'm taking a *nap!*"

"Suit yourself! Come on, boys!"

They walked to the elementary school and Ray and Patrick shot baskets on the blacktop. Dad smoked a cigarette and stubbed it out, looking around. It rained, and they tumbled home under the power lines, coats pulled over their heads, Dad and Patrick laughing the whole way. Back in the den it was video games, two very small beers, and, at Mom's insistence, a ceremonial reading by Dad from *A Christmas Carol.* They got as far as Jacob Marley rebuking Scrooge for calling him "a good man of business."

"*Mankind was my business,*" Marley retorted (sounding, in retrospect, like a Bounty Bag board-meeting transcript excerpt). "*The common welfare was my business; charity, mercy, forbearance, benevolence, were all my business. The dealings of my trade were but a drop of water in the comprehensive ocean of my business!*"

The sun was down, surprising everyone a little. Dad traded Dickens for crowd-pleaser *Superman II*, his favorite childhood film. In his annual act of baking, he prepared a round of hot blueberry cobbler dishes topped by vanilla ice cream, by this means perfecting the atmosphere of cozy lassitude that had been gathering all day. It was akin to the peaceful state that Ray found Dad in after school most days, a bare foot dangling over his chair and his nose inserted in an "excellent" whiskey. Ray wondered if this sober Thanksgiving version of Dad could be extended through the year. Why did Dad need to drink to get there? Didn't blueberry cobbler and ice cream and TV and his family cut it? *Superman II* wrapped up, Zod and his junior partners once more vanquished, a superkiss that always felt like a downer wiping out Lois's memory of the Superman-Kent connection. Now he was just Clark Kent from Kansas again. Dad switched to endless football. Players blazed through snow walls in far-off colder places like Montana. It only warmed Ray, his feet roasting in holiday socks.

At supper time, Mom and Ray compiled leftover sandwiches and Ray removed the crusts for Patrick, only to find him asleep on the floor. Dad sat in his recliner and rubbed his temples.

"Can I get another beer, hon? And aspirin."

"One more, and that's it."

"Yes, ma'am, thank you, ma'am!"

This last bit of good news roused Dad, and he hammed it up, saluting and grinning. One eye open and aiming, he tried to loop in Ray, who shunned him. The ever-obliging Patrick quickly roused himself from his nap to click his heels and return Dad's salute. "Attention!"

Dad guzzled the last one in seconds. He washed the glass and polished it dry with a small cloth, then flipped it 360 degrees in the air, caught it smartly, and hooked it on the rack.

"Nighty night."

Off to bed at eight o'clock.

Fragile as it was, this family happiness contrasted sharply with what happened at Christmas. One memory in particular stood out.

That year they had a late-night dinner at a real downtown steakhouse, another occasion to "break bread together," a phrase Dad used to frame basically any restaurant meal. Dad's blessing of his meals with the language of Eucharist opened the door to an extended bout of drinking. "Let's hit the Nines and *break bread together.*" "Climb in the car, kids. Time to *break bread.*" It got so Ray cringed at the phrase no matter who said it or when, even Father Travassos from the pulpit.

The steakhouse impressed Ray. It was a dark lounge of green leather chairs, cherry-wood blinds, and elaborate rugs that led to another world. The décor recalled the home office of Vito Corleone, who was Dad's favorite *adult* movie character, even though the two of them, like Dad and Kal-El, seemingly had nothing in common. About the closest Dad got to the Corleones was a failed stab at Tom Hagan's profession. Before computers and retail Dad had washed out of law school. Toward the end, he sometimes subbed at Mom's school, his only remaining source of employment, and Ray's worst fear, never realized, was Dad's face at the front of one of his classrooms.

"And how would you like your porterhouse?"

The waiter struck Ray as some kind of steak professor he knew so much about the different cuts and means of preparation.

"Pittsburgh style," Dad said. Three martinis deep, he stared at his tapping fingers.

"I didn't catch that, sir. What did you say?"

"Pittsburgh style. Pittsburgh style. Pittsburgh style!" He banged the table. "Don't you know squat?"

Dad didn't complain about the below-decks saturation, maybe didn't feel the massive expanding wet spot. They had chocolate-lava cake and Dad, forgetting even to perform his somber ritual of crafting a judiciously meager tip, hobbled out of the leather booth with a napkin still tucked in his shirt.

"I'll take that, hon." Mom moved in to yank out the napkin.

"Wha – Oh yeah. Thanks. Thanks for a great night. You too, kids."

"Welcome, Dad," Patrick said.

Right then Dad's knee wobbled out to the side and he went down and the waiter swooped in and clamped his elbow to raise him to his feet.

"My husband's sick."

"I think so."

Years earlier, the third of July. Dad, half in the bag, drove Ray and Anne home from summer rec. He had swung by the packie in Tyngsborough, and his paper bundles filled the back seat. Ray and Anne sat in the ancient station wagon's backward-facing bench, their bony legs touching. Ray hoped Dad would keep his trap shut because Anne was special.

Summer rec was primitive but adequate and cost a pittance to family and town. It ran from late June through July and had the kids playing kickball on the dusty baseball diamond and, on the hot blacktop, four square and an obscure sedentary sport called zoneball invented long ago on Cape Cod. The rules were missing from the zoneball kit and not even available on the Internet, so Rec Director Sam made them up. For refreshment, they slurped water from the middle school's concrete outdoor bubbler, and on a special day Rec Director Sam split a watermelon on the concrete table.

Ray had already gone there for a couple of summers and, ten that year, sauntered in the first day feeling manly and independent. He signed the attendance sheet, thinking of three-year-old Patrick stuck back home in the plastic toddler pool filled with garden-hose water. But days of torment followed. As usual Ray badly needed a haircut and the other boys, dubbing him "Raccoon," ushered him toward a fist-fight. After Anne joined them the second week and paired off with Ray, however, the others lost interest in hunting Raccoon.

That spring Anne's family had migrated from Monticello, Georgia, to one of the other elementary-school districts in town. Her lilt made him want to hear more. She was a reader like him, she said. It turned out she couldn't read well at all. She was nine years old and stuck on Richard Scarry, but her glasses made her look smart and she had a mild face and listened carefully as Ray bragged of the swollen volumes he had tackled.

"You like books about dogs?"

"Oh yes."

"You ever hear of Jack London from Alaska?"

"No."

"He wrote a couple on dogs. At least a couple. I guess *Call of the Wild* is more famous, but I like *White Fang* better. It's about a wolf-dog."

"Is that a wolf or a dog?"

"Both, like it sounds. It could be any percentage, but White Fang is half of each. He gets domesticated though."

"What's domesticated?"

"Means he starts off wild but then becomes for people."

He was always explaining words to her.

"It sounds very interesting. Why do you like it better?"

"Happy ending. White Fang has babies. He's a dad."

"Tell me more."

She used her nimble fingers to pierce his mylar juice bag and wipe a crumb from his lip.

One day temps hit the 100s and Rec Director Sam (saying, "I don't care, I don't fucking *care* what they do to me") busted into the cool, shaded middle-school gym with a crow bar and called a free-throw contest. Anne and Ray dropped out in the first round and slipped off alone, chasing each other under the fold-out wooden bleachers. The game had no point. It was something like hide and seek but without the hide part of the equation. They kept discovering each other and being dazzled, or at least Ray was.

"*This* is where you live?" Dad asked as they pulled into the mobile-home park on July 3rd.

Hers was one of the older and rustier ones. A true trailer, like The Rock.

"What's wrong with that? It's her house."

"That's no house."

Anne patted his knee. "He's right. It's not a house." Her moist thigh sucked free and she climbed out of the wayback. "Bye, Ray."

"See you tomorrow."

"Tomorrow's the Fourth."

She picked up a broom and brushed stones, her dirty-blond hair lifted in the wind.

She never came back. Years later, after a long time thinking about Anne and then some time not thinking about her at all, Ray asked Mom about her.

They were in the kitchen surrounded by spaghetti strips hanging from racks like snake skins and over-yeasted mutant bread loaves. These were the residue of Dad's abandoned homemade pasta-and-bread project, which he'd yielded to Mom. Just like he'd yielded unjamming the mower, assembling Ray's scooter, and even hooking up the clown-head sprinkler. "It can't be done!" he explained each time, and gave up.

Mom massaged one of the bread loaves and said Anne's dad had moved her away a couple years back, but then she had died from leukemia.

"Are you sure?"

Mom turned and stared at him.

"What do you mean, 'am I sure'? It was in the paper."

"Are you sure it was her with leukemia. Anne."

"I suppose it could be the other one. She had a sister. At least I think she did."

"Because I don't remember that. Her having a sister."

"Well then maybe it was her."

"How can you not know that? How can you not remember? A girl *dies*, and you don't even know if it was her?"

"What has gotten into you? You know what? I don't have time for this. I have to cook. I have to clean. I have to wash your—*everyone's—filthy* underwear. I'm not the only one in this house who can clean up, you know."

She slid the loaves into the oven. *Clankety clank.* Like a prison. "Anyway, they're gone." She flipped the oven shut.

But one Easter morning long before that Mom confronted the worst of it and nipped it in the bud.

Mom was pregnant with Patrick and snoring and Dad smelled sour again like bread. When Ray touched him he only groaned. Ray said "Happy Easter" twice, the second time a shout. His plan was to give Dad a quick back massage and then ask for his basket and the egg hunt. Dad's snore jagged but fell back into its groove. With so much at stake, Ray was not easily deterred. He poked Dad hard under the armpit and his red eyes flicked on, his arm flinging out, slamming him back against the dresser. The pictures on top flopped down and one slipped over the edge and knocked him under the eye, cutting him open.

"What's wrong with you?! Can't I get a goddam moment's rest? Can't I get a minute to myself! Stop it—you're bleeding on the rug!"

"What's wrong with Dad?" he asked Mom in the kitchen.

"Stop dropping the ice pack. Hold it up."

"Can I show him my picture?"

"After."

"It's a bunny picture."

"I said after."

"Okay. After what?"

Wrapped high in golden cellophane, his basket sat right there on the table. All sorts of things might be in there. Baseball cards, yellow birds. He could see two hidden eggs. Mom ignored his question and leaned over the stove. She made him some bunny-shaped pancakes, her hand shaking over the pan. Eager for the pancakes, Ray said, "Yum."

Dad stumbled in.

"Hey, hon. Coffee?"

"If you ever—ever—hurt my babies again, I will kill you."

It was like nothing else she ever said, before or after. At bedtime she read him *If You Lived in Iroquois Times*, which recounted Earth's beginnings as a mud daub on a turtle's back. She closed it and smoothed back his hair.

"Do you know what a 'frigate' is, honey?"

"No."

"It's a kind of ship. A warship, actually."

"Oh."

"There's a poem I want you to memorize. The first two lines, for starters."

"Okay."

" 'There's no Frigate like a Book / To take us Lands away.' Can you say that?"

He said it.

"Good. Do you know what that means?"

"Books float."

"No."

"They might. If it's salty."

"It means books can help us escape our troubles, by taking us to faraway places or times. They don't only do that, but (I will tell you a secret) it's one of the things I like best about them. You like story books, don't you?"

"Yes."

"Good. Can you say it again?"

He did.

"One more time."

"Okay." He said it.

"Try to remember."

He stared at his pineapple nightlight and breathed twice slowly.

"Can you stop talking about books and sing to me now?"

"Of course. Close your eyes."

Ray remembered the poem and showed it off to teachers. On another Easter he decided to share the poem with Patrick. They were in bed. Ray was on the cool top bunk with the ladder. Patrick was on the bottom bunk and had no complaints, even said he liked the darkness. Ray told him the poem and also what it meant.

"Understand?" Ray asked at the end. "Get it?"

Patrick rolled over, candy wrappers crinkling underneath him. Ray's voice had lulled him to sleep.

Patrick didn't show up for Thanksgiving so Ray ate the stuffed vegan turkey roll alone, liberally dunking it in Marcin's Cranberry Sauce from Dennisport, on Cape Cod. He had pie and walked over to Liberty's basketball courts, where he shot hoops and rebuked himself for all this brooding. The happiness books agreed that what you were supposed to do with the past was be grateful for the good stuff and toss the rest. With too much free time, was he becoming Patrick?

Local History:
The Diary of Mary Chestnut

BEFORE CLASS, MR. GRANT USED HIS LIMITED breath to speech-coach a member of his after-school mock-trial team on a finer point of pronunciation that, he conceded, eluded even certain adult members of the Pennacook bar such as second-best divorce attorney Joe Delahunt.

" 'Wanton.' Say it."

"Wonton."

"No, wanton. Emphasis on the '*wan*.' "

The bell rang.

"*Won*ton."

"Forget it. We'll try again at practice."

By the time Thanksgiving week rolled around, Mr. Grant had moved from four-point cane to walker, then switched to double canes. He had an oxygen mask now and took an occasional hit, pausing mid-sentence to turn on the tank and clamp the mask over his mouth and nose. The coughs continued. Today, after a long jag of them, he made room for a brief, uncharacteristic personal statement. Wind howled over sharpening knives and a wall of thumping heartbeats as he spoke.

"I'm sick and live alone. In fact, I'm dying. You may wonder why I come into this school at all to teach. Why don't I quit? I could. But if this school is going to kill me — and it is — I insist that my death be witnessed. In the meantime, I hope you're enjoying my class."

Patrick was. Local History's rigorous demands came as a relief. It was like Mr. Grant had handed him a card reading "Historian," giving him permission to stop thinking only about his own past or about books or videos, or even about Mr. Grant dying before their eyes, and to start looking at the broader context. After all, Patrick's childhood — which he'd gone over in his head so many times that he remembered remembering it, and then remembered *that* — didn't just spring from the vacuum via some random quantum-field fluctuation. Even Dad's drinking had echoes in the annals of American history. Weren't inebriated honkies a staple of Jacksonian Democracy?

"But enough of my whining. I want to set you loose on *this*."

Kaff.

He sent down the fresh packets, which required a short paper on Mary Chestnut's views on slavery and equality, based on fifty pages of diary excerpts. Patrick set to work immediately, circling passages that mentioned slavery and marking them with an "S" and circling those mentioning race and marking them "E." Later he'd collate them and tease out some ideas.

Mary Chestnut was a fascinating woman. She was married to one slaveholding North Carolina senator and daughter to another. Yet she came to despise slavery in the most acid terms. Patrick had already tabbed his paper's money quote. "God forgive us, but ours is a monstrous system, a wrong and an iniquity."

In addition to the diary, she wrote two novels. She was by any modern standard a bigot, and somewhat homely, but Patrick found her wit and intelligence charming and developed an unseemly crush. When Mr. Grant played the Civil War ditty "The Homespun Dress," something of a "California Girls" of its time, though one where the regional women were singing their own praises, Patrick thought of Mary Chestnut's oval portrait.

We scorn to wear a bit of silk,
A bit of northern lace
But make our homespun dresses up,
And wear them with a grace.

He felt a twinge of guilt, as though his lust had led him to betray his Radical Republican and Freedmen allies from the Reconstruction Role Play, but as with L. Frank Baum he was unable to judge. Did he have to?

"Why don't you begin with understanding?" Mr. Grant asked him after class. "Walk a mile in her shoes."

"What about her slaves' shoes?"

"Walk in theirs too."

"If they had them."

"Right. And even if they didn't."

Then Mr. Grant lost control again and folded over coughing.

Patrick wondered if this *To Kill a Mockingbird* shoes-wearing approach, even when the subject *had* no shoes, could help with personal history too. Then again, he didn't think as much about Mom and Dad lately. He was too busy with his Local History assignments.

A pack of barking dogs escorted Patrick to his locker. From there to lunch, branches crashed in forests all around him. A grandfather clock tolled midnight over an atonal organ during his fruit-cup dessert, and for a moment he was scared.

Back at Muscles Carbonara's he headed straight for the basement. As he crossed the pungent pine-incense barrier that separated the first few steps from Muscles Carbonara's underground lair, he doubted that his increasingly detached friend would even attempt to write the Mary Chestnut paper. When not off on some mission he lay about in the basement high on his brownies, playing shooter games, listening to New Hampshire's own GG Allin (long-dead coprophagist rocker), and staring up at the basement's perennial Christmas lights, now coming back in season. Sometimes he read aloud from *The Origin of Species*, savoring, Patrick suspected, not the lucid prose but the unforgiving principles of natural selection. (*"We behold the face of nature bright with gladness, we often see superabundance of food; we do not see, or we forget, that the birds which are idly singing round us mostly live on insects or seeds, and are thus constantly destroying life...."*) Muscles Carbonara could be scholarly in his own way, one of the qualities that had attracted Patrick to him in the first place, but his scientific curiosity typically ran to salacious arcana like the Coolidge effect.

"How now brown cow," he said.

Pine incense gave way to acrid steam produced by breakfast sandwich-flavored e-juice, yet another test product that Pennacook was pioneering for all the world, billowing from Muscles Carbonara's e-cigarette as its atomizer hummed along. He removed the e-cigarette and frowned at it.

"Not the same."

Like Ray, Muscles Carbonara was a bit of an analog man. He favored real tobacco. He even savored the cartons, including the minor thrill of exercising his enlarged arm muscle to crumple them up and toss them on the floor or ground wherever he found himself.

He was wearing his Boy Scout uniform. He cleaned up once a week for Troop 555 meetings, like the one later tonight, which Patrick planned to skip in favor of Mary Chestnut. Suspiciously, Muscles Carbonara was taking Scouts seriously now. He had nixed the boots and cargo shorts in favor of dress shoes and khakis and ironed his shirts meticulously. He had also begun seeking challenging merit badges with disturbing themes and implications. Shotgun Shooting and Nuclear Science; Wilderness Survival and Fire Safety; Welding and Composite Materials. At this rate, he wouldn't be a Tenderfoot for long. He'd be the Marathon Bomber! In contrast, Patrick's most recent merit badges, Indian Lore and Basket Weaving, suggested a harmless boy who perhaps lacked direction.

Patrick grabbed a game controller and fell into the couch. He liked video games. It was an art form, to be sure, perhaps the finest for diverting binges. Sometimes he met cool weird people on there too. Like Ludvig. One afternoon Ludvig had beamed into Patrick's Minecraft Parthenon from his mom's weather station on Svalbard spouting ardent Norwegian idioms like "That's completely Texas!" They became pals, but one time Patrick briefly took offense. Before the statue of Athena, he confessed to Ludvig that he wasn't feeling well. Ludvig, intending only sympathy, blurted in his imperfect English, "What's WRONG with you?" "A lot," Patrick typed into the chat bar, once he'd caught on. "But mainly just this belly ache today." Though for all the intriguing gamers he'd encountered, from Rio to Kyoto (places he'd also enjoyed touring on Google Maps, zooming in on storefronts, temples, and—let's face it—women), he rarely met Pennies online. They seemed to prefer solo or unplugged local gaming. Or else they were playing something sinister that Patrick hadn't sniffed out yet.

"I'm hearing those sounds," Patrick said. "The ones you mentioned. Slamming doors and wolves. It's a haunted house, right? It's playing all the time now. Everywhere."

"As planned. The beauty is it's all parasitic. You wouldn't believe the tracks Principal Chong's laying down in that school. Recording devices, wireless-networked listening nodes. Ultraviolet cameras. Putin would be jealous."

"You should stop it. Makes the whole school feel like a graveyard."

This was true up to a point. Muscles Carbonara had generally kept the volume low, and the patches of sound effects were just intermittent enough that a balky bureaucracy could overlook them or give up. Too hard to trace the source. During sixth period today, for example, Muscles Carbonara's soundtrack swelled up in the form of scratching fingernails, only to recede just as quickly to silence. And Dr. Chong may have balked at dismantling the network anyway if the prank truly was integrated into some secret surveillance system.

"It is a graveyard," Muscles Carbonara said. "Ask Mr. Grant. '*Kaff kaff.*'"

Muscles Carbonara glanced at the packet. He removed the cover sheet and pinned Mary Chestnut to the basement dart board.

"I've decided I'm not an anarchist anymore." On his third dart, he pierced Mary Chestnut's sternum. "I'm a fascist."

Escape to Castle Eaton

ONE FRIDAY IT WAS OFF TO A LONG-DEFERRED arm-twisting appointment with the Pennacook Gaming Association, or PGA, to promote the TCO. It was her first campaign stop in some time and to her good fortune it made little difference that she forgot her notes.

The gamers convened in the entire second floor of the Pennacook Free Town Library. They proved a paragon of distraction as she spoke off the cuff, hitting a few bullet points while beyond the windows late-November snowflakes slowly tumbled by. Several members gamed through her talk. One fellow in the back, mouth agape, wore some sort of experimental gaming goggles and seemed to be sacking groceries in a virtual supermarket. The fellow beside him, also goggled, appeared to be scanning items at a supermarket register and handing them to the first man, though their hands never touched. Despairing, Dr. Chong stopped mid-sentence to pose what she thought would be a provocative question.

"Why do you even have a club, guys? Isn't the whole idea that you los—gamers can do this without meeting in person? When you're totally and abjectly alone?"

The men—it was nearly all men—perked up.

"It's the beer," said one man.

"Yeah, beer," said another.

"Beer."

They looked all around, taking turns saying "beer."

Dr. Chong skipped to the end but while she was still stumbling through it the men started to get up and walk out to the reception room for their wings party. They shook their heads and cast hurt looks.

That weekend Skip's wife and their son Blake—who, it turned out, was not the sailor-suited munchkin that she had imagined but a stout twenty-three-year-old—were out of town, and Skip brought Dr. Chong "up campus."

The visit was made possible by Kat's patron grandfather, Elliot, who was hosting from Edgartown this weekend and who was the source of all sweet things in their lives. The Cohasset deck house, their securities portfolio, the possibility of a career teaching at Rorsch School not followed by a campground retirement. Elliot would prefer not to see Skip if it could at all be arranged. Thanks to Skip's sports and dorm and Saturday classroom duties, it could.

Skip's wife Kat was well aware that Skip was up to something with an older woman but let him play. Nevertheless, Dr. Chong drew the blinds and huddled in Skip's apartment all afternoon, waiting for Skip to return from squash practice. She drank water from the sink and poked around. A peek through the blinds revealed the regal head of school walking his Pomeranian and smiling at all passers like "the bourgeois monarch" Louis Philippe I, a popular if less potent Napoleon successor, a laughable pose at Andrew Johnson that she envied for that reason. Behind him on a frosted patch next to the boathouse (bit of an off note), a little graveyard for teachers. She drank more water and plopped down on Skip's leather club chair with piping to play games on her phone. Her hand slid down and brushed clandestine boogers. The dried boogers made the club chair and the matching ottoman seem somehow unearned.

Eaton Living gave the latest on Eaton Moat, which had brought Eaton and Rorsch School together, town and gown against the turmoil beyond. It also bound them in sorrow. As *Eaton Living* reported, its unfinished banks had already washed up two high-achieving-teenager suicides, one each from Eaton High and Rorsch School. Gymnasts and math champs, respectively. Terrible, terrible, but it was a story unfamiliar only in its particulars. Pennacook's suicides were more numerous but skewed old and male. Two cheers for Pennacook! She drank a glass of water as she read.

When Skip came home from squash she pounced at the door, but not for the reason that he likely expected.

"I need to go to the bathroom."

"I forgot: the toilet's broken. Exploded, actually."

"I know that. It's locked and it smells. Why didn't you text me back?"

"I was on the courts. You could've used the library. That's what we do. It's right next door."

"It's closed."

"Ah, but there's a way."

Skip led her, shivering in his poncho, down a dusky path to a drainage grate behind a stone wall.

"I learned this from the kids," he said. "I've caught them at it."

He took Dr. Chong by the heel and vaulted her through a library-basement window—into the most romantic bathroom she had ever seen. Towel baskets, filled to overflowing, graced ebony sink tops. Fresh flowers rested on bamboo beside a well-pruned bonsai as Ben Webster, wielding his tenor, serenaded the moon across a tiled wall.

The next stall rustled. "Oh shit. Penis patrol!"

"I'm just an old lady relieving her bladder."

They politely refrained while she finished her business and mounted an aromatic rosewood footstool to escape.

Back in the apartment, she asked, "Why don't you fix your toilet?"

"Oh, they take care of all that."

"Apparently not."

"Are we fighting?"

"I just don't understand why you don't fix your own toilet. If mine broke, I'd fix it. If I didn't know how, I'd call someone."

"I did. They haven't fixed it yet."

"Why not?"

"They're busy."

"How long has it been?"

"Oh, two weeks. I can't believe it's been that long! Wait. *Has* it been that long?" He counted on his fingers. One, two. "It *has* been two weeks!"

"For two weeks you've been breaking into a library to go to the bathroom."

"Not when they're *open*. There's a hall toilet in Howell House too. Sometimes we use that, and the gym has nice showers."

"Why don't you fix it or hire someone else?"

He considered this. "I can't. It's their bathroom."
"We're fighting."

Monday night she called Archie to strategize about the TCO and caught him roaming Pennacook's back roads in his camper van, where he always seemed to be these days, hunting votes. A man alone, except for Cornelius the Yorkie.

"I'm afraid the gamers were underwhelmed," she admitted. "It's all over Twitter and *The Beat*."

Her aborted statement that the gamers were losers had gained the wrong kind of traction for the TCO debate. *The Beat* had built two full-length articles and their lead editorial on the seemingly unpromising foundation of her brief rambling appearance. "ANDY J.'S CHONG DUBS PENNIES 'LOS-'ERS." "INFLUENTIAL GAMERS SWING AGAINST TCO." "RESPECT LOCAL GAMERS; THEY'RE OUR CHILDREN TOO!" The editors stamped her an "autocratic snob." The PGA re-tweeted the pieces, and all of them went viral.

"Water under the bridge," Archie said, putting the best face on things. "Pennacook Senior Center?"

"Also a flop."

"Tough crowd. A real T.A.P.S. hotbed. And my walk-out idea?"

"Faculty nixed it again. Which actually makes me sort of like it more."

Indeed, the faculty's ultimate "nay" vote, by a three-fourths majority, had stirred the Napoleon in her, breathing new life in the concept. She told Archie that her new plan was to muster the iconoclasts. A hardened core. The vanguard, the elite! Janice Chance, Tito Tiggs, and — if he could make it out the door — Keith Grant.

Archie spoke quickly as though sensing desperation. "Walkout sounds like maybe a dead end. Sorry: my fault. But how about door-to-door? Like on a Sunday afternoon, when everyone's around? People crave the attention. It works for me."

"Do I have to?" she asked.

Archie sighed and let the question dangle.

Local History:
The Anti-Federalists

BREATHING TUBES LOOPED THROUGH MR. GRANT'S nose and the line ran diagonally across his chest like a shoulder-bag sash. They had installed a massive maroon leatherette hospital recliner over the weekend, but Mr. Grant mostly avoided the recliner, preferring to wheel his oxygen around on the gurney, other hand free to gesture.

He'd put up a chart for them. He didn't explain it, which only made it more intriguing to Patrick, who at first just observed it, like he might a flower or a poem's shape. Except it was facts. He took a closer look.

Year	Top Marginal U.S. Income Tax Rate	Marginal U.S. Estate Tax rate	Real GDP Growth in U.S.
1951	91.0	77.0	8.1
1964	77.0	77.0	5.8
1985	50.0	55.0	4.2
2005	35.0	47.0	3.3
2010	35.0	0.0	2.5

SOURCE: Holzer, Harold, and Norton Garfinkle. *A Just and Generous Nation: Abraham Lincoln and the Fight for American Opportunity*. Basic Books. P. 262 (internal citations omitted).

He had explained on the board that "marginal" meant the tax applied only to a certain part of the taxpayer's income, in the case of the taxes featured on the chart, the highest income and the amount of the estate over a given threshold. So those taxed at 91 percent weren't taxed 91% for all of their income; only for the part that made them richer than everybody else. He also wrote on the board that "GDP growth" meant how much more stuff per person the economy produced over the prior year.

Patrick put two and two together and inferred this was a shot across the bow at Mr. Dobson, Patrick's business teacher, who believed lowering taxes *always* fostered growth. What interested Patrick was the poisonous intrigue of it all, how Mr. Grant just planted the idea and let the kids run with it back to Mr. Dobson. Then again, Mr. Grant wasn't up for man-to-man combat anymore.

Mr. Grant pulled down the chart and turned to today's class proper. He lectured between coughs and when the coughs overtook him projected typed all-caps answers to their questions. He started off talking about America generally, but at one point the class took a sharp and unexpected turn back to Pennacook.

He was giving them the inside scoop on the 1787–88 constitutional-ratification debates. Everyone of course knew all about the legendary figures arguing in the *Federalist Papers* for approval of the U.S. Constitution. (Actually they didn't, but the more obscure the fact referenced, the more likely Mr. Grant was to say "of course" about it.) But what did they know of the *Anti*-Federalists, the American patriots who opposed the Constitution? Cato, Brutus, the Federal Farmer? Mr. Grant diplomatically positioned the Anti-Federalists as defenders of "Don't Tread on Me" small-r republican virtue and provided a small sample of their handiwork critiquing the Constitution.

> The evil genius of darkness presided at its birth....

> If anarchy...were the inevitable consequence of rejecting the new Constitution, it would be infinitely better to incur it....

> To preserve liberty it is essential that the whole body of people always possess arms and be taught alike, especially when young, how to use them.

LOCAL HISTORY: THE ANTI-FEDERALISTS

> The Lawyers in particular, keep up an incessant declamation for its adoption; like greedy gudgeons they long to satiate their voracious stomachs with the golden bait.

Okay, so the last bit rang true, but if "guns-'n-anarchy" was the real America—some political historians estimated the Anti-Federalists had more popular support but didn't mobilize so well and got outclassed by Madison, Hamilton & Co.—it all made Patrick briefly entertain the message he found in yet another Anti-Federalist paper.

> Idiots and maniacs ought certainly to be restrained from doing themselves mischief, and ought to be compelled to that which is for their own good. Whether the people of America are to be considered in this light and treated accordingly, is a question which deserves, perhaps, more consideration than it has yet received.

All considered, maybe not the best way to win votes.

In the end, despite Mr. Grant's best efforts at non-partisan balance, the Anti-Federalists came off like a bunch of paranoid yeoman-farmer cranks, disturbingly reminiscent of modern-day Pennies in their rank pessimism bordering on despair. The Constitution a "hideous daemon of Aristocracy" packed with "treacherous measures"? What did these people want? A different currency and militia for every block?

Much to Patrick's surprise, some data backed up his intuition of an Anti-Federalists-Pennacook link. Mr. Grant threw up an Early Republic map digesting the best available demographic, newspaper, and voting information from the 1780s. The chart broke down the Federalists/Anti-Federalists by town and color-coded each town by level of estimated ratification sentiment. The urban areas were typically shades of orange, showing firm support for the U.S. Constitution. But farther out in the country things gradually transitioned to purple until, sure enough, a telltale grape-dark blotch, which Mr. Grant blew up with his stretching fingers, featured Pennacook as the Commonwealth's least supportive town. These were not hard numbers, mind you, but perhaps 90% of Pennies opposed ratification.

Mr. Grant wrapped up the Anti-Federalists and, continuing his swerving rear-drive through American history, handed out a chronology of the lead-up to the American Revolution. This event he described as conservative, "but only in a limited sense." For instance, the colonists were used to pushing aside Indians when it came time to expand westward, but King George III's Royal Proclamation of 1763 had barred settlement of choice lands won in the French and Indian War (1754–63), marking them as an Indian reserve. This change in approach bred white-colonial resentment. But probably more important, Parliament had indulged in two centuries of "salutary neglect" (Edmund Burke, 1776), allowing the colonies largely to self-govern. Strong elected assemblies dominated the royal governors and made the colonies into thirteen flourishing schools for democracy. The tone-deaf British eventually tuned back in, but by that time they had unwittingly trained these backwater eccentrics into a people distinctively accustomed to self-rule, to talk and to protest. Parliament and George proved arrogant and bumbling and severely underestimated their problem when they tried to take these things away.

An early misstep, the Stamp Act fiasco of 1765–67, exemplified this. Parliament unilaterally required that a tax be paid and, as a receipt, an unsightly foil seal applied to colonial newspapers, almanacs, playing cards, wills, even dice—basically anything other than books that the colonists might put in front of their eyes to remind them of the tax and replenish their rage. Conspiratorial organizations like the Sons of Liberty and the Committees of Correspondence organized to block stamp-tax distributors and tax collection. Parliament backed down. First, bloodless cut of revolt.

Mr. Grant called a break but waved Patrick over to his screen. "DO YOU LIKE SCHOOL?" he typed.

"It's... boring. Not this class, and not Art. But in general."

"WHAT'S WRONG WITH A LITTLE BOREDOM?" Mr. Grant typed.

Patrick didn't have an answer for that.

"I OFTEN SEE YOU READING. WHAT DO YOU LIKE TO READ THE MOST?"

"Classics and, uh, k-kids books."

Mr. Grant's eyes had closed but as Patrick began to move away they slowly re-opened.

"YOUR PAPER ABOUT THE MALL AND THE POLYNESIAN RESTAURANTS. I HAVE IT HERE FOR YOU."

Patrick stiffened. He'd been in the groove while writing the paper, but he wasn't sure it counted as history or was any good.

"AS I WRITE HERE ON THE BACK, YOUR 'FINE WORK' IS 'INDICATIVE OF EXCEPTIONAL PROMISE IN A TEENAGER' AND 'YOUR MIND IS ALREADY OPERATING AT THE COLLEGE LEVEL.' I'M GIVING YOU AN A+, THE FIRST OF THE DECADE."

Mr. Grant's hand shook as he handed over the paper. The A+ was unheard of and would've made Ray proud. Too bad he wouldn't see it.

"I'VE JOTTED SOME OTHER STUFF TOO. MAYBE WHEN I'M GONE YOU CAN USE THIS FOR YOUR COLLEGE APPLICATIONS NEXT YEAR."

Patrick shifted his feet. The plan was no plan.

"YOU'D LIKE COLLEGE. IT'S NOT LIKE THIS." He paused for a moment, then re-commenced typing. "YOU MAY MISS THE BOREDOM."

He hacked into his handkerchief. Patrick took this as a laugh.

Muscles Carbonara was incurious about the American Revolution but surprisingly rallied to the Anti-Federalists' defense—or so it seemed at first.

"Didn't they corner James Madison into supporting the Bill of Rights in order to get enough votes for the Constitution?" he asked.

He was smoking a bong but rubbed his spikey head in agitation. Against all seasonal logic, he'd given himself a wiffle. Hair tufts tumbled about the basement.

"You know you're right," Patrick conceded. "I guess the Anti-Federalists weren't so useless after all."

"Are you kidding? The Bill of Rights was a *terrible* idea. People running their mouths off. Turning away soldiers who just needed a hot meal and a haystack to crash on for the night. 'Need to take a piss, officer? Get a warrant, pal!' I guess *some* of them made sense."

He fired a hand-pistol at Patrick.

"People are lazy complainers," he continued. "Sheep. They need a strong hand to tell them what's what. If they don't have that, they'll only complain more."

Patrick climbed into the hammock and Muscles Carbonara settled back on his couch, humming the melody to "When Johnny Comes Marching Home," a Civil War anthem that Mr. Grant had covered together with "The Homespun Dress." After a time, Muscles Carbonara began singing, his lyrics a variation on the Scout-camp version.

The ants go marching two by two
  Hurrah! Hurrah!
The ants go marching two by two
  Hurrah! Hurrah!
The ants go marching two by two
  And the little one stops to beat up a Jew

Rise and Fall of the Third Reich, its first half dirtied by close reading, and some untouched Nietzsche rested on the end table atop the well-meaning *Boy Scout Handbook* and *The Origin of Species*. At least no *Mein Kampf*. Though what a thing to have to say!

"How many Jews do you even know?" Patrick asked.

Muscles Carbonara ignored this but, having exhausted his anti-Semitic lyric pool, retreated to his grating hum.

"That's what I thought, you jerk. Are you really this bored?"

He was thinking of the only Jews he had known, the Rosenbaums of Waltham. They'd taken him in while Ray roamed the earth in search of this paradise. Patrick still wore the Star of David necklace they'd given him.

"I hope you know what you're getting into with this haunted-house business," Patrick continued. "It's bigger than your other pranks. This isn't ordering Hawaiian pizza from the local-cable call-in show or setting up fake detours."

"Or stealing chickens—which, by the way, has gotten exceedingly difficult for me since you ran away from home."

Add to the list the things they'd done together since Patrick moved in. A forest fire behind Pike Middle. Bologna applied to a neighbor's babied Mustang, causing bologna-shaped hood corrosion. Piss balloons through the same neighbor's window. They'd committed crimes against innocents as well, pouring cherry Kool-Aid in a Boys and Girls Club wading pool and, as November turned to December, using stolen loaves of Ray's scrumptious Deli bread to lure Pennacook boars to the dam across the icy Pennacook River, where Muscles Carbonara kicked them in and drowned them. True, Patrick had backed out of this last spree when he realized Muscles Carbonara's lethal intent. But how would that stack up in a court of law when he'd done nothing to thwart him?

One thing they had not done: chase girls or get them drunk or stoned. Patrick wouldn't say it, but he had concluded that Muscles Carbonara, so ribald in his humor, either feared real girls, thinking that he repulsed them, or—more likely—was gay, a "friend of Dorothy." Patrick could easily have cast himself as the sympathetic ear for a coming out, but Muscles Carbonara did not welcome such topics. Something in him did not care for introspection or for chewing on its fruits with another.

Sober when they did these pranks, Patrick felt liberated, then imprisoned. Each post-prank crash mandated another and bigger prank, to up the ante and earn another high and fresh smiles from his friend, who never laughed. Though after the boar-killing a kind of exhaustion set in. Punishment. He had wanted out even before the hateful turn in Muscles Carbonara's thinking.

"And you aren't paying me anymore," Patrick said, relative to the chickens.

"You live here."

"It's messing with the wires," Patrick said, returning to the topic of Muscles Carbonara's aggressive new prank.

"And tapping phones too, and recording conversations. I didn't tell you about that. A federal offense, I get it. Like selling heroin, which I also do to the good citizens of our fair town. Does this mean you won't help me with the next phase?"

"Phase?"

Escape to Castle Eaton

GOOD NEWS AT LAST ON THE TCO. JANICE CHANCE e-mailed that, yes, she would walk out "arm-in-arm" with Dr. Chong on the appointed day, now two weeks off. "Let's *do* this," she wrote. Was there a set time and place? As if to tantalize her with his distinguishing chromosome, hyper-masculine Tito Tiggs wrote simply "y." Crotchety Mr. Grant went radio silent for days but then replied that he would participate on one condition, that Dr. Chong agree to jettison her STEM (Science, Technology, Engineering, and Math) program in favor of a new one that Mr. Grant had devised and that was represented by an alternative acronym inspired by his cancer cough: *AHEM*, or Art, History, English, and Music.

Dr. Chong counter-proposed "STEAM," adding a compromise A for the Arts. Softening, Mr. Grant questioned the sincerity of her A but also thanked her for "trying to try" to accommodate him. Dr. Chong took this as a "yes" and wrote to all three faculty members that they'd meet inside the main entrance at 7:20 A.M. on Tuesday, December 17th — the day before Election Day — and walk out together.

She opened a new e-mail and typed "PRESS RELEASE" in the subject line. She sent the finished e-mail to Graham Bundt at *The Beat*, urging him to put down his juice box at Jack's Four Lounge and hit the presses with this breaking news, and posted a follow-up message to her fake website. Next she caught up on the series of weekly maintenance e-mails from Head Janitor Kyle Gherkin. The e-mails only tangentially related to the TCO drive and the first one reported standard building issues.

62 loose tiles & intercom wire dangle in the Sick Building. loose knob B-Room.

Have a splendid day
Kyle

"KG," she replied, "We don't call it 'the Sick Building.' —Dr. RC."
More ominously, a week later:

84 loose tiles & loose snaking wire bundles in the Cancer Wing, B.-room nob removed. Also there's funny sounds in the walls. I think it's g-g-g-ghosts.

Have a splendid day
Kyle

"There's no such thing as ghosts," she wrote. "Go home."
Most of this, the ceiling tiles, the loose wires, a loose boiler-room knob, was good PR for the TCO campaign. Heck, she'd welcome a small brush fire or minor faculty injury at this point.

She did not, however, want the haunting noises publicized, and for a simple reason. It had to do with her potentially controversial tech upgrade, the first-in-its-class twenty-first-century accountability system. It seemed that system occupied the same Andrew Johnson innards that hosted the means for this prank. "Deny deny deny" had been her motto up to this point, but *The Beat* was already clamoring for an investigation of "Halloween High." No telling where that would lead.

Her morning hall-walk brought further discouragement. Eerie sounds pervaded Andy Johnson and undercut her caustic response to Kyle Gherkin's g-g-g-ghost-fearing e-mails. The sounds still faded in and out and eluded precise pinpointing, but when they did play, they were louder. Old doors creaked. Chains clanked. Thunder crashed. Women screamed. Rain pattered. Very, very slowly, echo-voiced children sang "Ring Around the Rosy."

She dialed Archie's van.

"You don't believe in ghosts, do you, Archie?"

Cornelius yipped in the background. He was an old dog but had a pup's spirit.

"What do you think?"

She smiled into the phone. "Me neither," she said, though she had her doubts.

"We have enough ghosts in our heads, don't we? Parents, the old fools we were when we were younger. I don't think we need the sticky kind that flicker candles and hide our keys."

Not such a fool, Archie Simmons.

As the hot rush of their first weeks faded, Skip circled back to Rorsch School in increasingly bitter terms, his revised portrait including a faculty as hemmed in and duty laden as English-manor butlers of yore.

"Last night I had to work a *bubble* cannon for *four hours* so these kids could frolic through the gym in their bathing suits. Who even heard of such a thing? See this arm? That's as far as it goes."

He also trashed his wife.

"Do women *need* to talk more? I just don't get it. I could be getting ahead on grading. Instead I listen to my wife complain. For hours. I can feel my lifeforce just *sucking* away. She's like this *noxious talking gas* that just expands to fill all of space and of time."

Sometimes he felt that his wife had trapped him. A Rorsch School alum, Kat had been in wealth management, but after helping Skip land the teaching gig at her demanding alma mater she had promptly traded that career for dorm duty and community theater. Meanwhile, their grown son Blake lived in their surplus balconied bedroom, from which he emerged three times daily to feed off the school. "I'm still growing my wings," he declared from the balcony, bathrobe open and flapping.

As she listened to *Skip* complain about his Rorsch School life, Dr. Chong considered where she really fit in this rarefied world, this Eaton within Eaton. If other prep schools that she'd heard about, such as the formerly all-girls Acton Academy, had a collaborative bent, Rorsch School, plainly, had gone full feudal. She pictured an elevator that descended from space. At its thermospheric top you'd find major donors and trustees, followed by their children. *Ding!* The head of school and students from royalty shared the next stop down. Then came the WASPs, both faculty and students, some secure, other names fading. Under them, the stratosphere thickening with ozone, fell the rest of the students. "No names," the head of school had called them in a faculty meeting. The newer, unhazed faculty and the married-in teachers like Skip who were of questionable origin (Skip's real name was Sal and he hailed from Malden) fell even lower, where the elevator sank into nacreous clouds. The laborers came next, mistily concealed but very much needed: the janitors and landscapers, the window washers and visored dining-hall staff. And then way way down at the bottom of the space elevator, where you struck ground zero—she could hear Ba clucking—you'd find your Dr. Chong. A true blow-in. Skippy's old side-dish, if only for a time.

The sex became bland. Dr. Chong wanted to push the envelope, smacks and pinches, nails and spanks, but this terrified Skip, who grew increasingly mechanical and flipped her over distractedly. Immediately after, he'd roll off fumbling for his pants, leaving Dr. Chong to clutch her stuffed manatee.

Once right in the middle of things he said "Kat." He caught himself and lowered his voice. "That's my wife."

"I know and I don't care."

"I wasn't thinking of–*her*. If that's what you were thinking."

She pulled loose. "I'm taking a shower."

"Sure!"

Skip had labeled Blake a slob and griped about him wearing Pennacook Rebels sweatpants to Rorsch School's yawning wood-paneled dining hall, as if for the very purpose of embarrassing him. "Lord knows where he found those wretched garments." But Skip had his own animal ugliness. Years of cafeteria eating, plates protected by underlying trays, had resulted in slovenly habits. Buttered squash and sticky rice from zongzi over-spilled onto her fold-out card table and her linoleum-asbestos flooring. He started to smell.

"Can you *not* pick your teeth in public?" she asked.

"Can you not *not* clip your toenails?"

"Can you *not* spill coffee on my floor, and if you spill coffee on my floor can you *not* just leave it there to dry up in splotches?"

"Why do you talk this way?" he had asked.

She ignored him but had an answer. She had once been married to an ornery Canadian man who, expanding upon Ba's curriculum, had taught her by example to stand up for herself, and who left her when she did. Ever since, she couldn't help being blunt about the grossness of men and her intolerance of it. If the guy couldn't brook a few hearty slaps (and a cuddle), then why should she let him stink up her bed?

That Monday a piece of paper crossed her desk. Mr. Grant was on his last legs. Worse, her manic decision while riding a Skip-induced high to ship in some goodies from *Lung Cancer Monthly*, an electric recliner-bed, heated pillows, anti-bacterial wipes, and fresh towels, had backfired. Tito Tiggs swung his Greek-god-like frame into her office and tearfully informed her that his friend Mr. Grant not only was dying but, finding the infrastructure more than adequate, intended to complete "the death process" in his classroom.

"We need a new school, chief. I don't want to die."

"Come. Sit down. Have a tissue. Talk to me." She patted the chair next to her. "Let's talk."

Tito demurred. "Badminton tournament."

Alone once more, Dr. Chong checked up on her earlier PR efforts. Somehow the four-person walkout had not proved newsworthy to *The Beat*'s editorial staff. And no one but Archie, not even the Pennacook boar who followed her on Facebook, had visited her website to read her urgent message publicizing the walk-out.

To top it off, she found another Kyle Gherkin note in her inbox: a testing probe drilling under the Sick Building's foundation had struck sand.

Inspection

A MID-DECEMBER FRIDAY. RAY STOOD OUT FRONT breathing ice crystals through nostrils that had, finally and blessedly, re-opened after a knockout three-day ailment, possibly the flu, which he had come to think of simply as "The Sickness." He brought his eyes down from the horizon's pink fingernail to the Christmas sales-item ads. The neat line of rectangular posters with big red numbers pressed against the store's plexiglass front windows like a giant stamp collection. To avoid mental overload and the "we're going out of business" vibe, a strict five-or-fewer limit applied to the ads. The Bounty Bag Code also required that they be keyed to Bounty Bag's primary and secondary themes, "fresh" and "cheap," respectively. They were. He raised his clipboard and checked off the box.

All-store Inspection was his first duty of the morning—and the perfect opportunity to do a pulse check on Bounty Bag post-Angie.

Though expected, Angie's firing had stunned them all. The phone call came late morning on Thursday, Ray's third and last sick day, and he hoped, through the murk of his NyQuil-dampened congestion, that the call was from Patrick, ready to make amends and come home. As he picked up his flip phone, Ray's soggy eyes dazedly drifted to the hula-girl clock and he found himself perversely checking out her shapely nut-brown legs and canted plastic hips (*Who you takin' to the luau, Hula Girl?*). But when he saw that it was an unprecedented sick-day business call from Stan, his lust turned swiftly to dread.

"Sorry to call you on a sick day"—always gracious, Stan—"But... they got her."

His voice broke and he hung up, leaving Ray mid-splutter on some Stoic nugget about not giving over your mind to be mystified and controlled by others. Or was it the more Stanish quote from Groof that Ray liked better, the one inviting you to try to enjoy the festival of life with other people? Ray always appreciated the modesty of that "try" because, I mean, let's not push it…. He was still a little foggy.

Stan was able to share more in a gabbier call that evening but first asked Ray to come back to work. Mary had once more called in sick. That left *The* Alfredo next in line at Deli, an impossible situation, and due to the general chaos Stan couldn't handle the daily Inspection and needed Ray to sub again on Friday. Ray assured him, and Stan gave the blow-by-blow.

It had happened two days earlier, right when Ray was taking to bed with The Sickness. The board terminated not only Angie but grandfatherly Ops director Pell Greene and four other Angie loyalists.

The specifics of Angie's termination were peculiar in that Chesley took a page from Hitler's vengeful playbook. After the Germans vanquished the French in June 1940, Hitler ordered that the French surrender in the same railway carriage, on the same spot, in Compiègne, France, where the Germans had surrendered to the French in the First World War. Chesley, similarly, planned to fire Angie on Lane Eight of Hennessey's Duckpin Bowladrome in Billerica. That, of course, was where Ernesta had once renounced Chesley and pledged her troth to Angie over pizza and a few frames.

Chesley also tried to mirror the timing of Angie's termination, initially setting it down for the Friday after Thanksgiving, the day that Ernesta had defected to Angie following Chesley's desecration of her fridge and her chukkas. But unfortunately that date didn't work. As a practical matter Chesley needed more time to draft a professional-plunderer replacement CEO from the ranks of our leading business schools.

Rumors swirled in the meantime that Chesley lacked resolve, that he had caved to associate pressure. Chesley adamantly denied this and issued a brief profane statement to a *Lowell Post* reporter over cocktails at the Top of the Hub. He read the statement from a piece of cream-colored stationery that he ceremoniously withdrew, together with his reading glasses, from the inner jacket pocket of his wool business suit.

"It's my motherfucking company. I own it," he read. He folded up the short note and his glasses and slipped both back into his suit. "The end," he added, knocking his knuckles twice against the oak table.

Though the date moved back to mid-December, Lane Eight was still ground zero. But when Chesley's executioner, a pug-nosed toady wearing bowling shoes, chuffed in on his moped to deliver the bad news, Hennessey moved into the door and held up his hand like a stop sign.

"Whoa whoa whoa. Hold on there, buddy. I know who you are. She's *not* here."

The toady found Hennessey's facts specious. After all, it was Tuesday at 11 o'clock. Prime time for duckpin, owing to a "large-and-a-liter" meal deal that without fail drew frugal Angie to the lanes. And the way Hennessey stressed "not" was a little weird too. He spat on Hennessey's bowling shoes and lunged.

Now, Hennessey wasn't what you'd call the muscle of the family. He wasn't even the toughie of his namesake establishment, or a particularly aggressive businessman for that matter. Years ago, he had sold out to Bounty Bag for a song, securing his joint as Angie's inner sanctum without losing the duckpin functionality. At that time, Hennessey handed over the reins and gave up all claims to profits. He freely shared that he just wanted to relax, duckpin bowl, and rub shoulders with Angie, who, long before she rose to become Bounty Bag's matriarch, had been welcomed as first among equals and "one of the guys" at Hennessey's. Sure enough, after the sale closed Hennessey remained on only as a ceremonial figurehead who mostly kept to the shadows, like a retired boxer you might find sipping a beer at his namesake clam shack.

But with Chesley's toady, Hennessey showed unexpected sand. First he used his body to plug most of the doorframe. Then when the toady tried to slip through the openings around Hennessey's armpits, knees, and flanks, Hennessey went amoeba and sealed him out. At last the toady threw the sheaf of papers in Hennessey's stiffened face and hopped back on his moped, headed for a Chesley spanking.

"And don't come back, you—*nincompoop!*" Hennessey yelled from the open doorway, and just at that moment someone earned a clamorous strike.

The board installed Conor Tweed in Angie's place. Tweed was controlled remotely by ear pieces wired to Chesley's voice box, or so it was rumored, and Chesley had programmed the new CEO to scrap

Bounty Bag for parts or sell it off to some cost-cutting conglomerate. The basic idea was the same either way. Turn the whole Bounty Bag *circus* into something much tidier, much greener, and much more stackable in Chesley's many-stickered briefcase (*Tahiti, Antarctica, Clark's Trading Post*).

Now Angie was holed up in the John Hancock Tower, in the offices of Enos, Omobono & Shenoy LLP. The scrappy sixteen-lawyer firm occupied the same building as Chesley and Ernesta's firm, Vines Hay LLP. But Vines Hay was much larger. It had one thousand associates, smeared out over eight muted floors.

Snow was today's first problem, or "opportunity to excel," as Stan would've put it, citing his managerial-optimism manual, which said any "problem" should be recast in this fashion. Historically, Bounty Bag gave substantial leeway to local management on most matters. But adherence to the core standards of the Bounty Bag Code was mandatory, and Section 4 explicitly required a wide berth at the entrance. This meant either no snow (ha!) or snow plowed into the summit abutting Worcester Road, a hot spot for Andrew Johnson's madcap midnight sledders.

Section 4 proved elusive at this early hour, so Ray left the box blank. The plowers with their pickups and the makeshift muscle-car plows should come through well before the store opened at 9 A.M. At Ray's urging, Stan had rewarded the plowers with an early bonus-cash spurt given the hard weather. If they didn't get here soon, it was unto the breach with shovels, spooled-out extension cords, and snow blowers!

The plowers were a motley crew. They came from Pennacook and lands beyond. Underemployed landscapers, retail part-timers juggling kids at home, and troubled souls who did only this accounted for most of them. And guess what? They got the job done, typically with humor and great élan. As a bonus, they'd gratefully accept a sub-and-cocoa party in Ray's deli, but Stan was usually able to offer more. The same holiday spirit of solidarity pervaded associates during a major snowstorm. It was just the opposite with Ray and Patrick. Ray would have to concede this was probably because Ray did all the shoveling, sheltering his little chick Patrick from the elements and then resenting him for it.

No drivers had arrived yet, but when Ray peered through the snow he discovered that there were dozens of new Tiger mini-plows parked together at one end of the lot. Three days ago, Store #28 had had only one Tiger. It was a tiny orange truck with a one-person glassed-in cabin and a small plow tacked on the front. It came in handy for smaller jobs that a single associate could handle. But now the Tigers were two rows deep, lined up all across the edge and hulking under the pine-tree line. They had a uniformity and order to them that was disturbing, like battle tanks poised for a blitz. No doubt at Chesley's behest, the company had mustered an entire fleet. This was bad news for the local guys, of course. Even if Bounty Bag let them drive the Tigers, they'd get paid less on account of not having to use their personal vehicles for the job. On the other hand, Ray supposed the fleet could be good for Bounty Bag's bottom line, after you costed it out over the life of the Tigers.

But then Ray looked closer and saw that Chesley's Tiger fleet was purple, not orange like the old mini-plow. As Stan had predicted, Chesley had gone for the cheapo version, the Tiger 204s. Stan had shown Ray the Tiger 204s last summer in the online Tiger catalogue. They had received an unheard-of two safety stars due to ice slippage and being dangerously top-heavy. One sign of the problem's, or opportunity to excel's, scale: personal-injury-lawyer ads auto-populated the website's margins.

"Can you believe this guy?" Stan had asked that July afternoon. Chesley had already signaled way back then that he was eyeing these death traps.

Ray now wondered. Chesley might be shaving short-term driver costs, but wasn't Bounty Bag taking a pretty big risk on lawsuits by fielding a garbage fleet? Another accountancy mystery above Ray's pay grade.

Ray shook off the disturbing implications of the Tiger 204s and moved down his checklist. He was relieved to see that Pennacook's wild boars had receded — if only for the duration of Exterior Inspection — and that some diligent associate had already been at work within the store's skirt. The exterior-prep tasks were cold and monotonous but had to be done. Ray's best guesses were Gary Snow and Shelly Frampton, both hard workers. One or both of them had wiped the snow off the quarter-hungry miniature carousels and given the sidewalk, also semi-sheltered, a last shovel before the morning's latest dusting. They'd even re-piled the remaining Christmas trees to expunge from the record yesterday's bedlam.

Ray jotted a note to dispatch a sacker to clear the fresh snow by the entrance and gave the parking lot another once-over. Bounty Bag had used green-, red-, and orange-tinseled wire to decorate Truble Cove's lampposts as Christmas trees. It was a classic decoration that evoked for Ray the doo-wop era. Ray eyeballed the tinseled trees for alignment. *Check.*

Even in such troubled times, Ray appreciated this added responsibility that Stan had given him, its breadth and its call for precision. Indeed, as Ray expanded through the store as a frequent substitute inspector for Stan these past two months, he had begun to question his one-foot-in-front-of-the-other policy toward the future. If the chain survived its latest crisis, he wouldn't mind cutting back on sandwich-making for a while. Leave behind Deli's dysfunction, focus more on the rest of the business.

Publications came next.

Ray removed the weekly store flyer (exp. 12/31) from the outside rack and double checked that the flyer matched the ads in every particular. *Check, check, check*—but Ray had other misgivings about today's flyer.

He didn't mind the hoary graphic design on tap. Like so much else at the chain, Bounty Bag's posters and newspaper-printed flyers had a no-frills, even crude quality that appealed to the Cotton Mather in him. So too did the monotonous star-bubble icons pitching deals ("Save 35¢") and the superfluous sheet-pizza-flavor key featuring Stan-drawn icons that had no rhyme or reason. A smiley face with sunglasses represented sausage. A mustachioed face, extra cheese. To its credit, Bounty Bag generally prized word and substance over image and panache, and these unmilled stylings, like other humble failures of Bounty Bag's low-budget, analog world, plucked a sympathetic chord in him.

Of course, his indifference to splashy appearances didn't mean he liked *smut*. Ray wasn't sure of the artist's precise intent in snapping this week's food pics, but the sliced hams and Chinese-flavored sausages poised before the groins of excited customers certainly raised an eyebrow. Ray removed his small spiral notebook and wrote a Note to Self. Next time he encountered Muscles Carbonara—not only Patrick's crony and a cashier but an AJMHS photography buff—he'd suggest an alternative. Why not remove the human models (and their groins) and return to the disembodied, irregularly sized product clipart that was the flyer's traditional hallmark?

That recent concern aside, Ray's main quibble with the flyer was that the word "fresh" lurked everywhere, with wildly varying modes of emphasis—worst of all, in quotes. The company's slogan also appeared within quotation marks, on its icon. "Stretch Your Buck." But Ray chose to take this as a direct Angie quote, instead of an unsightly misuse of quotation marks for emphasis. Masochistically, Ray focused anew on the flyer. The "fresh" contagion was rampant again this week, and the severely overworked adjective infected every special. *"Fresh Quality,"* "**Fresh Sliced**," *"Made with* **'FRESH'** *Grilled Chicken Breast...,"* "**Made Fresh in Store**" "Made Fresh Daily," "<u>Fresh Sushi Made 'Fresh' Daily By Our Sushi Chefs</u>," *"Always Fresh."* The word itself had lost all freshness. Was the author joking who penned a runner at the bottom insisting *"Fresh* means *Fresh"*? The flyer had a decided thou-doth-protest-too-much quality to it, a minor tragedy because Bounty Bag's food *was* fresh. Moreover, by striving so hard for ads that would "pop," Bounty Bag was playing hard against type. Always risky.

The flyer had other issues. The use of non-words like "instore." A persistent allergy to phrasal adjectives, an example being this week's "bacon like flavor," a phrase that, without a hyphen between "bacon" and "like," resembled the confused utterance of a very young cave person. The flyer did have a disclaimer, *"Not Responsible for Typographic or Illustration Errors."* But this was just there to scare off legal claims. A customer could blame Bounty Bag—but not sue it—for the occasional pricing misquote on an apple-cinnamon Danish ring, deceptively sweeping in appearance on the flyer.

As a balm for the eyes, Ray swiped the information-rich *Common Items* from the same rack. Refreshingly "fresh" free, *Common Items* was a list of, oh, one-hundred popular products and where to find them. The nameless authors belonged to a prior generation, the sage Ancients, who, on account of bureaucratic wizardry you sometimes heard assigned to New Deal savants, could uncannily discern that, to your own surprise, you yearned for "Mushroom, Can," and thus would need to visit Aisle Three during your visit. *Common Items* had landed on Ray's lap for updates, and one day after work he and Gary Snow had made light revisions over sudsy root beers and 25¢ hot dogs in the break room.

"Vienna sausage," Ray had mused. "Do we still carry that?"

"Let me think.... Aisle Four: yes."

Gary Snow had a good head for it.

As he returned *Common Items* to its rack, his eyes fell on a publication of another and less attractive variety: a political solicitation, which had no place in the aisles of a supermarket.

"SAVE ANDREW JOHNSON!" the purple flyer screamed from the top of the stack.

Ray peered closely and saw that this interloper also had fine print.

Principal Chong and the FAT CATS in town hall want to bulldoze
the high school with you're tax dollars. "Fight the waste!" "Save" The
Original Andrew Johnson™! VOTE YES ON QUESTION 2 – THE
PENNACOOK UNDERRIDE! AND VOTE NO on QUESTION 1:
MORE TAXIS hert are kids! (Over 35? Join T.A.P.S. now!)

Like all Pennies, Ray knew that T.A.P.S. was the Taxpayers Alliance of Pennacook Seniors, a force much respected, if not always admired, for its potency in shaping local affairs. The T.A.P.S. flyer, however, was a disaster of salesmanship. It claimed to be pro-school but was riddled with errors, including the superfluous trademark symbol, an apparent stab at cuteness. Ray generally left political judgments to finer minds, but this flyer alone persuaded him to vote the opposite of however the flyer's authors wanted him to vote, and not only because it was illegally trespassing on his store and poorly written. The logic didn't hang together. He didn't quite get why voting to cut funding would save the high school and strongly suspected that it would not. Plus, who could object to more taxis?

But where the store was concerned, so far, so good—with one glaring exception. Ray noticed a new starburst-shaped sign, just above the "'Save' The Original Andrew Johnson™" flyers. It read: "Holiday Hours—Revised and Expanded!" The new hours included a full day, 9 A.M.–9 P.M., on Christmas. First Ray had heard of this abomination! For goodness' sake, even Bob Cratchit had December 25th off.

Ray dumped the "'Save' The Original Andrew Johnson™" flyers in the exterior recycling bin, re-pinched his tie's prongs, and passed through the automatic doors to *Kapow!*

―――

The store was still only in prep mode when Ray entered, but he was pleased to find the spigot already open on the idiosyncratic holiday soundtrack that he and Stan had recently perfected. It was a mixture of old mellow Christmas favorites that they both agreed upon, Patti Page, Nat King Cole, and Andy Williams; secular mood music that evoked warmer climes and that a shell-shocked Ray had a hankering for year-round (the exotic sounds of Martin Denny, chiefly); and, Stan's choice, potentially offensive holiday comedy classics. A glitch, or Stan prank that he wouldn't cop to, had Yorgi Yorgesson's "I Yust Go Nuts at Christmas" on triple repeat each time it surfaced, and the bawdy novelty record "The Freckle Song" also made an appearance. Orgastic standards from more recent decades reflected a limited concession to one silo of contemporary taste, but they brushed up uncomfortably against Ray and Stan's choices from the Roosevelt-thru-Eisenhower years.

Like Exterior, *Kapow!* betrayed no signs of imminent collapse. *Kapow!* encompassed the first thirty feet of the store. As its name suggested, *Kapow!* dressed to impress the entering customer, but Angie was ambivalent about the whole concept as sort of a con. "There's a firm difference between 'welcome, friend' and 'step right up!'" she said. Consistent with this, Bounty Bag's *Kapow!* area was pretty basic and you had to walk around the bulky but highly profitable Bounty Bag Cola machines to get to it.

Today, a deep-bedded locker featured "fresh" shrimp platters, ungarnished on ice, tilted toward the customers as they entered. Shrimp platters weren't too pricey but were a luxury nonetheless and an old *Kapow!* standby.

Then-vegan Patrick had stopped short at *Kapow!*'s shrimp platters during one of his rare princely visits to Ray's store. Fingers clenched on the icy locker, he gruesomely highlighted that although the shrimp were placed directly in the customer's line of sight the crustaceans' own "really amazing" light-polarization-detecting eyeballs, and their heads, had been torn off before some human arrayed the pretty carcass platters for viewing. Why did people desire to remove shrimps' eyes/heads before noshing the remainder? Was it so they couldn't stare back?

"Way more comfortable for people this way," Patrick said.

Ray lifted his thumb to his chest. "I stripped 'em, buddy."

Ray never relished an animal-welfare debate with Patrick. He quickly found himself in morally indefensible terrain and didn't handle the turned-tables dynamic very well. Patrick would take up a sympathetic animal, the playful, family-loving, curious-minded (domestic) pig, for instance, its life emotionally rich as a child's, and ask Ray how he could possibly slay and eat that li'l guy. Ray lacked an answer, beyond he didn't do the slaying with these ten fingers and as he ate the pig its having lived never crossed his mind. So he became a wisecracking nihilist instead and proposed pan-frying Wilbur and eating Freddy-derived bacon for breakfast. Curiously, the very next day after one of these debates he found Patrick elbow-deep in the fridge, twisting off a hunk of smoked ham with his grubby fingers and downing it all while he was still in there.

"Need some floss?" Ray had asked him. "I know meat gets in your gap."

Patrick slammed the fridge shut. Red-faced, he crossed his arms in a *bras d'honneur.*

Ray moved on to Pivot Point, where *Kapow!* surrendered to dewy Produce and thence to Aisle One. Pivot Point was decked out for the holidays but also honored religious pluralism. Pennacook's Jewish community was vanishingly small, but sufganiyah and Christmas cookies shared a glitter-spangled table and bathed under electric-menorah light. On the floor beside that, customers had their first chance to select a hand basket. This was a calculated delay that subtly favored the selection of carriages. When returned by the customers to their natural state (filled to collapse), carriages extended the customer's register tape an average 200%. All passed muster, or as Toothless Mary, an unlikely Air Force veteran who should have known better, would have it, *passed the mustard.*

Ray exited Pivot Point and made a beeline for Registers. The first and last were already lit up, as they should be.

It was an old trick, but the cashier at Register One could do double duty as a greeter. The cashier at Register Eighteen, their last register, had a contrasting and less cheery assignment: spy for shoplifters hustling shrink out the door. "Shrink" was a general trade term. It covered all product loss, from shoplifting and expiration to *The* Alfredo's messenger bag crushing it. To minimize shrink from theft, they typically put a male toughie on Register Eighteen, someone who could scare the bejeezus out of shoplifters and extract a prompt confession. Patrick's new housemate Muscles Carbonara had asked for the job and, on account of his muscle, got it.

Today, long, slender Natasha Romanov stood at Register One. The great-grandchild of Russian immigrants, Natasha had a true-blue sideline in magazine modeling and a rumored blood relation to the deposed last Czar. She could be haughty and detached and right now she was *painting her nails.*

"*Natty!*" Ray shouted, too hard. He felt an addled lung detach and carom about his chest like a deflating balloon. The Sickness had felled him swiftly after work the other night, spawning fever dreams. Patrick in a prison cell. Patrick being buried in the rain. Himself being buried—alive, with Patrick haphazardly shoveling the dirt over him while chortling about the whole business to someone just out of sight. In the dream, Ray chastised Patrick on his form. "Pay *attention.* It's my first time dying!" In yet another dream in this genre, a Pennacook boar dangled his snout over Ray's open grave. "Are you man or beast!?!" the boar taunted.

Natasha gazed up, eyelids heavy. She had a nail-polish brush in one hand and petite smelly jar in the other. Ray mimed blowing on his own nails—*foo! foo!*—and spread out his fingers at arm's length to google-eyedly admire the results, then shook his head twice severely.

"*Nyet!*" he said. He raised a flat hand to his neck and pretended to slice his head off.

"I do *zis* because I *vant* you," she said in her baloney accent, more Transylvania dungeon than St. Petersburg ballroom. She rolled her eyes and screwed in the cap-brush.

Ray smoothed his jacket and marched off. He'd have to get a better handle on his temper in these situations if he wanted a long-term future outside a torpedo roll. As Epictetus might have pointed out, there was plenty of wrestling with the gods to do even at a supermarket.

Ray noticed that a black tarp, pulled tight at the bottom and secured by bungee cords, covered Register Two. *That* was strange.

He backtracked to Natasha.

"Any intel on that?"

"*Vy* are you asking *me*."

Ray's best guess: Stan had prevailed in his unorthodox proposal to tear out a register to test increased traffic flow. But the resulting gap risked added shrink, and Ray opposed the idea for that reason.

At Register Four, Bonnie MacNutt, a seasoned veteran and a real tower of a cashier, folded cash and neatened the rack. This morning she moved with the lumbering deliberation of a sad but friendly giant. Her soaring hair wall was extra frizzy today and she had missed a button on her coat. Was Angie on her mind? Or was it just a long night?

Ray decided to distract her with B.O.B., M.I.T.C.H., and L.I.S.A., an established method for combatting shrink while minimizing confrontation with merely clumsy shoppers. He grabbed a stray carriage and a twelve-pack of grape soda. Eyes down, he moved into her lane, posing as "Customer Ray." When he pulled astride her register he briefly switched roles to "Manager Markham," who had a pivotal one-line walk-on for each part of the B.O.B., M.I.T.C.H., and L.I.S.A. test.

Manager Markham raised a hand to his mouth. He turned his head to the side as if to throw his voice to a distant point from which a manager might be shouting a command to Bonnie and asked, "Bonnie, any word from *Bob* this morning?"

Bonnie gave him a little half-smile but quickly got into her role. "No, Mr. Markham. Must be on his way."

Ray switched back to Customer Ray. He tapped his fingers on the carriage handlebar and rolled his eyes around the ceiling.

"Sir, there's a soda case in the B̲ottom O̲f your B̲asket. I'll *need* to scan that."

"Good," Ray said.

He glided the carriage out and then back into Bonnie's lane, re-setting the scenario.

This time Manager Markham hollered, again as if from a great distance, "Sure thing, *Mitch*. Cream corn's Aisle Seven, same place as always! Didn't think we'd hide it on ya, did ya? [*Snort snort*]."

Customer Ray snatched some peanut-butter cups from the candy rack and waved them in the air. He scrunched up his face and balled his other hand into a tight fist, pretending to maw on it.

"Looks like *baby* wah-wahnt *candy*," Bonnie said. Much lower, she added, "May I scan that for you, mister?"

M.I.T.C.H. stood for "M̲erchandise I̲n T̲he C̲hild's H̲and."

Ray re-set once more, this time popping open the child's seat and tossing in a tabloid with the headline "Elephant Kills Man Dressed as Giant Peanut."

Manager Markham crooned the first line of the old tune "Mona Lisa," putting an exaggerated emphasis on its subject's last name.

Bonnie grabbed the tabloid—which had been L̲eft I̲n the S̲eating A̲rea.

"Bravo," Ray said, moving away.

Because he had issued a compliment, Ray started to move one of the ten pennies from his left pocket to his right, but then out of the corner of his eye he caught a glimpse of Bonnie patting herself on the shoulder, and his hand seized up. Criminy. What had he been thinking? Bonnie was *the last* person he should have subjected to the B.O.B., M.I.T.C.H., and L.I.S.A. test. In stressful situations she was known quickly to lose it and she'd harangue customers on incomplete forensics, her tirades frequently requiring Stan-level intervention. One memorable time it was a "cupcake shape" in the pocket of a curly-haired little boy's baseball jacket. Turned out to be an unsolved Rubik's Cube.

There was so much that Ray had yet to learn. Still, it was a minor comfort to think that if Ray had to make the move to another chain at least some of this would come in handy. B.O.B., M.I.T.C.H., and L.I.S.A. haunted every grocer.

After Registers, Ray paced the aisles with dustpan and broom, collecting remnant sawdust from yesterday's clean-up jobs. He took it slow, his energy flagging.

Here and there faithful stockers bent to their loads. They had just started. At most grocery chains, stockers were your nightshift, but Bounty Bag had an abbreviated schedule (Mon.–Sat., 9 A.M.–9 P.M.; Sun. 10 A.M.–6 P.M.) and didn't use a night shift. This cut down on overhead. It also upped vitamin D intake and meant more associates around to help customers find stuff. This morning's stockers moved at something like half speed. Ray chalked this up to understandable discouragement at Angie's departure. They had the main things right though, accurate placement and aiming against traffic so their faces were open to customer questions.

At the end of the freezer aisle, he removed a tape measure from his pocket to confirm the six-inch elevation of the end-cap pallet—and thus of all jumbo tri-flavored-popcorn tins on it—from the grocery floor. He Scotch-taped a peeling beef-stew label back into place and saved the can from Discards. At Bakery he paused for some quick-hit cookie-carton straightening and to lift his nose.

Alas, he smelled nothing. Debbie Hays was running late today on the cinnamon rolls, but her paper hat bobbing behind Bakery's counter calmed him. She was a cake decorator and one of his favorite associates because she had a natural way. He discovered this shortly after his promotion. He was negotiating a Deli buy back there when a little boy approached Bakery and gravely brandished his Cookie Club membership card like it was an explosives license. Debbie handed him two warm chocolate-chip cookies.

"Oh, you don't need to show me that honey," Debbie said. "Any time you're here, you come on by, okay?"

The customer nodded and moved away, one cookie already vanished.

Debbie's statement was simple enough, treacly even, if you missed the everyday tone. Yet it affected Ray strangely. Her voice was sincere, not fake-nice or strained by obligation or self-congratulation. It was a very small act of kindness to the boy, but she took visible pleasure in it, and unselfconsciously so, as it was a kindness that she took for granted in herself. Maybe this was a touch of the "more love" that Angie had admonished Ray about when he was angrily re-aligning Bridge's Bacon. If so, it was a terribly delicate and baffling thing. Ray envied it and, so far, couldn't pull it off. His clipped voice ("What can I get ya'?" "Hots?") projected at best a restless soul eager to produce an excellent sandwich, and that right quick. At his worst Ray let his stern patrolman emerge. As it had once last summer.

It was late morning on a beach day, clutch hour at Deli, and an expanding, vague line had predictably stirred up customer friction. Ray, who had gone so far as to craft an acronym for these situations—"alp," for "ambiguous line problem"—empathized too much with those at the back of the line, got real stressed, and barked at a tall drink of water who maybe had elbowed his way to the front.

"Excuse me: that guy's next. I saw him! You are last, sir. Last."

And he carried the feeling home.

"That's what people are like," he told Patrick.

"We're dwelling in opinion here," Patrick replied.

"You wait and see. You just *wait*."

Certainly Debbie's love—if the word fit—was more precious than Ray's sandwich-making skills. People made bad sandwiches because they didn't care. Anyone could learn how to do it right. Debbie's love was different, perhaps unteachable. Jeremy Wiggins, a career sacker with Down syndrome, had the same touch. That was one reason why he'd always have a place here. His assiduous sacking was another.

Overall, Inspection reassured him. There were a few irksome downgrades, of course. The holiday hours and the tardy cinnamon rolls, for instance (plus, late discovery, unsightly upchuck from a torn dog-food bag all over the exit lane, visible while you paid and a real "fuck you" to tap dance around on your way out the door). All things considered, however, he anticipated an "all systems go" report to Stan this afternoon. Perhaps everything would be okay after all. Maybe Bounty Bag, only slightly diminished by Angie's absence, would run itself, the CEO's greatest legacy a perpetual-motion grocery machine.

But just as this thought crossed his mind, over in Magazines a new prop flashed at him. Down one whole shelf, a Chesley agent had stacked a series of thick, pea-green, hard-cover books. The books had frayed edges and velvety ribbons with strange numbers and unfamiliar abbreviations stitched into the spines with golden thread. The medieval-looking books resembled something you might see at a furniture store's leather room, meant to strike a note of class. Ray wasn't sure how effective they'd be in flattering *Us Weekly*'s customers but, curious, he picked one up and opened its cover. The frontispiece said "Ala. Code (1833)" and some other stuff. He opened to a random page of the Alabama law book.

> Any person or persons who attempt to teach any free person of color, or slave, to spell, read, or write, shall, upon conviction by indictment, be fined in a sum not less than two hundred and fifty dollars, nor more than five hundred dollars.

Some books classier unopened.

It was 9:15. The store had opened and the first thin stream of customers trickled in. Inspection's generally auspicious first two phases and the rising buzz of commerce restored Ray's spirits, The Sickness retreating to a small, dim ache at the back of his head and some soreness in his raw gut.

An elderly couple paused restively in Produce to chat in quiet tones about, it appeared, anything other than their grocery list. Snow melted on their jacket-folds and on the man's Irish driving cap. A young man zoomed past both the elderly couple and Ray, who stood nearby un-denting plastic limes containing lime juice. He had giant clear-framed eyeglasses and spiked, frosted hair and he had loaded his arms with French bread, a cheddar-parmesan Bounty Bag crunchy hybrid cheese, and a netted bag of vine-ripe tomatoes. His red sneakers squeaked across the tiles.

The young man—Turbo Boy, Ray dubbed him—followed a zig-zag course from Produce to Bakery, then back to Dairy for a forgotten block of muenster. Next he shot up three aisles to condiments. A jar of mayonnaise prompted an eleventh-hour retreat to *Kapow!* Hors d'oeuvres, or perhaps a simple lunch, had added up as usual to more than the customer had imagined.

Turbo Boy finally barreled his way to Deli where Ray — slipping behind the counter — snapped on gloves and intercepted him with a smile.

"Can I try the Italian roast beef?"

"Sure thing."

He tried it.

"How bout the Angus?"

"You got it."

"Maybe a little thinner?"

"Okay."

"*Thinner.*"

"Yes."

"And how about the cheap stuff? Can I try that too? Many thanks."

Ray was really beginning to dislike Turbo Boy.

"Half pound, no less. *Please.*"

While Ray worked, *The* Alfredo leaned on the steel slicers counter, uncritically enjoying the deals flyer that had so troubled Ray earlier this morning. With his usual low standards, *The* Alfredo considered Bounty Bag's flyers well-wrought food porn, though thanks now to Muscles Carbonara's photography it was sort of just porn. A restorative tub of yogurt rested in *The* Alfredo's giant palm.

Ray glared at him, as if to say, "Can you please put down your yogurt and help me slice this a-hole's roast beef?"

"I'm taking my breakfast," *The* Alfredo said.

Ray taped and priced the order and shunted Turbo Boy to Registers. "Taking" was a Britishism that *The* Alfredo had picked up from a movie about Edwardian merchants, a nationality and class with which he occasionally identified. There were two types of people, Ray figured. Those who understood and those who did not that breakfast was to be "taken" at home, not on the job. For *The* Alfredo, of course, the conflict was all in Ray's head. By definition, home was wherever *The* Alfredo plopped his yogurt and his tush.

Ray looked up to find Turbo Boy performing a leisurely post-Deli victory parade to the front of the store. Fully provisioned, Turbo Boy moved with a lighter step and unlocked shoulders, and Ray felt a pang of guilt for judging an honest customer and for letting *The* Alfredo's antics color his view. A grocery customer had a multi-faceted nature. Hungry or time-pressed, as sample-happy Turbo Boy apparently was, a customer was liable to turn selfish and inconsiderate. But make abundance plain with a well-wrapped pound-plus roast-beef pack or boundless birthday cakes "to choose from" and watch a very different person emerge. Forgetful of budget, funny bone restored.

A new sign hung above one end of Deli's counter. It read, "U.R. Kind Dogs. *Natural*™" and featured as a logo a smiling hot dog with the requisite sunglasses. It also featured a not-so-happy new price ($2.99!) and a disclaimer that "Natural" only meant it was "meat." Ray sighed. The 25¢ hot dog special, the go-to budget option for associates needing quick sustenance on the 15-minute afternoon break, would be dearly missed. Almost as off-putting, it seemed from the name that Chesley was riding the *I'm-a-good-person-because-of-what-I-eat* marketing trend, and with Angie on the outs, there was no one left to veto. The overpriced frankfurters, green-mottled and slitted, were now Ray's to hawk.

Back to Inspection, except when Ray turned to exit Deli he bumped right into a clear trash bag full of *chickens on ice*. What the heck?

Clearly we had shrink. But of what variety? Ray picked the chickens up by the bag's top-knot and let their dimpled yellow-and-pink bodies dangle before him, their blood running down the plastic in pink rivers to an icy bulge.

This could be the work of a desperate Toothless Mary. The new trash compactor would see its grand opening on Presidents' Day, when it would briefly chomp for public view. This meant the end of Bounty Bag's dumpsters and of Toothless Mary's access to them. In response, for the past several weeks the increasingly erratic departmental manager had wavered between taking to her bed and flipping into overdrive. For her "on" days she drafted the wheelbarrow and manpower of her latest boyfriend Dusty Grimes, who, perhaps as a result of his Toothless Mary liaison, was looking particularly harried these days, his orange jumpsuit fraying, and his brother Harry, who managed sewage treatment and sludge making for Pennacook. She rarely interrupted final excavations to work Deli and then only for grouchy bouts of salad mixing, during which she turned her back to customers and refused even to touch sandwiches.

"I'm covered in trash," she said with apparent surprise.

So perhaps these chickens were claimed garbage, flawed birds with a second shot at a meaningful posthumous existence in Toothless Mary's home? It didn't add up. Toothless Mary was out today, and the chickens looked fresh. Furthermore, any imaginable home use was a stretch. What would she do, scavenge them for chicken-bone jewelry or attempt a farfetched taxidermy project?

Almost certainly, then, this was theft. But who would be rash enough to try this right under Ray's nose? Last year he'd had Stan replace the old green-lined garbage bags with clear ones because Bonnie MacNutt had caught a kid stealing beef jerky and energy drinks, disguised as discards, with the opaque bags. Not so easy anymore.

Ray lugged the chickens to one of the meat lockers for reclassification and an evidence tag. He weighed various suspects, from photographer Muscles Carbonara to cashier Natasha Romanov. But he kept coming back to *The* Alfredo. He doubted the man had the initiative even to cook stolen chickens, let alone the enterprise to sell them. But if someone else was involved, Ray pondered, *The* Alfredo might be willing to play the middle man and pop them out back for the right price.

Ray shook off the theft for the moment—he'd interrogate *The* Alfredo soon enough—and seized his clipboard. He tramped off toward Inspection's final stop, the alternate universe they called "the Outback."

The Outback housed the restrooms, but its significance went well beyond that. To begin with, it was huge. It took up a solid one-third of the store's footprint, the fringe around its inner border serving as a kind of liminal zone where associate hands loading frozen sausage and ice-cream tubs briefly noodled into customer view.

The Outback had many uses. A dismal unlit corner bunghole housed the cleaning equipment, buckets, mops, and industrial sinks. When Ray was on-duty at closing, he would pull a mop and join the gang of blue-aproned sackers. Sign of his premature decrepitude, twenty-two minutes sliding a mop back and forth was enough to fire his endorphins. Just behind the bunghole, a short set of stairs led to the Outback's well-magazined breakroom, and a rope ladder went from there through a black hole in the ceiling to a special circle of hell reserved for suspected shoplifters. Interrogation was a tight windowless room with a theatrical chained single lightbulb, a small steel table, a pre-loaded typewriter, three chairs (two more comfortable than the third), and a box of tissues.

"The Big Show" was in the Outback too. A broad term that covered all things Inventory, the Big Show included Unload, Storage, Discards, and Re-Shelving. Every day was Omaha Beach, June 6, 1944, at the Big Show. Two, three times a day, fleets of trucks backed up to the Open Sesame-scale receiving doors sounding their horns of victory. Their ramps dropped, and out rolled legions of loaded dollies and cubes on wheeled pallets. The Big Show foreshadowed the world-historical abundance available to shoppers out front, and it had impressed Ray from the first, even as a cocksure eighteen-year-old trainee.

The Big Show was central to the Outback, and "everything in its right place" would be Ray's standard of review.

Only Ray never reached that part of his checklist.

As he passed through the double doors into the Outback, he was stunned to discover that the instruments of revolt, enough to field an army, had already been assembled, sorted, stacked, and hung.

His eye caught first the vastly expanded arsenal of homemade pro-Angie signs over in Dairy Unloading. Since their first appearance sometime in September, the signs had grown into something of a home-hobby group project for craft-loving associates, mostly some gal cashiers, a converted knitting circle. But they had never attempted something on this scale, hundreds of signs, if not a thousand—too many to count, really, from any one spot in the Outback. And somehow they had done this on Ray's three days off.

Ray moved in for a closer look. Associates had nailed and taped the signs to pickets and dowels and crowded them into the racks and shelves. They had hit a point of overload and had imprudently—or deliberately, as sabotage—stuffed the last of the signs into half-shut freezers, spawning melted ice-cream shrink that pooled out on the floor and already stank. The associates were working with new materials now and had built and painted the signs with seemingly anything at hand that seemed equal to the moment. Gone were the *apropos*-of-nothing glued-on bits of yarn and popsicle sticks and cutesy cat cartoons that sort of resembled Angie Martini. In their place, metallic house paint, oversize black and red markers, a lump of charcoal—*blood?*

The text on the signs had fiercely sharpened too. The earlier signs had been vague in their demands and projected an uncomplicated affection for Bounty Bag. Some poor bastard had even internalized Chesley's propaganda, scrawling "I ♥ My Job!" in jagged purple crayon on a bed sheet drawn taut over a large wooden frame (when Ray, with scalding humor, later pointed out this foolishness to Stan, his friend copped to playing some role of unspecified depth in creating the sheet). The associates brought clarity and focus to the new signs and to their simple but momentous demand.

GIVE US BACK OUR STORE!

ANGIE IS OUR CEO!
DON'T TREAD <u>ON</u> ME. [?]

<u>ONE</u> LEADER, <u>ONE</u> DIRECTION, <u>ONE A.G.M.</u>!

BRING BACK ANGIE

IBSEW LOCAL 123 [electrical-workers union] STANDS WITH BOUNTY BAG

<u>FIGHT</u> THE POWER!!! [with a softening peace sign]

SAVE BOUNTY BAG

IN ANGIE WE TRUST

Last but not least:

ALL TOGETHER NOW.

Ray looked at the back wall and saw that things had taken a turn to the surreal. Soaring murals depicted Angie in modified roles from American history. In one of the murals, a Brillo Pad-bewigged Angie crossed the Delaware in a boat filled with Bounty Bag associates and private-label products. In another, a top-hatted Angie delivered 272 words on bargains and freshness to a rapt host of customers, associates, and Civil War amputees at Gettysburg. In a third, she sat in a wheelchair by a fireside, mike to mouth, presumably chatting. Under the murals, Ray spotted a giant stuffed-animal turtle, some ten feet from head to tail, some kind of mascot.

The associates had set aside other duties to accomplish so much. As Ray walked deeper into the Outback unexpelled fish garbage—worst smell on Earth—cut through the melted-ice-cream stench and shot through his nostrils (*reeking of havoc*) while yesterday's milk soured on packed pallets. The scene recalled the sanitary issues of well-intentioned Woodstock. Whatever else you were up to, someone had to keep things clean.

Ray was about to grab a mop himself and beep out front for reinforcements when he heard with the relief of a reprieve the intercom's familiar *coo-coo*, followed by Stan in a tin can, summoning him.

Local History: Chimpanzee Politics

THE WEEKS HAD BEEN CRUEL. MR. GRANT'S FACE was a wet tissue that might tear or slide off and his body was laden over like that of a one-man band or one of your more flamboyant Jacob Marleys—or a soldier. A sash of boxes crossed his chest. Hair gone to wisps, he concealed it with a square hat, crushed to a cocked tricorn. Backed-up fluids had him in knee-high compression stockings. Canes shot from his arms like muskets. Gas masks and bendy tubes of fluid snaked in and out. His equipment—gurney, tanks, and bags—had him circled.

He stood at attention at a stand-up desk and typed the Friday lecture as it came to him in bursts. After a time he reached into a zippered leather pouch, removed a small stick, and proceeded to swab the inside of his cheek with the stick and work it under his tongue.

"What's that?" Muscles Carbonara asked. It was his first day back from mononucleosis, a bogus ailment for which he had a standing doctor's note.

"FENTANYL."

"Experiencing BTCP?"

"THAT'S RIGHT," Mr. Grant typed. "I'M HAVING BREAKTHROUGH CANCER PAIN AT THE MOMENT. YOU SHOULD CONSIDER A CAREER IN MEDICINE, MR. CARBONARA."

Breakthrough cancer pain: more proof God cares.

Snow piled up outside. Today's topic was Mr. Grant's *bête noire*: Pennacook's inability to pass a tax-cap override to build a new school. Formal override petitions had only started in the 1990s, but cancer-cluster grumblings extended at least to the early 1970s, when Mr. Grant started at the school. He traced his town's failure—he'd lived here forever—and its political culture generally, to aspects of the Pennacook Town Charter. Impliedly, he blamed the Charter for his imminent death.

"SINCE PENNACOOK'S FOUNDING IN 1684, A MEDIEVAL ETHOS"

—*kaff*—

"POINTING BACK TO THE FEUDAL SOILS OF EUROPE, HAS DOMINATED YOUR HOMETOWN. THE TOWN'S RULING FACTION FAVORS HIERARCHY, TRADITION, AND ORDER, TAKING AN ESSENTIALLY KNIVES-OUT POSTURE TO ANY PROFFERED CHANGE OR REFORM."

Kaff kaff kaff kaff kaff.

"BY 2010 THE FEUDAL FACTION'S REDISTRICTING HAD REACHED SUCH PROPORTIONS THAT OTHER FACTIONS, THEIR FORCES SCATTERED, WERE LOCKED OUT OF MEANINGFUL PARTICIPATION ON THE BOARD OF SELECTMEN."

He flashed on the overhead the crazy-quilt map of Pennacook's board of selectmen districts, then switched to a town-meeting-rep map, much neater.

"THE FRAMERS OF PENNACOOK'S GOVERNING CHARTER (1802) SHARPENED THIS BIAS WHEN THEY ESTABLISHED TOWN-MEETING-REP DISTRICTS THAT ARE FIXED REGARDLESS OF POPULATION.'

Kaff kaff—ka hoo!

Patrick kept expecting back-row snickers, like what you heard if a teacher flipped out and started roaring at a kid, but by now he should have known better. With the exception of Muscles Carbonara they were, to a person, sober if not somber in this class.

"THIS PRINCIPLE OF EQUAL REPRESENTATION PER GEOGRAPHIC DISTRICT, IRRESPECTIVE OF POPULATION, GIVES YET ANOTHER TILT FAVORING PENNACOOK'S MORE PASTORAL CORNERS, WHERE FIRM FEUDAL MAJORITIES PREDOMINATE. SOUTH OAKHURST, FOR INSTANCE, HAS ONE REP FOR EVERY 40 RESIDENTS. PENNACOOK CENTER HAS ONE REP FOR 600."

Kaff kaff.

"NEEDLESS TO SAY, THE RURAL FACTION HAS ALWAYS OPPOSED THE NEW-SCHOOL PROJECT. GIVEN

THIS SLANT, PENNACOOK IS NOT QUITE WHAT IT SEEMS IF YOU JUDGE IT ONLY BY ITS MUNICIPAL ORDINANCES, THE WRITINGS AND SPEECHES OF ITS ELECTED OFFICIALS, AND THE GENERAL REACTIONARY VIBE COMING FROM TOWN HALL. BUT WHILE THE FEUDAL FACTION DOES NOT REPRESENT A TRUE PENNACOOK MAJORITY, IT HOLDS ALL THE PLUM POSITIONS IN TOWN GOVERNMENT."

He flung aside his keyboard but as he blasted through the pain his words still boomed out all caps.

"THIS LENDS IT THE DOMINATING STANCE OF A BRANCH-DRAGGING"

—*kaff*—

"ROCK-THROWING"

—*kaff*—

"FOOT-STOMPING"

—*kaff kaff kaff*—

"CHIMP."

Blood pooled in his lip and ran down his chin.

"FOR THIS REASON, EVEN THE MOST SENSIBLE INITIATIVE, FROM SEWAGE-PLANT UPGRADES TO THE NEW-SCHOOL TCO, IS LIKELY TO FAIL. SIMPLY PUT"

—*kaff*—

"YOUR REPRESENTATIVE GOVERNMENT *DOESN'T* REPRESENT. NOT IN ANY NORMAL SENSE."

Kaff.

"WORSE, IT IS LEADING THIS TOWN TO MISUNDERSTAND AND UNDERESTIMATE ITSELF."

The students from the rural districts he had maligned didn't raise a peep. In fact, one of them, Doreen Robinson, of both South Oakhurst and Grand Bend, Alabama, filled her thermos cap with water and walked it over.

"Why you don't have some water, Mr. G?"

Maybe Patrick had been wrong. Maybe there were worse things about teaching than dying in front of teenagers.

Muscles Carbonara, who had been strangely attentive during Mr. Grant's lecture, stirred in his seat.

"These electoral districts. Sort of a 'might makes right' situation, don't you think?"

"I DO."

"I like it."

Mr. Grant shuddered.

On her way back to her desk, Doreen handed Patrick a real paper note, which he slipped in his pocket unread. Patrick waited for Muscles Carbonara to leave—last one in, first one out—before opening it.

"Please come home. I love you. —Ray"

Mr. Grant died during C lunch, and they shut down the school.

Escape to Castle Eaton

D R. CHONG AMBUSHED KYLE GHERKIN IN HIS office, where she found him sitting behind his desk peering into a glass paperweight and threw the "negative-energy extraction" bill in his face.

"What's this? I want answers."

Behind her back her head janitor had turned ghost buster.

"That's David," he said.

Sage burned in a clay pot behind him. Flapping shutters and banging hammers filled the air.

"David."

"Entity and spirit remover. Loose spirits, unconnected energy cords. That sort of thing. Good news: he's cleared the high school. The sick building, too!"

"Cleared?"

"I, for one, am feeling much, much better," he continued, but his eyes were two knives aimed at his terrarium. "*Those* worry me. Infested with demons, but David says there's risks if we drown 'em."

"If he's 'cleared' the school, how come it still sounds like the Haunted Mansion?"

"We-ell—"

"Look, I don't care what otherworldly powers your turtles may or may not possess. This"—she swept up the bill and flapped it around—"I will not pay. Either 'David' backs off, or we're calling the town solicitor. You hear me? The gloves are off."

"Don't think that'll work."

"And why not, pray tell?"

"The town solicitor recommended him. In fact, David *is* the town solicitor."

Defeated, her ego changed subjects.

"And what about the boiler?"

Suddenly (and insanely) composed, Kyle answered, "Pressure-relief valve's balky, as per usual. Well, a tad more than 'as per usual,' but you catch my drift. Water-level monitor's also on the fritz. What we *really* need is a package boiler."

"You know what I think? Your ghosts and your boiler and your hundreds of missing ceiling tiles? They aren't a poltergeist. They're some kid running a prank. *Find* him. Find him, and we find our ghost *and* our boiler fiend. As for your package boiler: it's in the new-school specs. Without the TCO, we're toast. It's why I asked you numbskulls for a walkout! *Have a splendid day.*"

As if to compensate for these troubles, her romantic life at last seemed to take a turn for the better when, for Dr. Chong's fifty-somethingth birthday, Skip invited her to dinner at the Colonial Tavern, Eaton's historic steakhouse, making time in his schedule for an irregular Saturday outing.

But as they walked up the creaky ramp to the Colonial Tavern's deck, Skip repelled to the side, clinging to the opposite rail. Then he vanished like a sprite into the lobby's cherry woodwork while moony Bronson Alcott, on loan from Fruitlands, cornered Dr. Chong, helpless in a low-slung chair.

"Do you want to hear a story?"

"No."

Skip materialized to fret about the wait time, rolling his eyes and tapping his foot.

"Table for Mr. and Mrs.... Bartleby?"

"Finally," Skip steamed.

They sat down and he stared at his plate. While Dr. Chong carefully buttered her first crumbly roll, Skip ate two of them. The mashed potatoes arrived and he scooped most of them onto his plate and rested the platter on his side of the table. He cut his steak into wide strips and, fork tines facing down, pitched it athletically into the side of his mouth.

"There's food on your chin. Can you *not* feel it?" she asked.

He looked over her shoulder at someone else. Behind him, raw steaks dangled in a cabinet. Long gone were the under-table footsie and steadily drained red-wine bottle of their first afternoon at Eaton Bistro.

Her birthday cupcake arrived.

"Happy birthday," he said.

She took a bite and pushed the plate away. Skip's long fingers filched the remains.

"Listen, we should talk," he said.

It was supposed to sound sad but instead came off like businessman bravado. As with everything else since they'd entered the restaurant, Skip moved and spoke with the purposeful, impatient confidence of Eaton, Rorsch School, and his wife's money at his back. Resolutions had been made, a new commitment. A circle redrawn.

Tears welled. Dr. Chong pounded her fist on the table, clanking the silverware and making Skip jump.

"You just took me here to feed me steak and dump me."

"No! I—I don't know what to do." He looked down at his fingers with fascination. "I can't stand my life." More theater.

"You hate me."

"I don't!" he said, but he looked surprised, his eyes asking, Do I?

"I—I hate myself."

Later he took her hands. "I worry about you, you know. I hope that, well, whatever becomes of 'us,' that you will keep an *open heart.*"

"Open your heart and you bleed to death. Surgeons know this."

In the parking lot he gripped Dr. Chong's shoulders and gave her a long kiss that was somehow both deep and flaccid, his tongue just spilling, while a kitchen staffer filmed the incident on his phone. *Whoot-whooo*, whistled Bronson Alcott, lurking in a shrub.

At his car, Skip turned to her. "Would you please tie my shoes?"

"You don't know how to tie your shoes?"

"I do know how to tie them, but my lower back is killing me and the *roundy* ones always come undone."

It proved more difficult than expected, but not because the laces were too roundy. There was some flawed looping through the rungs. This made the laces too long on one end and too short on the other. She stripped the shoes and rewove from scratch. It wasn't hard. Even so, she didn't understand why Skip would assume that she could do it if he could not.

"My advice? Try loafers."

The next morning, Dr. Chong decided to bring matters to a head.

"Maybe we should just stop each other," she texted, then corrected herself: "Stop seeing each other." Despite everything, she didn't really mean it.

"k," Skip texted back.

She saw him that evening through the Eaton Bistro's purple window dropping off bills in one of Eaton's cordial talking mailboxes, his feet dry on the heated sidewalks. At the corner he unchained the new electric bike he had been talking about. Next stop Rorsch School, to rouse Blake for supper.

Back in her dripping basement home that night, she dialed up Archie of all people for consolation. Before she could say a word, Archie blurted out, "Is it really okay to break up over text?"

"How did you know that?"

"How did I know what?"

"How did you know I was just dumped over text?"

"I didn't. *I* was dumped over text."

They laughed.

On the night of Mr. Grant's death there came a knock at the door. There were just days to go until the override vote and for just a moment she fantasized that it was the cops come to haul her off for killing Mr. Grant, thereby relieving her of more complicated problems. But it was her nephew Tommy, beaded with sweat yet shivering in the winter air. He had his compound bow under one arm and trailing on a child's red wagon—dragged here, apparently, all the way from Pennacook, through slush and falling snow—was a boar carcass. A steel-tipped arrow had impaled the boar's head.

"Hi, Auntie. How are you?" He regarded his defeated quarry. "I tried to find you at the high school and, uh, do you by any chance own pliers and a meat saw?"

Inspection

On his way to Stan's office, Ray scrambled around an unfamiliar white-plastic blinking monolith in Aisle Five. It had hit the floor sometime after Inspection and appeared to be some kind of newfangled movable mop closet. Ray spared the device a second thought and jogged up the management-only front stairs to the long hallway that wrapped around the side wall.

Ceiling cameras encased in glass augmented the elevated hall. The hall and the cameras allowed management to scan the floor for shoplifters, including the occasional criminal element among the associates. The cameras had a warm-and-fuzzy secondary function too, ensuring swift-moving aid to shoppers in distress. You'd often find lonesome men down there, unaccountably searching the Home/Cleaning aisle for a favorite soda or cheese-and-caramel popcorn mix. Sometimes it was grandparents getting thigh-clobbered by the junk-cereal demand curves of their hard-kicking carriage passengers.

Right now, in fact, Ray spotted a customer in need of aid. The woman looked hungry and morally vexed as she squeezed a boxed product. A little thought bubble above her head read, "*Can I bust into the Keebler's right now or do I really have to pay first?*" Some chains frowned upon it, but at Bounty Bag she could. Ray did a slow, stretched-arm wave, caught her gaze, and flashed his Hollywood smile. He made an exaggerated scooping-to-the-mouth gesture, followed by a fat thumbs up. A moment later he heard the satisfying crash of fingers into cookies.

Ray scanned the rest of the store. Things looked mostly normal at first. If anything it was busy for a Friday morning, and after Turbo Boy traffic had quickly picked up. The lines had expanded and multiplied, with four registers open and a fifth one already on break. Sawdust had memorialized a tomato-sauce spill, result of excessive enthusiasm for today's two-for-one special, and the perimeter teemed with stocking, baking, and customers ordering sandwiches and fish. Was the Outback a mirage?

But on closer examination, all was not well.

Ray looked out through the massive fiberglass storefront windows and saw good-egg Gary Snow out in the parking lot shagging carriages, even though he was a senior-associate stocker, only a notch below deputy assistant manager and the pride of a purple coat. The plowers should have been here by now and cleaned up this mess with Chesley's fleet of Tiger 204s. But there was still no sign of them and Gary, caught in a snow squall without a proper winter parka, was paying the price for their extreme tardiness. The accumulating snow was making it especially hard for him to get the job done. He struggled to combine and corral the carriages but the wheels kept getting caught in slush pools, the hinges between the carriages jammed, and renegade carriage snakes slithered threateningly into parking rows. Snow caked Gary's bare head and his indoor-jacket sleeves, and as Ray watched, Gary's dress shoes slipped out from under him and only a lucky grab at a carriage handle prevented him from tumbling face-first into the snow. He reminded Ray of the arctic-dwelling musk-ox from one of Patrick's kiddie picture books, hunkered down for winter on his windswept feeding plain. Ray silently promised himself that after Stan's meeting he would bring Gary his own parka and his boots.

Even accounting for the unplowed snow and perilous ice patches, Gary's step had slowed severely, enhancing the somber atmosphere that — Ray realized in retrospect — had permeated the entire store during Inspection. If in earlier times like the now distant seeming day of the "I ♥ My Job!" T-shirts, Ray had been keenly attuned to bad omens in the store, denial or something very like it had led him to turn a blind eye to this day's portents. It ran from Bonnie MacNutt to Bakery to Gary. What Ray had fancied mere lethargy or repose had been the hushed ceremonial pall of a funeral parlor. Even *The Alfredo*, reading the deals flyer, had been less garrulous than usual today (though a botched chicken theft could account for his behavior).

Ray stepped into Stan's office and found his friend subtly altered as well. He stood at his desk with his sleeves rolled up. His purple jacket with the golden store-manager stripes still hung on the coat-hanger behind the door, and he appeared more preoccupied than usual with whatever business or marketing decision he was worrying. Indeed, by all appearances Stan hadn't even left his office since Ray saw him unlock the automatic doors at 7 A.M. and scurry up the manager's stairs. Whatever he had to show, he had been working on it all morning.

"Let me know what you think, and I want you to be honest," Stan said.

He gestured to two poster boards he had set up on easels.

"'Truth never damages a cause that is just.' —Gandhi," Ray said.

"Idea number one."

Stan flipped over one poster and revealed two wobbly rectangles with aqua and pink squiggles between them. Underneath, he'd scrawled, "*Simple food for simple people!*" If Ray hadn't known Stan's familiar symbol for bread, signaling that this was a sandwich concept, he might have guessed this was a flag design for some newly christened Pacific island nation. The squiggles, however, were a mystery. Vegetable? Meat? Hummus or other spread? Nothing seemed right.

"Uh — BLT? We have that."

"Frosting sandwiches."

"Let me see idea number two."

Stan turned over the other poster. It showed a big circle with what looked like a couple of crudely drawn snakes inside of it.

"Behold the Double Dog. Two hot dogs *in one bun*. I'm thinking gold-star special."

"Everything's a gold-star special. Have you seen our flyer? Besides: 'Gilded honor, shamefully displaced.' —William Shakespeare."

"You hate them. I knew it." He whacked the boards hard and they flipped violently off the easels onto the floor.

"Now why'd you go and do a thing like that?" Ray asked. He sensed something larger, e.g., revolution, was troubling Stan. Ray wanted to play it cool because if Stan stayed, Ray would too, but if Stan jumped...

"Frosting and dogs aren't selling, and I'm all out of ideas," Stan confessed.

"That's all?" Expecting something urgent, Ray was confused. He refocused on Stan's dilemma and quickly divined a strategy that just might work. He sat up in his chair and leaned forward interestedly.

"Well?" Stan asked, uncharacteristically impatient with Ray's professorial stance.

"Loss leaders."

Stan's eyebrows rose. "How so?"

"Simple. Promote the dogs or, rather, the buns at, oh, two for one. Do that, and the dogs might go along with them. Same thing for frosting. You could discount the other cake stuff, like maybe the mix or some butter. And you don't need me to tell you this but be sure you pair the items for display. We don't need a wild-goose-chase to throw off the cherry pickers. In these types of cases, selling is key."

Cherry pickers traveled from store to store sniffing out the loss leaders. Loss leaders were popular items, such as soda cans or ground beef. They priced these low to sell at a loss in order to attract customers into the store. Once inside, most loss-leader customers would buy a full load of weekly groceries — and the store would end up back in the black. But if the loss leaders weren't somehow protected against them, the cherry pickers would quickly deplete the stock. This would leave the store with nothing to offer its other customers, which could be extremely alienating.

Quantity caps were a solid first line of defense against the cherry pickers. "Two-per-customer on the seltzer, ma'am." This sent an egalitarian message that Bounty Bag treated each customer the same while also providing a little something for everyone. The strategy also scattered all but the most devious cherry pickers, who wore disguises. But too many quantity caps evoked the specter of hard rationing ("Moderation in all things, especially moderation." —Emerson).

Ray liked quantity caps but, at least in Pennacook, the best way to undermine cherry pickers was to hide the loss leaders. Cherry pickers were, after all, a rather lazy bunch who had nothing better to do than fart around town exploiting retailers. Ordinary customers coming into the store would receive ready directions on where to find the loss leaders. Known cherry pickers could be, well, lied to or, to satisfy Kant, told the God's honest truth. Most cherry pickers were too skittish to ask.

Cherry pickers weren't even customers, really; they were *leeches*. Stan thought Ray was too hard on the cherry pickers, that it was a symptom of his managerial greenness that he wanted to fight every battle like a Viking. But there you have it. "A little less duty, a little more love," Angie's personal words of advice, came back to Ray at surprising moments.

"Gosh darn it, you're a genius!" Stan pulled Ray's head down and kissed the top of it.

It had been a false alarm after all, Ray thought. Stan was just stuck on frosting and dogs. But then San's face darkened once more, and Ray was back on tenterhooks.

Stan's hand roiled with nervous tremors as he tossed an opened manila envelope on the table like a dead fish.

"I need your help with something else."

"Anything."

Ray half-expected his own termination or a draft store-closure announcement for proofreading. He withdrew the letter and noticed, in a Michael Corleone moment, that his own hand was steady. Inside the envelope, he found a simple thank-you note from Giuseppe Alvaro, their leading giardiniera vendor. False alarm number *two*.

Giuseppe lived in New Hampshire but hailed from a village of Mariotto, not far from the Martinis' own ancestral home in Turi. His domestic tendrils extended as far as Colchester, Vermont, and Austerlitz, New York. From his sprawling network of farms, he trucked down to his Portsmouth plant an array of fresh vegetables, bell peppers, celery, gherkins, cauliflower, and carrots. There Giuseppe and his five assistants jarred and pickled the veggies with oil and white-wine vinegar. But he was known best for the hot-mix variety, which he enriched with a sprinkle of chopped pepperoncino imported from Diamante, Calabria, and branded with the image of Christopher Columbus, who had first brought the pepper to Europe from the New World in 1492. The pepperoncino were the subject of the note, which, as always, Giuseppe had made out in the tiniest print.

Caro Angelica:

È passato così tanto tempo dall'ultima volta. I am very happy my hot-mix like your customers. The samples of new Hot Mix I send February.

Un abbraccio grosso [A big hug]
Giuseppe Alvaro

The note's first sentence was a dramatic and inaccurate, but typical, greeting for Giuseppe Alvaro. It meant, roughly, "it's been so long since we've last communicated." In fact, Angie and Giuseppe, an old bachelor, met in the North End for espresso every week. Stan occasionally joined them. Angie had flown solo ever since the heart attack that had taken Stan's father, and Stan often wondered aloud at Giuseppe's true intentions. Cautious but amorous, both Stan and Ray had concluded.

"What's the big deal?" Ray asked. "It's a simple thank-you. I don't think he's even asking for anything."

"He's not asking, but we always give. He's a key supplier—and a friend."

The local "sourcing" of most of Giuseppe's ingredients was typical for Bounty Bag. The chain's suppliers came from all over the world, but the scales tipped decidedly toward New England, New York's long eastern border, and the borderlands of Quebec ("The French Crescent," as Angie referred to that area, a wordplay, Ray suspected, on "the Fertile Crescent" of Mesopotamian fame. Stan mutilated it to "the French Croissant," which Ray tetchily told him was redundant). Bounty Bag's slant toward regional suppliers had little to do with the preferences of foodies, locavores, or even nutrition-minded parents. It mostly reflected Angie's premium on trust and friendship in business relations. The care and maintenance of firm vendor relationships was paramount, and Giuseppe Alvaro was a much-loved vendor, not to mention a possible suitor to Angie. It was obvious to Ray what they had to do with the pepper king's letter.

"A gracious reply and a 'free gift,'" Ray prescribed. "So what's the issue? Send him a crate of hams. I can write the letter if you're stumped."

"The issue—do you even *read* the paper?"

As a matter of fact, he didn't. Sure, he'd browse *Supermarket Happenings*, but even that fell by the wayside during The Sickness. As for broader news, he caught a few stray headlines with WBZ in the morning or in the *Pennacook Beat*, on rare occasions when his guard was down and he threw a buck away. But he generally didn't read newspapers, finding the news salacious or dread-inspiring or both. When the convention called to congratulate him on the presidential nomination, Ray supposed he'd have to bone up on current events. Until then he typically favored a half-century delay in his non-fiction reading, with narrow exceptions for optimism and parenting literature.

Thus, right now as far as Ray was concerned Lyndon Johnson was mobilizing national sentiment for a War on Poverty. Meanwhile, the decentralized approach of the shadow RFK administration focused on community development corporations, like this one he got behind in Bedford-Stuyvesant, that brought power and money to the local level. America, Kennedy disclosed, was a generous country, compassionate and kind. It would reconcile its disenchanted, black and white, young and old, and take care of its poor children. *Come, my friends, 'Tis not too late to seek a newer world*, RFK quoted Tennyson. Which of these paths would the country choose? Future volumes would reveal all…though of course Ray knew the bitter outline.

Stan swung around and pointed at his mission-control dashboard panel from which, in ordinary times, he presided cheerfully over the store floor like a celebrity DJ.

"See that button over there?"

Ray's eye caught the chrome glimmer of an unfamiliar rainbow-colored button. He edged toward it.

Stan frowned. "Chesley installed it yesterday. Sent lackeys to drill us—three hours straight. Told *me* to follow *their* orders. Go on. Press it."

Ray walked over and smacked the button hard with his palm.

Beyond the dashboard the store lights dimmed, then rapidly brightened in multiple, swirling colors. The security cameras—upgraded overnight—descended from the ceiling and converted to disco balls. Speakers blared through jacked-up amps, and the looped chorus of the 1974 Bachman-Turner Overdrive hit "Takin' Care of Business" flooded the floor.

"I know you can't hear it from up here, but it's on," Stan said.

Stan was right. Triple-thick plexiglass prevented any sound from coming through, but Ray knew the song and could imagine it playing below them.

Instantly, all the associates already at work, even poor snowbound musk-ox Gary Snow out in the parking lot, fell into a frenzy. Wiped counters. Loaded watermelons. Stuffed shelves. Swept floors. Mopped aisles. Dumped drumsticks in the hot-wings bar. Shelly Frampton plunged her mop like she was drowning a rabid raccoon.

Ray looked at the dashboard. The counter ticked down from 15 to zero, again and again, resetting after each run of the chorus. A little red digital note above the timer spelled out and repeated the song's title: TAKIN' CARE OF BUSINESS.

Already spent, a watermelon stocker flung himself back against a wall of crackers and slid to the floor, boxes of Ritz raining down on him—*donk! donk! donk!*—and cartoon birds twittering around his head satellite-fashion. Outside, Gary Snow shoveled like a madman. Snow clouds flew up in the wind and back in his face.

From what the dashboard said, "Takin' Care of Business" continued to pound through the store. Ray couldn't hear or read the lyrics but he watched the song's title scroll across the screen: TAKIN' CARE OF BUSINESS! TAKIN' CARE OF BUSINESS! TAKIN' CARE OF BUSINESS! The volume dial turned itself up up up. The digital letters trapped Ray's eyes and held them in a cage. He imagined indicators he'd seen earlier in the Bounty Bag weekly deals flyer superimposed over the song's title.

> TAKIN' CARE OF *BUSINESS*!
> TAKIN' CARE OF "BUSINESS"!

Ray felt queasy. He broke loose from the dashboard and looked down at the floor. Customers fearing an active shooter clumped together for safety or ran screaming for the automatic exit doors which, terrifyingly, opened at their usual stately pace. *Bzzzzhhhhhhhhhhht.*

Others stayed behind. One woman shielded her unpaid-for items from assault by draping her body over her filled carriage, crying "*Oooh Oooooooh.*" On the floor between Register Four and Aisle Seven, three elementary-school boys—who must have been playing hooky from school—had also misidentified the precise nature of the threat and were performing the "stop, drop, and roll" technique, their exuberant log rolls carrying them halfway across the store. Coming closer to the comically humiliating heart of the matter, a gaggle of young guys and a shaggy old man wearing a bathrobe and flip-flops and holding a paper-towel cube back-slapped, guffawed, and pointed through the whole performance.

The song title rolled by:

TAKIN' CARE OF BUSINESS!
TAKIN' CARE — OF *BUSINESS*!!!

Late-responding associates burst from the breakroom and spilled out onto the floor to prance about and work to the piercing soundtrack. Even *The* Alfredo—who, as Ray had witnessed time and again, still peed with his pants pressed down to his ankles like a three-year-old who has yet to master the urinal—waddled out of the restroom, one hand clenched to his sagging waistband, the other uselessly painting the floor with a dry mop head.

The crew moved desperately in a tight range of repetitive tasks like cuckoo-clock figurines or cursed Amish carpenters chained to their hand saws in some high-stakes handmade furniture factory in Lancaster, Pennsylvania.

Again and again, Ray read the title as it scrolled nightmarishly across the digital screen.

```
TAKIN' CARE OF BUSINESS TAKIN' CARE OF BUSINESS
TAKIN' CARE OF BUSINESS TAKIN' CARE OF BUSINESS
TAKIN' CARE OF BUSINESS TAKIN' CARE OF BUSINESS
TAKIN' CARE OF BUSINESS TAKIN' CARE OF BUSINESS
TAKIN' CARE OF BUSINESS TAKIN' CARE OF BUSINESS
TAKIN' CARE OF BUSINESS TAKIN' CARE OF BUSINESS
```

TAKIN' CARE OF BUSINESS TAKIN' CARE OF BUSINESS
TAKIN' CARE OF BUSINESS TAKIN' CARE OF BUSINESS
TAKIN' CARE OF BUSINESS TAKIN' CARE OF BUSINESS
TAKIN' CARE OF BUSINESS TAKIN' CARE OF BUSINESS
TAKIN' CARE OF BUSINESS TAKIN' CARE OF BUSINESS
TAKIN' CARE OF BUSINESS TAKIN' CARE OF BUSINESS
TAKIN' CARE OF BUSINESS TAKIN' CARE OF BUSINESS
TAKIN' CARE OF BUSINESS TAKIN' CARE OF BUSINESS
TAKIN' CARE OF BUSINESS TAKIN' CARE OF BUSINESS
TAKIN' CARE OF BUSINESS TAKIN' CARE OF BUSINESS
TAKIN' CARE OF BUSINESS TAKIN' CARE OF BUSINESS
TAKIN' CARE OF BUSINESS TAKIN' CARE OF BUSINESS
TAKIN' CARE OF BUSINESS TAKIN' CARE OF BUSINESS
TAKIN' CARE OF BUSINESS TAKIN' CARE OF BUSINESS
TAKIN' CARE OF BUSINESS TAKIN' CARE OF BUSINESS
TAKIN' CARE OF BUSINESS TAKIN' CARE OF BUSINESS
TAKIN' CARE OF BUSINESS TAKIN' CARE OF BUSINESS

Ray reeled to the side, only to find that Stan wasn't there. Ray caught the last of him turning the corner down the stairs. He reappeared seconds later down on the store floor in full uniform with an enormous pasted-on grin.

I can't get enough of this stuff! the grin unpersuasively urged as he used a box-cutter to shave a piece of gum while bobbing his rump.

Panic rose in Ray's throat, and he turned back to the store. The disco-lights receded and the music faded. The blitz had crushed the associates and they slumped back down to their work or off to the breakroom or toilets or to the sports-drink aisle where they cashed in store credits for a sodium-potassium top-off. Customers looked fragile in the aisles but they gradually un-huddled. Some returned to shopping. Others calmed one another by quietly negotiating a restoration of the pre-crisis lines.

Ray thought the tsunami had finally subsided but just then two cottage-sized men dressed in safety coats and carrying hammers closed in on the tarp-shrouded Register Two that he had asked Natty about earlier. They tore off the tarp and knocked at the equipment from odd, seemingly random directions. A huge box behind them contained—how could he not have guessed it?—an automated register. Chesley was moving fast with those plans!

Ray was only beginning to digest this development when he spied in the distance a demon of far greater menace. It was the white-plastic tower he had spotted earlier, mistaking it, fool that he was, for a harmless mop closet. Ray could now see that *this* "mop closet" had eyes. Cute, round, blue bubble-eyes. More disturbing, the baby-faced tower was working. It blurped and bleeped, scanning the shelves with a red laser matrix and soaking and crunching data from the passing stacked items. *Inventory robot*, with—Ray could just make out—a little rotating claw and mechanized arm for truing shelves, even stocking. No doubt an army of Tin Man siblings was already on the container ship, blinking in the darkness; at the pier, latter-day Dorothys ready to oil their joints and turn them loose on Stores 1 to 74. The robots would be charmers, but Ray could easily guess what foul dust floated in *their* wake. Mothership drones to dump groceries on your head. Deli machines that didn't talk at all, let alone follow Garner's or AAVE's strictures. In short, a whole world, or "ecosystem," a fishy term he'd read in a Chesley board-transcript entry, set up for Howard Hughes in his less presentable days. Ray was a bit of an introvert, but this was ridiculous. What did Aristotle (well, Groof) say about people being political animals who needed society? If Chesley had his way, as it now seemed he would, we'd all be shut-ins, nothing more than shoppers: the associates' only purpose to hang up their coats and go home; the customers' only function to keep funneling to Chesley all of their cash—whatever little they had left after their own jobs started "doing the robot"—and continue eating; the communities'—*what* communities? *Pace* the sanguine posture of the unreliable *Supermarket Happenings*' editorial pages and the understandably complacent 1997 assessment of *Grocery Business*, one of Stan's older volumes ("People generally don't like to grocery shop on the Internet. 'They want to see their food, and touch it. They also like the experience, and chatting with our people,' one Arkansas grocer explained"), the future was clear. Bounty Bag and all that it stood for were doomed!

Stan rounded the staircase corner and removed his golden-striped purple manager's jacket. He plopped into his roller chair, looking spent but relieved and like himself again, as though he'd just figured something out. He carefully set the jacket on his lap and while they spoke he petted it gently like a kitten.

Ray held up Giuseppe's letter. "You're leaving."

"Correct."

"And you want me to reply."

"Yes, but..."

"Fill me in."

"Later. Maybe *much* later. But let me tell you this:

"Mom always carries this old green leatherette pocketbook. One night last winter outside The Chateau, she dropped it and a note fell out. Said the damnedest things that I can't get out of my head. Part of it was something she picked up at the Waltham Civic Society, I think, when they gave her a plaque for that bookmobile? This I don't know, but the note was written on their stationery and it was very old, so many times Mom must have kept it when she could have thrown it away.

"Anyway, on one side it's got this quote from this 'Louis Brandeis, J.' You know the guy? Says, 'We can have democracy in this country, or we can have great wealth concentrated in the hands of a few, but we can't have both.'

"You know what Mom wrote on the other side? 'The supermarket kills the little man — Papa's last words.' 'Papa' was my great grampa, guy who founded this place. Thing must've haunted the both of them, Papa *and* Mom. I'm thinking this whole debacle might be a test of sorts, of whether these things Mom wrote down are true."

"I'll quit with you," Ray said.

Though what was he thinking? Who'd pay for Patrick's food? If he quit, Ray wouldn't even be eligible for unemployment. Then, he supposed, it was time to drain Patrick's college fund or beg a handout from Stan — the same Stan who, despite possibly being a millionaire, found only flies in his own wallet and hit *Ray* up for cash when they grabbed the occasional lunch out at Pat's or H. T. Pasta. Ray could, as an unsatisfying last resort, head right back to Dusty Grimes's

Pennacook Food Pantry. But the PFP was no adequate substitute for Bounty Bag, as Ray well knew from the Markhams' first rocky canned-food-only days in Pennacook all those years ago. Ray had told eleven-year-old Patrick, at that age still basically a trusting boy, that it was like they were camping, but they had been very poor. The fragile equilibrium that Ray had sustained these past years, ever since the Bounty Bag paychecks kicked in, now faced its greatest threat. Stan, fortunately, had something else in mind.

"You can't quit. We need you in the store." Stan leaned back and swung his arms behind his head, grinning. "But if I told you more, like what to *do*, well then as you know Mom and I could be held legally responsible."

"Breach of fiduciary duty," Ray said, taking the hint. "Intentional interference with business relations. *Emotional* distress. Chapter 93A. Frottage." Most of these were practically boilerplate counts in Chesley's annual National Homemade Cookies Day Superior Court complaint against his twin sister. The last one, though, he had tossed in for the first time this year. It was wholly fabricated and served for media catnip.

"Our old friends. Listen, you always wanted to wear the purple jacket. You didn't know it but you did. Here it is." He tossed the golden-striped purple manager's jacket across the room and Ray caught it. "Take it and wear it."

Ray didn't believe a word of what Stan said about wanting the jacket, but he decided for the moment to play along with Stan's Prince Hal fantasies for him. He'd save for a later hour his dread at this colossal responsibility.

"What about Giuseppe?" he asked.

"Oh, just send him a ham or something."

Manager Markham

STAN'S RESIGNATION MIGHT HAVE BEEN THE END of the day's ample drama, but he lingered in his chair, saying he wanted to go over the books and show Ray how to operate the panel's more advanced features. Ray knew this stuff, but he could see it calmed his friend to teach it again and that he was reluctant to depart. Then they both sat back down and, buying time, talked Groof and sipped coffee from Stan's thermos. Stan finally accepted the inevitable and reached for his purple manager's duffel bag. It was swollen with extra dress shoes and clip-ons, Stan's Billerica Memorial High School diploma, and a framed photo of Angie from her high-school days. In the photo, Angie, in a female sacker's billowy smock, sportily sacked some veggies. That was back in the '60s, when the smocks were a forgettable mauve.

Stan rose to go, but just then the smaller Deli crisis came back to Ray in a rush and he waved Stan down.

"One more thing," Ray said.

"Criminal shrink, one of our own," Stan fumed as, seconds later, they marched down to Deli, Ray in the golden-striped purple jacket, Stan in his shirtsleeves and no clip-on. "On a day like this."

"I know."

He saw them closing in fast to the counter and didn't try to escape. They seized him roughly by the upper arms, one man on each side.

"Oh no," *The* Alfredo said, his eyes red-rimmed and bulging.

He went limp. They caught, turned, and pulled him, *The* Alfredo sobbing "*No! No! No!*" and "*Oooh hoo hooo!*" and his knees dragging across the floor as they hauled him around the corner, through the double doors, and up the short set of stairs. At the rope ladder leading through the black hole to Interrogation, they halted.

"You'll have to do this part yourself," Stan intoned.

"Okay," *The* Alfredo said, regaining his poise with breathtaking speed. "If you'll excuse me."

He motioned for them to step back so he'd have more room to

climb the rope ladder through the black hole. But after picking some lint off his brown Deli jacket, he made a run for it—right into their waiting arms.

"You're not going anywhere, pal," Ray said.

"*Oooh ho hooo! Boo hooo hoooo!*"

Upstairs, as expected, *The* Alfredo quickly spilled the beans.

Ray's instinct had been right. *The* Alfredo hadn't acted alone. He'd had an accomplice, Patrick's slimy host. In describing Muscles Carbonara and their arrangement, *The* Alfredo showed a surprising flair for storytelling in an animated style. It occurred to Ray that the narrative element had been missing from all of *The* Alfredo's other stories (Doughnut Dayle, etc.), which really amounted to simple anecdotes. Ray wondered if, in a way, it was the need for story that had attracted *The* Alfredo to crime. Was he, in a word, bored by too much time behind the counter?

The Alfredo reached the part about his compensation. "So *I* said to *him*, 'Magnum only, please. Smaller ones would harm my unit.'"

"We don't need this level of detail," Stan said.

"It's what *happened*."

He filled them in on Kluck Klucker's villainy—Ray had always hated that stupid "Kool Bird."

"So why'd I find a chicken bag in my deli today?" Ray asked.

"Planned delivery. But Mary called in sick, and then after I bagged the chickens, well, you got here. I didn't do it when you were supposed to be here. Then I got caught."

The Alfredo shrugged and looked down.

"I don't want to see your face again," Stan said. "You're lucky I'm not calling the fuzz."

"You mean I can go home now?"

Ray caught Stan's eye.

"No," Stan said. "Finish your shift."

The Alfredo bowed his head. One foot on the rope ladder, he turned back, face drooping.

"Best job I ever had."

"Sorry, pal. You blew it," Stan said, his voice thick with regret.

Ray escorted his friend to the automatic doors, stopping to chat one final time in the utilitarian exit lane, just beyond the doors' activation radius.

"You're in the driver's seat now, buddy. What do you think's gonna happen?"

Ray put on his pundit's hat. It didn't fit.

"Best guess? Protests tonight, but then everyone comes back to work tomorrow, mad as hell. Oh, we'll put on a good show for a few days, more after-hours flyers and shouting. Maybe a march around the parking lot with a bass drum. But they'll bring in a benign-sounding imitator, saying all the right things. 'No cuts to profit-sharing,' 'Bounty Bag values.' Clear malarkey, but we'll roll over anyway. War doesn't appeal to anybody, especially supermarket employees. It's not like we have cash to burn."

Stan frowned.

"What?" Ray asked.

" 'You may not be interested in war, but war is interested in you.' "

"Churchill?"

"Trotsky."

Ray thought of the Angie signs and the stuffed turtles in the Outback. Then again, that was only the Outback. How many of those signs would make it out front in a way that even mattered to Chesley and the board?

"My bigger concern is this robot."

"What robot?" Stan asked, looking confused.

"Old Blue Eyes, doing Inventory."

"Oh, him? Mom's idea."

Before Ray could demand an explanation for the robot stocker, Stan's phone buzzed and he held up a finger to pause Ray.

"Gotta go. Late for meat loaf. Can't make the old lady wait! So long, chum. See ya' around."

Stan stepped through the automatic doors, leaving this mystery in his wake. With his box of personal effects clutched to his chest, he looked like any guy that got fired, not a billionaire's child displaced from his birthright.

The store drifted in the doldrums until closing.

Ray holed up in Stan's old office. At one point an urgent dashboard message ordered him to hit the TAKIN' CARE OF BUSINESS button again, but Ray ignored it. As they completed their shifts, the associates one by one retrieved their pro-Angie signs from the Outback and formed a modest but growing picket line on the edge of the parking lot, over by the neat rows of Tigers.

The usual snow-removal crew never came. Instead, far too late for Gary Snow's health or well-being, a pack of contractor drivers arrived in a white prison bus with caged windows. They wore peculiar all-black costumes and face masks. Mounting the Tiger 204s, they started them up with some effort and cleared the snow, then returned the purple mini-plows to their neat line facing the parking lot, climbed back on the bus, and left.

On an instinct, Ray pressed the all-store buzzer—BLOOP!—for an improvised message. *"Ahem. Attention all associates. This is Ray Markham here with you. As of this announcement I am hereby unlocking the Faraday cage and releasing all smartphones for unlimited associate usage, for any and all purposes, both on and off the floor, until further notice. Take care and...be safe!"* BLOOP-BLOOP!

Not exactly Churchill, or even Trotsky. In fact, more like a snowstorm warning toward the end there. And why did he say "usage"? Why not "use"? He'd been store manager for all of an hour and already he suffered from bureaucratic slippage! But at least he'd thrown a bone to the rebels by unleashing the phones. At the same time, he'd kept his own purposes and allegiance vague—suitably, for a store manager hoping to keep his head attached to his neck awhile longer.

He slipped off to Deli where he toasted a turkey club. He brought it back to Stan's office and looked out over the store while he ate it (The Sickness had miraculously vanished, as if his new duties had displaced it). The lights blinked out in patches by department. Deli. Seafood. Bakery. Produce. Associates chatted, plotting who-knew-what, just outside the automatic door's ambit. He saw that over in Aisle Two they'd already carried out a first act of violent defiance. Someone had toppled Chesley's monstrous robot — or Angie's, rather, if Stan's disheartening intel on the robot was accurate — but its blinking persisted as it scanned the ceiling for canned tomatoes.

He set the sandwich on the desk and went over the tumultuous day. He was strangely dissatisfied by, of all things, *The* Alfredo's termination and returned to his story with a nagging sense of unanswered questions. *The* Alfredo had said he'd been caught because Ray was there, subbing for Mary as a surprise. "I didn't do it when you were supposed to be here," were his words. But to deter *The* Alfredo's work-shifting shenanigans, his malingering and the rest, Ray always carefully secured his paper schedule from prying eyes, posting it at home for no one else to see. How did you know when I wasn't here? he asked *The* Alfredo in the mental re-play, and *The* Alfredo's mouth formed a circle. There was only one answer.

PART THREE

The Take-Home Message

T HEY WERE IN MUSCLES CARBONARA'S BASEMENT watching *The Take-Home Message* for the second time that day. The infomercial with the surprisingly hyphenated phrasal-adjective title aired for the first time during the early afternoon when on a normal day they'd either be in school or at track. Because Mr. Grant had died, they'd already watched it once this afternoon. Now it was night, and they were watching it again. That was okay. Numbing repetition was the genre's main point after selling.

The format was a mock talk-show. Women behind empty coffee mugs opened the program, their banter quickly centering on the nuisance-du-jour. Today, unaccountably, it was autumn leaves. They brought out the protagonist and customer stand-in, a different dunce for every episode and the slapstick highlight of the program for Muscles Carbonara and Patrick. Today's victim was named Ray and eerily resembled his brother. He even wore a thin tie like they wore at Bounty Bag, though without the green coat.

Ray fretted about his personal leaf-removal situation. "*Every October it's the same story. I rake and I rake, but then how do I clean up the mess? Trash bags are useless.*" The infomercial cut to Ray in his yard. He used his bare hands to push leaves and what looked like dog shit onto a huge rake but the rake's strategically missing tines led to critical spillage even before Ray failed to mash the leaf pile through a narrow-slitted trash bag. The rake dipped before the ever-narrowing bag and reminded Patrick of his failed attempt at sex with Stacey Larusso last spring, when his penis shriveled as he fumbled with the condom. "I feel like I can never have you," she said a week later, dumping him for some dolt from New Hampshire. A heartbroken Patrick had consulted one of Ray's parenting manuals and concluded that his impotence was situational, symptom of teenage nerves. It didn't make him feel any better. After all, he was a nervous teen.

"I'm not going to the funeral."

"I didn't think you would."

"*How do I get the leaves into the trash bag? And even when I do...*" Ray marched off across his yard, but the trash bag full of leaves and shit exploded in his hands. Upended, Ray landed on his ass on a dirt pile. An artistic close-up showed a spinning leaf eclipsing the sun. "*Leaf blowers are no better.*" Ray's leaf blower had a jet engine's propulsion. It shot him back against the house. "*And who needs the noise?*" Bleeding-ear close-up.

"It's not that I don't care but, well, I don't."

"I didn't think you did."

Clock ticking, Ray moved swiftly from discouragement and skepticism to unbridled enthusiasm for a new product that had been invented seemingly just to help him. "Television Host," read the caption under Rhonda Jade, who showcased the product. "Rake-A-Mania" might appear to be nothing more than a doctored bedsheet, Rhonda Jade acknowledged. But this was no mere linen. The inventor had *folded it over* and sewn down the four edges into sleeves; he threaded a thin rope *through* the sleeves but left slots in the corners for handles to poke out. Rake-A-Mania's patent was pending, and the chances to buy one had dwindled.

As usually happened around this point, Patrick was persuaded that the product was worthy and that the infomercial format wasn't doing it any favors by making it sound like a con. How come they only used infomercials for cool inventions and saved the slick Hollywood ads for uncreative crap like cars?

"Anyway, I'm going to blow up Andrew Johnson."

"I don't think you should do that. What if there's someone inside?"

"When it's empty. Sort of a punishment for Mr. Grant, and also a barrel of laughs."

Patrick didn't believe him. He didn't believe Muscles Carbonara would do it and he didn't think he could.

"Where's the money in that?"

"This isn't about money. Ever hear of the Reichstag Fire? Or Rome burning? It's the best way to turn the tables on these cowards."

Patrick looked around. "What cowards? Teachers? Listen, if this is about grades—"

"Not *just* teachers. Voters. Supermarket managers. Big brothers. *Dads*. The whole weedy system. Clear the path, then walk on through it."

"I—I don't get it. Are you planning a mayoral campaign? Because as you know we have a modified New England Town Meeting system here and—"

"I don't know what comes next. I just know it will be better."

He took the dumbbell down from his shelf and curled his namesake muscle, still formidable but somewhat fatty from over-eating and too much lying around. Like toenail care, arm curls were a preferred, regal way of communicating, "We're finished here." Fine by Patrick. He still didn't believe him and had nothing left to say.

Muscles Carbonara's phone bleeped. An instant later, Patrick's buzzed.

"Sonofabitch just fired me. Calls me a thief!"

"I know it was you," Patrick's message said.

Patrick opened his duffel bag and started pushing clothes in. "I'm leaving."

Muscles Carbonara raised a finger to his lips. *Shhh.*

Ray loaded the leaves into Rake-A-Mania's center and pulled taut the corner loops, forming a noose-tight sack.

He meant to go home to The Rock to take his medicine, but after he'd slipped out of Muscles Carbonara's house into the boar-filled night, his feet started walking toward Andrew Johnson, and Patrick, as usual, followed them. In Mr. Gherkin's office he fed and watched his turtles.

They looked old. A. Lincoln was half on top of Eleanor Roosevelt like she'd fallen asleep mid-hug. Satchmo was off to the side doing some slow-but-funky in-and-out thing with his head. He looked like he was blowing a cornet, actually.

Patrick twisted and pushed in his earplugs to block the haunted sounds and drifted off to sleep.

The Supermarket Revolution

A MILD WIND SWEPT THROUGH THE LOT. THE lampposts dripped and the snow cracked and collapsed mildly in heaps.

Ray stood on the ridge overlooking Truble Cove. Around his neck, binoculars. Under his arm, an overnight pouch, received from the offices of Chesley Martini. The pouch contained a cover letter from Chesley, a chronology, a list of contacts from the all-new managerial squad, bennies information for Ray as a new manager, and recent clippings from *Supermarket Happenings*.

The paper reported that after Angie's firing Leroy Soots's online petition had exploded from 10,000 signatures to 40,000, and tech-savvy associates had expanded it to a threaded discussion and a rousing blog. Yesterday, while Ray was saying his goodbyes to Stan, the blog announced an associate walk-out and called for a customer boycott. Store #28 and two other claimants to flagship status, one each in Tewksbury and Billerica, were the initial targets. The walkout would start there and spread across New England—if the company did not take back Angie.

The pouch spoke of other matters, either not yet reported or just making their way to the blog. The biggest news concerned Warehouse, which at Bounty Bag was responsible for both the warehouses and all deliveries. Citing purported accounting discrepancies, Chesley had fired the entire staff at midnight and hired an overseas firm to fill their spots with strangers, "smoothing the handover."

Ray could understand why Chesley would want to be done with those guys. Warehouse was a boisterous bunch. For sport in all seasons, the associates staffing Warehouse #2 cannonballed into the Pennacook River, upstream of Harry Grimes's outflow. They also held all-night hockey games at Hallenbuck Rink, typically interrupted—but not ended—by at least one ambulance ride. Their riotous energy prodigious, they formed the nascent Sam Adams wing of the erupting supermarket revolution.

And it wasn't just their grit that threatened Chesley. Warehouse had leverage. If they wanted to starve the chain to death, all they'd have to do was lock up and Bounty Bag's shelves would go barren. From a $4b company to nothing in an instant. Then try to sell your rotting chain to Hoggly Woggly.

Given this, the Warehouse mass firing was well worth the storm of wrongful-termination lawsuits inevitably to follow. Bounty Bag associates, including Warehouse, knew their rights. They had, after all, studied the Martini family disputes for decades, making them far more attuned than most supermarket staffs to the law's peculiar windings. Every store, it seemed, had its own supermarket lawyer. Seafood's Huddy Packer was Store #28's. Ray had once overheard Huddy explain a finer point of Massachusetts tort law to a hair-splitting high-school trainee, a veteran member of Andy Johnson's mock-trial team.

"I don't think physical injury is an element of intentional infliction of emotional distress," Huddy insisted. "What's that? *Negligent* infliction? Yes, of course you have to prove it with *negligent* infliction. But you didn't ask about negligent infliction. No, you didn't. Now, shucking clams. First you slip the paring knife between the two shells. Next, twisting the knife, you cut around the seal. Like so. Are you listening to me? Watch the hands, guy."

Warehouse was no exception. They, too, had in-house counsel — currently pro bono.

Chesley's communique also laid down Ray's re-cast managerial duties.

"Keep the lights on," "maintain status quo."

Open the Outback, accept groceries from the drivers "without word." "They are not your enemy, but they are not your friend."

Shelve the groceries and sell them.

He was to remain unarmed.

He was to report armed associates to the police.

He was to leave undisturbed the Tiger 204s. "It may snow."

He was not to leave the store while on duty, except for Exterior Inspection, during which he was to look mostly down.

He should not "fraternize," or spend break time with, "any associate not working as scheduled." "Fraternize" was defined to include "providing such an associate with restroom access."

He "shall not feed them."

He "shall process replacement job applications with dispatch."

The letter warned, "Agents of Bounty Bag Grocers, Inc., can and will, as necessary, enter the premises and, using reasonable force, eject trespassers from the store or the lot." With these efforts Ray was "not to interfere."

Chesley had affixed a handwritten note to the letter. "Welcome aboard, Ray. I see big things in your future at 'the Bag.'"

No one called it "the Bag," which sounded like some kind of self-asphyxiation equipment.

Ray also found a card in the pouch. It outlined an intensely escalating bonus structure that spanned the next eight weeks of Ray's employment. It applied only to managers and only during this time of "extraordinary transitional duties." The card promised an added $100 the first week, $200 the second, $400 the third, and then $600 per week each additional week of "satisfactory employment" after that through the two-month period. Next on the menu, a permanent bump.

The cover letter had one final detail of interest. *Ray's store would lead the counter-offensive.* Big Data required this. Chesley's Kendall Square "team" had merged Mr. Grant's extant course website with *The Beat*'s latest stats. The regression confirmed their political consultant's assessment. Because Pennies lacked ballast, Store #28 was the rebellion's soft underbelly. "Strike there first."

Ray helplessly proofread the pouch's contents but found little to correct except the high and formal tone, which ran against the plain-English counsel of Bryan A. Garner and other contemporary style experts. It was, in fact, the cleanest prose he'd read from the company, Corporate or Store #28, in years.

He raised the binoculars and glassed the lot. Still no sign of the early-morning Saturday crew. Frayed Christmas-color tinsel drifted among garbage from last night's after-hours protest. Pennacook boars picked through the slop. Ray lowered the binoculars and walked down the hill. Come what may, he had rolls to bake.

If You Would Be Loved

THE WALK-OUT IDEA DIED WITH MR. GRANT. A grieving Tito Tiggs begged off, leaving only one teacher, Janice Chance, to join her in what would've been the most pathetically under-attended walk-out in protest history. Yet the propaganda value of Mr. Grant's death did not escape Dr. Chong, who achieved something of a media coup on the exceptionally mild Saturday morning after he died. By all rights the town's attention should've been focused on the chaos at Bounty Bag, but Dr. Chong arranged with PTV and *The Beat* to have cameras and reporters at the ready for when the *Lung Cancer Monthly* furniture was removed. Tommy came along for the ride, carrying his compound bow, on the lookout for Pennacook boars.

"Do you see any connection between Mr. Grant's death and reported carcinogens on the Andrew Johnson campus?"

The puffy red mike pressed against her mouth.

"I'm not a scientist," she said, "but this scene disturbs me."

The maroon hospital chair passed behind her into the moving truck. Gurneys followed and bags filled with tubes and dirty rags.

"How has this affected your views on next Wednesday's TCO?"

What must have been the last of Mr. Grant's refuse and equipment sailed by the cameras in a giant bulbous trash bag. A compelling image—if Pennacook was watching.

"It has only strengthened my resolve that we need a new school. I call on all voters to vote 'yes' on Question One!"

Tommy lurked in the background, practice-shooting a shrub.

After the interview, she took Tommy to Pat's Café for an early brunch. They split a pu pu platter and as they talked she peered at the strangely quiet Truble Cove parking lot. The lot should be half full with customers and the supermarket's workers by this hour, but it was practically empty, except for one small patch of cars in a small corner far away and another by Pat's.

"I just can't work for Agong anymore," Tommy was explaining. "I don't want to be a tailor, and he can be, well, *difficult* at times."

"You said a mouthful."

Speaking of full mouths, Tommy's bulged with teriyaki beef skewers and sopping wet chicken fingers. Duck sauce trailed down his chin.

"What is this stuff?"

"Chinese food."

"It's terrific. It's really sweet and like eating dessert for lunch. How come we don't have this at home?"

"Because it's not really Chinese. It's American Chinese, or Polynesian." She paused to look at the stuff, then threw her hands up in defeat. "Something or other anyway."

Tommy had largely avoided such food. You could do that in Flushing, where he'd lived all his life except for the one semester at Springfield College. He grabbed breakfast pastries and lunch around the neighborhood, and his mother, who slaved all day behind a fried-fish take-out counter on Roosevelt Ave., was a skilled Sichuan chef who made his dinners. Perhaps Dr. Chong should've brought Tommy to the more authentic Sichuan Surprise. Then again, he was happy as usual and even seemed enchanted by this food, so mundane it was exotic, and was eating very quickly, a family tradition. In fact, Tommy was accelerating through his meal and seemed to be approaching some sort of climax.

"Only the best of it here," Dr. Chong said.

She explained that Pennacook had half-a-dozen American Chinese restaurants, most of them costumed like Hawaii or the South Pacific, even though the town had no more than a dozen Chinese residents. Pat's particular charm was the well-spaced sea of booths, guaranteeing privacy and comfort. Pat also had an expansive bar overhung with TVs. This kept sports-fan Pennies at a safe distance and made the dining room feel even more expansive.

"Who are all those people?"

Tommy planted his elbow on the table and pointed with a chopstick to the all-Chinese staff. Pat, Pat's wife, and the waiters stood behind a lobby podium stocked with toothpicks, mints, and paper menus.

"The Pats live here, in an apartment out back. But the chefs and the waiters are mostly from Chinatown. There's a bus that comes up, and at night it takes them back."

"So white people prefer to have Chinese people serve them non-Chinese food in a place that looks like Honolulu but they don't want them to live here? I am confused."

"I wouldn't go that far. Most Chinese don't want to live here, but while it certainly isn't perfect, I've always felt welcome."

"Always" was a little strong. Some Pennies were hateful bigots who showed their stripes with abandon, while others, more numerous, saw her as the unfathomable other (*Do you know kung fu?*). But those, she was persuaded, were a minority. Sure, most Pennies might resent her for costing them some tax dollars, but not, generally, for being Asian or Chinese-American.

"Too welcome, in fact," she added between bites, thinking of all the times Pennies had buttonholed her, before, during, and after public hearings, to spill forth their life stories and their grief. "As for the food, well, they don't know what they're eating." She turned an egg roll in her hand, then chomped it. "Or care. As far as they're concerned, they served this in the Forbidden City."

"I see."

"Or Fiji. But they think we make it best. I'll take you to Sichuan Surprise next time. It reminds me of your mom's food, but not as good."

His face lit up. "She sends her love. I should've said that sooner."

Always the adorable favorite, her little sister. "Tell her I said ditto."

"Sure, Auntie. Whatever you say."

Selectman Archie arrived, too tied-up with a hearing for lunch, and slid into the booth next to Dr. Chong.

"Good news. The job came through!" Archie reached across the table and shook Tommy's hand. "Remember what we talked about. Safety first, you hear?"

Tommy was hard up for cash and accepted the offer of a day's employment helping to test and install Pennacook's voting machines for next week's TCO vote. Dr. Chong was grateful for Archie's prompt aid.

"Where's he stationed?" Dr. Chong asked.

Archie pointed out the window.

"Right here."

T.A.P.S., angling for advantage, had once again volunteered its Truble Cove space for Election Day.

Dr. Chong edged deeper into the booth to avoid Archie's warming touch, which was pleasant (even enticing!) but she didn't want to send the wrong signal. The fortune cookies came, and she let Archie grab hers.

" 'If you would be loved, love and be lovable —Ben Franklin,' " Archie read.

"Guess I'm O for two," she said, frowning at Archie as he handed the fortune over.

"I'd say you're halfway there," he said. "Like—most of us," he added, as if to cover his tracks.

Tommy's eyes flicked between them.

"All paid up?" Dr. Chong asked. "Let's go." She shoved Archie. "Out!"

The Supermarket Revolution

ROLLS PREPPED AND LOADED, RAY EMERGED TO find himself alone. He paced the perimeter turning on the lights and performed a mockery of yesterday's Inspection. Christmas-tree section not cleaned up. Check! Coin-op rides uncovered. Check! *Kapow!* too was a mess. Discount lawn chairs from last summer remained tossed in a pile, just like the customers had left them. No Natty or Bonnie MacNutt at Registers. No stockers facing the right way. No cookies baking for Debbie Hays's Cookie Club members, even if they had their membership creds. Not even the faithful Jeremy Wiggins was up front, Jeremy who hadn't missed or been late for a single day in over eight years of sacking. The meat and veggie cases, like Cereal, were a jumble. The Outback, in contrast, had been stripped clean of its signs, though the fish stink had expanded to fill the vast space.

Beyond the windows, the courteously distant associate-parking quadrant remained a ghost town. Ray's Buick was there, plus a compact hatchback. Bernie, a Pennacook homeless man and Bounty Bag regular, had taken advantage of the mild weather to sleep on the outdoor park bench. Say what you will about Bernie but he was faithful. Always here or just around the corner, Bernie spent at the store whatever nickels he collected.

A few feet from Bernie, a woman clutching a long coupon tape stared at the entrance with dread, as though a mighty beast could erupt at any moment from the automatic doors. It was Jennifer Harney, mother of one of Patrick's classmates. She worked long hours as a waitress at Tiki Shed and supported two daughters. Clyde Harney, her husband, was still around, but an opioid addict who didn't shoot straight at Pennacook boars and had been jailed twice for it.

What to do? At 9 A.M., he lifted the latch and opened the store. Jenn Harney gingerly rolled her carriage over the rubber-matted entrance.

"I can't afford to go anywhere else. I'm sorry."

"We're not sorry to have you."

Bzzhhhht!

Gary Snow, bless him, walked in behind her.

"I have something for you," Ray said as Jenn set off. He left Gary by the door and returned seconds later with his old green jacket.

"I know, I know. This is department-level colors, but when I get into the lockers, I'll pull you the unstriped purple. I'm making you my first deputy assistant manager. But right now we need hands on a register, pronto."

Gary looked at the jacket, then at Ray, then back at the jacket.

"I—I don't even know if I can work for you yet."

"Who's going to take care of Jenn Harney?"

This got him.

"Okay," Gary said, taking the jacket. "Green's fine. But I'm not making any promises."

"I owe you a root beer."

Gary buttoned up and Ray climbed the stairs for a bird's-eye view. There was a deeply unnatural quality to the place. Supermarkets had been a central image in countless apocalyptic movies, TV shows, and books, but they were never quite like this. Well-stocked, open—and empty.

Not, apparently, for long. Something caught his eye through the front windows. A neat line of five cars, blinkers on like a funeral train, had turned in the lot and crawled toward the store. The cars parked illegally in the yellow zone (Gardening, in springtime), their doors opened, and a crush of Bounty Bag associates piled out. Ray counted twenty in all—some 3,000-plus pounds of Bounty Bag to contend with. They blitzed for the doors carrying Angie posters in stacks and rolled up. Once inside, the bulky-coated associates swiftly marched around the obstacle course of holiday-cookie and candy-apple displays, rushing through the store applying posters to every free space, a task requiring ingenuity in a supermarket (even at a moral chain like Bounty Bag, "free space" was precisely not the point). They plastered "BRING BACK ANGIE" posters to Deli's and Bakery's plexiglass and strung an "ALL TOGETHER NOW" ribbon from Aisle Seven's coupon tree. Mimi from Produce raised a grappling gun and fired it — *pop-pewww!* — toward the rafters. Rope secured, she worked an attached pully to raise the Gettysburg and FDR murals like championship banners at the Garden. Ray's store was *in protest against itself.* Finished, they moved for the exit, where Ray waited, hoping to have a word.

"Traitor if you take them down," the kindly Debbie Hays said, looking Ray dead in the eye.

"Traitor," said a man behind her before Ray could open his mouth.

"Can we leave our stuff here?" Bonnie MacNutt asked. "It's easier than lugging it around."

"Absolutely," Ray said, glad to draw on some of the old civility.

The associates climbed back into the cars and drove off to the far quadrant for parking, then walked their stuff back to the store, hanging up their extra bags and umbrellas and, more out of habit than anything, lodging their car keys in the Faraday cage for safekeeping.

Bzzzhhht! went the doors.

Enter Doreen Robinson. "Daddy said you need me."

Doreen plus Gary a skeleton crew made. Ray promoted Doreen on the spot, assigning her Mary's green jacket with the bronze stripe and sending her to cover Deli, Seafood, and as much of Bakery as her remaining energies allowed. Gary, up front, continued to jockey Register One, cashiering and sacking. Between those duties he and Ray shagged carriages from the small half-row of spaces that their few customers had used.

In this manner they passed the first day.

He arrived home after midnight, dog-tired and ready for a snack. He flipped on the stove light and shook two packets of dehydrated-onion-soup mix into a bowl of sour cream, whisking the mixture into California dip.

California dip was a classic. Decades ago, early in the supermarket era, Lipton made it up to boost sales of its mix pouches to the gentile masses, but the name and the cool savory flavoring still evoked the balmy beaches and creative-yet-low-workload leisure-time refreshments one associated with the sunny West Coast. Cynical perhaps, but Ray wouldn't let a product backstory skunk his enjoyment of a tangy treat that went perfect on a scoop-shaped corn chip.

His pocket buzzed and a glossy dollop of California dip slipped his mouth and plummeted to his lap.

"Congratulations!" the text said. "We are pleased to offer you early-action admission to Hampton."

It was supposedly from Dean Max Page—even the name sounded fake—of Hampton College in Hadley, Massachusetts.

A new vista in college-recruitment fraud. They teased you with a bogus admittance notice, only to get you to open their cascading promotional mail. Then a "follow-up" deflating disclaimer would arrive under separate cover. "This could be you next year!"

Sure enough a thick paper package from Hampton College awaited at the mail center. Ray curled it up and slipped it into his soiled purple jacket. He left it unopened, but the text message and thick envelope did give him pause. Maybe some poor schmuck had gotten in, and Ray would have to play middle man. If so, this could wait a few days. He had a mail pile like Old St. Nick's and if he didn't send out some checks soon and keep the lights on how was he going to sort out Hampton's admissions snafus?

Too bad the college admission wasn't real and he wouldn't accept it even if it was. Hampton had its appeal, starting with location. The Pioneer Valley was populated by affable country hippies and by credulous farmers and townies whose folksy demeanor owed more to Cleveland than to crusty New England. Ray was different from these people but he liked them. Back during his grand search following their parents' death, in fact, he had almost settled them out there. He even had his eye on a rental, an old Haydenville ranch house with a peace-sign-shaped garden. But at the last minute, his courage failing, he left the rental papers unsigned and drove the Buick back over Mount Tom's hump, the rooftops and spires of Easthampton receding around the corner and the Connecticut River glistening below.

While he was out there, he'd driven by Hampton, a Brutalist campus behind red maples. The school was supposed to be flakey, but it had potential, its membership in a six-college consortium enabling its spacey kids to cross-register at Amherst and U-Mass. And maybe the world could use a place for young dreamers, who only needed some time among their own. Like Deli's frozen rolls, placed on trays to defrost overnight.

Bounty Bag was just now breaking into that region. Three new stores, the largest one in Northampton, were already under contract. Ray knew all about the Valley stores because Stan had asked him to revise the Deli menu for regional vernacular. He'd decided that in Northampton subs would be grinders. Frappes, however, became shakes, and tonic, a term fading fast even in their Boston-area stores, was just soda, as it was now in Pennacook. Jimmies still reigned across Massachusetts as the term for chocolate-flavored sprinkles, but that was Bakery.

Ray pushed books and bills off the queen bed and climbed under the covers. He worried about Patrick, who hadn't replied to his *j'accuse* text. He set the alarm for 4:30 and slept.

On Sunday, the second day of protests, the weather was mild again, enough to excite the colony of boars who lived between the store and the river and to draw them in clumps to the lot's fringes. But temperatures were forecast to drop, a wind to come down from the hills, and a light snow to dust Pennacook that night.

The first rally swarmed into the parking lot at noon, and the associates filled in quickly from the center. Most were Ray's staff, but as the rally expanded, associates from other stores swooped in to join them. The associates had caught whiff of Chesley's plan to confront them here and had coordinated and combined their forces. Familiar faces — Natty Romanov, Bonnie, Debbie, and (head poking out) *The* Alfredo in his orange-belted karate uniform, stained pink from being washed with Benvolio's tablecloths and napkins — milled through the crowd, shaking hands and flashing smiles like envoys from a consulate. Ray recognized other faces from the regional tour Stan had taken him on back in October. Stan had claimed then that it was a standard part of management orientation. Ray realized now that Stan had been preparing him for this day.

Truculent Hank Ramapriya led the roguish sackers from Store #42 in Waltham. On some kind of pact, this troupe had started together junior year of high school. The passing years shed a few of them to college or other work, and the remaining sackers formed a hardened core of Bounty Bag lifers.

The imperious and polyamorous Denise Nedelros, a Framingham store manager, had delegated her duties to her assistant manager and drove her off-duty crew down in a donated school bus. The bus emptied into Ray's lot, and the associates lugged sleeping bags, battery-powered space heaters, barbecue sets, and coolers out onto the slick blacktop. Her two boyfriends opened up a fold-out chair, her throne. She sat on it and whispered orders as her people set up camp. The associates unfolded before her a larger foldout chair that could accommodate eight fannies, ample seating for whatever audience or counsel was required. In addition to the boyfriends she'd brought a menagerie to keep her company. Puppies and kittens climbed over her, and a bird hung beside her in a heated cage.

The Bedford and Carlisle associates, their bonds forged at summer softball, arrived in cars packed for camping. They assembled tents and set up lines to relay sleeping bags and other equipment from the car trunks to the tent entrances. In the tents, associates unrolled and smoothed out the sleeping bags and inflated air cushions until they were blue in the face.

Chelmsford brought a spit for roasting. Somerville installed a stereo for blasting gangsta rap and anthemic rock. Warrior music. Stuffed-animal turtles, pinned to lampposts throughout Ray's lot, represented fortitude or persistence or something-or-other that was never made clear.

There was an uncertain period of overcrowding and cooking, but after lunch an aproned staff swept through the crowd poking up garbage with ski-poles. A bevy of jacketed protestors convened post-cleanup for a pow-wow. (As a general rule, management protested in uniform, associates in jeans and sloganeering T-shirts.) The meeting broke up and associates were dispatched to re-arrange the tents in a well-ordered grid. They started with one inner box of six rows by six, and the camp expanded outward from its corners. They reserved four squares within each 36-site box for community use, one each for a teaching/meeting space, a fire pit/kitchen, garbage, and the toilet. The portable toilets arrived and the in-store restroom traffic, which Ray had allowed despite Chesley's injunction, trailed off. Hot cider and fruit punch poured from tureens and a series of "Hurrahs!" went up. Generators deployed and power cords bound in electrical tape went out to centralized stations where they recharged phones and the portable heaters.

Nervous but impressed, Ray coined a nickname for their camp: the Pnyx (*pr.* puh-'niks), after the Athenian hill. The Pnyx was a thing he'd happened upon in Groof while using the breakroom toilet and taking a shine to the annotated Pericles speech. The Athenians held their densely packed assembly there. In Pennacook, of course, the boars controlled the hill itself, relegating the Pnyx to the parking lot's plane.

Up front the associates built a small, store-lit stage that overlooked the Pnyx. In the late afternoon, they gathered before the stage with the signs that Ray had seen in the Outback and started the cheering and the speeches that, interrupted only for sleep, eating, and cleanup, were more or less continuous from that point on. One of the first speeches ended with a voice from a bullhorn leading the crowd in a chant of, "TRAITOR! TRAITOR! TRAITOR!"

Doreen, Gary, and Ray were sitting ducks.

> HEY HEY. HO HO. CHESLEY'S THUGS HAVE GO TO GO!
> HEY HEY. HO HO. CHESLEY'S THUGS HAVE GOT TO GO!

Arms chopped, ending in fingers pointed at Ray and his crew. One poster featured a poor likeness of his replacement-manager's face.

Other cheers sounded a similar theme.

> TELL ME WHAT BOUNTY BAG LOOKS LIKE.
> *THIS* IS WHAT BOUNTY BAG LOOKS LIKE!

"We the good guys, right, Mr. Ray?" Doreen asked.

Ray didn't answer.

When a family entered the store, Ray tugged on Gary's sleeve and led his people back in. The morning shipment had not arrived, and Ray jogged up to the office to check the latest from *Supermarket*

Happenings. As reported there, the Warehouse scabs literally could not find the light switches. And even after they found the light switches, and divined the correct direction in which to flip them, the place descended rapidly into chaos because the scabs had no idea how to operate the myriad exotic vehicles that were required to do the department's vital work. Mini-trucks and mini-forklifts. Scooters and electric wagons. Even a clown car retired from the Topsfield Fair. In ordinary times, the fleet sailed through Warehouse like a delicately orchestrated Dyson swarm, one of those space things that Patrick was obsessed with. The scabs, in contrast, played what amounted to an extended-bonus-length round of Crash Derby with the vehicles. As a result, they had missed morning delivery for the second day in a row.

Ray weighed a response. Conference call to the other managers? Dispatch Gary Snow, an organizational wizard, to aid Warehouse? Paralyzed by indecision, Ray tapped an eraser against Stan's congested desk blotter and sighed. At 4:15, finally, the trucks pulled in.

By this time most of the associates from beyond Pennacook had gone home for Sunday dinner, leaving behind the Pennacook associates and a small band of chaos junkies who smelled a party. The campers finished dinner, tidied up the Pnyx, and started bedding down for the night. Ray stayed late to take in the shipment. He stored the excess in the Outback and carted the rest out to the floor. The last step, emptying the meat cases of expired product, he left to Doreen and Gary, and he awarded each a discretionary spot-award and $50 bonus. This freed up Ray to balance the books and make reassuring calls to vendors and pay them.

As two days of protest turned to three, Ray's tasks were unfamiliar. During the day, he manually took in deliveries from the dilatory Warehouse scabs, loaded them onto the shelves, and transported the swelling carriages of expired goods to the Outback. At the front entrance, Dusty Grimes's Pennacook Food Pantry truck made twice-daily stops now to exploit the unprecedented bounty of excess product, and Ray found the orange-jumpsuited man uncharacteristically wired and loose. "Keep 'em comin'. That's the ticket!" Dusty exclaimed, hauling in Ray's hardening French loaves and softening green peppers. In a role reversal, Ray sulked as the unsold stock drifted away, albeit to a worthy cause.

On the fourth day the customers turned. When Ray got to work Tuesday morning, he saw the first long white piece of register tape stuck to the automatic entrance door, a receipt in the amount of $122.89 from Wegman's. Stop & Shop and Star receipts, even one Great Foods, followed. Ray couldn't imagine a more eloquent statement of Bounty Bag's lost revenue and of the sacrifices made to punish Ray's store.

Ray turned to the protestors, olive branch in hand. After school Doreen helped him fill the front windows with the enormous slogan that'd come to him the previous night in a dream.

WE ARE BOUNTY BAG, they wrote in red paint-chalk.

It would be just like Mom had said. Words—words and *reading*—would save him.

But by day's end the associates had smashed hundreds of eggs against the windows.

FLASH! FLASH! A news photographer caught Ray standing behind the egg-soaked windows.

That night Ray and Gary wheeled out a cart of hot drinks and old rolls toasted with cheese and wrapped in aluminum. Most campers rebuffed them, but a small group huddled at a fire drum snatched greedily at their food with fingerless-gloved hands. They were willing to talk, and he listened to their woes. Chesley had—punitively, illegally—put a stop on last week's paychecks, and the squeeze was on. The two-associate families had it the worst. In one of them, while the wife camped, the husband went door to door asking for dollars to sweep sidewalks, put out family garbage pails, or, calling on an old talent, do oil-painting portraits.

By now the protests were general across the chain. A last token of lingering trust remained at Store #28 though: the associates hadn't removed their keys from Ray's Faraday cage. Occasionally an associate or group of them emerged from the Pnyx and cycled through the store to get warm.

What the Higher-Ups Were Doing

D R. CHONG MONITORED WITH GROWING ALARM the supermarket war that threatened to swallow Pennacook's essential taxpayer and all hope for a new Andy Johnson High.

First there were the self-destructive protests that were driving it all. On TV, "44 *Action* News" broadcast dangerously naïve grocery workers driving their gravy train right into the gravy. All of the chain's other stores had followed Tewksbury, Billerica, and Pennacook into the parking lot. To Dr. Chong's surprise, the reins at the giant Pennacook store behind AJMHS had passed to the puppyish Ray Markham boy, now plugged in as some sort of hate-inspiring substitute manager. Talk about promotion beyond your capacity!

Meanwhile, warring Martinis gathered at the John Hancock Tower, to schedule, convene, and walk out on meetings, the corporate death-spiral commencing. Angie Martini wanted her job back, but Dr. Chong couldn't tell if Angie fully supported the associates' goals, which included banning automatons, a powerful new profit center according to the papers.

The other side, Chesley's, was cagier still, but its basic business aims were more comprehensible to Dr. Chong, who'd tussled all her life for control. The board-appointed management, those folks one step below a conference-room invite to the John Hancock, stressed that their "number one priority" was to persuade employees to "come home to Bounty Bag." Or as the company's replacement CEO put it, shrieking at Angie loyalists over company loudspeakers, "Get back to work!"

That man made the *Lowell Post* the next day, in a syndicated piece picked up from an extremely casual trade paper called *Supermarket Happenings*.

Tough day at the office, fella? Tell that to Bounty Bag CEO Conor Tweed!

It's been only days since Bounty Bag fired Angie and all is not well with her replacement. We caught up with Mr. Tweed at the Spalding Rehabilitation Hospital in Cambridge, Massachusetts, where he is currently recovering from a fractured femur incurred when he slipped on a banana peel in the company cafeteria.

"First day was touch-and-go, but now I feel I'll be hitting my stride."

Er, once he's walking again, that is!

In a related development, the last few Angie loyalists at the company's Wilmington headquarters tendered their resignations amid ongoing associate protests.

Chesley's people paid lip service to a "return to normalcy," but what they mainly wanted—this made perfect sense to Dr. Chong—was to sell their profitable chain and retire. While the board stonewalled Angie in one Vines Hay conference room, in the next one over it interviewed Hoggly Woggly, Albertson's, and three other chains and invited corporate valuations and bids from each.

The protestors were misguided, but their core demand was clear and insistent: it was Angie or no one. This being the one hard fact, Dr. Chong had to face its implications. How much was this supermarket really worth without Angie? The land it sat on. And if Bounty Bag was practically worthless, then so too were Pennacook and her school.

But her work was done. The TCO was one day off, and it was in the voters' hands now—theirs and Bounty Bag's. On Election Day, she planned to sleep in.

Meanwhile, Tommy appeared in her kitchen doorway, bow in hand, requesting another driving tour through the mean streets of Pennacook.

Patrick Returns

ON MONDAY HE SLIPPED OUT BEFORE DAWN SO he could be seen walking into the school from Worcester Road instead of emerging from Kyle Gherkin's office. He ran track after school, just like normal, then showered in the locker room and, carrying his clarinet, walked as far away from town center as he could for dinner. Then he circled back to the school to feed his turtles and sleep under their light. His kiddie bike was busted, and anyway he liked walking better. Each night he had ventured farther, and on Tuesday he made it all the way to Oakhurst, stopping twice along the way.

The first stop was for basketball with eight-year-old brother-and-sister twins, who hailed him to join their game on the Pike Middle blacktop. Carol and Harold quickly succumbed to frustration and fell to bickering, confirming Patrick's long-held belief that it was impossible for elementary-school kids to enjoy regulation-height basketball.

"What's that?" Patrick asked to distract them, and he pointed to two white trash bags leaning on the park bench.

"That's our animals," Carol said.

"Wanna see?" Harold asked.

With the deep feeling of their kind, Carol and Harold dived right in, showcasing their projects to Patrick. Distraction was one of the favored techniques in Ray's psychology worksheets. They told you to use it to escape bad feelings, and it was startling when it worked well, as it seemed to be doing with Carol and Harold. But how did an older person decide which bad things he should just distract himself from and which he needed to pay attention to even more *because* they felt bad? He didn't want to end up the kind of person who, say, distracted himself for five-plus years from the fact that he hated making deli sandwiches just so he could die without having to admit it and make a career change. Ray's books were full of such logical holes.

Carol had softened her hyena with doe eyes and a gently lapping tongue, and she had dedicated one thick poster margin to debunking hyena myths that unfairly maligned the species (Myth #2: "hyenas are just stupid scavengers"). While Carol demonstrated her findings, twin-brother Harold scuffed his shoes and spread a dust cloud over the three of them — he really seemed like a younger brother. Harold had been relegated to the lowly, nearly harmless garter snake of North America, but he valiantly tried to macho up his randomly assigned animal, highlighting its lesser-known powers such as venom, which they had though it was weak and couldn't kill you (more like it numbed your fingertip for a half-hour), and squeezing, which like king cobras they did (but again the effect was rather mild).

Patrick bade them farewell. "Go home. It's late."

He walked off and went *pffft pffft pffft* with his teeth pulled over his bottom lip to deter boars.

He walked about a mile and sneaked into the old abandoned shoe mill overlooking Micassic Falls, swung his legs out over the water, and put his clarinet together. He streamed a play-a-long rhythm section on his smartphone and played "Ain't Misbehavin." After that he did the "One Dime Blues" without accompaniment. He didn't know the dominant 7th and other chords he'd need to improvise on "One Dime," but he ran through the melody on the clarinet and sang all the verses in a high-pitched, miniaturized tone that imitated the way Blind Lemon Jefferson sounded on his antique recordings. He switched over to the G-blues scale and let loose for the boars and for Mr. Grant. He started crying and felt dumb about it.

It was closing in on midnight when he reached the Kluck Klucker, his second stop. An old man at the counter drank coffee, his dog asleep, tied to his stool. Patrick splurged, seating himself at one of the dining-room tables where they waited on you. His waitress, unusually, was an African American girl. She looked like his classmate Doreen Robinson, because she was.

"What are you doing here? I thought you worked for Ray."

"I got three jobs now," she said, and smiled at his reaction. "Don't you worry! It's just practice."

"Ray says I should work, but I don't want to work for him."

"He needs you." She wiped her hands on her apron. "That's all I'll say."

"Mr. Grant," Patrick began, but his stupid shoulders shook and he couldn't breathe.

"I know." She sat down next to him and rubbed the center of his back.

He kept the sobs down but when he looked up she was watching him curiously.

"You gotta sleep," she said.

"My next stop."

With a diet soda to sluice the ol' meat-chute, he shamelessly devoured a juice-dripping orange piece of chicken, his vegan better self, reflected in the window, sneering at him all the while. The bill came and he paid a 40% tip, one percent for each acre they'd failed to grant Doreen's Alabama ancestors in the Reconstruction Role Play. It may sound silly, given his own lot as a homeless sloppy schmuck and when the recipient was a really together person like Doreen, but it was at least as morally defensible as doing nothing. Plus the chicken he'd eaten, he'd probably stolen. And if he was honest with himself, since it was Ray's money, it sort of counted less. Easy to play the big shot for Doreen.

He heard Mr. Carbonara, Kluck Klucker's sous chef, out back berating Doreen for some failure or slight. Imagined, Patrick was certain. He'd forgotten that guy worked here and his raging voice drove Patrick to the exit.

The door bells jangled, releasing him from this slaughter pen. Kluck Klucker was the last business open at this hour for a solid mile in either direction. It was pitch black—"stygian," as the SAT might say—but for the starry vault. He kept to the road's edge, with one foot on the pavement and the other in the dirt to keep his place, using the last of his smartphone battery to light his shoes down the first hill and then it died. The cold silent pocket of December seemed to open all at once and his nostrils stiffened to a crust. The welcome smells of mud and river, which had risen from the ground during the warm patch, vanished, sucked off into space. He felt closer to space, as though winter had shucked the Earth of its atmosphere, leaving only its crust and his scraping shoes. He pulled his hands up high into his coat sleeves except for one index finger hooked around the clarinet's handle.

There were lights up ahead. They came closer, and he was caught.

"What are you doing out here at this hour?"

"Just walking, Principal Chong. Walking and playing my clarinet. What's that thing your friend's got?"

"Bow," the young man said. He aimed it at the stars.

"This is my nephew Tommy."

"We're boar hunting," Tommy said sheepishly.

"You came to the right place."

"Where you headed?" Dr. Chong asked.

"Bounty Bag." He squinted up the road. "Gone to check on my brother."

"Get in."

He hopped in back of her Mini, which was cramped and overheated.

"This is a small car," he said. He tried to sound light but it came out loud and rude. "Sorry," he added, too quiet and polite.

"Can you just lemme off here?"

"This is far from the store."

"This is the lot. It's where we meet."

"When?"

"He's late. Don't stick around and worry about me," he said. "He's—kind of a jerk about being really late like that," he added, thinking he needed to lose these two.

Dr. Chong pulled over, and Patrick gave the wide-eyed, amiable Tommy a vigorous handshake. Then the devil grabbed ahold of him and he invaded the front seat, giving Dr. Chong a firm hug and smooching her on the cheeks, a la Dorothy Gale greeting Queen Ozma in *The Emerald City of Oz*. It was nothing more than a French hello, but the stunned principal's head bounced back against the seat and her jaw dropped.

"Thanks for the ride," he said, hopping out.

Funny, you didn't think of principals as fully human but it turned out they were, at least in the outside world when they had other people around to soften them. Maybe Principal Chong was Tommy's hyena project, and Tommy her garter snake.

Back at AJMHS, Patrick urinated in a stall beside a note informing him that this was where Napoleon came to rub his bone apart. In the next stall over, a boar lapped at a toilet. Ghosts in chains slumped ever closer. Kyle Gherkin's ceiling dripped fluid and the ambient spooky sounds swelled. The sounds penetrated his ear plugs and curled through his brain, killing his focus and making it impossible to continue with *The Boxcar Children #15: Bicycle Mystery*. He'd bet dollars to doughnuts that the vibrations of Muscles Carbonara's soundtrack bothered even his deaf turtles.

He decided to check the headlines and plopped into the beanbag with his laptop. He had gathered that Ray's job might be in trouble, due to some dispute involving his eccentric boss, Angie Goode Martini, and wondered if it had made the papers.

To his shock, Ray was right there on the front page of the *Lowell Post*. This was big enough, but when he clicked around he found Ray's image on the *Pennacook Beat*, the *Worcester Gazette*, and, buried a few sections in, even the *Boston Globe*. It was the same photo in each publication. Ray stood behind a smeared glass wall of egg and something illegibly drawn in chalk. His whole body wept egg.

"WHO IS BOUNTY BAG?" the *Lowell Post*'s headline asked.

The journalist explained that the smashed eggs had visually obscured the "WE ARE BOUNTY BAG" message that Ray had painted. She speculated that, by writing "We," Ray had meant to refer to himself and his allies, not to Bounty Bag associates as a whole, and she interpreted the egging as a violent rebuke. The other papers followed. Civil war, not protest or rebellion, was the theme they hit on. The protestors, according to the storyline (comments suggested the public agreed), were supporting Angie, the humble-looking woman on their posters, but they had a committed and shrewd foe in Ray Markham of Pennacook. The store manager, it was reported, was a Chesley stalwart, willing to court his colleagues' undying wrath in the interest of principle. Which principle was that? No one seemed to know or approve.

Ray was sure making a mess of things. Patrick felt an unexpected surge of energy and packed up and decamped once more. He crossed the baseball diamond, lighting a small space in front of him with his recharged phone and going *pffft pffft pffft*. At the river he slipped his arms through the duffel-bag handles and made it into a backpack, fell belly-down on a log, and shimmied across to the other side. Then it was up the last hill to Truble Cove. His other key got him in the store and he slipped into their bathroom with his box of dye, scissors, and a comb.

The Supermarket Revolution

A MAN IN BLACK ON A BLACK ELECTRIC MOUNTAIN bike stormed through the Pnyx, splattering the tents. He rode up the grand central lane to the store, hand-delivered a pouch to Ray, then zipped around the camp and out the exit to Worcester Road. Dawn had not yet broken on the fifth day of protests.

The letter told Ray of a major delivery planned for the afternoon, enough groceries to re-stock fully. The *last* truck would drop its ramp and unload a full staff of scabs. The scabs would march off the truck and into Ray's store, already uniformed and armed with pricing guns and gleaming new mops. They'd "secure" the store and take "reasonable measures" to clear the lot. With Store #28 as their foothold, scab forces would swarm the other Bounty Bags, all across New England. And the war would be over.

It went without saying that Ray was to cooperate, but Chesley said it anyway, reminding Ray that Warehouse had the keys and could get into Loading without him.

"Bounty Bag is *back!*" Chesley wrote at the end of the letter.

Supermarket Happenings and the protestors' blogs updated Ray on corporate negotiations. A reporter asked Chesley what he thought of the protests, and he gave a mushy answer that didn't really respond to the question.

"I'm not going to comment on hypotheticals at this point in time," he said. "As we move forward," he added meaninglessly.

Bleh.

As Ray suspected, Angie was trying to buy the company herself—and facing stiff resistance. Angie had written that she would personally pay the *pre*-protest value of $4b, and three governors—Massachusetts, Rhode Island, and Maine—penned a joint letter asking, in a non-binding sort of way, that the board "weigh and consider" Angie's bid. The other chains' valuations of Bounty Bag Grocers, Inc., started off larger than Angie's, ranging from $4.1b all the way up to $5b.

But their corporate accountants exhausted another eraser with every passing day of protests as they chased Bounty Bag's declining value down to zero. According to the latest rumor, Angie and Hoggly Woggly were the sole remaining suitors. "The Hog" dangled a higher price but had one eye trained to John Hancock's emergency-exit stairwell.

It was Election Day in Pennacook and, as it happened, a snow day for the schools. Soon after the man on the electric bike, T.A.P.S. staff arrived to open up their storefront for voting and Pennacook contractors lugged in the machines and started working out some of the limb-imperiling kinks. An unfamiliar Asian man was among the town's staff but he stood outside with what appeared to be a compound bow and stared off wistfully to the boars, which were patrolling the ridgeline and snorting through the campground refuse.

Excused from school, Doreen Robinson braved the budding storm to join them. Meanwhile, a cash-strapped Bonnie MacNutt crossed the protest line that morning to retake her place at Register Four. An early-bird Penny came through the line, and Bonnie, referring to a weekly special that the customer had failed to exploit (two two-liters for 99¢ each), asked: "Do you *like* Coke products?" The special was a regular in the rotation, and Ray must have heard Bonnie MacNutt use this line a dozen times. Now its familiarity brought him solace (though it didn't work), and he had visions of a return to normality—a temporary return, of course, in light of the stocking robots.

He still fretted that Angie, not Chesley, was behind Old Blue Eyes. She must have concluded that the end of supermarket life was upon them. Supermarkets had once ended the small family grocers that Angie had ruminated upon in the gloomy pocketbook note that Stan had uncovered. Now Old Blue Eyes would retire the big chains too. Of course, if automation was their destiny—if the supermarkets would now obsolete themselves, effectively transforming their own stores into self-serve warehouses—then Ray preferred to have Angie guide them gently into the furnace. But it wouldn't make much difference in the end. That's why he still felt, despite Chesley's greedy machinations, that the protestors mine—*might* as well come back in and work. At least they could make some money in the meantime.

He had another reason for keeping the store lights on. He shared it with Patrick after discovering him in the freezer, sleeping with dead chickens and nearly frost-bitten — and after dealing with this chicken-theft business.

Ray melted Patrick with a cup of hot water, a bowl of instant chicken-flavored rice-and-sauce mix, and a steaming bowl for his feet. When Patrick turned pink, Ray ordered him up the rope ladder to Interrogation.

"Just what the hell were you thinking, stealing my chickens? Do you know I could call the police?"

"It wasn't about the money, not like you think. I tried to pay it back."

"You're a day late and a dollar short!"

"I know."

"And I want every red cent back. Do you hear me, buster?"

"I don't have it."

"What about all that cash I left you? I guess nothing's ever enough for *you*."

"I know. I was just…"

"What?"

"*Angry* and trying to hurt you, I guess. 'Get your attention,' like your books say."

"What books?" Ray asked, but he knew. This language could have been lifted from any of several volumes on rebellious teens that he kept in The Rock's built-in bookshelf. Nearly everything, it seemed, was a "cry for help" to these authors, which made perfect sense. Except when the one doing the crying was fully aware he was doing it, and why, yet did it anyway, and made excuses.

"You should know better," Ray said. "In fact, it sounds like you did. How many times have I said it? We need to stick together. We're all we have now."

"I'm sorry I left."

"Why did you do it?"

"I needed a break. And I guess I wanted more."

"More what?"

"More than 'all we have.' More than you."

The golden-striped purple manager's coat was a sham. He wasn't qualified to wear it. To manage a store or to be a brother's parent. He'd always thought Patrick was the viscous one, the gentle-lamb brother who stuck to you and wouldn't wipe away. Turns out he had it all backward. All Ray's Hawaiian daydreams had been nightmares, visions of a change that he simply could not handle. Like he couldn't handle any other change, including Patrick's leaving.

"How's the drinking?" he counter-attacked, instinctively feeling for the moral high ground. "Still trying out for 'Father' from *The Boxcar Children*?" *Or Dad*, he resisted adding, to spare them both.

"I quit. The day I left you, I practically quit."

Ray couldn't say why, but he knew this was true.

"So what do we do now?" he asked.

Patrick touched his raven-black hair. "I was hoping I could work here. Like you said."

Ray thought of giving him another lecture, about the impossibility of hiring a thief to work in his store, particularly after they'd just canned *The* Alfredo and Muscles Carbonara for the same scheme. But Ray was practically alone and could use extra staffing to help take in the massive delivery, absorb the replacement staff, and cope with today's parking-lot rally, the largest ever planned for Truble Cove.

He unhooked an apron and threw it at Patrick.

"Today only. And only because it's an emergency. No thief works in my store."

"Great," Patrick said sarcastically, but he put on the apron.

By 10 the gently falling snow had swollen into soft clouds that fell blue under the lights, blanketing the Pnyx. Ray took Patrick outside with the wide broom, the salt bag, and the shovel. Midway through his explanation of how to clean up out front, Patrick interrupted him.

"Can I ask *you* something, Ray? What exactly are you hoping to accomplish here?"

"What do you mean? We're clearing the sidewalk."

"I mean, why aren't you out there with them?"

He pointed to the camp.

"I am with them. I bring them coffee and extra food every night." Ray considered explaining about the Inventory robots and his fatalistic calculation that they were all better off coming back inside and working and maybe thinking about revamping their skill sets to include robot repair. But the other reason seemed more direct. "Like them," he said carefully, "I prefer to have Angie in charge. She's always taken care of us and generally lets us do what we want in the store."

"Within limits," Patrick interrupted, pointing at his head.

"But *Chesley*," Ray nearly spat out, "would rather *end* us than return control to his sister. Lose billions instead of share. That's how deep his aggression runs."

Patrick thought about this. "Chimp, not bonobo," he said mysteriously.

"That being the case," Ray continued, "it's crucial that we keep this store open. If we shut down, everybody loses. Chesley, yes, but also Angie, me, and that whole encampment of brave, loyal associates. Our only hope is to keep this place open, and if we're lucky Angie will get it back somehow."

"So you think the protestors are just playing into Chesley's hands."

"I think they're applying pressure," he corrected. "And while I'm not sure it's even worth it"—he paused, deciding again not to bother explaining the more subtle robot issue—"I'm here to make sure it's no *more* pressure than the store can handle. We need to stay open."

Big Jim Tuohy, one of their long-time sackers, saw Ray and Patrick standing out front with the snow-removal equipment and stepped out under a lamppost. He grinned and waved his arms wildly at them until he got their attention—and then his face turned to stone.

"Hey! Yo! Yo, hey, Ray! Hey, *fuck you*, Ray! *Fuck you!*"

"They don't seem to get it," Patrick said.

T.A.P.S. opened at 11 A.M., and Pennies lined up to vote. Question One asked if they'd override the tax limit to fund the demolition of Andrew Johnson Memorial High School and build a replacement. Question Two asked the opposite, if they'd lower the current tax cap, precluding a new school and probably a lot of other projects.

Ray was dimly aware of the record-breaking low turnout ordinarily seen in Pennacook and was surprised, especially considering the snow storm, at the initial brisk traffic to the T.A.P.S. voting station. It was mostly Bounty Bag campers at first. But something of their spirit must have moved through the town because after they departed the line only grew and didn't let up for the rest of the day. For or against, Pennies were turning out.

Ray passed the baton to Gary Snow so he could vote.

"Keep this kid busy," he said to Gary, putting his hand on Patrick's shoulder.

"Hey, Ray? After you get back, I'm leaving."

"Sure, Gary. We all need to vote."

Bounty Bag gave employees up to a half-day paid leave for voting.

"Not just that."

"You're leaving me?"

"I'm *joining them*."

"I'll give you $200 to stay."

"Keep it. You'll need it."

"I'm giving it to you anyway."

Ray removed the cash wad and peeled off ten twenties. Gary waved him off, but Ray folded the bills, stuffed them in Gary's pocket, and gave the pocket a gentle pat.

"I always wanted to do that," Ray said.

Gary have him the old Gary Snow smile. "No hard feelings."

Ray slumped off to vote. T.A.P.S. staff hovered while he read the questions carefully and answered. He voted "yes" on Question One. It'd be nice to get a new high school for the kids. He voted "no" on Question Two, as logic required given his answer to Question One. He slid his ballot into the machine, but his sleeve caught and the machine reeled him in. He yanked hard and finally tore his sleeve loose from the machine's gnashing teeth and listened apprehensively to its gears' angry crank as the box began to rumble like an overloaded washing machine. It was as if the box understood, but objected to, Ray's answers. Ray backed away, feeling the heat coming off the thing as a black smoke plume rose from its backside. Finally the box settled back to the floor and a purple bulb on the top lit up, marking the end of the machine's fit and its surrender.

A T.A.P.S. banner above the door read, "NO TAXIS, EVER." Ray opened the door, stepped out and *FWOOMP!* — an arrow shot past and smacked wetly into the side of a boar just steps away.

Ennngh! squealed the boar. *Eeeennnngg!*

FWOOMP! went another arrow, piercing the boar's head with a thud and the boar fell over.

The man with the compound bow swept past Ray and crouched over the fallen boar, pressing two fingers deep into its neck.

"Good," he said. "Her suffering's over."

He turned his head and looked up at Ray.

"I usually get them on the first shot, but it was too risky. I didn't want to hit you."

Ray nodded and edged away. Back at the store, he watched the young man conferring with Mr. Robinson under a lamppost, just within the Pnyx's tidy border.

"I've been thinking about what you said and it sounds like *BO-LOG-NA.*"

They were in the breakroom eating 25¢ hot dogs and BBQ chips and drinking root beers. Ray's one rebellion had been to dismantle the "U.R. Kind Dogs" promotion, including the criminal pricing. Mangled old magazines were scattered randomly about the breakroom like shot birds.

Ray slurped his root beer. "Continue."

Patrick was wearing Gary's foresworn green jacket, which, a mere week ago, had been Ray's. He leaned back and bobbed annoyingly in the chair, folding his hands behind his head and staring up at the wall behind Ray.

"You said your job is to keep the place open because Chesley would rather shut the place down than sell it to Angie. If you keep it open, at least Angie will have some time to buy it, to bid against Hoggly Woggly."

"That's right."

"But you're assuming Chesley has no feelings for his sister."

"That's a fact. Not an assumption."

"Be that as it may, you're *also* assuming that he'd rather starve himself than share a little bit of food."

"So to speak."

Patrick pushed his foot against the table, suspending the front chair legs in the air.

"I'll say this. You're not much of an 'optimist.'"

He hoisted the word optimist high above his head in scare quotes. It was like he already knew what Ray was likely to say next, that "optimism" of the kind he was talking about had little or nothing to do with the kind of "stay on the sunny side" optimism of the naïve past. It was more complicated than that. It involved at least three Ps, a couple of Ds and Rs, practical exercises, and copious, well-thought-out checklists. But just when Ray was going to cut him off with this analysis, Patrick pressed deeper with his attack.

"You always say 'tend your garden.'"

"Cultivate your garden."

"Whatever. Same thing. Well, that doesn't tell you how big your garden is. Is this your garden?" Patrick reached across the table and flicked Ray's name tag. "Is this?" He pinched Ray's jacket at its striped shoulder. "This godforsaken room? This store? This state? This country? All of humankind? Animals?"

"What are you getting at?"

"This is America in the twenty-first century." Once more he precariously leaned his chair back, front legs loose in the air. "Forced to choose, most people would rather make money than harm other people. That may not sound like much of an accomplishment, but I'd say it's the base minimum of what this country stands for. It's historically correct."

The image of Turbo Boy, so anxious but only until he'd gathered his load, flashed through Ray's mind.

"'Without a struggle, there can be no progress.' It's from your own quotes book."

"Frederick Douglass."

"Listen," Patrick continued. "If Chesley is anywhere close to the national average, if he's not some kind of criminal cartoon like you make him out—well, then I think he'll bite."

"Bite what?"

"Angie's offer. *If it's the only one he's got.* If I were you? I'd shutter this joint." He slammed down his chair's front legs and, leaning forward, made a scattering motion with his arms. "Drop the fence and drive off The Hog."

Two things happened at about the same time that afternoon. A mushroom cloud rose from Andy Johnson and a team of some thirty men wearing the same ninja-like costume as the pouch-delivery boy slipped into the back end of the lot and mounted the Tiger 204s. A couple of inches of fresh snow had accumulated. The protestors had shoveled clear their makeshift camp-roads, but the rest of the lot was a long blue sheet. Between the snow sheet and the Pnyx, associates had constructed a thick barricade from pinewood pallets and assorted supermarket debris. Chesley's forces would want to push through the barricade to dismantle the camp and make room for customer parking. If Chesley's latest threat was sincere — of this Ray had no doubt — they'd also be taking dead aim at the protestors, using "reasonable force" to evict them.

"My turtles," Patrick said.

They were standing out front watching the Tiger 204s' lights come on and their engines fail.

"What?"

"I gotta go to the high school, Ray. My pet turtles are burning."

"You can't," Ray said. *I need you,* he thought.

"I have to. Besides, I've told you. There are reinforcements coming. They promised."

Ever since lunch, Patrick had been out at the Pnyx, working the crowd. He had strategically swapped Gary's green coat for the humble sacker's apron, darkened now with melted snow. Ray unhitched Gary Snow's walkie-talkie and handed it to him.

"You know how to use this?"

"You think I'm an idiot?"

Patrick snatched the walkie-talkie and sprinted back into the snow. Doreen Robinson appeared at Ray's elbow wearing Toothless Mary's battered bronze-striped green coat. Beside her, Toothless Mary wore a stocker's blue coat in lieu of her green one. *The* Alfredo stepped up behind them, towering in his thick-heeled snow boots and the pink karate uniform with the orange belt.

"Kwee help?" he asked.

Patrick liked the smell of burning leaves. The practice was illegal but widespread in Pennacook. It kept away the boars and, for those not possessed of *The Take-Home Message*'s "Rake-A-Mania," was easier than hauling leaves out back. The Markhams' yard was a postage stamp, so they didn't have this chore to contend with, but Patrick had ample exposure, while training for the two-mile, to aromatic leaf smoke, wood smoke, and burning turf.

Andrew Johnson's smell was different: charred meat and chemicals and plastics. Nauseated, Patrick had to pause while crawling over the log to cross the river to the baseball field. He reached the field and hopped the fence in one quick sideways swing that felt almost glamorous until his pant-leg caught on the fence-top and tore at the calf. His shoes sank into the snow and muck but he pounded through the last of it, spilling out onto the blacktop and rushing toward the burning school. His skin throbbed and his eyes peeled as a hot gust howled down his throat. He reached the entrance, tripped over the steps, and slammed into the steel doors.

"Keys keys. Keys keys keys." He found the master key, inserted it, and grabbed the handle. "Ow! Hot! Hot!"

The door wouldn't open all the way but he wedged inside and hurtled down the hall to Mr. Gherkin's office.

He was too late for A. Lincoln and Satchmo. A falling ceiling tile had knocked the terrarium off the counter and smashed the turtles together in a mound of glass and mud. A boar reeking of blood and bacon, smoke rising from its hide, greedily snapped at their scrambled flesh. But Eleanor Roosevelt had somehow survived and stood at Patrick's toes, looking at them.

Patrick scooped her up.

"Ow! Ow! Hot!!"

He tucked the scalding Eleanor Roosevelt in his apron's kangaroo pouch.

Brrrrscht! went his walkie-talkie.

"Sorry, Ray. No time to speak," he whispered, as loudly as he could.

He headed for the door—only to stumble upon Muscles Carbonara in his Boy Scout uniform. He'd apparently paused mid-inferno to recover one of Mr. Grant's stray fentanyl wands and lodge it in his cheek. But it—or the smoke—had knocked him out. Something lower down caught Patrick's eye. Oh, Christ. Muscles Carbonara's legs had caught fire.

Ray and his Deli crew waited 1.2 seconds for the automatic door to open, then burst into the store and bolted for the Faraday cage.

"*You. You. You. You.*" Ray handed out four car-key sets to Doreen.

"*You. You. You. You.*" Four more to Toothless Mary.

He distributed another four to *The* Alfredo, then five to himself.

"Aw, hell." He dumped the Faraday cage's contents on the table and, drawing on a slogan they'd used for the pre-packaged lunch case, shouted: "Just grab! *Grab-'n'-go! Grab-'n'-go!*"

Ray would've tried to enlist the cars' owners but they were entrenched in the camp and only Deli trusted him now.

They ran out the front doors, weaving in and out of the camp. Eggs smashed around Ray and as he danced through the yolk the associates showered him with insults and names.

"Traitor!"

"Brutus!"

"Benedict Arnold!"

"Eazy-E!"

"Nah, Eazy was all right."

They made it to the associate quadrant, the one politely distant from the store entrance to allow customers ample parking close to the store, "generous" parking, as Chesley's latest cloying directive would have it. Confusion reigned. Which car went with which key?

"I got the Suburban!"

"Who's got the Chevy!?"

"Impala ready to roll!"

Outraged associates railed at them.

"Hey, asshole! That's my car!"

"I can't believe it. He's finally crossed over the line into stealing."

The front line of cars bumped forward into the snow. It was coming down hard now and Ray, inside a beat-up Nissan Maxima from the late '90s, slipped over a hardened old mound onto a rough, icy plane. Only one of the low-quality Tiger 204s had started up, but it had moved swiftly, clearing a thick snow-wedge between the Tigers and the Pnyx.

Boars had gathered on the Tiger side of the pockmarked ice-plane and were tentatively hoofing their way out to explore. Others dotted the ridgeline, the cheap seats for the unfolding drama. But the largest group of all that night, as Ray would later piece together from associate accounts, marauded through the Pnyx. They picked over garbage and poked into tents, flaring their mouths and flashing baby-banana tusks and purple dripping gumlines. Terrified, the associates clung to flaming trash-drums and swung sticks to ward off attack.

The Maxima fishtailed and threatened to spin around but Ray regained balance and shot off over the edge to the snow. Snow brushed the car's underside as he crossed beyond the last lamppost into the void, where a light-devouring silence descended.

He checked the rearview mirror. Toothless Mary's orange troll-hair and her sunglasses wobbled above her steering wheel and she neighed with glee as she sped the Impala through the ice-plane. *The* Alfredo—after all a great driver—barreled a ramshackle beige GMC Suburban with a "HERE COMES TROUBLE!" bumper sticker around Toothless Mary and joined Ray at the hip, flashing a thumbs up. Ray returned the gesture with unexpected joy. Doreen Robinson eased through the snow in a green Volkswagen Golf. Like a seasoned cowgirl she herded them with grace to the Golden Mile.

Patrick hitched up his pouch to secure Eleanor Roosevelt and dived back into Mr. Gherkin's office. He wrapped a hand in a rag, opened the fire-axe case, and removed the axe. Back in the hall, he crouched in front of Muscles Carbonara's motionless gut, noting from the green-and-golden badge that his fellow Scout had finally made Second Class. Patrick gripped the axe, jumped, and swung hard at the exposed blue water pipe.

Whack! Whack!

Nothing happened. He bent over and heaved but nothing but hot air came out. He rose again with the axe.

Whack whack whack!

The pipe split open and water gushed down into the hall, a long red line of flame extending from Mr. Gherkin's office to the cafetorium.

Recalling proper fire-safety techniques from the Fireman's Chit, Patrick loosened Eleanor Roosevelt's pouch and untied his Bounty Bag apron. While he doused Muscles Carbonara's flaming legs with the still-damp apron, Eleanor Roosevelt rested on his friend's still chest.

"Come on, Muscles Carbonara! Wake up! *Wake up!*"

He slapped his face. The bicep twitched. It suddenly occurred to Patrick that the bicep was the wrong muscle for JV shot put. You barely used it to hurl the shot! All that time in his basement Muscles Carbonara had been working the *wrong muscle.*

Patrick ran in a fury, water spewing and smoke all around, smashing at the pipe, cutting and hacking as far as he could make it. He got as far as Mr. Grant's before a swirling wall of flame and whirring metal from the boiler's direction made a joke of pressing farther. A *bang-metal-clang* rolled toward him. Behind that, a whoooosh like a waterfall or many-nozzled fountain. He swept up Eleanor Roosevelt in one arm. With the other, he mustered some kind of temporary superhuman strength to drag Muscles Carbonara by the ankle. He made it around the corner and out the rear doors to where a fireman, an ambulance, and three cops waited.

"Dick" was stitched into the fireman's jacket.

His walkie-talkie crackled.

"I'm okay, Ray," Patrick said, realizing it was true.

"Patrick." *Brzhhht.* "Get back. Over and out."

"Roger."

A broad passage, the Golden Mile led from the store's rear corner all the way to Unloading—and thence to the Outback and the shelves of Ray's store.

Patrick didn't have this specific idea, but Ray had to credit him for the revelation that destruction, not keeping the lights on, was their goal. Destroy the business, and Chesley might, just might, sell to Angie. Then Ray and the other associates could enjoy a couple more years of humane treatment before the robots took them down.

But how do you do it?

Ray thought he knew.

He moved deep into the Golden Mile. All was silent. Two conical lights on the roofline made whirling golden snow-clouds. The Maxima slipped again, this time over the edge of the tar into the boars' riparian empire between the store and the Pennacook River. He yanked the wheel too hard in the other direction and spun out facing the wrong way down the Golden Mile's entrance. *The* Alfredo also spun around but bobbed and rolled and sprung back into place. Ray shifted into reverse and, slowing to a crawl, eased the Maxima back toward Delivery's farthest loading door. He angled in and blocked the edge, then turned off the car and got out. *The* Alfredo slid the Suburban in beside him. Toothless Mary and Doreen followed.

Ray popped open the door and rushed them through the shimmering rectangle into the Outback. Seconds later they were squeaking across the lavender-and-egg-white tile floors — "I Yust Go Nuts at Christmas" playing again, seemingly in slow-mo — and Ray hurdled over a boar that had cleverly cracked open a tri-flavored-popcorn tin but then not-so-cleverly trapped its snout and most of its head in the tin, which it dragged down the canned-foods aisle like a shattered limb. At Registers they dodged five more feast-maddened boars and Ray threaded his crew through Chesley's wider-laned automated register to the exit area where, silently pressed together like polite elevator occupants, they again waited 1.2 seconds for the automatic door to buzz open — *bzzzhhht!* — then sprinted back out through the Pnyx to the distant associate lot and seized more cars.

Patrick easily dodged Pennacook's finest, including Fireman Dick, who was tending to Muscles Carbonara, and ran down the stairs to Hallenbuck Rink, where he mounted the Turtle, the school's luxe ice resurfacer, and inserted the funny-shaped key dangling from his

Andrew Johnson key chain. At 18 mph it was perhaps the fastest way back to the store and he had a rough idea how the equipment could be useful. He switched gears from RS—which he guessed meant the gear for resurfacing—to D for Drive, turned the Turtle around, and guided it up the ramp to Mediterranean Avenue, making a hairpin turn onto Worcester Road.

The Tigers were still having engine trouble. The black-clothed goons had dismounted and were busy with repairs. They watched warily as Ray and his crew drove the associate cars around back.

By now the protesting associates had figured out that something more than conspicuous mass car theft was afoot. With renewed swagger they muscled the boars aside and mounted the barricade to watch. Ray's group, exhausted and sweat-soaked, made the last trip out back, then joined the protestors. An unknown associate with a T-shirt with Ray's motto, "We Are Bounty Bag," embraced Ray and handed him a Bounty Bag cap. It was only then that Ray realized he'd lost his in the whirl of driving.

He thought of peeling out for Andrew Johnson but then eight Mack trucks pulled in, each bearing the Bounty Bag logo and slogan across its length. They slithered behind the Tiger 204s, headed toward the rear lot and Unloading.

Ray watched the first truck disappear around the side. Then the second. Then the third. When the fourth and fifth turned, he started to worry. Had they found a way around?

But then the sixth truck stopped, its ass hanging out, and the seventh halted behind it. The eighth truck barely nudged into the parking lot. Its scab driver turned off the engine and stepped out of his cab. In an unlikely gesture of defeat, he leaned on his truck and scratched a bare flank.

Ray updated Patrick on the walkie-talkie, and a moment later Patrick hailed back with his idea. Overhead, the snow clouds thinned and the moon broke through.

Some of the Tigers had finally gotten moving and started rolling toward the ice-plane. By the time Patrick turned in the lot, Ray had brought out the rack of fresh rolls, the afternoon batch still warm in the locker. He wheeled the rolls down to where the Tiger 204s were getting started. Pennacook boars leered from all sides.

"Howdy, guys!"

Ray waved at the goons, then slid out the rolls, tray by tray, and dumped them in a line before the Tigers. Starch-deprived boars bolted, coming down from the ridgeline and emerging from the Pnyx to brave the ice-plane.

Patrick entered from the side, behind the charging boars. Eleanor Roosevelt perched on the dashboard, looking about with gentle curiosity, as Patrick shifted to RS and aimed along the barricade's border. He made a clean, wet, slippery ice line that covered its length, then turned to the side and filled in the next line, and the next and the next.

The fresh ice trapped all but a few of the Pennacook boars in a thin margin with the Tiger 204s. Their feasting and the slippery, resurfaced ice halted the Tigers' advance, but one had made it around the side and bowled toward the Pnyx.

His own handiwork complete, Ray ran back to the camp.

The Tiger closed in. It scooped up some snow and pushed it to the side. The driver flipped on a spotlight, lifted a megaphone, and addressed them sternly.

"PER ORDERS OF CHESLEY MARTINI, YOU ARE ALL *TRESPASSERS*. LEAVE NOW OR REASONABLE FORCE SHALL, CAN, MUST, AND WILL BE USED TO REMOVE YOU."

The associates pummeled the Tiger with bits of garbage and shaken-up two-liters and with expired burger meat that Doreen Robinson had, in a moment of inspiration, carted out for this purpose.

"YOU HAVE BEEN WARNED!"

The Tiger made a loud crack and shot forward in one big rush, smashing through the barricade. Shattered wood crates burst into the Pnyx, planks shooting up in arcs like missiles and then a low groan and a kid was down and the crowd pinched and swelled and pulled back. The driver steered to a tent and jammed his plow through the darkened flaps and lifted the tent high and flung it. A cooler tumbled out and a propane stove and blankets. He jolted back and took aim at another, lit tent where shadows moved on the surface like puppets. He lifted his boot and the wheels turned and the crowd pushed forward but the driver kept rolling, until an arrow whizzed by Ray's ear and went *fwomp!*—right into the mini-plow's engine.

Fwomp! went another. It pierced the driver's calf.

"Ach!" screamed the driver.

Fwomp! came a third arrow, driving deep into a tire.

The driver jolted into reverse and backed out to the resurfaced ice-plane but his balance was off and the cabin tilted and toppled, crashing down on four squealing piglets. A sow charged in and tore at the driver's pant leg and the arrow-punctured calf, rooting in the wound.

"Oh!" screamed the driver. His hands flew up, straining to grip.

Fwomp! went a final, tragic arrow. Through the sow's brains.

The driver slipped out and cycled his forearms to climb from the wreck.

Staff from the Pennacook Walk-In, who for days now had been placidly watching the protests from their converted Pizza Hut, scrambled with gurneys toward the fallen child—just a slip and bruises after all—and the bleeding, crumpled driver. Mr. Robinson arrived in his boxy white barbecue truck and delicately eased the sow in.

"Closing time," called one of the miserly old ladies from the T.A.P.S. voting station. "No more voting!"

The Bounty Bag associates of Pennacook always had hockey skates at the ready and knowing a good thing when they saw it, they quickly laced up and glided onto the moonlit ice. Other Pennies caught wind of the fresh ice and converged on Truble Cove until it was packed with Pennies like any other free skate. Some time later Mr. Robinson returned with the sow. Dressed, butchered, and barbecued for feasting.

AFTER

Pioneers

RAY SPENT MOST OF THE NEXT DAY EMPTYING THE shelves of expired food, locking down the equipment, and closing down the store. When struggling customers like Jenn Harney showed up, Ray directed them to the Pennacook Food Pantry, where a newly responsive Dusty Grimes gave them double loads.

The other stores copied Store #28's tactics, blocking off Delivery with car jumbles and assembling pallet-barricades to backstop that. Revenue collapsed. Hoggly Woggly retreated to Dallas, Texas, its tail spiraled behind its legs, leaving Angie as the sole bidder. At the John Hancock Tower, Angie renewed her offer to buy the chain for its pre-protest value, and as Patrick had predicted, Chesley accepted.

In Deli, Ray re-hired a redeemed *The* Alfredo, and Toothless Mary came back to manage. Shorty's Rib Cage had a strong opening in the New Year, and as expected, Doreen Robinson resigned to join her father. As a direct result, Ray's Carolina Smoker was slated for retirement; that spring, they'd post it for sale. Stan, meanwhile, returned to the store and re-claimed his jacket, but he ordered a fresh one for Ray, naming him co-manager, with a part-time Deli presence.

News of the AJMHS explosion briefly went national. A distant aunt, recognizing Muscles Carbonara's authoritarian potential, took him in, supervised the rehab that was part of his sentence, and trained him to assistant manage the family's sweltering chocolate plant in Aiken, South Carolina. Patrick, who agreed for the time being to stay on as a sacker at Store #28, never again saw Muscles Carbonara.

On Presidents' Day, Toothless Mary sobbed through the grand opening of their new compactor, which heralded her dumpsters' removal. But she didn't quit. Angie pulled Ray aside after the ceremony to thank him.

"For what?" Ray asked, thinking he'd only done less than the others, and almost too late.

"Love. For all of the love you showed the people."

Ray couldn't ask the great woman directly, but immediately after the mildly androgynous CEO pulled her Ford Fiesta out of the lot, he jogged up the stairs to their shared office to confront Stan about the thing that'd been gnawing at him ever since the day Stan resigned.

"What's going to happen to us?"

"What do you mean?"

"With these robots."

The robot fleet had expanded. There were four of them already in Store #28 alone. Like Old Blue Eyes, two of the new ones were stockers, wearing blue jackets, their empty sleeves hanging. Another guy surveyed Inventory and generated polite, articulate reports on Expireds.

"Since we're co-managers now, you should fill me in on this stuff."

Stan smiled. "Not to worry."

"I am worried. We all are."

"Whoa whoa whoa, pal. You sound like you're getting ready to revolt again! It's normal time now, remember?"

"Pax Angie. I get it."

"Normal time" included that the smartphones, so useful in a rebellion, were sent back to the Faraday cage. But soon, Stan said, they'd loosen the regs so associates could use their phones for work stuff and emergencies and on break. "It's only humane. We're cutting them off from family and friend." They were expanding the company intranet, too. It would have e-mail accounts for all associates and comment boards for ideas and complaints. No more walkie-talkies. "Times change," Stan had said, removing his smartphone and aiming it at Ray. It showed Stan and his wife with their four kids on beach swings. "You should consider catching up. It ain't 2005."

Ray had his doubts about these changes. As if to up the ante, Stan now removed a piece of paper from his jacket pocket, unfolded it, and handed it over.

"THE ROBOT EQUATION," it said at the top.

Ray didn't understand all the symbols — it wasn't plain math — but right there at the bottom he found the dastardly grid projecting work hours.

"So you're going to reduce hours, cutting wage costs as the robots come online? I suppose this is better than firing people. But not by much."

"Look closer, my friend. Yes, we're reducing work hours, but not compensation. So, you see here, it's an immediate drop to 38.5 hours per week. That's full-time. By 2020, we're looking at 37 for full-timers. Maybe even lower, depending."

"Leisure time," Ray said with wonder.

"That's right. Do what you want with it. Climb a hill. Take the kids to the seashore."

Ray didn't know if the Robot Equation would work, but it was right in tune with Bounty Bag to try it. Why not? A century ago John Maynard Keynes, quoted in Groof, had called for something more.

But how would Bounty Bag keep up when the other chains automated? Forget about Chesley's chunky automated registers. With sensors working wonders in Great Foods labs, shoppers would soon avoid check-out altogether. Even *Supermarket Happenings* flashed concern.

Ray put these questions to Stan.

"Funny thing about the future," Stan said, looking down at the store floor. "More questions than answers, but we've always done well."

"I like Bonnie MacNutt and everything but I don't really like checking out," Ray admitted.

"Me neither."

A curtain of melancholy fell between them. Tearing through it, they switched topics and chuckled over the Hampton College "admission" packet that Ray had received in the mail and for some reason kept bringing up.

"Imagine a sucker like me going to college at my age."

" 'History is a nightmare from which I am trying to awake,' " was all Stan said.

"James Joyce."

"Well, Groof," Stan specified. "We really should double check these things."

"Or read the original books."

"Unlike you, my friend, I've never been a reader. Or 'thinker,' as Groof calls 'em."

"Too bad we don't have a real library in this town. I might yet convert you."

Stan only smiled.

The following week Hampton College's dean of admissions phoned Ray at the store. Dean Page somehow routed his call to Bounty Bag's sacred red line used for associate-hiring calls, which, Stan had assured Ray, would remain a fixture. He invited Ray to take a day off and bring his brother out to "sunny Western Mass" for "a little talk about this Hampton College business."

Ray gathered the basic picture and confronted Patrick in The Rock that night. It had begun, Patrick confessed, as an art project. What would a college application for his older brother look like? But gradually at first, and then very quickly, it snowballed to the point where it came to seem almost inevitable that he would take it all the way.

"You have to stop acting like these things just happen to you, like they are out of your control," Ray said.

"I know, but I didn't think you'd get in."

Now here they were, facing Dean Page in his office. Ray's most fervent hope was that by crying poor they could deter police involvement. Unless, of course, it was already too late.

"Who *did* apply to Hampton this year?" asked the dean, tenting his fingers.

Behind him in the window a crane moved beams into place. The dean also taught English and book towers surrounded him, with a small path for egress. Ray was impressed. Truth was, despite all his attachment to the medium, Ray did not count himself a good reader. Sure, he'd read Mom's standards, but he knew *The Bounty Bag Look* and Groof far better than *The Great Gatsby* or *My Ántonia*, and even these he had clung to, instead of branching out like a real reader, just as he'd clung to supermarket life, seeking permanence in both. But books were ships. Warships, Mom had said. They were motion and change, and Ray had been their foe. He wished he could have some more time to read, time to read rightly, and felt an animal yearning for the books piled around Dean Page and for the time he'd been spared with them.

"It's hard to say," Patrick said.

"He did, but with my materials. Some of them."

"Some of them," Dean Page repeated.

"The original scores were his, but I re-took it last spring—"
"Using *his* identification."
"Right. And then sent them to the school."
"Who wrote the letters?"
"I did."
"Whose grades do we have here?"
"His."
"Who made this?"
"Mine," Ray said.
"*Yours.*"

It was Ray's long-ago color-pencil drawing of his mother reading on a straw chair by the window. He'd won a school prize for it, but it lacked distinction. As with a sandwich, his goals had been accuracy and neatness. The drawing's only artistic virtue was integrity. Mom was sad again that day, and that's how she looked in his picture.

"And this?"
"Mine," Patrick said.

A little half smile pulled at the dean's mouth.

It was a baby in a onesie, painted in oil on a blue-and-white curtain. The painting was enormous and had cluttered The Rock for weeks until Ray forced Patrick to find it a new home at the school. A partly translucent belly had the immateriality of a hologram, but the thickly-painted parts, head and heart and limbs, were robust. The mass of the thing amplified both qualities, the immateriality and the robustness. To Ray it said something about the paradoxical vulnerability and resilience of babies, or of humans, or of life generally. Or maybe of just this one baby here. Ray had as usual found the wrong question where Patrick's art was concerned. "Who is it?" he had asked. Patrick frowned. "Who's *she*. I dunno. Mine."

"And who wrote this?"
"Me."
"And who drew that?"
"Him."

And so on. As they answered his questions Dean Page separated the materials into two neat piles. *Crash—boom—bang!* The crane dropped a beam.

"And, lastly."

"What's that?"

"*The Tiki Boom of Post-War Pennacook: A Study in Fantasy Nostalgia.* Received as an application supplement."

"Mine."

"Some high praise on here from a Mr. Grant."

Patrick looked down.

"And this other supplement—very late—about your, uh, dad's troubled history and how your brother 'sort of' saved you? 'Father of the Year,' I believe, is the title."

"Mine."

"I thought so. Listen, no college takes application fraud lightly. Even we Hampton eccentrics depend on our applicants to tell us the truth. That's how we make fair decisions. And when a liar slips by, well, it's more than a scandal. It's a crime. Not against the state, perhaps"—Ray sighed with relief; this meeting was just a time-waster, not a prelude to handcuffs and fingerprints—"but against the other applicants and, frankly, the whole exhausting process."

He furrowed his brow and raised his palms above the two piles.

"But there are big crimes and there are little ones. Now, *Patrick* has the higher test scores and the more impressive portfolio. Setting aside grades, a tertiary consideration here, he is the stronger candidate."

"Hear that, dummy?" Patrick elbowed him.

"But he is a high-school junior. We don't admit them. Ray, you've graduated from high school, and your application also would be strong. But you have no real letters of reference, outdated SAT scores, and no personal statement. In addition, neither of you has submitted a complete and honest application form. I cannot offer admission to Hampton."

"I get it," Ray said, rising. "Sorry for the mix-up. We couldn't afford this joint anyway. Besides, I like my job." He picked at Patrick's elbow. "Come on, let's go."

He did like his job but at some level knew he was running on fumes. As usual Stan had called it. Just yesterday, in fact. They were in his office reviewing Ray's most recent lackluster list of ideas for Bounty Bag improvements, lead among them a "Two-Stall Solution" that would relieve bathroom occupants of much of the psychological pressure to rush their business. Stan had set the plans aside and rested a hand on Ray's shoulder. "Stay as long as you like, buddy, but I don't think you're a lifer."

Dean Page didn't rise. Instead, he gestured for them to sit back down.

"I can't admit you *today*. But next year, all else being roughly the same, we'll eagerly welcome you both to the college."

Crash! Another beam landed in the pit.

"As for funding, well, let's just say it's not a factor in this case. Some people are lucky."

"What's that over there?" Patrick asked.

"Funny you should ask. That's our new library. There was a funding drought and for many months it was touch and go, but now all of that's cleared up and they're back at it like gangbusters."

Ray caught the mischievous tone. "What's it called?"

" 'C. Richard Groof Thinkers' Library.' We had suggested 'Stanislaus Martini,' but our patron had other notions. Anyhow, the grant came with several strings."

"Two of which sit before you today."

"Great," Patrick said. "We bribed our way in."

"Not at all. My decision on admission stands regardless. The money to pay for your time here, on the other hand…" He trailed off. Rousing himself, he slapped his thigh conclusively and rose. "Well then!"

Split Decision

SLANTING SNOW WET HER FACE AS DR. CHONG CROSSED Truble Cove, entertaining a play for the handsomeish Ray Markham boy, puppy-cute master of the chicken-salad sub. She had just wrapped up a round of after-school disciplinary hearings, the first ever convened at Andrew Johnson Memorial High School @ Bounty Bag Warehouse #2, and meting out punishment always roused her soul for feast and adventure.

Word from her secretaries, who'd done the paperwork for Patrick Markham's transfer, was that the brothers were hitching up their trailer and heading west into the sunset, albeit only as far as the Pioneer Valley. Ray was to open up the new store in Northampton, and next year they'd both enroll in college on some unheard-of supermarket grant, Ray held on retainer as the company's part-time editor-in-chief, whatever that meant in a grocery chain. Strange family; even stranger supermarket.

Now or never, she thought, approaching Bounty Bag. But just as she tripped the automatic door she spotted an admirer of her own, Archie Simmons, lurking behind a concrete beam in his track suit. Archie straightened himself, feigning a calf-stretch, then zipped up his jacket and calmly approached.

"It all worked out in the end."

"Worked out? Our school reeks of produce and diesel. It's one enormous room!"

"And we live to fight another day."

"Ever the optimist."

"Why not?"

Turnout had been heavy, and the TCO had passed. Graham Bundt at *The Beat* persuasively credited the Bounty Bag mojo for this. But by the slimmest of margins the *underride* passed too. The town applied the override first because it was the first ballot question, but then it applied the underride—which, small consolation, had received fewer votes—to this higher figure. The net result, absurdly, was a slight revenue-cap decrease. Hard times ahead.

There was good news too, however, surprisingly connected to both Bounty Bag and the destruction wrought by Mortimer ("Muscles") Carbonara and, unintentionally, by Patrick Markham. She still didn't quite get how Bounty Bag's protestors did it, or why, but their success shored up the town's meager tax base. As for the school attack, the water had done more damage than the explosives or the fire. The insurance was going to get them back in the building by August and was covering toxic removal and a partial renovation, modest improvements that nevertheless had eluded her for years. In the meantime, Bounty Bag was putting them up in its warehouse and had cleared one-third of its floor for this purpose.

Archie shoved his hands into his jacket pockets and stared past her. "Cornelius died."

"I'm sorry."

"Had to. He was old."

She hooked his arm and walked him next door to Hungry Tiger Pasta.

They ordered Vic's eggplant and a bottle of red wine. Dr. Chong disclosed that she'd had a change of heart about her faculty while working alongside them in the warehouse these past weeks, and under conditions far worse than at AJMHS. She had discovered a newfound respect for her teachers (well, for some of them; deadwood Hitch still wore a target). It wasn't easy managing kids while meeting the state's curricular demands. She decided that when it came time to return to Andy J. she'd dial back surveillance.

They had tiramisu and espresso. Then it was off to Archie's well-stocked camper van, special-ops vehicle of this loneliness-twisted, public-minded man. They played backgammon and drank diet soda. Archie flicked on a battery-operated red plastic candle and, starting up the engine, let the van's heater rip and played Chet Baker.

"Oh, what the hell," she said and matter-of-factly removed Archie's shirt. Archie, naturally, took off Dr. Chong's.

They embraced and fell with laughter on his thick down blankets. When they kissed, she bit his tongue and held it, making him drag it out through her teeth, a little sadistic preview that Archie, tongue tunneling right back in for more, plainly enjoyed. Eagerly and for far longer than she would've dared imagine — up, over, and beyond what she needed — they locked limbs and strained together on his mattress.

"I can't believe it," Archie said. "I just can't... *believe* it."

Dr. Chong gazed up at the snow falling on the moonroof and scratched his heaving back.

Finally calming down, Archie asked, "How's your nephew?"

"Tommy? Got a job."

"Doing what?"

"Slaying boar."

"For the town?" He was suddenly incredulous. "I ought to know about that."

"No, for Shorty's Rib Cage."

"Makes sense. We know he's a great shot."

Shorty's Rib Cage, which had branded the boars a local delicacy, was herding them for breeding into a farm fenced out of Bounty Bag's massive Pennacook holdings, finally clearing the town of this menace. The local Martini princeling had anointed Shorty's the supermarket chain's rib vendor of choice, and the Robinsons would soon supply New England's four corners. The daughter, Doreen, was still only a junior at AJMHS@BBW#2, but she had picked up accounting online and would keep the company books. Come summer, Tommy would open and manage their second joint, in Billerica. Patrick Markham, his new and departing friend, disapproved of all this killing, and of the anticipated manure run-off, but she gathered it hadn't soured their relations.

"What?" Archie asked, touching her arm.

"Tommy's moving out."

"I knew you looked sad. I've never seen that!"

When would she stop making Archie so excited?

"Tell me one reason why you like me, Archie. I can't think of any."

"I'll give you two. I need you and I *think* you need me."

"Maybe," she began, then stopped and re-started. "Maybe if I hadn't *wasted* all those weekends in Eaton..."

"Maybe we would have won?"

"Yes."

"Of course," said the selectman, who of all people knew. "But I'm inclined to forgive."

THE END

Afterword

I wrote this book before the COVID-19 pandemic but its subject matter and themes seem, in this respect, perhaps more relevant than anyone would wish. Like much of the world right now (I'm writing this on June 5, 2020), Pennacook suffers from economic paralysis and depends on supermarkets as almost the last bastion of normality and abundance. The valiant and sometimes fatal willingness of grocery and other essential workers to report for duty during the early months of the COVID-19 pandemic, not to mention their grace, warrants our deepest gratitude and admiration.

But George Floyd's murder has, for now, dwarfed COVID-19 in the public's imagination, and with good reason. It is sickening and reflects deep rot in our system. As a humorous novel of ideas, *Ring On Deli* is not keyed to the precise mournful note of this moment. But it is about some of that same rot, the warping deficits in our democracy—voter suppression, gerrymandered districts, a decaying Fourth Estate, and gaping economic inequality, much of it, for African Americans, caused by official government-sponsored racism in particular on the issue of housing—that, in the real world, are emboldening bigots from Charlottesville to the White House.

In an attempt to save Bounty Bag and themselves, its workers place a wild bet on one another and collective action. It seems to me that we must do the same.

Acknowledgments

Heartfelt thanks to Mom, Dad, and Chris; Nanxian Chen and He Tong; Dan Visel, the finest reader and editor I know (and an exceptionally patient man); Robert Cohen, whose support has been stalwart; Stewart O'Nan; David Eric Tomlinson; Hillary Read; Jill McCorkle; Lauren Groff; Rion Amilcar Scott; the Millay Colony for the Arts; Bread Loaf, Writers in Paradise, and my fellow workshop participants at both conferences; the gentlemen of Burdick; Mark Travassos; Ignacio Montoya; Charlene Postell; Andrew Palid; Lawrence Pisto; Tim Holohan; Ivan Kostadinov; David Marder; Morgia Holmes; the Honorable Ernest C. Torres; Ragan Willis; Adriana Schick; Jennifer Brady; Ogawa Coffee, Archie's New York Deli and Sam LaGrassa's; and the associates of Demoulas Super Markets, Inc., and, in particular, Larry Frost.

I am indebted to the authors of several books. *Beyond Words: What Animals Think and Feel*, by Carl Safina, supplied the bonobo-starling anecdote. Harold C. Lloyd's nifty *Supermarket Rules!* disclosed the "B.O.B., M.I.T.C.H., and L.I.S.A." test and informed certain other aspects of Ray's supermarket inspection. *We Are Market Basket: The Story of the Unlikely Grassroots Movement that Saved a Beloved Business*, by Daniel Korschun and Grant Welker, was especially relevant and among business books is perhaps uniquely entertaining. *Garner's Modern American Usage* (now *Garner's Modern English Usage*), which Ray overreads with scholastic consternation, is an elegant and invaluable reference book of astonishing depth and precision, whatever your leanings in the Descriptivist-Prescriptivist debate. Richard Rothstein's *The Color of Law: A Forgotten History of How Our Government Segregated America* and Harold Holzer and Norton Garfinkle's *A Just and Generous Nation: Abraham Lincoln and the Fight for American Opportunity* helped carry Mr. Grant through his terminal semester at Andy J.

Finally, I am most grateful to my wife Jasmine and our two children, Rose and Woody. Without their forbearance, good humor and love, this book would not have been possible and my life while writing it not half as good.

About the Author

Eric Giroux grew up in Billerica, Massachusetts, where he sacked groceries for Market Basket and ate large quantities of American Chinese food in his hometown's unaccountably numerous tiki-themed restaurants. He graduated from Harvard College and Harvard Law School, extracting academic credit from both institutions for fiction-writing workshops. Along the way, he worked the deli counter at a Tedeschi's convenience store. Like Ray, he makes sandwiches both swiftly and neatly.

Eric's fiction writing has received support from the Millay Colony for the Arts, and he has contributed to the Bread Loaf Writers' Conference and to the Writers in Paradise conference at Eckerd College. His publications in *Massachusetts Lawyers Weekly* have included a range of oddball topics, from Epictetus to Abraham Lincoln. He has also published travel guides for Let's Go and the legendary Cognoscenti Map Guides.

Eric is a senior counsel for the U.S. Securities and Exchange Commission. He lives with his family outside of Boston, not far from Pennacook. *Ring On Deli* is his first novel.

Printed in the USA
CPSIA information can be obtained
at www.ICGtesting.com
LVHW040424250524
781390LV00023B/141